CAN YOU SOLVE THE MURDER?

Can You Solve the Murder?

Book Two:
The Forest of Death

ANTONY JOHNSTON

bantam

TRANSWORLD PUBLISHERS

UK | USA | Canada | Ireland | Australia
India | New Zealand | South Africa

Transworld is part of the Penguin Random House group of companies
whose addresses can be found at global.penguinrandomhouse.com.

Penguin Random House UK, One Embassy Gardens,
8 Viaduct Gardens, London SW11 7BW

penguin.co.uk

First published in Great Britain in 2026 by Bantam
an imprint of Transworld Publishers

001

Typeset in 13/16 pt Garamond MT Pro by Six Red Marbles UK, Thetford, Norfolk
Printed and bound in Great Britain by Clays Ltd, Elcograf S.p.A.

The authorized representative in the EEA is Penguin Random House Ireland,
Morrison Chambers, 32 Nassau Street, Dublin D02 YH68.

A CIP catalogue record for this book is available from the British Library.

ISBN: 9780857506948

Penguin Random House is committed to a sustainable future
for our business, our readers and our planet. This book is made
from Forest Stewardship Council® certified paper.

In memory of Joe Dever

HOW TO SOLVE
THE MURDER

The Forest of Death is no ordinary case . . . and this is no ordinary book.

Can You Solve the Murder? is an *interactive* novel. Unlike a normal book, you shouldn't read it straight through from front to back. Reading the text sequentially won't make any sense, and will spoil the experience – because this story is also a puzzle, in which YOU play the part of the detective and YOU must solve the crime by making decisions about the investigation.

Who will you interview? Which leads will you follow? What clues will you find? And, finally, who will you accuse? The choices are yours – and only by following the correct path can you solve the murder.

Here's how it works:

NUMBERED SECTIONS

The story is divided into *sections*, each of which is numbered. First, pay close attention to the text, as important clues are hidden within – but be wary of red herrings.

At the end of each section, you will be given a choice of what you, as the detective, want to do. Each choice directs you to a different number; make your decision, then turn to the section matching that number and read on.

For example, let's say you've just read a section and it ends with the following options:

   🔍 *To examine the body, turn to* **35**

   🔍 *To search the murder scene, turn to* **143**

You must now decide which of those two actions to perform. If you choose to examine the body, flick through the book until you find section **35** and read it – remembering that you're looking for the section number, *not* the page number. If you choose to search the murder scene instead, find and read section **143**.

(These numbers are only examples, and don't reflect the actual contents of those sections within this book.)

If you're reading the ebook edition, you don't need to manually find each section.* Instead, simply tap the bold number '**35**' at the end of the option to be taken automatically to that section.

**Except in a few unique circumstances, which you may discover as you progress . . .*

YOUR DETECTIVE'S NOTEBOOK

Every good detective carries a notebook to record information and evidence vital to solving the case. At the back of this book, you'll find blank pages to use as your own notebook, and to record Clue Numbers.

(You'll have to supply your own pen or pencil, though. Department budget cuts seem to get worse every day . . .)

If you'd prefer not to write in your copy of this book, you can use a separate notebook or even a digital document; whatever you feel comfortable with. What's important is that you can easily write in it and review it while reading, as you'll be performing both actions many times.

Record information about the story, the suspects and your theories. Write down each section number you visit, in case you later want to check something in the text. Solving a murder requires making good notes, and *The Forest of Death* is no exception.

CLUE NUMBERS

From time to time, you'll be told to write a Clue Number in your notebook.

Clue Numbers consist of a letter and number, such as G2, P5, A4, and so on. It's important you write these down when instructed, because later sections will ask you to check if you have a particular Clue Number in your notebook. You'll then be directed to a specific section.

(There are many different paths to take in this story, so you may sometimes be told to write down a Clue Number you already have in your notebook. This isn't an error – in fact, it's a sign that you have good clue-finding skills! So don't worry about it, and move on.)

Let's say a section tells you to write **P5** in your notebook. Then, later, a different section presents you with these choices:

If you have P5 written in your notebook, turn to 45

Otherwise, turn to 118

In this example you would turn to section **45**, because you have **P5** written down. If you didn't have that Clue Number in your notebook, though, you would turn to section **118** instead.

Sometimes you'll be asked to check your notebook for *multiple* Clue Numbers. When this happens, compare them against your notes in the order listed and act on the first that applies.

For example, imagine you now have both **P5** and **A4** written down. Later, you read a section which ends with the following instructions:

Check your notebook in the following order:

If you have G2 written down, turn to 87

If you have A4 written down, turn to 165

If you have P5 written down, turn to 45

Otherwise, turn to 118

Your notebook doesn't contain **G2**, so you ignore that instruction. You do have **P5** written down – but you *also* have **A4**, and the instruction for that Clue Number precedes **P5** in the list. Therefore, in this example you would turn to section **165**.

Clue Numbers are vitally important to solving the case, and also determine your Detective Score once justice has been done, so pay close attention to them.

Remember: YOU are the Detective, and it is up to YOU to solve this dastardly crime! An attention to detail, combined with your sleuthing skills and good notes, will be required to successfully determine whodunnit.

🔍 Now begin your investigation by turning to section 1

'A young woman, wearing strange clothes, found dead in a forest at midnight. Doesn't get any more suspicious than that, does it?' Sergeant McAdam says grimly as she changes gear and leans into a corner.

'The devil, as they say, is in the details. What more do we know?' you ask from the passenger seat, clinging to the over-door handgrip.

'That's all anyone told me. Constable Zwale's already at the scene, though. No doubt he'll fill us in.'

McAdam focuses on the road, racing through the dark as you head deeper into Grenholme Forest. You watch tree branches whip by at speed, making the full moon strobe in your vision, and hope the local wildlife is sensible enough to hear McAdam coming and stay well away. You've been working with the sergeant for a while now, since her transfer from Northumbria Police, but the night forest creatures are encountering her rally-like driving for the first time.

You bring up a map of the area on your phone. Reception out here appears to be slow and spotty, so it takes a while to load, but finally you see Grenholme village and its namesake forest, which completely surrounds and isolates it. The woodland is extensive, stretching for a mile in each direction around the village. Just one main road traverses the forest, and you're currently on it. You notice several marked points of interest within the wooded area: viewing platforms, lookout points and even an area of marshland.

McAdam turns off the main road on to a narrow single-track lane through the trees, and soon you see flashing lights ahead. Police vehicles and an ambulance occupy a hammer-head parking area at the end of the lane, near the banks of a narrow river. If you crossed the river on the way, it was too dark to notice.

Also parked here are a few civilian cars, including a Transit van from a rental company. Judging by their positions, these vehicles predate the police presence.

McAdam pulls up and you get out, stepping into a low, inter-mittent mist that hugs the ground, sweeping across your feet and out on to the water. You shiver in the springtime night air, looking around in vain for the familiar blue-and-white crime scene cordon tape.

A uniformed officer, tall and wide-shouldered, approaches to greet you. You recognize him as Constable Zwale, an eager young man with ambitions to transfer to CID. He's a good constable, if occasionally prone to distraction, but in your opinion needs more experience under his belt.

'Evening, Inspector. We've secured the scene,' he says.

'Thank you, Constable. Um . . . where is it? I don't see a cordon.'

'A few hundred metres in that direction,' Zwale explains, pointing into the trees. 'This is as close as vehicles can approach.'

'Do we need boots? The air feels damp.'

'I gather that's normal around here, but the ground's mostly dry. The main problem is finding our way. I got the lads to tape a path between the trees so we don't get lost.'

'Good work. Lead on.'

He takes you and McAdam deeper into the forest, lighting the way with a handheld torch. Sure enough, police tape has been strung between trees to guide you to the crime scene. You pass uniformed officers and a pathologist's assistant, all heading in the opposite direction, back to the parking area. After an almost ten-minute walk you see lights some distance ahead, hazy and indistinct through the trees.

'The victim has been identified as Lori Velvet,' Constable Zwale tells you, stepping over thick tree roots that wind across the path. 'Female, twenty-two years old, unmarried, no children.'

'Lori Velvet?' McAdam says, surprised. 'As in the singer of Killer Velvet?'

'That's right, Sarge. They were out here filming a music video. The other members of the band have positively identified the body.'

McAdam chuckles. 'So much for the reports of strange clothing. I suppose folk around here don't go much for leather and studs.' The sergeant's taste in music runs to the loud and raucous, so it's not entirely a surprise to you that she should know of this rock band.

'Who found her?' you ask.

'A local astronomer, in the forest with the village club,' Zwale explains. 'I've informed him, and the victim's bandmates, that you'll want to talk to them.'

At that moment the ground fog rises and sweeps across the path, obscuring your vision. An owl hoots somewhere near by. Then the flap of broad wings, a rush of air—

'*Aaah!* Bloody hell,' McAdam yelps, stumbling backwards.

You turn to find her doubled over, hands on her knees,

with a pale expression. McAdam is short and wiry, the sort of copper who looks like she punches things to relax, and you've never seen her so spooked.

'Are you all right, Sergeant?'

'Like a face . . . came out of the fog . . . at me,' she says between breaths.

The hoot comes again from somewhere in the trees.

'Just an owl,' you say, trying not to laugh. 'Come along.'

She grumbles about how inconsiderate it is of people to get themselves killed in places like this rather than, say, a nice shopping centre with bright lights and ample parking.

The thought makes you wonder: why would a rock band choose to make a music video here?

You break through the trees into a clearing, and what you see suggests an answer.

Eleven pale, waist-high stones with strange chalk markings on them stand in a circle, fifteen metres across. The markings are abstract shapes of some kind, possibly ritualistic in nature. You don't recognize them, but pagan symbolism is far from your area of expertise. Presumably the rock band thought the monument would make a good backdrop for their music video.

Unfortunately, that turned out not to be the case. At last, you've found the familiar blue-and-white cordon; it surrounds the stone circle, in the centre of which stands an equally familiar white forensics tent. Uniformed police officers guard the cordon, talking to a surprisingly large number of people who have gathered around, while forensic investigators in protective gear move in and out of the tent.

'These are the known as the Lock Stones,' Constable Zwale explains. 'Dr Wash is in there with the body.'

Ribbons of mist sweep out of the trees and through the circle as you take in the scene.

'Blast. No signal,' McAdam says, checking her phone. 'I was going to look up the stones.'

You duck under the cordon and make your way to the tent, followed by McAdam. The interior is illuminated with bright LED lamps. A police photographer takes pictures of the scene, while an elderly white-haired pathologist examines the victim. Seeing you enter she stands upright, groaning as she straightens out her back. You've worked with Dr Wash many times before, and trust her judgement implicitly.

'Good evening, Detective Chief Inspector,' she says, beckoning you over. 'I'm afraid it's not pretty, though at least it's clean. Let us be thankful for small mercies.'

Lori Velvet lies on her side, with one arm outstretched and legs crooked. You might think she was asleep, if not for her glassy, staring eyes.

Her clothing is even stranger than you expected. She wears baggy trousers and a billowing top, both made of multiple layers of coarse fabric with tears and holes in them, and over it all a heavy coat, also worn and holed. A variety of accessories such as feathers, twigs and scarves are sewn and clipped on to the skirt and sleeves. Bracelets and bangles cover her wrists, and she wears heavy black boots, as if she was about to go hiking.

'We may have different definitions of the word "clean", Doctor. Sergeant, weren't you expecting leather and studs?'

'Aye,' she confirms, peering at the strange outfit. 'I've never seen her in anything like this before. She must have been trying out a new look.'

Behind Dr Wash is a fold-up table holding tools and

equipment. From it she retrieves a sealed evidence bag, which she hands to you. 'We found this just a metre or so from the body.'

Inside the bag is what looks like a hood made from fur and hessian, covered in twigs and moss, with plastic goggles over the eyeholes. Its bottom edge is soaked in blood.

'How odd,' you remark. 'Sergeant, you're sure this wasn't how she normally dressed?'

McAdam shrugs. 'I'm not their biggest fan, but I reckon I'd remember this.'

'Perhaps she wore it for the music video,' you suggest. 'How about these rips and tears in her clothes, Doctor? Also part of the costume, or signs of a struggle?'

The pathologist shakes her head. 'None of the cuts look fresh, so I think they're by design. As was the manner of her death, if you take my meaning. Despite the rather eerie surroundings, which I don't mind telling you give me the heebie-jeebies, for once it's fairly straightforward. Look here.' She indicates the woman's throat. 'A single, clean cut rupturing the carotid artery. Exsanguination would have been rapid, causing the victim to quickly lose consciousness and die shortly thereafter. I doubt she would have had time to even register what had happened.'

'Like you said, small mercies,' Sergeant McAdam murmurs, crouching to examine the wound. You hang back a little – even from here you can clearly see the crimson ruin of the victim's neck, the blood having covered her skin and soaked into her upper clothing.

'Looks left to right,' McAdam observes, glancing at Dr Wash to check.

'I concur,' she says. 'Very well done, Sergeant.'

Her tone is somewhat patronizing, and you brace yourself to step in should things escalate. Sergeant McAdam is old-fashioned, aggressive and unfiltered; Dr Wash is well-bred, vegetarian and erudite. The two have clashed before, both giving as good as they get – particularly on McAdam's first case when she was newly transferred to this area. Tonight, though, she doesn't rise to the bait.

'So it's either a left-hander from the front,' the sergeant says, 'or a right-hander from behind. My bet's on behind, or they'd be covered in blood. Not that you can see much out there.'

'It would be a very brave or foolish killer who relied only on fog to conceal their bloody clothes,' you say. 'On the other hand, it could have concealed their presence from the victim. Look at the blood on the bottom edge of this hood. It seems reasonable to assume Ms Velvet was wearing it when she was killed. Those two factors combined would make it easy to sneak up on her, so I agree it's likely she was attacked from behind. Finding the murder weapon may help.'

'On that point I have good news and bad news,' Dr Wash says, holding up another evidence bag for your examination. To your surprise, it contains a bloody knife. 'I see that look in your eye, but don't get too excited,' she warns. 'The good news is that, like the hood, this was found near the body so there's a high chance it's the weapon you seek. The bad news is that it's symmetrical, so doesn't help you determine left or right-handedness. It also appears to be a regular knife that you can buy in a thousand places. There's nothing really distinctive about it at all . . . except this.'

She lifts the bag up to the light and something catches your eye. 'Sergeant, could you shine your torch on the hilt, please?'

McAdam does so, using the torch she keeps in her pocket. You peer closely at the knife and, beneath the blood, make out a shallow carving in its hilt that seems to have been scratched with a penknife. The strokes form an unusual pattern . . . but it's one you've seen before.

'This is the same as those symbols chalked on the stones outside. What the blazes is going on here?'

Dr Wash shivers a little. 'I fear you may be looking for a ritualistic motive.'

A rock singer, in a bizarre costume, filming in a forest on the night of a full moon, killed inside a stone circle with a knife that bears a symbol found on the stones.

'It certainly doesn't feel like a random, impulsive killing,' you murmur in agreement. A silence falls over the scene.

'What a waste,' McAdam says at last. 'Poor woman had her whole life ahead of her.'

'Doctor, do you have anything more to tell us?'

'Not at this time. Frankly, I'll be glad to get out of here as soon as possible. The last thing I need is ghosts looking over my shoulder.'

'You never struck me as the superstitious type.'

She regards you over her glasses. 'There are more things in heaven and earth, Inspector, than are dreamt of in your philosophy. I've lived long enough to understand that only a fool discounts the unknown.'

You bid the pathologist goodbye and step out of the tent. The haze has lifted, and you look up at the sky in time to see a shooting star pass overhead; a momentary streak of light slashing across the dark before it vanishes. You return your gaze to the more mundane crime scene, and the people around you.

Having now seen the body, you recognize a certain uneasiness in some of the uniformed police standing guard; shuffling of feet, murmurs of disquiet. You're not superstitious yourself, but a murder scene like this would be enough to make anyone uncomfortable.

'If this wasn't an act of impulse, who knew Lori Velvet would be here at this time of night?' you wonder aloud. 'Who else would even have been out here at the time, besides her bandmates?' You look at the people gathered beyond the cordon, who appear to be massed in three groups, as Constable Zwale approaches.

'More than you might think,' he says. 'As I mentioned, in addition to the band and video director, the Grenholme Stargazers were out here. It was their secretary, Glenn Davis, who found the body.'

'What was an astronomy group doing in the forest?' McAdam asks.

'All the fields around here are private farmland, so off-limits,' Zwale explains. 'And Grenholme Forest has some good overlook points and clearings with a view if you know where to find them. The Lyrids are out at the moment, you see. Quite exciting.'

You both look questioningly at the young constable.

'The what-ids?' McAdam says. 'How do you know all this, lad?'

Zwale looks abashed. 'Sorry, sorry. The Lyrids are a meteor shower that come around once every year at this time. I was planning to watch them myself at home tonight, but then we got the call out here.'

You wouldn't have pictured the young constable standing in his back garden with a telescope, but it takes all types.

'Sounds like that's our suspect pool, then,' McAdam says. 'Unless Aaron Warrior finally killed her, it's likely not someone from the band, so let's talk to Mr Davis.'

'Not so fast, Sergeant,' you say. 'First of all, who's "Aaron Warrior"?'

'Killer Velvet's guitarist. He and Lori used to be an item, and everyone knows they've had ups and downs, as they say. Come to think of it, maybe we should speak to him first after all.'

Zwale clears his throat. 'There's more. A local pagan group, known as –' he checks his notebook – 'The Disciples of the Green. They were also in the forest, on their way to the stone circle for the first night of the full moon, when they heard Lori Velvet scream.'

'Did you say *first* night?'

'Yes, Sarge. Technically a full moon phase lasts for three days, you see. Tonight is the first.'

You exchange glances with McAdam. If tonight's killing really is linked to the full moon in some way, that doesn't bode well for the next forty-eight hours.

'All right, then we'll speak to the beardy weirdies as well,' McAdam says. 'Who's in charge of them?'

'Bill Thomas,' Zwale says, pointing out a man standing beyond the cordon. 'Calls himself the "First Disciple".'

'It's going to be a long night,' you say, and McAdam groans. But she knows as well as you that this is the job. The first hours following a murder are vital, and even in this dark post-midnight time you must learn all you can.

The first decision to make, then, is in what order you'll interview people.

⚲ *To talk to Aaron Warrior, the guitarist, turn to* **38**

⚲ *To talk to Glenn Davis, the astronomer, turn to* **113**

⚲ *To talk to Bill Thomas, the pagan leader, turn to* **148**

2

You call McAdam over and point out the plastic rounders set.

'Didn't you say you wanted Douglas to get outside more?'

'Aye,' she says, taking it from the shelf hook. Hanging behind it are child-sized fishing nets, the kind of thing you'd use to trawl rock pools on the beach or the shallows of a river.

'Or you could look for minnows with him in the local stream,' you suggest.

McAdam shakes her head. 'He needs to be doing stuff that doesn't rely on me,' she says quietly. 'It's great that he's bookish, but . . . plenty of other kids at his school aren't. He's got to toughen up and gain some confidence.'

'I understand. A tricky situation for any parent.'

She calls out to Raven, holding up the rounders set. 'Can I get you to put this aside, and I'll collect it at the end of the day?'

'So long as you pay for it, you can do what you like,' the shopkeeper replies.

McAdam does, and Raven puts it behind the counter. 'Come and collect it any time.'

⚲ *Write* **R5** *in your notebook*

⚲ *Then turn to* **30**

3

'I told you, it's ceremonial,' Bill says, getting to his feet. He walks to the shrine you saw earlier: a display cabinet featuring the Disciples paraphernalia. Inside is a knife with an intricately carved handle and a slim blade. He opens the cabinet's glass door and withdraws it.

'All this blade ever cuts is ferns and leaves, when we perform a ritual. We're planning one tonight, seeing as last night's ceremony was interrupted. But you can see for yourself, it's clean.'

He's right. It's possible for microscopic blood traces to remain on knives after they've been washed, of course, but there are certainly none visible to the naked eye here. Combined with the fact that you already have a knife that Dr Wash confidently believes to be the murder weapon – Lori's own, which is quite different – you're satisfied this one wasn't involved.

Nevertheless, one question remains: is it likely that Bill would simply forget to take his knife on a Disciples outing?

🔎 *Turn to* **115**

4

'Thank you for the tea,' you say. You only took a couple of sips, but it was a polite gesture to get Glenn talking, and it worked.

'I won't be bullied, you know,' he says suddenly. 'Tonight is forecast to be ideal for meteor-watching, and I intend to take to the forest over any objection.'

'I wish I could join you,' Zwale says, smiling. 'The Lyrids were superb last year. I managed to swap shifts so I could be out observing three nights in a row.'

Glenn smiles back, despite his earlier enmity towards Zwale. Given recent events, perhaps he senses that any ally is worth cultivating.

'I don't think the rest of the group would be too pleased to see a policeman this evening. But there's always next year.' He turns to you. 'If you want to do something useful, tell Bill and his pagans to stay away tonight. You know they're planning to perform some nonsense ritual at the stones, don't you? They may claim to respect nature, but they have none for the dead.'

'Lori Velvet was removed from the circle in the small hours of last night,' you tell him, 'and as I understand it, forensic examination of the site was completed this morning. There's no reason the Disciples of the Green shouldn't be able to gather at the circle.'

Glenn grumbles his disapproval, and you take your leave. Outside the street is clear, with no sign of angry locals or other trouble-makers.

If you have A1 written in your notebook, turn to **197**

Otherwise, turn to **143**

5

'Doctor,' you ask as a thought forms, 'could Lori Velvet have done this to herself? Is there any possibility the wound was self-inflicted?'

The pathologist shakes her head. 'You know I don't deal in one hundred per cent certainties, but in this case the chances are so low as to be effectively zero. The cut was too deep, too confidently done.'

You ponder what this all means.

'For some reason, Lori carried a knife with her into the woods. But her attacker took it from her, killed her with it, then dropped the knife on the ground and fled. This raises all sorts of questions. Was she already holding the knife, because she saw her attacker and feared for her life? That would fit the bruise and her screaming. Or is it possible the attacker knew she would be carrying the knife? Did the killer wear gloves simply because it was a cold night in the woods . . . or did they go with the intent of killing Lori?'

'That's your department, not mine,' Dr Wash says. 'And there's more I've still to show you. Look at this.'

With an assistant's help she removes the sheet covering Lori's body, revealing many more tattoos, then turns her over. It takes you a moment to see what the doctor is showing you, amid the swirling shapes and colourful patterns. There, in between her shoulder blades, is a symbol you've seen before.

'That's the same as what's carved into the knife hilt,' McAdam notes.

'And also chalked on one of the Lock Stones,' you add.

'How old would you say that tattoo is, Doctor?'

14

'Dating body art is always tricky,' she says, turning Lori's body upright once more. 'That particular piece isn't brand new, but neither is it very old, as there's no fading and very little spread. Given she's only aged twenty-two, it can't be more than three or four years old anyway.'

So it's possible Lori had the tattoo done as soon as she was old enough. It must have been important to her.

'You were right about the surprises, Doctor. This is already shaping up to be a very tangled case.'

Dr Wash snorts. 'Oh, I'm not finished. There's the matter of the victim's identity, for a start.'

'What do you mean?' McAdam asks, gesturing at Lori's face. 'She's a rock star. I know she looks different without the make-up, but thousands of fans could tell you who she is. Her bandmates identified her. There's no question this is Lori Velvet.'

You see a glint in the doctor's eye, and recalling Lori's enigmatic behaviour in interviews, hazard a guess at where this is going.

'I'm sure you're right, but I suspect the real issue is of a deeper nature. Doctor?'

'That's correct. To wit: *who is* Lori Velvet? Yes, she's a rock star. In my experience with such people, what you see on stage, in videos and in interviews is only what they want you to see. In a way they are their own creations, and "Lori Velvet" was a prime example.'

McAdam rolls her eyes, realizing what the doctor is implying. 'It's a stage name.'

'Yes and no. I assumed the same, and attempted to find out her real identity. What I found is that she almost certainly adopted the name for the stage . . . but it is also her legal name, because she changed it by deed poll. Her birth name was Lucy Isherwood, something which I don't think is common knowledge. Even her Wikipedia page doesn't mention it.'

'That could explain why she never talked about her past in interviews,' you observe. McAdam looks at you with surprise. 'I may not be a fan of her music, but research is research,' you say. 'Not to mention that her appearance "in character" was highly stylized. Seeing her like this, you'd hardly know it was the same person.'

'Was she running away from something?' McAdam suggests. 'Wouldn't be the first kid to change their name and join the circus.'

'Indeed. I wonder if the name change and tattooing were done around the same time, too. On the bright side, at least now we know where to look for her family. Perhaps they can help us understand what happened, and if it may have some connection to her murder.'

'She was born in London, but I didn't dig any deeper than that,' Dr Wash says. 'Before you talk to her family, though, there's one more thing you should know. I'm sorry to tell you that Lori Velvet was pregnant.'

Silence falls across the mortuary room. Not of shock so much as an acknowledgement of tragedy.

'She doesn't appear to be showing,' you observe quietly.

'No, it was early,' Dr Wash explains. 'But there's no question.'

'So, who was the donor?' McAdam asks. 'I mean, she was in a relationship with a woman, remember. Emma and I adopted both our kids, but first we were offered IVF. I assume that's the case here.'

'But she was previously in a relationship with her bandmate Aaron Warrior,' you point out. 'Evidently Lori was bisexual.'

'Aye, but that ended months ago. If it was his child, she'd be a lot further along.'

Dr Wash consults her notes. 'I found no record of IVF, which does rather imply the pregnancy was from good old-fashioned intercourse. Are you sure she wasn't seeing a man?'

'I suppose she must have been,' you say. 'The question is, did her girlfriend Julie know anything about it?'

You exit the mortuary in low spirits. It's bad enough dealing with the death of a young woman, whom you strongly suspect was already troubled, but to learn that she was also carrying a baby somehow makes solving this case even more important.

'Do you think the killer knew?' McAdam asks.

'It would have to be someone very close to her. Neither her bandmates nor her director-slash-girlfriend mentioned it, and one assumes they would have if they knew.'

'Unless they were hiding something. What if Julie found out, and killed her in a jealous rage? She knew where Lori would be, and that she was wearing the costume.'

You climb into McAdam's car, ready to return to Grenholme.

'Remember that the band and Julie are each other's alibi. Lori herself aside, they were all together. I could imagine a band member perhaps slipping away without the others noticing, but it seems unlikely the person actually filming them could have.'

Your phone rings with a call from Constable Zwale.

If you have P3 written in your notebook, turn to **63**

If you have P6 written in your notebook, turn to **97**

6

You proceed into the village, contemplating your next move as you wind through the old, narrow streets. Passing a small cafe, you recognize Keith and Steve, the Killer Velvet rhythm section, taking brunch in the window.

You nod in greeting and walk on, but after a few yards someone calls out from behind you. Turning, you see one of the musicians – you think it's Keith, the drummer, though you wouldn't swear to it – running to catch you.

'How's it going?' he asks.

'Not bad,' McAdam replies. 'Yourself?'

Keith looks confused, then tries again. 'No, I mean, how's the investigation going? Everyone's talking about it.'

'Oh? What do they say?'

His enthusiasm to talk evaporates. 'Well, you know. Just . . . stuff. About Lori, and the guard bloke.'

'The Stone Warden.'

'Yeah, him. I mean, it's obviously someone just dressing up, isn't it? But there are people saying Lori deserved it, which is totally out of order. They didn't even know her.'

It occurs to you that they actually did, though perhaps without realizing it. Certainly, Lori Velvet was a very different person to Lucy Isherwood, if nothing else by having grown up and seen the world.

'Julie's in bits, too, after they argued and everything. Imagine that, you call someone a bitch and it's the last thing you ever say to her . . .'

'Wait a moment,' you say. 'Julie and Lori argued? That's news to us.'

Keith looks worried. 'Oh, I – I thought she'd have said . . . I've put my foot in it now, haven't I? Typical.'

'It's OK. Tell us what happened.'

He takes a deep breath. 'Lori got mad at Julie because she only filmed half the encore last night. Julie thought we'd finished, and she was packing away her stuff when Lori came on in the costume. Then the situation blew up again later, filming in the woods. Lori said everything was taking too long, and we were going to miss shooting at midnight in the stone circle unless Julie bucked her ideas up. She, uh . . . she threatened to fire her.'

'What happened then?'

'Julie called her a bitch, and Lori stormed off,' he says quietly.

This shines a new light on things. By all accounts, Julie isn't a big-name director, so she was probably hoping this job with Killer Velvet would increase her credibility and worth. Not to mention that she was Lori's lover, of course. To have both her job and relationship threatened gives her plenty of motive. Could this have been a crime of passion after all?

You thank Keith and walk on to the village square. It doesn't seem to have become any busier while you were in the forest, and you notice that Stones & Spirits has closed for lunch. But the quiet is shattered by the unmistakable sound of smashing glass, followed by raised voices – from inside the Watching Warden.

McAdam is already running towards the pub. You follow, and quickly assess the scene. Patrick the landlord is behind the bar, telling everyone to calm down; Aaron holds a smashed bottle in his hand, threatening Glenn; beside Aaron stands Raven, looking stunned; Bill remains at the bar, watching with detached interest; and Julie is filming it all with a handheld camera.

'What the hell's going on here?' McAdam shouts. For a small woman she has a surprisingly large voice, and everyone freezes in their tracks. 'Aaron, drop that bottle immediately!'

He wavers for a moment, then relents and throws the bottle to the floor where it smashes among the shards of its other half.

'He said I killed Lori,' Aaron growls, pointing at Glenn. 'I'll sue him for defamation!'

'For something said in a pub? Don't be daft,' McAdam says. 'Mr Davis, why would you accuse Aaron of such a thing?'

Glenn huffs. Wearing tweed, a fly-pinned hat and wellington boots, you assume he came to the pub directly from fishing. 'I should think it's obvious. They're heathens, practising blood rituals and black magic. They sacrificed that girl on the altar of fame in order to become more popular.'

'You can't seriously think they killed Lori for publicity,' Raven says, stepping between the men. 'Glenn, be serious.'

'All right, I don't need you to defend me,' Aaron says tetchily. 'Especially when I'm not the one drumming up publicity from it.' From his back pocket he pulls a piece of paper, unfolding it and turning on Raven. 'This was you, wasn't it? Trying to generate some extra business. And you lot call us sick!'

Patrick emerges from behind the bar holding a long-handled dustpan and brush to sweep up the broken glass. This action neatly forces the arguing parties to separate; as Aaron moves aside, distracted, you pluck the sheet of paper from his hand.

Handwritten in black marker, it reads:

THE STONE
WARDEN HAS
A HUMAN FACE

The same words Lori Velvet spoke on stage last night.

'Where did you find this? Did Lori write it?' you ask.

'Pinned to the front door of the pub,' Aaron explains. 'I saw it this morning when I went out for a smoke. It's not Lori's handwriting.'

'It's not mine either,' Raven protests. 'Aaron, believe me, I would never do something like this. You know I wouldn't.'

You look at the note again, and a memory triggers in your mind. Raven is telling the truth; she didn't write this. How interesting.

Having watched proceedings with amusement up until now, Bill peels himself away from the bar and puts a comforting arm around Raven. Then he turns on Aaron.

'Look, you cocky sod, you can see how upset she is by all of this, especially now it turns out she used to know your singer. We don't need to stir up trouble to generate business. We were doing fine long before you got here, thanks very much.'

Glenn tuts loudly. 'Your pocket is all you ever really care about, isn't it, Bill? How much extra business will tonight's ridiculous pageant bring in, do you think? Are you planning to get her to film that, too?' He flings an accusing finger at Julie, who smirks from behind her camera.

'Maybe I will,' she says. 'After the gig, of course.' She glances at Aaron.

Patrick finishes sweeping up the glass and turns to her. 'I

think we've all had enough of cameras, don't you? Stop filming, please.'

'Freedom of the press!' Julie protests. 'This is a public place.'

'No, it's a public *house*,' he corrects her. 'Which is still a private establishment, and I didn't give you permission.'

'He's right,' Raven says, turning on Julie. 'You've got no right to be filming us like this, you ghoul. You were supposed to be in love with her! Give me that.' She reaches for the camera.

'No!' Julie recoils, moving out of the shopkeeper's reach. 'I'm making a documentary. The public has a right to know.' She turns the camera on you and McAdam. 'Tell me, Inspector, are you any closer to finding out who murdered Lori? Or are you running around in circles, as usual?'

To you, such insults are water off a duck's back, but McAdam's temper matches the woman herself: short and explosive.

'How dare you!' she shouts at Julie. 'Every minute since we got here has been spent trying to find Lori's killer, with less help from most of you than we'd prefer, I might add. You're not a journalist, and you've already been asked to stop by the establishment owner. Now put that thing down before I put it down for you!'

Julie is backed into a corner, and McAdam reaches for the camera.

Perhaps this has gone far enough . . . or perhaps Julie needs to be shown that a murder investigation is serious business.

   To prevent McAdam doing something rash, turn to **185**

   To let McAdam carry out her threat, turn to **74**

7

Before you leave, one final question comes to mind.

'Mr Davis, you said you've lived here all your life, so I assume you're familiar with the legend of the Lock Stones and the Stone Warden. Did you know the band had written a song about it?'

He sighs. 'Yes, I gathered. I consider it even more evidence they were merely out to exploit the good people of Grenholme.'

'I'm not so sure. It seems Ms Velvet herself composed the song, and her fellow band members didn't know it was connected to this place until they arrived in Grenholme today. It's why they came here to film a music video.'

'Didn't know? Absurd. People visit the Lock Stones from all over, you know. No, it's impossible.'

You wonder about that. It's natural that a man who's always lived here would assume everyone else has heard of a local legend. But you don't live so far away yourself, yet this is the first time you've encountered the Lock Stones. Is Aaron telling the truth when he says he didn't know about the song's connection? If so, and Lori was insistent they come here to film the music video . . . why didn't she tell them?

If you haven't yet spoken to Bill Thomas the pagan leader, turn to **148**

Otherwise, turn to **88**

8

'You told us you were with the band the whole time last night, shooting the video in the forest,' you say, and Julie nods. 'Is there anything more you'd like to tell us?'

'No, I don't think so.'

'Ms Grafton, we've been advised that you were in fact absent from the shoot for about ten minutes, around half past eleven. Ring any bells?'

The director thinks for a moment. 'Oh, that. Well . . . yes, I suppose technically I was by myself for a few minutes. I was shooting B-roll footage of the forest, so obviously I wasn't with the band.'

'I keep hearing this term "B-roll". What is it?'

'It means shots that don't feature people or sound sync, so we can use them as cutaways and interstitials. In the edit we might show Aaron playing for five seconds, then cut to the woods at night for one second, then Lori singing for five seconds. The shot of the woods in the middle is from B-roll.'

'Why didn't you mention your time apart from the band earlier?'

Julie shrugs. 'It's standard practice.'

'One that took you out of sight for ten minutes.'

'All I did was film some trees. I can show you—Oh no, I can't, because someone smashed my camera.' She glares at you resentfully. 'Someone's aura is going to be well out of alignment for that, I tell you.'

    If you have J2 written in your notebook, turn to **93**

    Otherwise, turn to **128**

9

Bill Thomas is not best pleased to see you again.

'Can we go home yet, or what?' he says when you approach. 'We've all given statements, and it's very late.'

'I thought you normally hang out here all night anyway,' McAdam says scornfully.

'Yeah, not in these circumstances,' Bill replies. 'Just because we're pagans, doesn't mean we perform human sacrifices.'

'Speaking of which . . .' You show him the bloody knife in the evidence bag, holding it up. 'If I could keep you for a moment more, Mr Thomas, I hoped you could possibly shed some light on this. Do you recognize it?'

'No. Should I?'

'I'm told you often carry a knife like this.'

Bill peers at it, looking puzzled, then groans with realization.

'You've been talking to Glenn, haven't you? I shouldn't be surprised he'd say that. Yes, I carry a knife, but purely for ceremonial purposes as First Disciple. It looks nothing like that.'

'Let's see it, then,' McAdam says. 'Or have you conveniently mislaid it?'

The 'First Disciple' narrows his eyes. He's almost twice the sergeant's size, and looms over her. But she doesn't back down, and you know which of them you'd put your money on in a scrap.

Suddenly, you wonder if that scrap might come sooner rather than later as Bill reaches under his robe and pulls out a knife. McAdam steps back, instinctively putting herself beyond his immediate range.

But he quickly flips the knife in his hand and offers it to her hilt-first. 'Ceremonial, like I said. Check it all you like, it's clean as a whistle.'

He's right. The knife looks pristine, as if it's never been used to cut anything more than an envelope, with a thin, smooth blade. It's also very different to the knife found by Lori's body, with an ornate hilt that's decoratively carved in a filigree style, and lacking any particular symbol like the one in the evidence bag.

McAdam grudgingly returns the knife to Bill, and you change tack.

'Mr Thomas, do you see this symbol carved into the hilt? It matches one of the chalk markings on the Lock Stones, over there. Does it mean anything to you?'

'No. We'll be cleaning those markings off the stones at the first opportunity, anyway.'

You raise a warning finger. 'Not before our investigation is finished, if you please. Those symbols could be important evidence.'

'It's vandalism,' Bill snorts. 'Local kids messing around. Do you know how many empty lager cans we clean up from the forest every week? How many fire pits and used disposable barbecues we find? Caring for this forest is practically a full-time job.'

'Nevertheless, I must ask you to leave everything here as it is for the moment. Let us do our job, and I promise we'll clear everything up when we leave.'

   Write **B10** *in your notebook*

   Then turn to **85**

10

McAdam counts off on her fingers. 'The same symbol here on the stones, carved into the hilt of her knife, and tattooed on her back.'

'And now we know it wasn't just chalked on any stone. It was specifically on the stone where her brother's blood was found after he disappeared.' A chill wind passing through the stones makes you shiver. 'That's no accident.'

You both stare in silence at the markings, wracking your brains. You simply can't put your finger on what it could mean.

Turn to **47**

11

'We are still in the early stages of both cases,' you say to the camera, 'but rest assured we're doing everything we can to determine who's behind them. Now would you kindly stop filming?'

'Or what, you'll smash my phone like your maniac partner did to my camera?'

'I fear you're mistaken, Ms Grafton. I understand you're upset about the death of Lori Velvet, but you can't go around accusing the police of such things and stirring up trouble.'

Julie curls her lip in disgust. 'You're an even worse liar than you are a copper, and that's saying something.'

> *Write **J7** in your notebook*
>
> *Then turn to **64***

12

'Thank you, Patrick,' you say, turning to leave. You're keen to talk to other witnesses and suspects.

Sergeant McAdam takes your arm and pulls you aside. 'Are you sure we're done here, Inspector? Maybe we should take a look at the room Lori stayed in first. Never know what we might find.'

She has a point. Perhaps you were too hasty?

> *To ask Patrick if you can see Lori's room, turn to **82***
>
> *To stick to your guns and leave, turn to **100***

13

Leaving Constable Zwale to deal with Julie and Bill, you slip out of the pub and creep around the square, sticking to the edges and relying on the thickening haze to mask your presence.

It works. You tuck yourself in the shadowy doorway of a

bakery, close enough to Aaron and Raven to overhear them without being seen. Their voices aren't raised, but they're not trying to be quiet either.

'—warning you, this has to stop,' you hear Aaron say.

'I swear I don't know what you're talking about.'

'You can deny it all you want, but I bet you'll change your tune once that detective sees your phone and emails, won't you?'

'Aaron, please. This isn't fair. The things I've done for you . . .'

'See? That's what I'm talking about. Man, I can't wait to get out of this place. Listen to me: I don't want you anywhere near the gig tonight. I'm serious. If I see you there, I'll call the cops and tell them everything.'

This is clearly Aaron's parting shot. You suspect you may know why he's angry at Raven, but to find out for sure you'd have to reveal yourself, and that could make them defensive.

   To reveal yourself and ask questions, turn to **68**

   To remain out of sight and let them go their separate ways, turn to **156**

14

You cross the circle and approach the remaining members of Killer Velvet, who stand among the trees outside the police cordon. You're looking for Aaron Warrior in particular – at first you don't see him, but as you draw closer you realize he's in the shadow of a large tree with his arms wrapped around Julie Grafton, seemingly comforting her.

'Sorry to interrupt,' McAdam says, startling them. She isn't sorry at all, of course. They separate awkwardly, and Aaron glares at the sergeant while Julie wipes a tear from her eye.

'What now?' Aaron says, annoyed. 'Can we leave, or what?'

'You can, but first I wondered if you might be able to help.'

You'd planned to speak to Aaron by himself, but having Julie here as well could be equally useful.

🔎 *Turn to* **164**

15

'Boss,' you answer. 'What's up?'

'I was going to ask you the same question,' he replies. 'You've only been on the Velvet case for a day, and you've already got one officer in the hospital and a second body from a cold case. What the hell's going on?'

You haven't actually been investigating for even a full day yet, but correcting your DCS will do you no favours.

'There are a lot of moving parts, and a fair amount of local resistance,' you explain. 'But we have around half a dozen suspects in the picture. I believe Sergeant McAdam was attacked by the same person who killed Lori Velvet, though I wasn't able to apprehend them. On the other hand, if not for that encounter we might never have found Daniel Isherwood's body.'

He grumbles. 'I'm sure I don't need to tell you that the press

30

are banging down my door. I tried to keep it from them as long as I could, but it was only a matter of time. I'm told it's spreading all over social media thanks to the band's fans. There's a magnifying glass on you for this one, Inspector, and the sun is ever brightening.'

Not around here, you think, looking around at the dark and desolate village square from your position on the bench. Instead, you say, 'Yes, there are some reporters here already. We can't stop them talking to locals, although the good people of Grenholme seem no more enamoured of the press than they are of the police.'

'Small mercies,' he grumbles. 'What *can* you give me for an announcement? Anything at all?'

You consider what you've learned so far. 'I'm not really sure there's anything yet. The one thing we know for certain is the victim's connection to this village, and her relationship to the second body, which is all but confirmed to be her brother Daniel. But the moment we release that information we'll be overrun by ghouls, wannabe detectives and worst of all: true crime podcasters. At the moment, all things considered, Grenholme remains fairly quiet. I'd like to keep it that way for as long as possible.'

The DCS is silent. You hope it's because he's seriously considering what you said, rather than thinking of how to word his rebuke.

'The parents are coming down from Scotland to see the body,' he says at last. 'I can't tell them nothing.'

'I'm not asking you to keep anything from the parents, just the press. It's not like we've never delayed releasing information before. I need more time.'

'Don't we all, but given the cold case as well, this is a sensitive one. In light of past failures, we must make ourselves look good to—'

Your phone beeps with another incoming call, this time from Dr Wash.

'Understood, boss, of course. Listen, I've got the pathologist calling me on the other line, I'll have to take it. Speak later.'

Before he can protest, you switch over to take the other call.

'Thank you for saving me from a dose of red-hot coals, Doctor. What can I do for you?'

'First of all, you can tell me how Ruth is doing,' she replies in her impeccable accent. 'I gather she's being kept in for observation. Are there complications?'

Dr Wash is the only person outside of Sergeant McAdam's family who dares to use her first name. They've had their differences in the past; following her first encounter with your then-new partner, the doctor was unimpressed and even warned you not to risk your career for McAdam if the sergeant went down in flames. But since then, a grudging respect has grown between them, as it often does in law enforcement. Harsh words may be traded, but they're colleagues all the same.

'I don't believe so,' you answer. 'I think the main purpose of the "observation" is to make sure she remains in bed, rather than trying to immediately come back to work.'

'Yes, I can see the sense in that. So you're working solo?'

'Actually, I have Constable Zwale assisting me for now.'

Dr Wash makes a noncommittal noise. 'You really do like a challenge, don't you, Inspector? Still, none of my business. Now, I have good news: I've cleaned up the bracelet found on the skeletal remains from the tree, and it all but confirms that this is Daniel Isherwood. Stay on the line, I'll send you a photo.'

🔍 *If you have P13 written in your notebook, turn to* **83**

🔍 *Otherwise, turn to* **188**

16

'For a start,' you say, 'it's no secret you were opposed to Killer Velvet performing and filming here in Grenholme. What you didn't tell us is that you'd gone so far as to organize a petition to have them banned from setting foot in the village.'

Glenn shifts uncomfortably. 'I'm within my rights.'

'Indeed you are, but considering current events I'm sure you understand why it's come to our attention. Why were you so opposed to them coming here?'

'I already told you. They're Satanist degenerates, offensive to all good and Christian-minded people. I saw no reason why we should welcome them to our home, and I knew no good would come of it. Well, I was right, wasn't I? That poor girl's death was a tragedy, and I pray for her soul as I would anyone's, but she led a life of sin.'

'Is that why you took matters into your own hands?' McAdam asks.

Glenn twitches, and he looks away. 'Surely even you know that His guidance is "Hate the sin, love the sinner". Given the chance I would have steered the girl on to a righteous path, not killed her for it. Besides, as I've already told you, I was with the Stargazers all night.'

🔎 *If you have B5 written in your notebook, turn to* **137**

🔎 *Otherwise, turn to* **78**

17

'Yet she did just that,' you point out. 'Can you think of a reason why? Given, as you say, that she was from the area and knew all about the Stone Warden.'

'I wish I could,' Bill says. 'I wish I'd got there sooner, too. Another few minutes and the Disciples would have arrived at the circle ourselves.'

You recall what Julie said, about asking Bill for help.

'That's why you declined to help the band coordinate the music video, wasn't it? Because you'd be working with the Disciples that night instead.'

'It wasn't just that. The full moon unlocks the stones, drawing back the veil between worlds. To enter at that time, with the Stone Warden abroad, isn't just desecration, it's stupid. I told her not to do it, and look what happened.'

Now it's your turn to roll your eyes.

'Mr Thomas, I appreciate your beliefs are sincerely held, but whoever killed Lori Velvet was not a forest spirit or mythological figure. It was a very human act, both cruel and tragic.'

🔎 *Turn to* **75**

'Let's just wait here for a while and people-watch,' you say. 'I'm sure Ms Moonwolf won't be long.'

McAdam grumbles, always preferring to be on the move and doing things, but waits with you.

The locals continue to avoid you and offer suspicious looks. A more superstitious detective might accuse them of giving you the 'evil eye'. Undeserved, perhaps, but you understand the motivation well enough. Small communities like Grenholme don't mistrust outsiders simply for the sake of it. They live by routines and familiarity, a necessary orderliness which allows them to exist peacefully in a place where they live cheek-by-jowl, seeing the same neighbours day in and day out, year after year. Your presence in the village signals a disruption of that order, a forced and unwelcome break in the routine that makes them see their neighbours in a new and potentially dangerous light.

A young woman, holding a toddler's hand, stops and asks, 'What you waiting here for?'

You would have thought that quite obvious, but this being the first local to speak directly to you since you arrived, you endeavour to keep the conversation going. 'For the owner to return. Do you know Ms Moonwolf?'

'Of course,' the woman says, with a confused expression. 'She runs the shop.'

'What can you tell us about her?'

'Who, Raven? She's lovely. Now listen, I heard that singer had her eyes taken out. Serves her right, I suppose.'

You glance down at the child, whom you assume is the

woman's daughter, and wonder if this conversation is suitable for her young ears. 'What makes you say that?'

'Well, you know. Coming here, singing about the Warden's eyes and dressing up like that. It's tempting fate, isn't it?'

'Her eyes were just fine,' McAdam says, annoyed. 'Who started this rumour?'

A voice from behind you asks: 'What rumour?'

You turn to see Raven Moonwolf standing there, once again dressed all in black, with a handbag slung over her shoulder. She holds a key in one hand and a loaf of bread in the other.

'The Warden took her eyes,' the woman says to Raven. 'I said she was tempting fate. Sorry, Ray, I know you liked her.'

With that, the woman leads her daughter away. The child looks back and sticks out her tongue at you.

While Raven unlocks the door, you ask: 'What did she mean? You told us you had no personal connection to Lori Velvet.'

She sighs and ushers you inside.

'Not exactly. Look, there are things I need to tell you. Come inside and I'll explain.'

Turn to **80**

19

Zwale groans. 'I just remembered I promised the Sarge I'd pick up that rounders set she bought for her son. If I find Raven, do you think she'll open the shop for me?'

'It can wait till morning. The main concern now is ensuring everyone's safety, not—'

You stop short, remembering what you saw in Raven's shop beside the plastic rounders toys: a selection of children's fishing nets, not unlike what the Stone Warden was carrying in the forest. Why? The answer seems tantalizingly close . . . but you have more immediate things to worry about.

'Never mind,' you say. 'Go and see if Raven's at home.'

🔍 *Turn to* **120**

20

'What about Lori?' you ask. 'Do you really think she'd have wanted this?'

'Of course she would,' Aaron sneers. 'We formed this band together, and we were partners for two years. Nobody knows her better than me.'

Sensing an opening, McAdam dives in wearing her most innocent expression. 'I'm a simple woman, Mr Warrior. Could you explain to me why your "partner" was planning to sue you for the naming rights to Killer Velvet?'

Aaron pales. 'I don't—What?'

'Would that be worth a lot of money?'

'Oh, I imagine it must be,' you say, playing along. 'It would allow her to release records under that name by herself, without involving Mr Warrior at all. What do you think were her chances of winning, Sergeant?'

'Quite good, I'd say. After all, she was the figurehead. She even changed her name to match the band.'

'Wait, wait, hang on,' Aaron protests nervously. 'Is this going where I think it is? First I'm accused of killing Lori for publicity, now you think I did it over the band name? You're more useless than you look. That lawsuit was nonsense. She couldn't take the name from me, we co-own the band.'

'So you did know she was planning to sue?' you ask.

Aaron scowls, realizing he's trapped himself. 'OK, fine. Our manager heard a rumour and told me, but I knew she wouldn't go through with it. She'd never have won. We signed a contract when we formed Killer Velvet, in black and white.'

'A contract that now means nothing,' you point out. 'With Lori dead, and her pending lawsuit never filed, nobody can challenge your ownership of Killer Velvet, can they? Or stop you taking her place on stage tonight.'

'That's – that's just a stopgap,' he insists. 'It's too early to decide what happens next. Keith and Steve are fine with it.'

That may be true, but the drummer and bassist are not running the show and making decisions. No matter what he says, the fact remains that with Lori out of the way, Aaron Warrior is now the undisputed leader of Killer Velvet.

Turn to **153**

21

'One last thing, Mr Davis. Have you seen this before?' You show him the scrapbook you found in Lori's room.

Glenn takes it from you and leafs through the pages. Understandably, he doesn't linger on the press reports naming him as a chief suspect in Daniel's disappearance.

'That poor girl,' he says again. 'Imagine the trauma. No wonder she fell into darkness.' He closes the book and hands it back to you. 'Not memories I particularly want to revisit.'

'You didn't answer the Inspector's question,' McAdam says. 'Have you seen the book before?'

'Never. Although, looking at it now . . . this rings a bell.'

He points to the symbol on the cover. The same one on the stones, and tattooed on Lori's back.

'Rings a bell how, exactly?'

'Daniel had a bracelet, a wooden beaded thing. He never took it off. I'm sure it had a symbol like that printed on it.'

That might explain why Lori seemed to place such importance on it. Something associated with her brother, and a way to keep his memory alive.

'Do you know what it means?' you ask.

'No idea, sorry. I never enquired. It was just a bracelet.'

⚭ **Add 1** *to your LOCATION number, then turn to* **100**

22

'It's no good,' you say, frustrated. 'I can't work it out.'

'Maybe we're looking at it wrong,' Zwale suggests. 'What if it's "Dan", not "Danny"?' In his own notebook, he divides up the letters. '*Dan – Nyis – H* . . . OK, maybe not. I don't suppose his middle name was "Nyis", was it?'

You smile ruefully. 'I don't believe he had one. You might be on to something, though. Let me think . . .'

Using this principle, try again to work out the message in the symbols. When you think you've got it, write out the full message, then assign each letter a number from 1 to 26 — but counting backwards. *So, in this case A = 26, B = 25, and so on down to Z = 1. Finally, add together all the numbers to get a total amount between 1 and 200.*

When you're confident you've found the solution, turn to the section matching that total number, but before you do note down section **178** *in your notebook. You'll know right away if you've deciphered it correctly. If not, you should turn immediately to 178 instead.*

    ⚲ *Alternatively, if you still can't work it out or don't want to try, turn to* **178** *anyway*

23

Deflated and upset, Julie sits at a table by herself near the window. Glenn is at another table; you noticed that when things became heated, he backed away to quietly watch events unfold. Aaron takes a cigarette packet from his pocket and steps outside to smoke. Patrick wearily brings out the dustpan and brush once more, this time to sweep up the remains of Julie's camera.

With the tension finally ebbing, McAdam releases Raven in order to retrieve the knife from the dartboard. The shop-keeper immediately goes to Bill.

'I'm confiscating this,' McAdam says to Raven, taking an empty evidence bag from her pocket and placing the knife inside. 'You'll be helping us with our inquiries.'

'I already have been,' Raven protests.

'I want to press charges,' Julie says to you. 'Then I want to get out of this horrible place as quickly as possible.'

'Unfortunately, neither is your decision to make,' you point out. 'I must ask everyone to stay in the area until further notice. As for making an arrest, that's within our discretion.'

McAdam looks at you expectantly. By rights you should be arresting several people here, after everything that's happened in the last few minutes, but you know from experience that doing so will only make everyone clam up and refuse to talk to you any further. You make a decision.

'However, as I was saying, emotions are understandably running high and I see no benefit in making this situation worse. The real issue at stake is who killed Lori Velvet, and everything else is secondary. Ms Grafton, I'll ensure you're compensated for the loss of your camera. I suggest we draw a line under things there.'

McAdam is agog, but you're confident it's the right decision.

As the formerly squabbling patrons separate, you approach Patrick at the bar and show him the note Aaron found.

'Apparently this was pinned to your front door,' you say. 'What do you know about it?'

'Anyone could have put it there,' Patrick says with a shrug. 'This place is like the village's living room.' He reads the note aloud. '*The Stone Warden has a human face.* She said that last night, you know. She told me she knew.'

'Knew what?'

'The Warden's face. We talked for a bit before she went on stage.'

'Good of you to mention this earlier,' McAdam says sarcastically. 'What exactly did she say?'

Patrick looks about to say something, then decides against it. 'I don't remember,' he says, turning away.

You hear a door slam, and look around to see Raven and Bill leave the pub.

'I realize our presence is disruptive,' you say to Patrick. 'But the more help you can give us, the sooner my officers will be able to leave Grenholme in peace.'

'Look, all she said was that we'd all learn the truth at midnight.'

You exchange glances with McAdam. Lori was killed at eleven forty-seven. Was she killed before she could reveal something?

You show Patrick the photo of the Bluetooth speaker found in the tree. 'Do you recognize this?'

'Speaker, isn't it? I use some in here, but they're bigger.'

'None of yours are missing?'

'No, look, you can see them.' He points to the room's high corners, where wireless speakers sit on small shelves. 'Is it important?'

'That remains to be seen.'

A movement outside draws your eye. You step closer to the windows and see Bill and Raven walk together into the square, then exchange words and a brief hug before separating. They leave in different directions.

'There's something about those two conspiring that I don't like,' McAdam says quietly. 'Should we go after them?'

'Frankly, there's something off about almost everyone we've met in Grenholme,' you reply. 'All we can do is work through the case as always, one step at a time.'

To leave the pub and go after Bill and Raven, turn to **84**

Or you can stay in the pub and talk instead to those who remain here:

- *To interview Aaron, turn to* **168**
- *To speak with Glenn, turn to* **111**
- *To talk to Julie, turn to* **55**

24

As you turn away, though, a thought strikes you.

'Mr Thomas, you and your Disciples seem very confident the Stone Warden is real and was abroad tonight in the forest. Meanwhile, the band were filming a music video. Perhaps they might have caught your elusive warden on film.'

Bill considers this, then laughs. 'No chance. I've tried to take a photo of him plenty of times myself. We all have. Nobody's ever managed it.'

'But you told us you've seen him,' McAdam says, pointing at the Disciple who spoke up earlier. 'Did you not have your phone with you?'

'You don't understand,' says the man. 'He doesn't show up in photos. You can only see the Stone Warden with mortal eyes.'

'How convenient,' you say. 'Well, on the bright side I suppose that means anyone who *has* been caught on film must be human after all.'

Leaving Constable Zwale to take Bill's statement, you and McAdam retreat to the stone circle.

'Let's remember to ask Julie Grafton for the footage she shot tonight,' you say. 'If Lori Velvet's killer was in these woods, it's possible they might have been filmed without knowing it.'

'Assuming it wasn't one of the band who killed her,' McAdam points out.

- _Write_ **J3** _in your notebook_
- _If you haven't yet spoken to Glenn Davis, the astronomer, turn to_ **113**
- _Otherwise, turn to_ **88**

25

You pass the parking area and enter the woods, soon enveloped by a frosty mist that reduces visibility to ten metres at best. Moving slowly between the shrouded trees, you carefully pick your way through roots, brambles and bluebell patches. Neither you nor McAdam speak, though you can hear her breathing even over your own. The lack of vision somehow seems to sharpen your hearing.

Within minutes, confidence that you're heading in the right direction begins to waver. The gloom obscures any view of your way back as well as forward.

The loud, sharp crack of a branch sounds. Near by or carried easily through the still, silent forest? You can't tell, but you glance at McAdam, who makes a barely visible nod. Whatever it was, she heard it too.

The answer comes soon after, when you hear another

snap followed by the crunch of brambles underfoot. You keep moving, resisting the urge to immediately turn around. Instead, you and McAdam instinctively move further apart, walking around opposite sides of trees and, step by step, drifting away from one another.

The footsteps remain, carefully shadowing your movement through the forest. So, your pursuer has decided to stick with you, rather than McAdam. You maintain pace, walking at an even speed. Who is behind you? Did they see you enter the trees and decide to follow, or were they waiting? Why haven't they announced themselves? Your breath quickens, anticipating danger. All you can do now is trust Sergeant McAdam . . .

. . . Who bursts out of the trees somewhere behind you, yelling, 'Police! Stop where you are!'

'*Aaah!* Jesus Christ!' screams a familiar voice. You turn to see Julie Grafton, one arm locked behind her back by McAdam. The other hand grips a phone, which Julie holds up to film you as she recovers her composure.

'Why are you following us?' McAdam growls.

'Last time I looked it's still a free country,' Julie protests, turning the phone on herself and the sergeant. 'This is police harassment!'

'Let her go, Sergeant.' McAdam does, reluctantly. You continue: 'Might I point out, Ms Grafton, that you were the one following us. If anyone is guilty of harassment here, it's not us.'

She turns the phone back on you. 'Is that your official statement? Where are you going in the forest, anyway? What have you found out about Lori's murder?'

It's an attempt to intimidate you, to make you aware you're being filmed in the hope you'll say or do something headline-worthy. But this isn't your first time dealing with the press, or, in Julie's case, someone who wants to act like they're press.

'We are visiting the crime scene,' you say. 'The place where your friend and partner was killed less than twenty-four hours ago, of which you should need no reminder. As I'm sure you're aware, we can't comment freely on an ongoing investigation. If you truly wish to make a sympathetic documentary about Lori's death, I suggest you return to the village and talk to those who knew her rather than following us while we do our job. *That* is my official statement.'

McAdam gives Julie one last warning glare, then you both resume walking through the trees, hoping the director does the sensible thing and stays behind.

'Well handled,' McAdam says quietly. 'Not sure I would have kept my temper as easily.'

'The last thing we want out there is footage that Julie can turn against us. As she said, we can't stop her entering public areas. We can only hope she sees sense.'

'Unless she's hassling us because she did it, and doesn't want us to find out. "Jealous lover" is an evergreen motive.'

Your diversion took you away from the path towards the circle, but you walk on through the trees and undergrowth, starting to recognize some landmarks. A tree with a particularly knurled trunk, rooted just before a dip in the ground, looks familiar and you estimate you're a hundred metres or so from the stone circle.

You hear footsteps again.

'For God's sake,' McAdam murmurs. 'So much for Julie learning her lesson.'

You let out a resigned sigh. You really hoped the director

would take your advice. You look from side to side, peering through the billowing fog, and see a silhouette about twenty metres away. When the mist parts, you can hardly believe your eyes.

The Stone Warden stalks through the trees. The avatar's moss-covered face and tattered robes seem to drift through the bitter air, like a limb of ancient forest come alive. He appears to be moving in the same direction as you, towards his domain: the Lock Stones.

Without taking your eyes from the Warden, you reach out and tap McAdam on the arm.

'Where is—' she begins, then gasps.

Alerted to your presence, the Warden turns his hooded eyes upon you. The moment seems to stretch in time as you stare at one another through the trees.

Then the mist closes around the Warden again, returning him to a mere silhouette, and he hurries away into the forest.

'Stop! Police!' McAdam shouts, breaking into a run. But what will you do?

⚘ *To chase the Warden, turn to* **89**

⚘ *To let the Warden go, turn to* **177**

26

You give McAdam the nod to interview Julie, then follow Aaron into his room and close the door behind you. The space is clean and tidy, with everything neatly arranged and in its place. Quite a contrast to Lori's room.

Aaron takes a guitar from beside the door and sits on the bed, absent-mindedly picking at the strings.

'I'll get right to the point,' you say, sitting in a rickety wooden chair by the window. 'How long have you and Julie been in a relationship?'

'A couple of months. Before you ask, no, obviously Lori didn't know and we intended to keep it that way. If she'd found out she'd have thrown Julie out of the flat, and fired her from the video.'

'Lori would have done that, despite Julie's talent as a director?'

Aaron snorts. 'She's hardly Spike Jonze. What Julie's got going for her is looks and charm. Lori thought so too, and that's how she got this job.' Seeing you're taken aback by this accusation, he smirks. 'Rock 'n' roll, Inspector. It's not like your world.'

'I assume you didn't mention your reservations about Julie to Lori.'

'Didn't want the argument, did I?'

'Especially if she found out you were sleeping with her girlfriend.'

He shrugs and strums a chord on his guitar. 'Julie knows which side her bread's buttered. She's even encouraged me to go solo. Maybe I will.'

You wonder briefly if that could be a motive for killing Lori: to get her out of the way so Aaron is free to pursue a solo career. But would that be necessary? Couldn't he just leave the band and strike out on his own?

Unprompted, Aaron says: 'I've got a stalker, you know.'

This abrupt change of subject catches you off guard, but is undeniably relevant. 'I understand obsessive fans are a common hazard of fame,' you say. 'Have they made contact? Do you know who it is?'

'No, they send me anonymous emails and text messages. I'll show you.' He puts aside the guitar and pulls a laptop from a backpack by the bed, opening his email.

You try to hide your feelings, but I know you're thinking about Me. The time isn't right, I understand that, but I need to know when you'll be ready.

Give me a sign to tell me when we can be together. You don't need that Bitch. Ditch her and it can just be the Two of us. For ever.

I know you can't reply because She might see it. That's why I'm always watching, so you can tell me without Her knowing. Give me a sign and I'll know. I know your signals better than your own mother.

'Loads more, all the same,' Aaron says. 'It started about six months ago, not long after I dumped Lori. I don't reply – I'm not an idiot – but it makes me nervous. I've changed my phone number twice already, but they keeping finding it again. Every time I step out on stage I wonder if she's in the audience.'

'Or he,' you suggest. 'I don't see anything in here to confirm it's a woman. Have you brought this to the police's attention?'

Aaron closes the laptop and puts it back in the backpack. 'Yeah, but your lot said there's nothing they can do unless she – or he, whatever – does something illegal. They can't trace anything, either. Burner email accounts and phones.'

You wonder if these messages are connected to Lori's death. Is it possible she also had a stalker? Or that this obsessive, jealous fan of Aaron's killed Lori because they saw 'Her' as a threat? If so, it would suggest they were here in Grenholme. They might even be on Raven's video of the crowd.

'Aaron, last night you said the band were all together, until suddenly you noticed that Lori had left the video shoot. Did she say anything to you before leaving for the Lock Stones? Or to anyone else?'

He shakes his head. 'Not about wandering off. She was kind of snarky, taking shots at me and Julie, but we're used to that. She often gets like that when she's nervous, though. I reckon it was because the gig was only half-full, thanks to her stupid idea not to promote it. Only the really hardcore fans found out about it.'

'Hardcore fans . . . like your anonymous stalker?'

Aaron's eyes widen as he realizes what you're implying. 'Yeah. I suppose so.'

You still have Lori's scrapbook, and are debating whether to show it to Aaron when he blurts out:

'I just remembered. Julie wasn't around for a while.'

'What do you mean?'

'Last night, in the woods. After doing close-ups of Keith and Steve she said she wanted to shoot some more B-roll of the forest, and walked off while I prepped. She came back about ten minutes later, and we were doing my close-ups when we heard Lori scream . . .' He trails off.

'Which means Julie was with you when Lori was killed,' you

reassure him. 'So she probably really was filming. Thank you, though. I'll follow up with her.'

Before you show Aaron the scrapbook you have another, more difficult choice to make: whether or not to tell him that Lori was pregnant.

*⚲ To tell Aaron about Lori's pregnancy, turn to **65***

*⚲ To keep Lori's pregnancy secret for now, turn to **104***

27

McAdam checks her notes. 'If the band is so import-ant to you, can you explain why you left them in the forest last night? Julie says you disappeared for about fifteen minutes.'

Aaron looks furious, but controls his temper and says quietly, 'I was on the phone to our manager. Had to walk back out to the edge of the forest to get a signal.'

'It seems an unusually late hour to have a phone call.'

'Rock 'n' roll time,' he says with a shrug. 'We don't operate on the same clock everyone else does.'

'What did you talk about?' you ask.

'Legal talk. You can check with him if you like.'

'Oh, be assured we will.'

*⚲ Write **A1** in your notebook*

*⚲ Then turn to **199***

28

So, the message on the stones, almost certainly written by Lori Velvet herself, reads 'Danny is here'. But now you have to ask yourself: why?

Did Lori somehow know that her twin brother's body was interred in the forest? Presumably she can't have known its exact location, or she would have simply led someone to it . . . wouldn't she?

As a child, Lori had told everyone the Stone Warden took her brother. Nobody credited her story because she was only seven years old and deemed hysterical.

What if she was right?

It would explain why she returned to Grenholme. Why she wrote a song about the Stone Warden, and insisted they film their music video here under a full moon. Why she declared to the crowd that 'The Warden has a human face', and even carried a knife with her into the forest.

Lori came to Grenholme Forest hoping to find Daniel's body . . . and his killer.

   Write **P13** *in your notebook*

   Then turn to **45**

(Or, if you came here after solving the symbols at some other time on your own initiative, return instead to whichever section you were reading when you solved the cipher, before you turned to 175)

29

You signal to McAdam to remain where she is, then step quietly into the narrow street, keeping to the same shadows in which the two men lurk. Bill and Glenn are too immersed in their argument to see you, and as you approach you overhear snatches of their angry whispers.

'. . . want to see you anywhere near the forest tonight . . .' Glenn says. '. . . police will hear . . . a promise.' Although he's the shorter of the two men, Glenn doesn't look at all intimidated by Bill.

The pagan leader makes a dismissive gesture. '. . . Hear what? . . . nothing on me.'

You draw closer, and their conversation becomes clearer.

'I saw you, Bill. I saw you arguing. Do you understand me?'

'You're not the only one—'

Unfortunately, your luck runs out as, unused to the cobbled street, you stumble on a stone and the two men immediately notice you. There's no sense in trying to back out, so instead you assert your authority.

'Good morning, gents. Anything you'd like to add to your statements?'

Glenn and Bill eye one another warily, then both shake their heads.

'I don't think so,' Glenn says. 'But while you're here, please inform Mr Thomas that his Disciples will not be welcome in the forest this evening.'

You turn to Bill. 'This evening?'

'Seeing as last night's protective ceremony was interrupted, we're going to perform a cleansing ritual tonight. To make sure the evil's all gone.'

Suddenly, a voice from behind you calls out: 'Inspector, what's going on?'

You turn to see Raven Moonwolf entering the narrow street, once again dressed all in black, with a handbag slung over her shoulder. She holds a key in one hand and a loaf of bread in the other. McAdam tries to usher her away, but Raven shrugs off the sergeant.

'I said, what's going on?'

'Ms Moonwolf, if you could please just wait a moment while I finish talking to these gentlemen . . .?'

'Looks like you're already done,' she says.

You turn back to Bill and Glenn and find they've taken their leave while you were distracted. The street is empty.

You sigh. 'Very well. As it happens, we were looking for you a moment ago. Could we talk somewhere?'

'Of course,' she says, returning across the square to her shop door. 'There are things I need to tell you anyway. Come inside and I'll explain.'

🔎 *Write* **B1** *in your notebook*

🔎 *Then turn to* **80**

30

McAdam places a business card on the counter. 'Thanks for your time, Ms Moonwolf. Please send me copies of those videos you took last night.'

Raven opens her mouth to say something, then thinks twice. She places the card in her handbag.

'Is there something else, Raven?' you say gently. 'You can speak to us in confidence.'

The shopkeeper shuffles nervously, as if weighing her options. 'I promised her I wouldn't, but . . . now she's dead it seems pointless.'

'By "she", you mean Lori Velvet?'

Raven takes a breath, then exhales. 'Lori came into the shop yesterday afternoon. Incognito, like, but I recognized her.'

'You already told us you're a fan of the band,' you point out. 'Why wouldn't you recognize her, even if she was incognito?'

'I don't mean she was wearing sunglasses. Well, she was, but that's not what I'm talking about. For a start, you should know that Lori Velvet was only a stage name.'

'Oh? Do tell.'

'Her real name was Lucy. Lucy Isherwood,' Raven says smugly.

McAdam catches your eye and presses on. 'She told you that, did she? So what was she doing in here? Looking at the Warden costumes, by any chance?'

Raven makes a face. 'I wish she had. My costumes are more accurate than what she wore on stage. You should have seen Aaron's reaction – she might as well have walked out wearing a bin bag. No, she was looking at crystals, the stone replicas, and stuff like that. We got talking, so I said I was looking forward to the gig . . . and then she called me "Angela".'

Raven's expression tells you this is obviously significant, somehow, but it means nothing to you.

'Speaking of birth names,' she explains. 'Nobody's called me that in years. Fifteen years, to be precise. That was when I knew. She made me promise I wouldn't tell, though.'

Despite her earlier reluctance, Raven appears to be enjoying stringing this moment out. Impatiently, you ask, 'Why didn't you mention last night that you'd spoken to her?'

'I was kind of in shock, sorry. It wasn't until I got home that I remembered.'

Given her enthusiasm for the band, it seems unlikely that Raven would have forgotten a personal encounter with the singer, but you let that pass for now.

'Where did Lori recognize you from? You told us you've lived here your whole life.'

'Oh, yes. Exactly.'

If one of Raven's crystals was measuring her level of smugness at this moment, it would glow like the sun. Nevertheless, you're starting to put together the pieces of what she's told you, and it does indeed seem significant.

'Are you saying that Lori Velvet had been to Grenholme before?'

'More than that, Inspector. The Isherwoods lived here . . . until Lucy's brother disappeared.'

This revelation hits you like a felled tree in the forest.

'Our records say she was born in London.'

'Maybe she was, but the family came to Grenholme when the twins were babies. I think they wanted to raise them somewhere quiet. They moved away again after Danny vanished, though. They couldn't cope.'

McAdam is furiously writing notes. 'Hold on, hold on. You're saying Lori Velvet grew up here in Grenholme . . . and had a twin brother who went missing?'

'Oh, Danny didn't just go missing. The Stone Warden took him.'

You step out of Stones & Spirits into the village square with a sense that this case has suddenly become an order of magnitude more complicated than it was already.

'Sergeant, pull the records on Daniel Isherwood's disappearance.'

'Already on it,' McAdam says, tapping at her phone. 'Did you recognize the song, by the way?'

'Song? You mean the New Age whale noises?'

'No, Raven's medication alarm. That was a Killer Velvet track, from their very first album. She really is a fan.'

It explains why the shopkeeper came running to the crime scene last night, concerned for the band's welfare. But you only have her word for it that she was at home. What if she was already in the forest, following them?

You recap what you know so far. 'Lori Velvet writes a song about the mythical creature who supposedly abducted her twin brother. Then she returns here, for what sounds like the first time in years, to play a concert and make a music video for that same song. She doesn't tell anyone her past connection to the place, but is recognized by Raven, whom she swears to secrecy. Later that evening, she surprises her band by wearing a Stone Warden costume on stage, then argues offstage with Glenn Davis. Later, the band begins filming in the forest, where both the Disciples and Stargazers are gathered. Lori wanders off and enters the Lock Stones circle . . . where someone kills her with her own knife.'

McAdam is engrossed in reading her phone and says nothing.

'The question, as ever, is *why*? Why did any of those things happen? What motivated Lori to concoct this scheme around Grenholme and the Lock Stones? Why didn't she tell anyone about her connection to the village? What motivated her killer to attack her? Come to that, if she once lived here, how come nobody else in the village recognized her?'

'I think I can answer that last question,' McAdam says. 'I found a BBC news story about it. Daniel vanished fifteen years ago, when the twins were only seven years old, and the family moved away not long after. Combine that with the make-up Lori wore on stage, and it's no surprise she went unnoticed. You said yourself, you hardly recognized her at the mortuary.'

'True, and Raven said it was only when Lori called her by an old name that she recognized her as Lucy from the village. What does that report say about the night of Daniel's disappearance?'

McAdam grimaces. 'Horrible story, really. The twins apparently snuck out of the house to play in Grenholme Forest, but only Lucy returned home. She claimed they'd seen the Stone Warden at the Lock Stones: that the Warden chased them, attacked Daniel and spirited him away. They found the boy's blood on one of the stones. But Lucy couldn't explain why the Warden didn't take her as well. Given her age, the assumption was that she'd been traumatized and her mind blocked out whatever really happened. No other witnesses ever came forward, and Daniel was never found.'

'What an unthinkably horrible experience for a child to go through. Fifteen years ago, you say? When exactly?'

'April twentieth, somewhere between eight and ten in the evening. The only precise timings we have are when their parents realized the twins had snuck out, and when Lucy came running home.'

A chill passes through your bones. You almost don't want to know the answer to your next question.

'Sergeant . . . what was the moon phase on that date?'

McAdam taps out a search on her phone. Her sharp intake of breath tells you the answer before she speaks it.

'It was a full moon. Like last night.'

Turn to **100**

3 1

Time is of the essence, but so is evidence, and you can't afford to ignore something so close to where Sergeant McAdam was attacked. You crouch down, peering into the undergrowth, and recover a stubby folding knife. A decorative fish-shaped outline is moulded into the handle. Picking it up with a handkerchief, you extend the blade . . . to reveal fresh bloodstains.

You pocket the knife in the handkerchief, then resume your efforts to reach the edge of the forest.

Write **P7** *in your notebook*

Then turn to **160**

32

'Is that why Killer Velvet asked you to help them coordinate filming a music video in the forest? Because you used to play music yourself?' you ask. 'I assume it would also have helped supplement your income.'

Bill's genial mood shifts.

'I had nothing to do with that, and I never took a penny from them.'

'According to Julie Grafton, you were quite keen to be involved at first, but then later pulled out.'

'That's right,' he grumbles. 'She said they wanted to be respectful, and benefit from what I know about the forest and stones. But then they insisted on filming during a full moon. I told them that was about as *dis*respectful as you could get, but the director wouldn't budge. So I washed my hands of it, and told them the Disciples would carry out the same ritual we always have. If we got in the way of their video, tough luck.'

'Why didn't you mention this last night?' McAdam asks.

Bill shrugs. 'I was kind of thrown by finding a dead body. Besides, this was all months ago.'

    Write **B8** *in your notebook*

    Then turn to **119**

33

You approach the remaining members of Killer Velvet, intending to speak to Aaron Warrior in particular. At first, you don't see him, but as you draw closer you realize that he's in the shadow of a large tree with his arms wrapped around Julie Grafton, seemingly comforting her.

'Sorry to interrupt,' McAdam says, startling them. She isn't sorry at all, of course. They separate awkwardly, and Aaron glares at the sergeant while Julie wipes a tear from her eye.

'What now?' Aaron says, annoyed. 'Can we leave, or what?'

'You can, but first I wondered if you might be able to help.'

You'd planned to speak to Aaron by himself, but having Julie here as well could be even more useful.

🔎 *Turn to* **117**

34

'Not so fast,' you say, preventing Julie from going inside. 'I believe you've taken Patrick somewhere, and I'm concerned for his safety.'

'Why on earth would I take him anywhere? You can check the van all you like, he's not there.'

'Then I'll ask you again: what have you done with him?'

'Nothing!' she protests. 'Look, this is harassment. Before you go any further, I reckon you should see this.'

She takes out her phone, and you think she's going to start filming again, but to your surprise she turns it to face you and presses play.

You watch a video of the moment in the pub when McAdam smashed Julie's camera and destroyed the memory card. You're clearly visible, looking on and doing nothing to prevent it.

'Where did you get this?'

'A source,' she says, smugly. 'They filmed the whole thing and sent it to me. Don't even think about smashing this one too, by the way. I've already uploaded it to YouTube. I wonder what'll happen when the press see it?'

You both know the answer to that question, and you don't even have to wait long for confirmation.

As you stand dumbfounded, watching Julie return inside the pub, your own phone rings. It's the detective chief superintendent.

Not only are you and McAdam both placed on immediate suspension, but you later learn that Bill Thomas and the Disciples of the Green found Patrick's body at the Lock Stones, with his throat slashed in the same manner as Lori Velvet's.

Could Julie have killed Patrick before returning to the van where you found her? It's possible, although she'd have had to move fast. His body is found to have been drugged, but otherwise offers no solid forensic evidence, and this time there's no sign of a murder weapon.

It doesn't matter anyway. You're off the case, and potentially off the force.

Lori Velvet's murder, and now Patrick's too, may yet be solved . . . but not by you.

*Wipe your notebook, return to **1** and try again – this time acting in a manner more befitting an officer of the law.*

For now, though, this is . . .

THE END

35

Delivering news like this is never easy. You take a deep breath and bite the bullet.

'Julie, I'm afraid I may have more bad news. Our pathologist's examination revealed that Lori had recently become pregnant.'

Before you can ask if she already knew, the director gasps in surprise. Her hands fly to her mouth, and she begins to weep.

'I'm sorry to ask, but I must: do you know who the father might be? It was an early pregnancy, so conception couldn't have been more than a few months ago. Did she talk to you about wanting a child?'

Julie shakes her head, sobbing. 'No, she never . . . never talked about children, or . . . or family. We've been . . . been together since last autumn. I don't know . . . don't know . . .'

'Is it possible she was still seeing Aaron during that time? You said their relationship was unpredictable.'

'No.' Even through the tears, there's a steel in Julie's voice when she answers. 'Lori would never do that. Not with him.'

*Write **J1** in your notebook*

*Then turn to **69***

36

You haven't yet spoken to Glenn since Constable Zwale told you what he'd learned from members of the Stargazers group, so it's time to confront him with that information.

'Mr Davis, you've maintained that you were with the astronomy group all through last night, correct?'

'That's right. Until I heard the girl screaming, at which point I ran to the stones.'

'But members of your group have told us you left them for several minutes last night, and from 11.25 until 11.38 you were nowhere to be seen. How do you explain that?'

Instead of answering, he turns to look across the bar. You're about to ask him again, when he says: 'Yes, I remember now. I returned to my car, to fetch my camera. I'd forgotten to take it with me when we first set up, you see. In all the excitement.'

McAdam views him sceptically. 'You forgot your camera.'

'That's right. I retrieved it, returned to Clearing Delta and eleven minutes later I heard the girl scream.'

You find it hard to believe a man as precise and orderly as Glenn Davis would forget his camera, especially on a night supposedly so important to the Stargazers. On the other hand, he's right about the timings. Whatever the real reason he left the group, Lori was still alive when he returned.

    Write **G9** *in your notebook*

    Then turn to **163**

37

Everything you've learned has pointed towards Glenn from the start. He was already with Lori when the others found him. He was the primary suspect in Daniel's disappearance. He protested the band's appearance, and has been caught spying on them in the forest. He might even have secretly recognized Lori as Daniel's sister.

Why would he take Patrick? Did the landlord see something he shouldn't have? Perhaps Patrick witnessed Glenn kill Lori. Given Patrick's loyalty to Bill through the Disciples, Glenn would be justified in worrying that he might give him up. It would explain the poison pen letter. You wish Patrick had been more forthcoming earlier. Now Glenn is going to silence him for ever.

If they're anywhere, it must be the forest. As leader of the Stargazers, Glenn knows it like the back of his hand, even on a fog-cursed night like this.

   Write **G8** *in your notebook*

   Then turn to **182**

38

Sergeant McAdam leads you beyond the cordon to where the band wait, still wearing what you assume are their stage clothes for the music video, all black T-shirts and leather jackets.

'This is Aaron Warrior,' she says, indicating a handsome young South Asian man with long, jet-black hair. He puffs nervously on a cigarette.

'Obviously,' Aaron says in a Northern accent. 'So hurry up and tell us which village idiot did this to Lori, will you? It's freezing out here.'

'We're not ruling anyone out at the present time,' you say, with emphasis on *anyone*. 'I'd be grateful if you'd introduce yourselves.'

A woman with pillarbox-red hair stands beside Aaron. Her eyes almost match her hair from crying. 'Julie Grafton,' she sniffs. 'I'm the director.'

'For the music video. Yes, I see. Is that your rental van in the parking area?'

'Yes. Oh, God, I need to pack up. Our equipment is still in the woods.'

'All in good time. It's quite safe with our officers around. Now, what about you two?' You look over Aaron and Julie's shoulders, where two more long-haired young men in leather trousers shuffle awkwardly. They introduce themselves as Keith and Steve, the drummer and bassist of Killer Velvet. Even with their names in mind, you have trouble distinguishing between them.

'That's not your real name, is it?' McAdam says to Aaron Warrior.

He sighs. 'Of course not. My name is Arjun Shankar, but everyone calls me Aaron, OK?'

'Aaron it is,' you say. 'Now please tell us why you're here in the forest, and what happened tonight.'

He and Julie exchange glances.

'Fine,' he says at last, exhaling a cloud of smoke that mixes with the haze and drifts away into the trees. It's clear he would rather be anywhere else, which makes you suspicious. His bandmate has just been found brutally murdered, yet 'Aaron Warrior' seems more concerned with his own personal inconvenience.

'We're here because of Lori,' he continues. 'She wrote this new song, "Eyes of the Warden", OK? It takes us in a new kind of gothic direction, really dark and brooding, with—' He catches himself. 'Whatever. Anyway, she wanted to come here to film the video. I said we should stay in London and do it in a studio, but she'd already arranged it without even telling me.'

'Including a low-key gig at the local pub,' Julie interjects. 'So the band would recoup some of the cost.'

'Not enough,' Aaron adds bitterly. 'Low-key is an understatement. Lori insisted we didn't do any promotion, so that the pub wouldn't have to deal with all our fans, and that we do it "stripped back", like in the early days, lugging our own gear. Stupid idea, man. We could have packed the place out if we'd done it properly.'

'You did post on Instagram,' Julie says to him.

He shrugs. 'For ten minutes, before she made me delete it. That nutter who tried to get us barred from the village needn't have bothered.'

'Oh?' That catches your interest. 'Someone objected to your presence here?'

Julie points across the clearing to where the astronomy group is gathered. 'Him, the telescope bloke. He thinks we're all Satanists.'

'Are you?'

'Of course not. Lori was a spiritual being, and she mixed

the dark with the light. But she was always focused on the goodness in people. I made sure of that.'

You catch Aaron Warrior rolling his eyes.

'Made sure how?' you ask.

'I'm sensitive,' Julie says, as if that explains everything. When she can see it doesn't, she adds: 'To auras and spirits. I was Lori's spiritual advisor, using my gift to guide her path. So you see, it's impossible for us to be Satanists.'

McAdam's expression is inscrutable. 'Oh, aye, and I'm the Wicked Witch of the West,' she says. You expect Julie to be offended, but instead she simply looks confused.

Aaron Warrior stubs out his cigarette underfoot and laughs. 'Look, I'm not even Christian. This is all showbiz, Inspector. We sing about dark subjects in the same way Lord Byron wrote about the darkness and hypocrisy of humanity. Nobody called him a Satanist.'

'Actually, I believe some people did.'

'Whatever. The point is, we're putting on a show. It's not real.'

'How did that show go?' McAdam asks. 'Was it fun playing to a small crowd again?'

'Not really, no. We played OK, and some of the locals were into it. The ones that weren't holding placards. But it was all a bit flat until Lori put that costume on.'

You look back to the white forensics tent, its brightly lit presence a stark contrast to the dark of the surrounding trees.

'The same costume in which she was found? So she wasn't just wearing it to film the music video?'

Aaron lights another cigarette, his hands steadier now as he warms to his subject. 'Surprised us all, I tell you. We always finish the encore with "Hell Town", but tonight Lori left the stage for a minute, then came back wearing . . . that. Not her usual look, and it didn't suit her figure at all. She said we were going to play "Eyes of the Warden" live for the first time, as our finale. Apparently, the lyrics are all about this stone circle? I didn't even know that's why we were here until we arrived.'

'Was she in the habit of keeping information like that from you?'

'Lori was an artist, Inspector,' Julie says. 'She didn't feel the need to explain herself.'

'So none of you knew she was planning to wear that costume?'

Aaron shrugs. 'I'd never even seen it before.'

'I had,' Julie says. 'She showed me the other night, before we came here.'

'Why would she tell you, but not her bandmates?' McAdam asks.

'She couldn't really hide it, she was making it in our flat. We weren't just colleagues, you see, we were bonded partners.'

Aaron twitches a little. You recall what McAdam said about his former relationship with the singer, and the sergeant picks up that thread.

'Aaron, everyone knows you and Lori fought like cats when you were a couple. How about now?'

He looks confused, then realizes what McAdam is implying. 'No, hang on. This had nothing to do with me! I was with the rest of the band when we heard Lori scream, OK? Then I ran here, and I saw those two weirdos standing over her in the middle of the stones.'

'That's as may be,' you point out, making a mental note to return to this later, 'but you didn't answer my sergeant's question.'

Aaron runs a hand through his hair. 'If anything, we got on better now than when we were going out. The others can tell you that.'

You look over his shoulder to the other band members.

'Mainly because they didn't talk much any more,' Keith says, nodding. Or maybe it's Steve.

'There was no jealousy? You were happy for your former girlfriend's new girlfriend to direct your music video?'

Julie smiles. 'What Lori wants, Lori gets. We all loved her, really. The band revolved around her.'

You wonder how much truth there is in that statement. Is it the sort of empty platitude people say because they're expected to? Everyone seems quite composed considering someone they supposedly all loved has been killed.

'Ms Grafton, I'm a simple woman,' McAdam says with mock sweetness. 'So perhaps you can explain to me why you weren't here with Lori in the stone circle? Weren't you supposed to be filming?'

'We were shooting B-roll first,' she says, gesturing into the trees. 'The circle was going to be the end of the shoot, after they'd warmed up and got into it. First the band together, then Lori solo.' Julie sniffs, holding back tears. 'It was going to be great.'

'Lori wasn't needed for the B-roll footage,' Aaron explains. 'She wandered off while we were filming, and I guess she came here to scout the place out. The next thing we knew she screamed.'

'What time was that?' McAdam asks.

The band members all shrug and look to Julie. 'About a quarter to midnight,' she says. 'I was taking my last shots of Aaron before we moved on to the stones.'

'Could you show us where?' you ask. 'Take us by the same route you used to come to the stone circle.'

'Good luck with that,' Aaron grumbles. 'Can't even get a signal out here.'

Julie rolls her eyes and takes out her phone. 'GPS doesn't need it,' she says, and explains to you: 'I keep a tracker in my kit, in case it goes wandering.'

'Very sensible. Lead on, Ms Grafton.' You call to Constable Zwale and ask him to coordinate some uniformed officers with torches, to walk with you while keeping an eye on the ground.

Julie takes you and McAdam through the trees, following her beacon's signal, while the uniformed officers follow. After a short walk you emerge into a small clearing with a rather surreal scene: a drumkit and two guitars lying on the ground.

'We dropped everything when we heard Lori scream,' Julie says.

Elsewhere, two cameras are mounted on tripods. Behind them are several lights on stands, powered by large battery packs, casting harsh lights and deep shadows on the scene. Open flight cases lie on the ground: large, empty ones to hold musical instruments, and smaller ones filled with cameras, lenses and filming equipment. Two folding chairs and a table hold other equipment, plus drinks and snack food. You recognize a square of black-and-white plastic as a clapperboard, with the video name and shot written in black marker. Near by is a large speaker, with a phone balanced on top and a cable connecting the two.

'That's for the band to mime to,' Julie says when she sees you peer at it quizzically. 'They need to hear the music, so I have the song loaded up on this old phone.' She demonstrates, tapping the screen of the device connected to the speaker. A song begins playing, all drums and guitars and wailing vocals. It drowns out the forest sounds, filling the dark night air. You shiver as the temperature drops even further, and deep shadows in the trees seem to dance on the breeze. Then Julie stops the music, and you return to your senses.

'Keith was here,' she says, walking around the space and pointing to the drum kit, then the space in front of it. 'Steve was here, and Aaron was over here. Camera one was group coverage, camera two I used for solos.'

You take in the scene. It's effectively an airtight alibi. It would have been impossible for any of the band to slip away unnoticed.

'You're sure that nobody except Lori Velvet left while you were filming?'

'We were all here,' Julie replies. 'Where was there to go?' She leads you back out of the clearing towards the stone circle.

You and McAdam follow, keeping enough distance to talk quietly without Julie overhearing. Constable Zwale is waiting alone outside the clearing; he confirms that the uniformed contingent found nothing unusual along the route and have returned to the stone circle.

'Unless they all did it and are covering for one another, there's no way one band member ran off and killed her without the others noticing,' McAdam grumbles.

'Yes, it seems far too risky. Even I know rock singers can happily antagonize their colleagues, but if someone wanted rid of her there are simpler ways to do it.'

When you reach the Lock Stones, you turn your attention back to Aaron Warrior, who leans against a tree with studied nonchalance.

'"Two weirdos",' you say to him. 'That's what you told us you saw, when you arrived at the stone circle. What did you mean?'

'What I said.' The guitarist gestures across the clearing. 'The old geezer with the moustache, the religious nutter, he was on the ground with Lori in his arms. The other bloke, the one in the robe, was standing over him. I ran up and pushed the nutter off her. It was obvious she was dead. Robe-guy backed away and started swearing, like he was in shock.'

'I don't think it was shock,' Julie says. 'I got here just after Aaron and the man in the robe was on his phone, trying to call an ambulance.'

'That's a point,' you say. 'I thought there was no phone signal here?'

'Satellites,' McAdam explains, pointing up. 'Same as Julie's GPS. You can use them to call emergency services.'

'Well, I never.' You look up at the night sky, where the full moon hangs over this grisly and inexplicable forest tableau. 'I assume you already arranged somewhere to stay overnight,' you say to the band. 'Please use it and don't leave the area. For now, Constable Zwale will take your statements.'

*🔍 Write **A3** in your notebook*

*🔍 If you already have B2 written down, turn to **161***

*🔍 If you already have G4 written down, turn to **73***

Otherwise, choose which witness to interview next:

*🔍 To talk to Glenn Davis, the astronomer, turn to **113***

*🔍 To talk to Bill Thomas, the pagan leader, turn to **148***

39

'Of course, they're not the only ones keeping secrets,' you say. 'Mr Davis, we know you attended the concert last night, despite petitioning to prevent it taking place. Yet you didn't mention this to us before.'

Glenn looks away. 'I don't know what you're talking about.'

'Would you like me to show you the video?' McAdam says. 'I have one of you in the crowd, watching the band . . . and another of you arguing with Lori Velvet after she came off stage.'

He considers this, gathering his thoughts.

'I tried to dissuade her from venturing into the forest,' he says at last. 'I'd been unable to prevent the concert, obviously, so instead I asked her not to invade the woods on such an important night.'

'You mean because of the full moon?'

'No! That's all superstitious nonsense, supposed sightings of the Stone Warden and what have you. Something that's only increased in recent years, I should add. Ever since that boy went missing . . .' He momentarily loses focus. 'No, I mean the Lyrids. This is an important time of year for the Stargazers, with many guests joining us for a night or two to see the meteors. The last thing I wanted was a rock group disturbing our peace and quiet.'

'Yes, about that—' you begin, but Glenn isn't finished.

'You know, speaking of Bill, he had words with her yesterday as well. I saw them outside the pub at 7.32 p.m. It looked to be far from a friendly chat.'

'Did you by any chance hear what they were saying?'

Glenn regards you with disdain. 'I'm not an eavesdropper, Inspector. But I couldn't help overhearing a few words. Bill said, "I'm telling you, don't mess with the Warden." The woman replied, "I know more about the Warden than you realize." That was all I heard.'

'I see. And when were you planning to offer this information to us?'

'I just did.'

McAdam rolls her eyes. You sympathise, but while Glenn Davis is proving to be far from an enthusiastic witness, at least he's talking.

'You seem very protective of the forest,' you say, to keep the conversation going. 'It must be dear to you.'

'It's dear to all of Grenholme,' Glenn replies, finishing his drink. 'That's why those ridiculous Disciples are so disliked.'

'Bill Thomas maintains he's well-liked by the community.'

'Only because nobody else is willing to stand up to him. But I knew his game the moment he came here. For years, the Stargazers happily coexisted with the forest, always leaving it how we found it. Then along came Mr Bigshot from the City, claiming to have found his spiritual calling, and accused us – us! – of failing to respect nature and the Lock Stones. We don't even go near the stone circle! It makes for a terrible viewing platform.'

🔎 *Write* **G5** *in your notebook*

🔎 *Then turn to* **87**

As the Warden looms over you, blade glinting, your hand closes around a rough, jagged stone on the ground. It feels almost the size of your palm.

You hold the Warden's gaze, tensing your arm, then whip it forward and throw the stone! It bounces off the Warden's hood, and with a muffled grunt of pain he staggers back. You scramble to your feet, picking up another stone and hefting it in your hand.

Even though the Warden has a knife, it's enough to make him think twice. He turns and runs into the trees, scooping up the cloth sack and securing its contents. To your surprise, you now recognize that the plastic handle you saw belongs to a small fishing net.

Regaining your composure, you throw the stone at the Warden's back, but it goes wide and ricochets off a tree.

After a quick check that you're not injured, you resume the chase. You won't let him get away!

🔎 *Write* **P11** *in your notebook*

🔎 *Then turn to* **125**

You direct Sergeant McAdam to ask Dr Wash whether Lori was killed here or elsewhere, and her preliminary thoughts concerning the bloody knife.

Meanwhile, you call over Constable Zwale and ask: 'Do I recall correctly that many stone circles were built to be crude astronomical tools?'

'Some definitely were, but I don't know about the Lock Stones. Shall I check?'

'Later. For now, I want you to look at these chalk markings with me and see if there's any connection.'

Pleased to be asked to accompany you, the constable smiles. 'Yes, Inspector. Let's take a look.'

You first walk a quick circle of the stones, looking at each symbol to see if there's anything you recognize, such as non-Roman alphabet characters, astrological symbols, perhaps even a form of semaphore. There isn't. What's more, contrary to what you originally thought, not every stone is marked. There are eleven stones, yet only eight of them, in a continuous sequence, feature a chalk symbol.

'What do you make of it, Constable?' you ask Zwale. 'Recognize anything? Astronomy symbols, perhaps?'

He shakes his head. 'I'm afraid not. They're like nothing I've seen before. If anything . . .' He hesitates.

'Go on. I asked you to accompany me because I want your opinion. Speak freely.'

He puffs out his cheeks. 'To be honest, they look more like, um . . . magical symbols.'

'Something to do with the pagans? Do you think they're lying to us when they say they didn't draw them?'

'It's possible. I mean, witnesses lying is always possible, isn't it? But the Disciples are adamant it wasn't them. Even if the symbols are magical, they don't look familiar at all. It's like something completely made-up.'

'Do you have much experience with magical symbols?'

Zwale looks a little embarrassed. 'When I was younger. A phase, you know.'

'I do indeed,' you reassure him. 'Fetch me the scene photographer, would you?'

Although there's nothing explicit to suggest these symbols are linked to Lori's killing, you're not taking any chances. Another spell of rain could wash them away in minutes. You ask the police photographer to take a picture of every stone, even the unmarked ones, while you also sketch them in your notebook for your own convenience.

You despair of making sense of them. What if it's just local children messing around? There probably isn't much for young people to do around here.

But then, as you stand before the final marked stone and focus your light on it, something catches your attention on the ground. Something that shines bright white when illuminated. You finish sketching the symbol, then crouch to investigate. Something lies by the stone, half-hidden in a clump of grass.

A piece of chalk.

Placing it in an evidence bag, you wonder if its presence explains why only eight of the stones carry symbols. Suddenly, you're back to assuming this has a connection to the murder. Did someone begin drawing these symbols, but was surprised and interrupted before they could finish? Could that person be Lori's killer, caught in the act when the singer unexpectedly entered the stone circle – alone and ahead of schedule? If so, it might mean the killer knew the band's filming schedule . . .

Your thoughts are interrupted by a woman's horrified voice from across the stone circle.

'Oh, Goddess! What happened?'

> *Write **P5** in your notebook*
> *Then turn to **183***

42

Like the Stone Warden earlier today, Glenn has you at a disadvantage by knowing Grenholme Forest better than you ever could. On the other hand, being in better shape, you move faster. And you're both at the mercy of the drifting fog, which randomly obscures paths and obstacles as you run. The cut he gave you bleeds into your eyes, half blinding you.

Nevertheless, you maintain your pursuit, neither gaining ground nor losing him. By now you're deep in the forest. Constable Zwale will never find you. If you're going to bring Glenn Davis in, you must do it alone.

Why did he run? Because he knows the game is up. You

should have seen it sooner, really. Many signs have pointed to Glenn from the start, but your mind should have been finally made up when, without any prompting or suggestion from you, he accused Raven of dressing up as the Warden to drum up publicity.

'*Cui bono*,' Glenn had said, hoping the thought would lead you towards his ex-wife and her shop. But Glenn also benefits from the myth, because the more people believe in the Stone Warden, the more easily they'll blame disappearances and deaths on the forest spirit rather than a man. A man like Glenn Davis.

As you clamber over a rise in the ground, keeping him in sight, a foul smell drifts upon the damp air. You're close by the bog where Daniel's body was found.

> *Turn to* **169**

43

You decide it's time to bring up the victim's past.

'Tell me, did you recognize Lori Velvet? Is that the real reason you attended the concert, and spoke to her afterwards?'

Glenn looks confused. 'Recognize? What do you mean?'

'So you didn't know she was, in fact, Lucy Isherwood?'

He recoils at the name and promptly sits down in his folding chair, breathing as if someone knocked the wind out of him.

'No, that can't be right. You can't be serious.'

'I'm not known for my pranks, Mr Davis. You remember her, then?'

'Of course I do. How could I forget? She and her brother Daniel were bright, promising young pupils of mine. Daniel especially was very precocious. But they were . . . goodness me. You know what happened, yes?'

'Daniel's disappearance? Yes, and I assume everyone in Grenholme does too. Yet you claim not to have recognized her last night.'

'Inspector, the twins were seven years old when Daniel went missing. You can't expect I'd recognize Lucy now, fifteen years later.' A mist drifts out of the trees on the opposite riverbank, crossing the water. Glenn rubs his hands over his face. 'Oh, heavens. What happened to that poor girl, to turn her into this?'

He seems genuinely surprised by the revelation that Lori was Lucy. Then again, you've known killers who could make a good living as actors if they were so inclined.

'We're still looking into Lori's background,' you say. 'In the meantime, if there's anything at all you can tell us about her time here in Grenholme—'

'I already told you people everything when it happened,' Glenn says with barely restrained anger. His hands curl into fists. 'I spent days in that bloody station going over and over it all again. Me! The family knew I would never do such a thing, but that didn't matter to your lot, did it?'

'You can't blame the police,' McAdam protests. 'Think about it. Who do we tell kids to run to, if they have a problem at school? Who spends almost as much time with them as their parents? Their teachers, whom we tell children to trust. The investigators would have been mad not to question you.'

'Questioning is one thing,' Glenn replies quietly. 'Marking me as a prime suspect and encouraging every curtain-twitcher in the village to watch and whisper is quite another. Besides, Lucy claimed she witnessed Daniel's abduction. Why would she tell everyone the Stone Warden took him, if it was actually me?'

'Perhaps she was scared,' you suggest. 'Imagine a young girl seeing her teacher attack and kidnap her brother, knowing that the next day she'd have to go to school and see that same teacher. Her word against his. That's enough to scare many adults, let alone children.'

Glenn remains silent for a while, then says, 'I was never charged. Eventually, the police admitted I wasn't involved. But the damage was already done. The Isherwoods moved away, and I . . . retired.'

'You didn't think of moving away yourself? Starting over somewhere else?'

He fixes you with a glare. 'This is my home. I did nothing wrong. Anyway, moving might have appeared even worse. Wherever I went, it would inevitably get out eventually and then I'd be accused of pulling the wool over their eyes.'

'Do you think Lori recognized you? Would she have remembered you, after all this time?'

'If she did, she didn't mention it. I wish she had.'

    *Write **G3** in your notebook*

    *If you already have P1 written down, turn to **21**￼*

    *Otherwise, **add 1** to your LOCATION number and turn to **100***

44

Bill straightens in his chair. 'Look, this might seem like a joke to you, but people around here take the Stone Warden seriously.'

'I assure you that murder is never a joking matter. What people believe is their own business. It only matters to me if it connects to Lori Velvet's death.'

He raises a sceptical eyebrow at you. 'She was dressed as the Warden, filming the video for a song called "Eyes of the Warden", at the Lock Stones, during a full moon. She even got up on stage and disparaged him.'

'Perhaps Lori intended to debunk the myth,' you say, recalling what Patrick told you.

Bill shakes his head. 'You should know better than to listen to village gossip, Inspector.'

A new angle occurs to you, one you hadn't considered before.

'Are you suggesting someone from Grenholme killed Lori because they were offended by her actions? That they thought she was mocking the legend of the Stone Warden?'

'Wasn't she?' Bill asks, sincerely. 'Mock the Warden, you mock the whole village.'

You consider his words as you take your leave. Could someone's belief in the local myth really be so strong that they'd kill for it?

'Where to now?' McAdam asks as you step out through the Disciple Chambers' gates.

'Back into town. I'm intrigued by this relationship between Bill and Raven, particularly as she failed to mention it before.'

🔍 *Write* **B9** *in your notebook*

🔍 *Then turn to* **150**

45

Constable Zwale collects you from the forest and drives you back to Grenholme. He keeps glancing down disapprovingly at your dirty shoes and mud-stained trousers. It hadn't crossed your mind before, but now you notice that the constable is a neat and orderly man. His uniform is always clean and presentable, and this police car, even though it isn't his per se, is likewise tidy and uncluttered, with every piece of equipment in its proper place.

'Sorry about the dirt,' you say. 'I expect you'll be the one who has to clean this out later.'

'Couldn't be helped, Inspector. You were chasing a killer, and without backup. That's obviously more important.' Zwale's body language suggests he's struggling more with that equation than he wants to let on, though.

His remark about backup makes you think of McAdam in hospital, who fared far worse than you. You felt terrible leaving her there, unconscious in the woods. Then again, if you'd stayed with her you'd never have found Daniel Isherwood's body. Perhaps Raven Moonwolf would call that fate, or karma.

Zwale has to leave the car on the street, as the pub car park is now full. You enter the village square together, where it seems that word has already got out somehow. A loose-lipped officer talking to a villager, most likely. This is annoying, but not

84

surprising. After fifteen years, the discovery of Daniel's body is undoubtedly big news, and once it leaked its rapid spread through the village was inevitable.

Killer Velvet fans now fill the pub, spill into the square and browse Stones & Spirits.

'Talk about a state of shock,' Zwale says. 'As if Lori's death wasn't bad enough, this lot are now having to process who she really was and what happened to her brother. It's a lot to take in.'

'Too much for some,' you note, seeing a fan weep openly and be comforted by friends.

Many locals are also gathered in the square, sharing stories and theories. Some eye you with disdain. One middle-aged woman sees you and cries, 'He was there all along! Why didn't you find him, you idiots? Useless, the lot of you!'

You decline to point out that you did, in fact, find him. 'Better late than never' is unlikely to appease anyone, and the truth is that you only located Daniel by stumbling across him, not because you were actively searching. Nevertheless, you *did* find him, and you're convinced all of this is somehow connected to Lori's murder.

With a note of distaste, you see the reporter who cornered you earlier standing on the edge of the crowd, typing something into his phone. You can already see several more journalists moving through the crowds, tapping at their phones and recording statements from the villagers. The discovery of Daniel's body will only make them eager for more.

As for you, with McAdam out of action in hospital, you must decide how to proceed. You could request a temporary detective assignment from your station, though you're not sure who's even free. Resources are already stretched, and even if they could get here tomorrow, you'd have to spend valuable time bringing them up to speed on the case.

'Now then, Constable, with the sergeant out of action—'

Before you can finish, your phone rings with a call from McAdam herself.

You answer it and say, 'I was just thinking about you. How are things?'

'Oh aye, never better,' she replies sarcastically. 'Whacked on the head, stabbed in the leg, minutes from bleeding to death, and to add insult to injury I'm stuck here with bad telly and worse food. I bet steak and chips isn't on the menu.'

You chuckle. At least there's nothing wrong with her mind. 'You need time to recuperate, Sergeant. I can't have you out here on crutches, threatening to start bleeding again at any moment.'

'Now you sound like Emma,' she grumbles.

'Well, I'm glad your family have visited. Though this may not be the best way of persuading Douglas to embrace the great outdoors.'

'Ha ha, everyone's a comedian,' she says glumly. 'Aye, they came by. The kids were fascinated, actually. Maybe a bit too much. They wanted to know all the details.'

'Well, I hope you told them something closer to a fairy tale than the mundane truth. Did you get a look at the Stone Warden when he attacked you? Any distinctive or recognizable features? Left- or right-handed?'

McAdam sighs. 'All I remember is that he came out from behind a tree and lunged at me. Right-handed, I'm sure. He stabbed me first, then when I went down he bashed me on the head. At least, I think so. To be honest, it's a blur, and even though we keep saying "he", I couldn't even swear to it being a man. Under all those layers, and with the hood on . . . it really could have been anyone.'

You've had similar thoughts since your encounter with the Warden, or rather whoever was dressed in the Warden costume. Man or woman, they came armed and prepared.

'That reminds me,' you say. 'The Warden was carrying a sack, with a fishing net inside. Do you have any idea why?'

'Not a sausage.'

'Looking for something in the river?' Zwale suggests.

'Possibly,' you agree. 'Surely they wouldn't actually go fishing while wearing the costume . . . would they?'

'Was that the constable?' McAdam asks, then winces with pain. 'Put me on speaker.' You do, and she continues: 'Listen, lad. While I'm not there you'll have to watch the Inspector's back, you hear me? I'm counting on you.'

'Don't worry, ma'am,' he says. 'I won't let you down.'

You nod, and make a decision. Instead of bringing in someone who doesn't know the case, why not use a resource you already have?

'I certainly hope not, Constable,' you say, 'because I'd like you to accompany me on this investigation while the sergeant recovers.'

Zwale's face is a picture of delighted surprise. 'Yes! I mean – yes, Inspector. Absolutely. It would be an honour. A privilege.'

'All right, lad, don't lay it on too thick,' McAdam says. 'You've come a long way and you show promise, but remember to engage your brain before opening your mouth, got it? You take care of the Inspector until I get back, or so help me I'll march you in front of the DCS myself.'

The irony of McAdam telling someone else to think before

they speak isn't lost on you (or on Zwale, judging by his wide-eyed expression) but you let it pass.

'Understood, ma'am,' the constable says. 'Get well soon.'

'Promise me you'll get some proper rest,' you say to McAdam.

'Aye, yes, I will,' she groans reluctantly. 'Keep me updated.'

You end the call. The crowd of locals in the square has thinned, leaving it to the band's fans. You wonder if Aaron Warrior is aware that they'll be playing to a packed house this evening.

'Where to next?' Zwale asks, and for the first time in this case you're not sure. There's so much to unpack: Lori's death, the symbols on the stones, finding Daniel's body, the many potential motivations for her murder and an equally large number of suspects.

'Why was she *really* killed?' you wonder out loud. 'I believe that's the key here. Figuring out their motivation will undoubtedly lead us to Lori's killer.'

Your phone buzzes, this time with a message from Penny at digital forensics, who's cleaned up the video you sent her as best she can.

You watch it right away. Once again, the band mimes playing their instruments by the light of the full moon, but that light has now intensified a hundredfold. The picture has been brightened so much, and the contrast so increased, that it's like watching a moving black-and-white drawing. The band members, whose faces were already lit, are now all but unidentifiable. But the same brightening means the figure walking in the background is now more visible over the drummer's shoulder. Instead of only a silhouette, what you now see is clearly a man wearing outdoor clothing. It's still indistinct, and to your eye could be any number of people.

But Zwale is sure. 'That's Glenn Davis. I'd recognize him anywhere.'

'Then I think you have your answer as to where we go next.'

You walk across the square in the direction of Glenn's house. When you're halfway across, Bill Thomas emerges from Stones & Spirits, hurrying over to you.

'I was just talking to Raven,' he says excitedly. 'Is it true? You found the boy's body in the forest?'

'We've found what appear to be human remains,' you reply, choosing your words carefully. 'However, a positive identification is yet to be made.'

'Come on, though, it's him, right? Where was he? The police spent weeks searching for him. How did they miss it?'

'I'm not really at liberty to say, Mr Thomas. Forensic examination is pending, and once we have all the facts an official statement will be made. Now, if you'll excuse us . . .'

You try to move on, but find your way blocked by another sudden appearance. This time it's Raven, who appears to have closed the shop and run into the square.

'Inspector,' she pants, breathless, 'you need to go to Glenn's house.'

'As it happens, that's where we're headed. Leave everything with us, Ms Moonwolf.'

'No, you don't understand. He just called me, sounding desperate. There's a mob outside his front door.'

To hurry to Glenn's house, turn to **131**

To stay here and keep talking to Bill and Raven, turn to **79**

46

You cross the circle and approach the remaining members of Killer Velvet, who stand among the trees outside the police cordon. You're looking for Julie Grafton in particular – at first you don't see her, but as you draw closer you realize she's in the shadow of a large tree with Aaron Warrior, who has his arms wrapped around the filmmaker, seemingly comforting her.

'Sorry to interrupt,' McAdam says, startling them. She isn't sorry at all, of course. They separate awkwardly, and Aaron glares at the sergeant while Julie wipes a tear from her eye.

'What now?' Aaron says, annoyed. 'Can we leave, or what?'

'You can, but first I wondered if you might be able to help.'

You'd planned to speak to Julie by herself, but having Aaron here as well could be equally useful.

Turn to **164**

47

'Inspector,' Constable Zwale calls out, breaking your concentration. 'Something odd here.'

You turn to see a group of officers standing just beyond the cordon, beside one of the trees surrounding the stone circle. Zwale is halfway up a stepladder and, as you watch, his top half seemingly disappears into the tree, while two officers bizarrely hold on to his legs. Penny from digital forensics stands with them, holding a tablet. She beckons you over.

You and McAdam duck under the cordon just as Zwale re-emerges from the tree, holding a small black object in one gloved hand.

'Odd is perhaps an understatement,' you observe. 'What's going on?'

'While I was checking the cellular signal, I detected an unknown Bluetooth device,' Penny says. 'Definitely not one of ours, but Bluetooth has such a limited range that it had to be somewhere near by. So I narrowed down its location, and . . . well, there you go.'

Constable Zwale hands her the object he found inside the tree. It's a Bluetooth speaker, with its power light flashing. 'You were right, Penny,' he says. 'It was halfway down the trunk. How it got in there is anyone's guess. Maybe kids messing around.'

'How on earth did you know it would be *inside* the tree?' you ask Penny.

'This is a wych elm,' she says, patting its rough bark. 'It's not uncommon for them to basically die inside, but stay standing because they're so old and big. You don't know the old story, "Who put Bella in the wych elm"?' Upon seeing your blank expression, she explains. 'During the war, in the 1940s, some boys went tree-climbing in the West Midlands and found a woman's skeleton inside an elm. She was never identified, and it became a local legend. My granddad told me about it when I was young.'

'What a delightful subject for the dinner table,' you say, teasing her. 'Now, can you tell me who that device belongs to?'

Penny turns it over in her hand. 'Unlikely with such a cheap model. What I can say is that the battery wouldn't last long with it left switched on like this. Even when idling, you'd be lucky to get more than a day out of it.'

'Meaning it was placed here no earlier than yesterday. How curious.'

You mount the stepladder and look inside the hollow tree trunk, then climb back down and reach up with your hand to gauge the height. The opening is just low enough that you can touch it, but high enough to be invisible from the ground.

'Maybe it was a prank,' McAdam suggests. 'Someone nicked a speaker, ran off with it and dropped it in there to hide it.'

'Perhaps. But it's too high to have been an accident, or be done by young children.'

'Unless they were climbing trees too. Plenty of kids still do, and there's not much else going on in a place like Grenholme.'

That's undeniably true, but it doesn't change your gut feeling. You can't explain it, but somehow this feels connected to the case.

Leaving Penny and Constable Zwale to finish up in the stone circle, you and McAdam make your way back through the trees towards the village. You've taken a photo of the speaker, intending to see if it belongs to anyone in Grenholme. Even if a tourist had lost it, you assume they'd have mentioned it to the locals. Julie Grafton showed you a large speaker that Killer Velvet used to film the video; if they'd lost another, wouldn't she have mentioned that too?

'Hey!'

Sergeant McAdam's voice snaps you back to reality. You're

immediately on alert, looking around to see what she's shouting about. Without another word, she dashes into the trees. You follow, careful not to trip on tree roots and brambles, but only a few strides later she stops and turns in a circle.

'What is it?' you ask.

She peers into the trees, her head darting from side to side like a dog chasing a squirrel. Then she relaxes and exhales heavily.

'Nothing. It must have been a trick of the light. This damn fog everywhere.'

'What did you think you saw?'

She sighs and turns back, her face pale. 'I don't know. Something, someone, moving . . . maybe it was just an animal. *Not* a bloody owl,' she adds before you can tease her again.

Minutes later, you reach the parking area and a blessed halo of warming sunlight. Your and McAdam's phones both bleep and ping with notifications.

Continuing towards Grenholme, you call an old friend in the Scottish force who puts you on to the Family Liaison Officer currently assigned to the Isherwoods. It's barely twelve hours since their daughter was found dead, and you haven't had a chance to talk to them yet. Having now lost both of their children, they'll be in the depths of grief, so rather than ask them directly you send the FLO your sketch of the chalk symbols, with a desire to simply know if they mean anything to the parents.

🔎 *Write **P8** in your notebook*

🔎 *If you already have P6 written down, turn to **194***

🔎 *Otherwise, turn to **6***

48

It's no coincidence that Lori Velvet was killed in the same place where her twin brother vanished fifteen years ago – and, you now know, where his body remained hidden.

'Danny is here'. The message Lori was writing on the stones when she was interrupted and killed. Did that message, along with the lyrics of her new song, seal her fate? Taken together, they strongly imply both that Lori knew who'd abducted Daniel and that she suspected his body was still somewhere in Grenholme Forest.

Julie Grafton has emphasized that Lori was a spiritual person. Could she have somehow regained a memory, perhaps through meditation or similar means? Something buried in her mind since she was seven years old, suddenly clarified . . .

Is that why Lori took a knife with her into the woods last night, then wandered off alone from where the others were filming? Did she hope to confront, and perhaps even kill, her brother's murderer?

Check your notebook in the following order:

*If you have A7 written down, turn to **81***

*If you have B11 written down, turn to **127***

*If you have G8 written down, turn to **171***

49

Glenn Davis lives along a short terrace of stone houses, but when you call there's no answer. A curtain twitches in the front room of the house next door, though, so you knock there instead.

'No good will come of this, you know,' says the elderly man who finally answers the door when you show your ID.

'Sorry – of what, exactly?'

'You. That girl. Incomers, the lot of you. Those stones are a curse, bringing people in from all over. Nothing but trouble since they came.'

Old as this gentleman seems to be, you're confident the stones were here before him. Rather than point this out, you ask: 'Do you know where we can find your neighbour, Glenn Davis?'

'Neighbour!' The man practically spits on the ground. 'Nuisance, more like. You want to arrest him, be my guest.'

'We really just want to talk to him.'

'Should arrest him anyway. I saw him leaving with all his tackle, like. He'll be up at the river, in his usual spot. Just a ways up from the car park. Take your handcuffs.'

The man slams the door closed. You exchange a glance with McAdam, then walk back to her car and drive into the forest.

Along the way you look up Glenn Davis. As he told you, he was formerly a schoolteacher here in Grenholme. Lori, or Lucy as she was then, and her twin brother Daniel were both pupils of his, and when Daniel disappeared, Glenn became the police's primary suspect. You share this with McAdam.

'Wonder if he recognized her,' the sergeant says.

'It's possible, but remember that Lori was only seven when she moved away.'

You pull up in the parking area, then walk upstream along the riverbank. The air is raw, and the dense forest prevents much sunlight from reaching the ground, so you're grateful for the break in the trees afforded by the river. A minute later, just as his neighbour predicted, you find Glenn Davis. He sits in a folding chair wearing tweeds, a fly-pinned hat and wellington boots, surrounded by fishing tackle. A rod is propped on a stand, its line reaching out over the water.

'Mr Davis, I wondered if we might have another chat.'

He glances at you, then returns his gaze to the river. 'I don't know what else you think there is to talk about. I told you everything I know last night.'

'Are you quite sure about that?'

'Whatever do you mean?'

🔎 *If you have B4 written in your notebook, turn to* **16**

🔎 *If you have B5 written in your notebook, turn to* **137**

🔎 *Otherwise, turn to* **78**

50

Seeing you approach, Glenn holds the door open. You and Constable Zwale quickly step inside, closing the door behind you, and Glenn leads you through.

Predictably, given what you've seen of Glenn's personality so far, the house is immaculate. Neat, tidy and spotless. A small crucifix hangs in the hallway, alongside a framed cross-stitched Bible verse. Following Glenn, you pass the lounge. He doesn't take you in, probably in case anyone threatens to throw a stone through the window again, but you pause and look into the room.

These walls are filled with pictures of planets, stars and the night sky. One particularly large picture hangs above the mantel, a photo of a half-moon surrounded by several streaks of light.

Zwale recognizes it. 'You took this one, didn't you, Mr Davis?' he says. 'I remember seeing it online.'

'That's right,' Glenn says proudly. 'A long exposure during the Perseids. Have you any idea how difficult it is to get the moon in shot without overexposing everything else?'

The constable nods. 'I do. I've never been able to take a photo this good.'

'Well, I'm glad someone around here appreciates that.'

Glenn continues on towards the kitchen and you follow, passing a cubbyhole filled with fishing gear. You haven't seen anything in here concerning the Stone Warden or Lock Stones, though that's not surprising. What does stand out to you is how old everything in the house seems, as if he hasn't bought anything new in years. Most houses nowadays are filled with technology; phones and laptops everywhere, smart appliances all over the place. Not Glenn Davis's home. It's a sanctuary from the modern world.

In fact, the kitchen is the one place modern enough to belong in this century, with fairly new-looking appliances in place. You notice a small Bluetooth speaker on the counter; it looks very much like the one found in the forest, though of course it can't be the same one.

You accept Glenn's offer of a cup of tea.

'I'm glad you believe I'm innocent, even if those savages out there don't,' he says, filling the kettle.

'Everyone is innocent . . . until proven otherwise,' you say. 'But whether or not you've done anything is a police matter, not something to be decided by a mob.'

'I'm telling you, I haven't done anything,' he insists. 'I've told you nothing but the truth.'

'A lie by omission is still a lie,' Zwale points out. 'Is there anything you'd like to tell us about your movements last night in the forest? Perhaps you'd care to revise your statement?'

You were about to bring up the same matter, and give an approving nod to the constable. You take out your phone and show Glenn the footage that Penny cleaned up.

'That's you,' you say, to drive the point home. 'Filmed at eleven thirty-six last night, walking within twenty yards of the band. The lack of any torch suggests you were intent on not being seen. Would you care to explain?'

Glenn sighs. 'Yes, all right, that's me. I slipped away from the astronomers' group for a while to see what was going on, that's all. I told everyone I'd forgotten my camera, which was of course absurd. As if I'd set off for an evening of astronomy without a camera!'

'Instead, you wanted to spy on the band as they filmed their music video.'

'Spying is a strong word,' Glenn protests. 'I wanted to make sure they weren't up to no good. For all we knew they might have been celebrating Satan just a few hundred yards from our own position.'

'But they weren't, were they?'

'No,' he admits reluctantly. 'They pretended to play their instruments for a while, then stopped and started again, over and over. At least, that's all they did during the short time I observed. It was quite dull, actually.'

You're fairly confident Aaron Warrior and the others would say the same about Glenn's stargazing that same night, but keep the thought to yourself.

'Was Lori Velvet present at that time?'

'Not that I recall. I observed them for six minutes, then returned to Clearing Delta and resumed work on my telescope. Not long after that, I heard the poor girl scream.'

The kettle has boiled. Glenn pours out three cups and watches them brew. You remain silent, patiently waiting for him to talk again. Eventually he strains the tea, handing you and Constable Zwale each a cup.

'I blame the parents, you know,' he says at last. 'They failed to discipline the twins from an early age. Daniel and Lucy were both bright and eager at school, but they had no interest in obeying their elders or following rules. Instead, they ran wild, positively encouraged by their mother and father.' He tuts disapprovingly. 'It's tragic that Daniel found his end so young in the forest, but one wonders if it was really so surprising given how they raised him.'

'The only person to blame for Daniel's death is whoever killed him, not his parents,' you say firmly. 'The same goes for his sister. Their parents are understandably distraught over the matter.'

'Yes, yes, I suppose you're right,' he says dismissively. 'I'm sorry for accusing Bill earlier, by the way. That was uncalled for.'

'Bill said you were "still mad about what happened",' Zwale reminds him. 'What did he mean?'

You're fairly sure you know already, but you'd like to hear it from Glenn himself too. He replaces his teacup on the counter and grips its edge. This is obviously a painful subject for him.

'Angela and I – Raven, I mean, Angela's what she was called then – were married for nine and a half years. We had a good, honest Christian marriage. Then Daniel disappeared, and as I'm sure you're aware, I was accused of abducting him. I was never charged, but the damage was done. It put an enormous strain on our marriage, especially when I was also forced to retire from teaching.' His voice becomes quiet. 'Finally, she left me for . . . him.' Glenn's knuckles are white against the countertop. 'He seduced her with folk tales and devilry, and she's never been the same woman since. Quite literally.'

'Raven even went into business with Mr Thomas, opening Stones & Spirits,' you add. 'So you took revenge by forcing her out of the Stargazers, is that right?'

Glenn laughs bitterly. 'Raven turned her back on science the day she opened that ridiculous shop. She was no longer fit to lead.'

⚲ *If you have P7 written down in your notebook, turn to* **118**

⚲ *Otherwise, turn to* **4**

51

It's times like this you wish you didn't have the detective's habit of leaving your baton and pepper spray at the station. Technically, every officer should carry them, uniformed or not, but you can count on a couple of fingers those detectives who do. Besides, they tend to spook witnesses.

So there's nothing else for it; you'll have to take on the Stone Warden barehanded. You take a deep breath and silently creep towards him.

He stands unnaturally still, like a statue of twigs and moss, and now you notice he carries a cloth sack over his shoulder. Poking out is some kind of plastic handle. You draw closer, the shape becoming clearer, until you recognize it – to your surprise – as a small fishing net.

Before you can wonder what this means, you step on a twig. Its snap alerts the Warden, who turns and rushes at you with unexpected speed, the statue animated in a burst of frantic motion. You react, trying to move out of his way, but stumble and trip on the uneven ground. The Warden crashes into you, knocking you to the ground and forcing the breath from your lungs.

You scramble to your feet, gasping for air as the Stone Warden flees. Catching your breath, you resume the chase. You won't let him get away!

⌕ *Turn to* **125**

<h1 style="text-align:center">52</h1>

You approach the remaining members of Killer Velvet, intending to speak to Julie Grafton in particular. At first, you don't see her, but as you draw closer you realize that she's in the shadow of a large tree with Aaron Warrior, who has his arms wrapped around the filmmaker, seemingly comforting her.

'Sorry to interrupt,' McAdam says, startling them. She isn't sorry at all, of course. They separate awkwardly, and Aaron glares at the sergeant while Julie wipes a tear from her eye.

'What now?' Aaron says, annoyed. 'Can we leave, or what?'

'You can, but first I wondered if you might be able to help.'

You'd planned to speak to Julie by herself, but having Aaron here as well could be even more useful.

⚲ *Turn to* 117

<h1 style="text-align:center">53</h1>

Raven refuses to tell you where Patrick is. You search her house, but there's no sign of him. When you arrest her anyway, she takes out her phone. You expect she's going to try to film her own arrest, but to your surprise she turns it to face you.

'I think you should see this first,' she says, pressing play.

It's a video of the moment in the pub when McAdam smashed Julie's camera and destroyed the memory card. You're clearly visible, looking on and doing nothing.

'Where did you get this?'

'Never you mind,' she says. 'Someone in the pub filmed the whole thing, and sent it to me. It's also backed up online, before you think about smashing this phone as well.'

'The whole thing? Including you pulling a knife on Julie Grafton?'

She shrugs. 'Didn't actually do anything, though, did I? Something tells me you'll come off worse if people see this.'

Raven is right, but you can't let that stop your pursuit of a killer. You arrest her and drive to the station, hoping the shock of being in a cell will loosen her tongue. You'll have to admit to the unethical behaviour — you can hardly deny it — but at least she'll be behind bars.

Or will she?

Not long after you arrive at the station, a call comes in from Bill Thomas. He led the Disciples of the Green to the Lock Stones this evening, to carry out a cleansing ritual. They arrived to find Patrick, with his throat slashed in the same manner as Lori Velvet.

Your case is thrown into chaos. Could Raven have killed Patrick before returning home to start the fire? It's possible, although she'd have had to move fast. Either way, you have no proof. When examined, the landlord's body is found to have been drugged, but otherwise offers no solid forensic evidence, and this time there's no sign of a murder weapon.

All that remains is your speculation . . . and a video of you and McAdam acting in a manner worthy of suspension, which is exactly what happens when the detective chief superintendent sees it.

Lori Velvet's murder, and now Patrick's too, may yet be solved . . . but not by you.

🔎 *Wipe your notebook, return to **1** and try again — this time acting in a manner more befitting an officer of the law.*

For now, though, this is . . .

THE END

54

'Not quite all,' you say. 'A witness told us you left for some time, around half past eleven.'

Bill eyes you suspiciously. 'Says who?'

'That's not important. Is it true?'

'Yeah, it is, as a matter of fact. We'd started walking to the stones when I realized I'd forgotten my ceremonial knife. So I came back for it, picked it up, then ran back. It only took about ten minutes.'

This immediately raises two questions in your mind. 'Why didn't you mention this last night?'

'Not relevant, is it? This was all before we heard the girl scream, and I hadn't been anywhere near the stones.'

'Very well. Second question, then: why do you need to carry a knife?'

🔎 *Write **B12** in your notebook*

🔎 *If you already have **B10** written down, turn to **99***

🔎 *Otherwise, turn to **3***

55

You sit down opposite Julie, with McAdam standing over your shoulder, and take out the sheet of paper Aaron found pinned to the pub's front door. Placing it on the table, you methodically smooth out its creases.

'You know Raven didn't write this note, don't you, Julie?'

She looks at the note, then out the window, saying nothing.

'I recognized the handwriting. Block capitals, black marker . . . it matches what I saw last night on the video shoot's clapperboard. As you work without an assistant, it's therefore a safe assumption this is your handiwork.'

Julie still doesn't reply, so you wait patiently. Sometimes saying nothing is the most effective way to elicit a response.

Sure enough, eventually she cracks.

'I thought it would be good content.'

'For what, exactly? Your sudden pivot to camera-carrying roving reporter?'

'Not reporting,' she says defiantly. 'I've decided to film a documentary about Julie's death, and your investigation. I can't finish the video shoot, can I, so I'm pivoting.'

'You're also provoking people,' McAdam growls, leaning on the table. 'If Aaron had used that bottle on Glenn, it would have been at least partly your fault. You could have been responsible for an injury, or something far worse.'

Julie flinches under the sergeant's barrage. 'It was only an argument. Aaron's all bluster, he wouldn't hurt anyone.'

'Really? You're sure about that, are you? How well do you really know Aaron Warrior?'

'I – I don't know how to answer that,' the director replies.

'Let's keep the focus on you, shall we, Ms Grafton?' you say.

If you have A6 written in your notebook, turn to 8

Otherwise, turn to 128

56

'We're almost certain the knife in question belonged to Lori Velvet herself,' you say, to Dr Wash's surprise. 'She was seen wielding it on stage during the band's concert yesterday evening.'

'Almost like it was part of the costume,' McAdam offers.

'That would explain why the only fingerprints I found belonged to the victim,' Dr Wash says, 'though one must always account for a killer wearing gloves. Fancy being killed in such a manner with your own knife, though. As if it wasn't bad enough already.'

Turn to 5

57

Sometimes you hate being right.

A crisp breeze clears mist from the stone circle. By the light of the full moon, you see Patrick on his knees, with the Stone Warden standing over him. Or rather, Bill wearing a Warden costume. You're sure of it.

He's ready to slash a knife across the landlord's throat from behind, just like how Lori was killed.

Several things made you suspect Bill, not least his past as a musician. Another was something Glenn said, about how there were almost no Warden sightings until Raven opened her shop, after which they increased significantly. He suspected Raven herself of dressing up as the Stone Warden and wandering the forest, hoping to be glimpsed by locals and tourists alike in order to bolster the myth and thereby support her business.

But Bill Thomas is the co-owner of Stones & Spirits, and had much more reason to want Lori Velvet dead.

'Bill!' you call out.

The Stone Warden looks up.

And runs at you, knife raised above his head.

Turn to **200**

58

'There is one more thing, before we go,' you say, and show Bill the scrapbook you found in Lori's room. 'Have you ever seen this before?'

He peers at the cover, then takes the book from you.

'That's the same thing that was chalked on the stones, isn't it?' he says, turning the pages. 'What does it mean?'

'We rather hoped you could tell us. Lori had a tattoo of the symbol, so it must have been important to her. We think it may have been her doing the chalking.'

'Fancy keeping a scrapbook of what happened to her brother.' He looks up from the pages. 'Did they ever find him?'

'Daniel? No, despite an extensive search. We believe that's why Lori kept this book. It may even be why she came back to Grenholme.'

Bill hands you the scrapbook. 'What, after all this time? He was probably taken miles away. He could be anywhere. I suppose he might even still be alive.'

'Indeed, but we must investigate all possibilities. Good day, Mr Thomas.'

🔎 **Add 1** *to your LOCATION number, then turn to* **100**

59

Fog drifts across the village square, chasing people into the warmth of the pub.

'Dannyish,' Zwale says, confused. 'Doesn't make any sense. Why would you write that?'

'I don't think that's it,' you reply. 'Look, three of the stones are blank. But I found a piece of chalk by the last marked stone, the "h". That's why I think Lori was interrupted. She was writing something that would use all the stones, but her killer surprised her and she dropped the chalk. Now think, Constable. What was the victim's name?'

'Daniel Isher—Oh, I get it. It's not "Dannyish", it's "Danny Isherwood".' He peers at the pictures again. 'Hang on, though, it can't be. You'd only get to "Isherw" before running out of stones.'

He's right. There are only three blank stones, not enough to complete the twins' surname. You're fairly sure they come at the end, rather than preceding 'Danny' . . . but what could they be?

You now have the full 'bracelet code' thanks to Dr Wash. The answer must lie within, somehow. With pen and notebook in hand, you wrack your brains trying to figure it out.

When you think you've worked out the missing symbols, there's one more step. Write out the full message, then assign each letter a number from 1 to 26 — but counting backwards. So, in this case A = 26, B = 25, and so on down to Z = 1. Finally, add together all the numbers to get a total amount between 1 and 200.

When you're confident you've found the solution, turn to the section matching that total number, but before you do note down section 22 in your notebook. You'll know right away if you've deciphered it correctly. If not, you should turn immediately to 22 instead.

⚬ *Alternatively, if you can't work it out or don't want to try, turn to 22 anyway*

60

You take McAdam to one side within the stone circle to show her the piece of chalk you found next to one of the stones, and your notebook copies of the symbols.

'My hypothesis is that all of the stones should be marked, but whoever was drawing on them was interrupted,' you say. 'Does anything look familiar to you?'

'It's all gobbledegook,' she says with a shrug. 'Maybe the

killer's one of those pagan nutters and the symbols are part of a ritual. What I don't understand is, why didn't they finish drawing after she was dead?'

'Perhaps there was no time. People came running when they heard Lori Velvet scream, remember. The killer would have had to escape quickly to avoid being seen.'

McAdam looks into the dark trees beyond the circle. 'They wouldn't have had to go far. Even with the full moon out it would have been almost pitch black. Half a dozen steps into the trees and they might as well be invisible.'

It's a good point. You've experienced the lack of visibility for yourself when accompanying witnesses through the trees. Combined with the forest haze, the killer could be confident of not being seen up to the last moment. They could have been only a few yards away yet invisible to both Lori Velvet and, subsequently, those who ran to help her.

'Do you think this might have been opportunistic?' you ask.

'Unlikely. Someone just happens to be in the forest, where they just happen to stumble across a young woman in the stone circle, who just happens to be dressed like a local legend, and because they just happen to be carrying a big old knife they just happen to decide to kill her? Pardon me, Inspector, but that's a stretch.'

You sigh. 'Which means we're looking for someone who knows these woods well, and knew Lori Velvet would be here.'

'By the sound of it, that's most of Grenholme.'

'Precisely. It doesn't narrow things down much. What was Dr Wash's verdict?'

McAdam shrugs. 'She's confident Lori was killed where she fell. There's blood on the ground, apparently. The doc's also pretty sure the knife found near the victim is the murder weapon, but won't commit to anything until she's examined it all properly. Kept insisting she won't be rushed.'

'Doctors do have a habit of requiring tested evidence before they'll commit to an opinion,' you agree. 'Nevertheless, that's good to know. Well done, Sergeant.'

'Aye. And on the bright side, most criminals aren't exactly masterminds. Like chalking these symbols on the stones. Hardly the sign of a stable person. Did Zwale recognize them?'

'No, and he maintains they're not astronomical. He suggested they might be linked to pagan magic in some way.'

'So, like I said, the Disciples rather than the Stargazers. How sure are you the lad knows what he's talking about?'

You have some confidence in the young constable, but he's only one source. You decide to get a second opinion about the chalk symbols. But who from?

 To ask Aaron Warrior, turn to **14**

 To ask Bill Thomas, turn to **142**

 To ask Glenn Davis, turn to **91**

 To ask Julie Grafton, turn to **46**

 To ask Raven Moonwolf, turn to **179**

61

You've had your eye on Julie since you first met. The director projects herself as a harmless creative type, spiritually minded and largely at peace with Lori's death. But is that because she was the murderer?

You wonder if Julie and Aaron might be in it together. Did they plot to kill Lori so she wouldn't be an obstacle to their shared future? The singer's pregnancy certainly would have put a dent in any such plans. And while Lori was her way into filming the band, Julie might have felt she'd extracted all she was going to get from the singer. She's obviously hoping to cash in on Lori's death with her supposed documentary. Killing someone in order to make them the subject of one's own true-crime film would be a cold act indeed, but all avenues must be considered.

Why would Julie take Patrick, though? Did the landlord see something he shouldn't have? They were all in the forest last night. Perhaps he witnessed Julie kill Lori, and Julie somehow found out. It would explain the poison pen letter. You wish Patrick had been more forthcoming earlier. Now Julie is going to silence him for ever.

The next question is: where? Julie isn't local. She doesn't know Grenholme, and there are only so many places one could hide a person in the village. Could she have gone into the forest? Besides the pub, it's the one place she's spent any real time. On a fog-cursed night like this, it's the perfect location for murder.

As you're about to set off, though, you hear a muffled sound. A cry, or perhaps a sob. Where did it come from? You're standing in the pub car park. It can't be from the pub itself, as you'd never hear it over the crowd. There are houses around the edges of the car park, but they're too far away. That just leaves the cars, the distinctive news broadcaster's van . . . and Killer Velvet's own rental van, parked a few metres from where you're standing.

You approach it quietly. There's no sign of anyone in the

cab, but the back area has no windows. You hold your breath and listen.

There's the sound again.

It makes sense. The van is a private area of sorts to which Julie has access. Nobody would look twice at her getting in and out of the back, even if she did so with Patrick. After all, he's the venue landlord.

You're no locksmith, and the best the pub could offer is probably a claw hammer. You could wait for Zwale to fetch a crowbar from a police car, but would that take too long? You could ask the band members if they have a key, but who knows what you might miss before you made it back to the van?

Your dilemma is rendered moot when the rear door suddenly opens and Julie steps out, with a laptop under her arm.

'Oh. Inspector. What are you doing here?'

Her eyes are red-rimmed, as if she's been crying. You look over her shoulder into the rear of the van, but it's too dark to see clearly.

'Wait there a moment, please, Ms Grafton.'

Using your phone's flashlight, you peer inside. Flight cases and canvas equipment bags line the edges of the van. There's no sign of Patrick. With a grim thought in mind, you double check for any bags big enough to hold his body, but they're all too small.

'What have you done with Patrick?' you ask.

Julie looks stunned. 'I don't know what you're talking about. I haven't done anything with him. I haven't even seen him since earlier this evening.'

'So what were you doing in the back of this van?'

Her expression turns cold. 'Not that it's any of your

business, but I was editing footage for my documentary and grieving the loss of a woman I loved. It hit me while we were setting up for tonight, so I came out here for some privacy. Now if you'll excuse me, I have a gig to film.'

Check your notebook in the following order:

🔍 *If you have J7 written down, turn to* **98**

🔍 *If you have J4 written down, turn to* **34**

🔍 *If you have J5 written down, turn to* **133**

🔍 *If you have both J6 and A6 written down, turn to* **158**

🔍 *Otherwise, turn to* **123**

62

You remember the emails Aaron showed you from his stalker. The way Raven talks about the young guitarist, as if she knows him . . . and the way she holds that diary, determined not to let you see inside it . . .

'Ms Moonwolf, have you ever sent Aaron Warrior an email?'

She looks puzzled by the question. 'Once or twice, I think. To tell him I enjoyed a particular song. Why?'

'What are your feelings towards him?'

Now she seems positively offended. 'I don't see what business that is of yours.'

'When you came to the stone circle last night, the first person about whose welfare you enquired was Aaron. Nobody has been more enthusiastic about the band coming to Grenholme, to the point of advertising it in your shop window. Your phone alarm is even a Killer Velvet song.'

'So I'm a big fan,' she says with a shrug. 'I've never denied it.'

'Do you know where that word comes from?' McAdam says. 'It's an abbreviation of "fanatic". Is that you, Raven? To what lengths would you go, to be with Aaron?'

The shopkeeper becomes flustered, her breath shortening as she looks between you and McAdam.

Then she laughs.

'Oh, Goddess. You think I'm obsessed with him! Ha!'

'It's hardly a laughing matter.'

'Wait till you've got a few more years on you, Sergeant, then it will be. Look, he's a gorgeous boy, but I'm twice his age. I love his music, his artistry, his spiritual depth. His music speaks to me, even more than Lori's lyrics. But that's all, I promise. If someone's sending him dodgy emails, I'm sorry about that and I hope he's coping with it, but they're not from me.'

'Would you allow us to see your email archives, to check?' you ask.

'Sure,' Raven replies. 'With a search warrant.'

Sergeant McAdam leans on the counter. 'You could have deleted them all, anyway. You have to admit, getting Lori out of the way clears your path to Aaron. No more obstacles.'

'They split up six months ago,' Raven says, fixing McAdam with a glare. 'Mainly because he can't keep it in his pants, by all accounts. So even if I did want to sleep with him, Lori wouldn't have been an "obstacle".'

'You told us you entered the forest last night after seeing police lights from your window,' you remind her. 'Do you want to revise that statement?'

'Why would I? It's the truth.'

You pace up and down in front of the counter. 'Your favourite band, featuring a man whose music "speaks to you", came to this small village. You advertised the performance, you attended it, you even filmed parts of it. You recognized that the singer was dressed as, and making reference to, a local legend from which you in particular make a living. Yet you expect us to believe that you didn't want to follow them into the forest while they recorded a video based around that same legend? You didn't even leave your house until you noticed a police presence?'

Raven folds her arms. 'I came back here after the gig, and watched a film like I told you. I'm *not* a fanatic,' she says pointedly. 'I certainly wouldn't interfere with the band's work.'

'What film were you watching?' the sergeant asks.

'The video of their gig at the Roundhouse last year, actually,' Raven says defiantly. 'OK, look, maybe that sounds bad, but it was a really good gig.'

'Can anyone corroborate that?' you ask. 'Anyone at all? Bill, Glenn, Patrick . . .?'

She shrugs. 'Of course not. Unlike me, they were all in the forest.'

Write **R1** *in your notebook*

Then turn to **195**

63

You answer the call, putting it on speaker so McAdam can hear.

'Morning, Inspector,' Constable Zwale says. 'I spoke to a few of the Stargazers like you asked. They were a bit cagey, to be honest.'

'You think they have something to hide?'

'Hard to say. It might be because they know me from the online group, and now they're suspicious that I never told them I'm police. Once I started talking astronomy and asking about the Lyrids, though, they relaxed.'

McAdam leans in. 'So what did you find out? Get to the point, Constable.'

'Yes, ma'am. It seems Glenn Davis omitted something quite important from his statement last night: namely, that he was absent from the group for about fifteen minutes.'

You exchange glances with McAdam.

'You're sure about this, Constable?' you ask.

'Three separate members of the group who were in the clearing say they noticed he was missing. I pieced together their timings. It seems he left at around 11.25, and didn't return until 11.38. But the thing is—'

'That's before Lori was heard screaming at 11.47,' McAdam says with a sigh. 'Still, it's interesting that he didn't mention it. Glenn definitely said they were all together in the clearing when they heard Lori Velvet scream.'

You think back to your conversation with Glenn, remembering what he told you. 'He did, and that part's probably true, but it doesn't account for those missing minutes beforehand. I wonder what he was doing.'

'Nothing good, I'll bet, or he would have mentioned it.'

'True. Constable, did you find anything else?'

'Not regarding people's movements,' Zwale replies. 'The Stargazers arrived at the clearing around eleven, and other than Mr Davis disappearing for a few minutes they were all there for the duration. I did ask about those chalk markings on the stones, just in case it was something I wasn't familiar with.'

'Good thinking. Any luck?'

'Unfortunately not. Everyone agreed they're not astronomical symbols, and a few even confirmed they're not astrological either.'

That last part surprises you. 'Aren't astronomy and astrology normally very much opposed?' you ask.

'I wondered that myself, but because of the Lock Stones legend a lot of people around here get into astrology when they're younger,' he explains. 'They grow out of it, though.'

The local mythology seems to have a wider influence on Grenholme than you realized.

   Write **G2** *in your notebook*

   Then turn to **159**

64

'I don't have time to stand here talking to a camera,' you say. 'Anyway, shouldn't you be preparing for tonight's performance?'

Julie shrugs. 'Not much point after Aaron stalked off.'

'Why? Where did he go?'

She points out of the square. 'He didn't say, just went off in that direction after he heard you'd found Danny's body.'

You all turn to look where she's pointing . . . In the direction of Glenn's house.

Minutes later, you reach the short terrace of stone houses where Glenn Davis lives. To your dismay, a large group is gathered outside his gate, yelling and shouting.

'Killer!'

'Kidnapper!'

'Nonce!'

'Come out here! You can't hide for ever!'

Glenn's curtains are drawn. Is he even at home? If so, there's surely no way he's going to emerge to face this mob – or the journalists who, you see, have followed the crowd here. You have no doubt they're loving this.

Behind you, Raven whispers prayers to her Goddess while Bill comforts her.

'Can't you do something?' Bill hisses.

'There's a lot more of them than us,' Zwale says nervously. 'Not sure they're in the mood to respect the uniform.'

Julie Grafton continues to film. 'Why should they?' she says. 'If he killed Danny and Lori, he deserves whatever's coming to him. I bet his aura's black as the night.'

'Whatever his astrological condition, Ms Grafton, we must truly establish a man's innocence or guilt before throwing stones.'

'Funny you should say that, Inspector . . .' Zwale says, pointing into the crowd.

Aaron Warrior is here, as angry and fired up as any local. While you watch, he reaches through a gap in Glenn's garden fence and picks up a large stone from the ground. He hefts it in his hand, ready to throw it.

   To attempt to stop Aaron and the mob, turn to **173**

   To stand back and let Aaron throw the stone, turn to **193**

65

This is never easy. You take a deep breath and bite the bullet.

'Aaron, I'm afraid I have more bad news. Our pathologist's examination of Lori revealed that she had recently become pregnant.'

He stares out of the window, frozen in place. For a moment, you wonder if he heard you. Then the guitarist's face crumples, and he looks on the verge of tears.

'It's . . . probably mine,' he whispers.

'I don't think so. This was a very early pregnancy, and you said you split up six months ago.'

He looks away, unable to maintain eye contact. 'Yeah, well . . . we've spent the night together since. Two, three months ago after a gig. We were both drunk. She didn't speak to me for a week afterwards.'

'You said you didn't speak much after breaking up anyway. And you've been in a relationship with Julie for several months.'

He nods, saying nothing.

'Aaron . . . your career is obviously on the rise. No doubt you have a bright future ahead of you. But a newborn baby would make that difficult, wouldn't it?'

His head snaps up and he looks you dead in the eye. No problems maintaining eye contact now.

'How dare you? I didn't even know she was pregnant. You think I'd *kill* her over it? We'd have worked something out! We always do – I mean, did! Bloody hell, what sort of person do you think I am?'

His protests sound sincere, but you've met many murderers who lie convincingly. Did Aaron find out Lori was pregnant, and kill her because she wouldn't end it voluntarily? It's a grim thought, but possible.

> Write **A2** *in your notebook*
> *Then turn to* **104**

666

Without warning, you find yourself walking through a forest, as the sun slowly dips below the treeline and shadows fall over the mist-shrouded undergrowth. Tree branches, angular and imposing, seem to grasp at you in the bitter air.

There's something on the ground. Reaching down for it, your hand closes around a tattered paperback, its pages damp and yellowing. Turning it over, you read the title: *Can You Solve the Murder?: The Forest of Death*, by Antony Johnston.

'Funny way of spelling his name,' you mutter, skimming the description on the back cover. An *interactive* story?

Feeling weary, you sit down. Damp earth and moss form a cushioned, welcoming seat as you lean back against a tree, embraced by its outstretched branches. The introduction of the book explains that it has numbered sections printed out of narrative order, and the one thing you must not do at all costs is read the book from start to finish – or visit sections you aren't directed to from within the text.

You shiver in the twilight gloom, feeling that, somehow, you've broken a taboo. If only you could remember how you got here! The sunlight dims, stretching shadows and darkening the forest floor. In the trees you glimpse a figure, fleeting and incorporeal, as if caught between worlds. With burning eyes, his gaze pins you to the tree, filling your mind with whispering fears. Then he turns away, breaking the spell, and night is here.

By the full moon's silver light, you turn to section 1 and begin reading . . .

67

Bill Thomas is not best pleased to see you again.

'Can we go home yet, or what?' he says when you approach. 'We've all given statements, and it's very late.'

'I thought you normally hang out here all night anyway,' McAdam says scornfully.

'Yeah, not in these circumstances,' Bill replies. 'Just because we're pagans, doesn't mean we perform human sacrifices.'

'Speaking of which . . .' You show him the bloody knife in the evidence bag, holding it so the symbol carved into the hilt is visible. 'If I could keep you for a moment more, Mr Thomas,

I hoped you could possibly shed some light on this. See this symbol? It matches one of the chalk markings on the Lock Stones, over there. Do you recognize it?'

'That's the murder weapon, is it?' Bill asks.

You shake your head. 'We're not sure of anything yet, but it was found near by so it's of interest. Do you recognize it?'

'No, nor the symbol.'

'Then why is it drawn on your precious stones?' McAdam asks. Bill has no answer to that, and the sergeant presses her advantage. 'Do you own a knife, Mr Thomas? For your little rituals?'

The 'First Disciple' narrows his eyes. He's almost twice the sergeant's size, and looms over her. But she doesn't back down, and you know which of them you'd put your money on in a scrap.

Suddenly, you wonder if that scrap might come sooner rather than later as Bill reaches under his robe and pulls out a knife. McAdam steps back, instinctively putting herself beyond his immediate range.

But he quickly flips the knife in his hand and offers it to her hilt-first. 'Purely ceremonial. Check it all you like, it's clean as a whistle.'

He's right. The knife looks pristine, as if it's never been used to cut anything more than an envelope, with a thin, smooth blade. It's also very different to the knife found by Lori's body, with an ornate hilt that's decoratively carved in a filigree style, and lacking any particular symbol like the one in the evidence bag.

McAdam grudgingly returns the knife to Bill, and you thank him for his time.

↗ *Write* **B10** *in your notebook*

↗ *Then turn to* **85**

68

You emerge from the doorway and show yourself. 'Wait there, please.'

Aaron and Raven are both startled by your sudden appearance.

'Were you eavesdropping?' Raven says, incredulous. 'You're the police, you're not supposed to sneak up on people. It's not on.'

'On the contrary, Ms Moonwolf, it is very much "on". My job is to determine who murdered Lori Velvet, by whatever means necessary.'

Aaron regards you with disdain. 'I've told you, I didn't do it. You should have a word with her, though.' He nods in Raven's direction.

'I'd rather talk to you both. For starters, which of you wants to explain exactly what Aaron is threatening to tell me about Raven?'

They hesitate, each warily eyeing the other, then both talk at the same time.

'She's been sending me creepy emails—'

'I swear it's not true, I don't know why he thinks—'

'Stalking's not funny, you know—'

'He's got no evidence—'

You hold up a hand for them both to stop. Amazingly, they do.

🔎 *If you have R1 written in your notebook, turn to* **191**
🔎 *Otherwise, turn to* **109**

69

You show Julie the scrapbook you found in Lori's room, pointing out the symbol on the cover.

'The same as her tattoo,' she says. 'She never told me what it meant . . .'

'Have you seen this scrapbook before? It relates to her childhood, when Lori was known as Lucy Isherwood.'

Julie looks confused. 'Really? She never told me that, either. Oh, she had so many secrets . . .'

You open it to some of the press clippings and tell Julie the story of Lori's twin brother Daniel, his disappearance and how the family subsequently moved away.

She turns the pages, shaking her head with a sad expression.

'I knew something was up. She insisted we come here because of the new song, about the Stone Warden, but I could tell there was more to it. My intuition is attuned to it, you see. But when I asked, all she'd say is that it was something she had to do.'

'Really? Those were her exact words?'

The director shrugs. 'Maybe. I don't remember. Why?'

'Because I wondered if Lori might have been trying to solve

her brother's disappearance, or even find his body. At the time, she insisted her brother had been taken by the Stone Warden.' You point out one of the press clippings.

Julie shivers. 'She must have dressed up as him to form a spiritual bond . . . oh, that's so dangerous.'

Less dangerous than having one's throat slit, you think to yourself, and take back the scrapbook.

'Is there nothing more she told you, while preparing the costume or planning to film the video? What about this symbol on the cover?'

She shakes her head. 'Lori doodled cosmic symbols all the time. It was a way for the universe to communicate through her, to channel the new wisdom. I said she should meditate and translate them. They could have made powerful lyrics.'

You wonder if there's something in that. Was Lori's new song connected to these 'cosmic symbols' in some way?

In the bar downstairs, you discuss what you've learned with Sergeant McAdam, and she reports her interview with Aaron.

Contrary to what Julie told you, Aaron claims they've secretly been lovers for months, keeping it quiet because Lori would have fired Julie if she'd found out. Aaron also believes he has a stalker: an obsessive fan sending him anonymous emails and text messages, telling him they're watching and waiting for 'a sign' from him that they can be together.

'Occupational hazard of being famous,' McAdam says. 'He seems pretty rattled by it, though.'

'Could that be connected to Lori's killing, do you think? An obsessive fan, perhaps jealous of her close relationship to Aaron?'

'But everyone knows they split up six months ago. Why kill her now?'

'I got the impression from Julie that Lori and Aaron's relationship was nothing if not unpredictable and chaotic. Perhaps someone was worried they might get back together, which doesn't seem an unreasonable fear given his propensity for bed-hopping. Notice how differently Julie and Aaron view their relationship, too. Aaron claims it's been going on for months behind Lori's back, while Julie insists that today was the first time.'

McAdam tuts. 'I don't know how reliably we can take his word when it comes to relationships, though. I told him about Lori's pregnancy, and he seems sure it's his. Insists they had a fling a few months ago, despite having split up. So much for love, eh?'

You hadn't expected McAdam to mention the baby to Aaron, but the guitarist's response is interesting. 'Love isn't really the word I'd use in this case, especially given that Julie now conveniently remembers how Aaron wandered off shortly before Lori was killed. It seems few people in this triangle were particularly faithful. Now, take a look at this footage.'

You take out your phone and show McAdam the video, with the indistinct figure moving through the background.

'You said Aaron has a stalker. Could it be them? Or Lori's killer, perhaps?'

'Why not both?' McAdam says. 'Sneaking around the forest at night is pretty extreme behaviour for anyone.'

McAdam's right, and by definition stalkers are not in the best of mental health.

'I've sent the footage to Penny at digital forensics. If anyone can clean it up so we can identify this person, it's her.'

Write **J2** in your notebook

**Add** 1 to your LOCATION number, then turn to **100**

70

You say nothing, hoping the silence will prompt Aaron to keep talking. Instead, he begins playing his guitar again. Constable Zwale arrives, catching up with you as requested, so together you arrest Aaron and rush him to the station for interrogation while other officers search the forest for Patrick.

Aaron maintains his innocence, and the truth is you have no hard evidence against him. You don't even have a strong motive, other than professional jealousy that Lori Velvet stole the limelight, denting his sizeable ego.

Then, while you're struggling to get a confession out of Aaron, Patrick's body is found . . . inside the Lock Stones, with his throat cut in the same manner as Lori.

Did Aaron kill Patrick before you found him at the river? Or was it someone else after all? Either way, you can't prove it.

The detective chief superintendent hauls you over the coals. Your sergeant is wounded in hospital; a second victim has been murdered; and you arrested someone without the evidence to back it up. It's simply not good enough, especially with media attention on this case rising.

You're banished to your desk, and the case is assigned to another detective. Lori Velvet's murder may yet be solved . . . but not by you.

🔍 *Wipe your notebook, return to* 1 *and try again – this time remembering to focus on obtaining the evidence to secure a conviction.*

For now, though, this is . . .

THE END

71

Before long, you see movement ahead through the trees. A minute later, you're close enough to see the police cordon surrounding the forest's central clearing, and a mixture of uniformed and forensic officers going about their business. One of them is Constable Zwale, who's talking to Penny from digital forensics.

'Don't often find you out in the field, Penny,' you say. 'Surely there isn't much digital work to be done here?'

She shrugs. 'After what you said about locating people's phone signals, I thought I'd come out and test the dead zone. The constable here has been walking me through the scene. Unfortunately, you were right and there's no signal at all.' She adds, 'Don't worry, by the way, my team are still working on that video back at the office. We'll clean it up for you.'

'Thanks, Penny.' You leave her to work and step under the cordon, into the stone circle. Eight of the eleven stones are still marked with chalk symbols, though they're already starting to fade in the cool, damp forest environment.

'Did Lori Velvet draw these?' you wonder aloud. 'What on earth do they mean?'

McAdam is looking something up on her phone. 'Inspector ... remember I said the original investigation found Daniel's blood on one of the stones? The photo's not the highest resolution, but I think I know which one.'

She points out the stone, and you nod. It makes perfect sense.

'The first stone with a marking after the three blanks,' you say. 'The one with the same symbol tattooed on Lori's back.'

'It's not proof that she did this, but it might be as close as we get.'

'So, the question remains: why?'

If you have P1 written in your notebook, turn to **132**

Otherwise, turn to **10**

72

Aaron has been in your sights since the first time you met him last night. Something about his contemptuous attitude towards everyone around him rubbed you up the wrong way. He may have protested that he was nowhere near the Lock Stones, but you now suspect that was a lie.

You wonder if Aaron and Julie might be in it together. Did they plot to kill Lori so she wouldn't be an obstacle to their shared future? The singer's pregnancy would have put a dent in any such plans.

Why would Aaron take Patrick? Did the landlord see something he shouldn't have? They were all in the forest last night. Perhaps he witnessed Aaron kill Lori, and Aaron somehow found out. It would explain the poison pen letter. You wish Patrick had been more forthcoming earlier. Now Aaron is going to silence him for ever.

They must be in the forest. Where else would Aaron go? The only parts of Grenholme in which he's spent any time are the forest and the pub. On a fog-cursed night like this, it's the perfect location for murder.

    *Write **A7** in your notebook*

    *Then turn to **182***

73

Before you leave, you have one final question.

'Why do you think Glenn Davis, the local councillor, objected so strongly to your presence?'

Aaron blows a thick cloud of smoke. 'Like I said, a lot of people think we're Satanic or whatever. Everywhere we go there's always a straight like him protesting, trying to stop us playing and stuff. It's pathetic.'

'But you maintain there are no grounds for these accusations.'

Julie laughs. 'We're about as Satanist as Peppa Pig. But like I said, Lori was very spiritual, and her lyrics were full of metaphor and symbolism. Women with a connection to the earth soul have always been oppressed, often by people like him. I wasn't surprised when he got worked up earlier.'

'Worked up? What do you mean?'

'After the gig he started harassing Lori. I didn't hear what they were saying, I was busy packing away my camera, but they were having a proper argument. Then he stormed off, and when I asked her about it she said he was a Bible-thumping idiot.'

Glenn didn't mention that exchange when you spoke to him. It explains how he was able to recognize Lori Velvet when he found her, despite her being dressed in a costume and covered in blood.

> *Write* **G1** *in your notebook*

> *If you haven't yet spoken to Bill Thomas, the pagan leader, turn to* **148**

> *Otherwise, turn to* **88**

74

Julie has nowhere to go, and McAdam is too fast. She snatches the camera out of Julie's hands and flings it to the ground. Once again you hear the sound of breaking glass, but this time from an optical lens. The director shrieks in horror, but McAdam isn't finished. She stamps on the camera, breaking it further, then reaches down to retrieve the memory card from within the wreckage. She holds it up in front of Julie's face and snaps it in two.

'Whoops,' McAdam says, letting the broken chip fall. 'Me and my butterfingers.'

The others look on in shocked silence.

'You can't do that!' Julie cries. 'You all saw what happened. That was deliberate!'

'Looked like an accident to me, Miss Director,' Raven says, mocking Julie. 'Now maybe you'll mind your own business.'

Write **J4** *in your notebook*

Then turn to **108**

75

'At least there's no danger tonight,' Bill says. 'They'll be safe here in the pub, not antagonizing anyone in the forest.'

'Anyone like who? You, perhaps?'

He shrugs. 'Our ceremony last night was interrupted. Tonight, we'll perform a cleansing ritual, to banish any trace of the fairie world that may have slipped through.'

'No matter what Glenn Davis and the Stargazers want.'

Bill smirks. 'Inspector, when you're top dog you don't pay attention to the mutts fighting for scraps. Glenn's hobbies don't concern me, and there's no reason for his little followers to go anywhere near the Lock Stones.'

You turn to Julie. She's holding up her phone again, recording everything. 'Ms Grafton, please put that away. Contrary to what you might think, this is not helping my investigation.'

She shrugs. 'Seems to me you need all the help you can get.'

Nevertheless, she pockets her phone. 'If you do catch Lori's killer, I want to be there. You owe me that.'

'The only thing I owe anyone is finding Lori's killer, as you say. Which would be a lot easier if people around here were more honest. Now, what are your plans for this evening? I assume you don't intend to return to the forest.'

The director sniffs. 'Not tonight. The time isn't right, and I can tell Aaron's not ready to face it. I know his signals better than his own mother.'

'Will the band even release the song, now that Lori's gone? Wouldn't that be rather macabre?'

She shakes her head emphatically. 'No, it'll be a beautiful tribute to her spirit. "Eyes of the Warden" was an important song to Lori, and now it'll be their biggest single ever. She'd want Killer Velvet to be remembered.' She looks to the stage. 'I should get ready for the gig. Aaron will want this one recorded, even it's only on my phone.'

She leaves you and Bill in the alcove.

*Write **J6** in your notebook*

*If you already have G5 written down, turn to **147***

*Otherwise, turn to **186***

76

'Let's have another word with Raven Moonwolf,' you say, walking across the village square. 'It seems she wasn't entirely straight with us.'

You enter the shop to find a young couple dressed in hiking clothes standing at the counter. They're buying a walking map and discussing local routes in the forest.

You want to speak to Raven privately, so you wait, browsing the shelves and listening to the soft New Age music. While contemplating a display of crystals which claim to enhance one's fertility, you suddenly hear a *hiss* followed by McAdam cursing. You turn in time to see the grey-furred cat leap down from a shelf the sergeant was browsing and saunter behind the counter. Raven tries not to laugh, while McAdam reddens.

After the hiking couple bid goodbye and leave, Raven turns to you and asks, 'How can I help?'

'By telling us the truth,' you say. 'You were keen to show us that Glenn Davis had argued with Lori Velvet when she came off stage last night, but you neglected to mention that you also spoke to her.'

Raven shrugs. 'Of course I talked with her. I told you—'

'You're a fan, yes. But fans don't normally stomp away angrily after meeting their idols, do they?' Raven's shoulders slump, knowing that whatever story she was going to tell you won't fly.

'OK, fine. I wanted to know what she meant about the Warden having a human face, that's all.'

'Why did that strike you as odd? As I understand it, the Warden is supposed to be the spirit of a druid. Why shouldn't he have a human face?'

'Because you never see under his mask,' Raven says, as if it were the most obvious thing in the world. 'I could tell she meant something significant by it, so I asked her and she confirmed it.'

McAdam looks up from her notes. 'Confirmed it? What did she tell you?'

'Nothing,' Raven says with a sigh. 'All she'd say is that we'd all find out soon. Until then, her lips were sealed.'

Later that night, someone sealed them for ever.

↗ *If you have P1 written in your notebook, turn to* **144**

↗ *Otherwise,* **add 1** *to your LOCATION number and turn to* **100**

77

'Profit's not the only thing you're interested in, though, is it?' you say. 'There's also Aaron Warrior.'

'I told you, he's barred me from ever seeing them again,' she replies quietly. 'Well, fine. I don't want anything more to do with him.'

'But you didn't have anything to do with him anyway. Your friendship with Aaron – your relationship with him – was all in your head. He's shown us the anonymous emails and messages you've sent, demonstrating your obsession. They border on stalking, and they're definitely harassment.'

Raven looks back to the fire.

'I haven't sent him any messages, and I'm not "obsessed",' she protests. 'By the Goddess, I'm old enough to be his mother.'

'An inescapable fact which only made you more jealous of Lori Velvet. Did you deem her unworthy of Aaron? Or were you angry at her for leaving him and entering a relationship with Julie Grafton?'

To your surprise, Raven laughs.

'Do you really think that's what happened? I killed Lori to get her out of the way, so I could be with Aaron? You're deluded, Inspector. Clutching at straws.'

You search her house, but find no sign of Patrick. You arrest Raven anyway and drive her to the station, hoping the shock of being in a cell will loosen her tongue.

But not long after you arrive, a call comes in from Bill Thomas. He led the Disciples of the Green to the Lock Stones this evening, to carry out a cleansing ritual. They arrived to find Patrick, with his throat slashed in the same manner as Lori Velvet.

Your case is thrown into chaos. Could Raven have killed Patrick before returning home to start the fire? It's possible, although she'd have had to move fast. Either way, you have no proof. When examined, the landlord's body is found to have been drugged, but otherwise offers no solid forensic evidence, and this time there's no sign of a murder weapon.

The detective chief superintendent points out that you have no case against Raven Moonwolf; only an accusation from Aaron, and your own gut feeling and speculation. That's not good enough now that a second body has been found while she was already in custody. You're forced to let Raven go, and the DCS reassigns the case to another detective.

Lori Velvet's murder, and now Patrick's too, may yet be solved . . . but not by you.

Wipe your notebook, return to 1 *and try again*

For now, though, this is . . .

THE END

78

'Come now, Mr Davis,' you say. 'We know you attended the concert, and also argued with Lori Velvet after she came off stage. If you truly are innocent, now is not the time to be coy.'

Glenn looks away. 'I don't know what you're talking about.'

'Would you like me to show you the videos?' McAdam says. 'Thanks to a concerned witness, I have one of you in the crowd, watching the band . . . and another of you arguing with Lori.'

The fishing rod twitches, bringing Glenn's attention fully back to the river. He stands, clutches the rod, and begins to carefully wind in the line.

'I tried to dissuade her from venturing into the forest,' he says. 'I'd been unable to prevent the concert, obviously, so instead I asked her not to invade the forest on such an important night.'

'You mean because of the full moon?'

'No! That's all superstitious nonsense, supposed sightings of the Stone Warden and what have you. Something that's only increased in recent years, I should add. Ever since that boy went missing . . .' He momentarily loses focus, struggling to hold on to the fishing rod. 'No, I mean the Lyrids. This is an important time of year for the Stargazers, with many guests joining us for a night or two to see the meteors. The

138

last thing I wanted was a rock group disturbing our peace and quiet.'

'Yes, about that—' you begin, but Glenn isn't finished.

'I wasn't the only person to have words with that girl yesterday. I saw Bill Thomas talking to her outside the pub before she went on stage, at 7.32 p.m. It looked to be far from a friendly chat.'

'Did you by any chance hear what they were saying?'

Glenn regards you with disdain. 'I'm not an eavesdropper, Inspector. But I couldn't help overhearing a few words. Bill said, "I'm telling you, don't mess with the Warden." The young woman replied, "I know more about the Warden than you realize." That was all I heard.'

By now, Glenn has wound the line in close, and is ready to land his catch. He reaches for a fishing net, resting on another telescopic stand.

'I see. And when were you planning to furnish us with this information?'

'I believe I just did.'

McAdam rolls her eyes. Glenn Davis is proving to be far from an enthusiastic witness, but at least he's talking.

You watch Glenn expertly snare the fish in his net and lift it out of the water. Working quickly and methodically, he unhooks it, lays it on a set of small scales, jots down the weight with a pencil, then releases it back into the river. The whole process takes thirty seconds.

'You look like a man who does this often,' you say. 'The forest is obviously dear to you.'

'It's dear to all of Grenholme,' Glenn replies, re-hooking his line. 'That's why those ridiculous Disciples are so disliked.'

'Bill Thomas maintains he's well-liked by the community.'

'Only because nobody else is willing to stand up to him. But I knew his game the moment he came here. Bill delights in being a big fish in a small pond.' Glenn casts his line out over the river once more, oblivious to his own pun. 'For years, the Stargazers happily coexisted with the forest, always leaving it how we found it. Then along came Mister Bigshot from the City, claiming to have found his spiritual calling, and accused us – us! – of failing to respect nature and the Lock Stones. We don't even go near the stone circle! It makes for a terrible viewing platform.'

   Write **G5** *in your notebook*

Then check it in the following order:

   If you have G9 written down, turn to **43**
   If you have G2 written down, turn to **176**
   Otherwise, turn to **43**

79

Zwale is ready to run over there, but you hold him back.

'Wait a moment. First let's have some context, please, Ms Moonwolf. Why is there a mob at Glenn's house? Is this why all the locals have cleared out of the square?'

Raven runs a hand through her hair, speaking anxiously. 'I was afraid of this. Glenn was the prime suspect in

Danny's disappearance, all those years ago. He was a school-teacher, you see, and he's always spent a lot of time in the forest . . .'

'So naturally the police investigated him, as they should have. But he was never charged,' you point out.

'That hardly matters. People were ready to believe he did it anyway. I never did, I always believed he was innocent, but he had to retire from teaching, and we split up because of the stress.'

'Split up?' Zwale asks. 'You mean you were together before then?'

Raven looks at him like it's the world's silliest question. 'Well, of course. We were married for nearly ten years.'

'You didn't think to tell us this earlier?' you say, amazed this is only now coming to light.

'Everyone already knows,' she says with a shrug.

'Everyone local, perhaps. So you and Glenn were together when Daniel Isherwood went missing, which led to your divorce, and then you opened Stones & Spirits?'

'More or less, yes. But it's all water under the bridge, and now I really think we should go and make sure Glenn's all right.'

Julie Grafton approaches from across the square, holding up her phone to film events.

'Apparently you now have two unsolved murders in this village, Inspector. What are the police doing about it? Are you simply incompetent?'

𝒫 *If you have J4 written in your notebook, turn to* **11**

𝒫 *Otherwise, turn to* **64**

80

Stones & Spirits is, to say the least, an unusual shop.

An old-fashioned bell rings when Raven opens the door, prompting the grey cat sleeping in the window to meow in protest and leap to a high shelf. You step inside to find a store teeming with tourist souvenirs and knick-knacks, from resin replica ornaments of the Lock Stones to local-themed bookmarks, badges, and plushy Stone Wardens. There are also guidebooks to the local area, maps for walkers and timetables for local buses.

Raven locks the door behind you and flips the door sign around to 'Closed', then makes her way to the back of the shop carrying her loaf.

You pass earrings and pendants in the shape of a Lock Stone; scarves imprinted with patterns of the stones; models of the stones with crystals in the centre; postcards and greeting cards; even T-shirts emblazoned with overhead pictures of the circle, or wolves howling at a full moon, or both. Behind them hang fancy dress costumes ranging from generic witches and vampires to costumes and robes specifically of the Stone Warden, and Disciples of the Green.

Raven walks behind the glass counter, placing her handbag on a chair. She taps on a tablet propped on the counter and soft New Age music starts to play quietly.

You step around a large rotating display case of crystals to approach her. To one side is a small fridge of drinks and snacks, so walkers can stock up before setting off. Underneath the glass-topped counter itself is more jewellery, and behind Raven is a bookshelf containing volumes on local legends, witchcraft, paganism and magic. Packs of tarot cards stand on a rack beneath the books.

'No Ouija boards?' McAdam asks drily, taking it all in.

'I keep those in the back with my inverted crosses,' Raven replies. You can't tell if she's joking.

McAdam prompts her: 'You said you had something to tell us.'

'Two things, actually. First of all, hang on . . .' She rummages in her handbag and produces a phone, then opens it and holds it up for you to see.

A video is playing of somewhere dark and crowded. The camera swings across the crowd, who mill around with drinks in hand, then back to what you now see is a small stage, covered in a layer of dry ice that reminds you of the forest. The camera zooms in on Aaron Warrior, who seems to be talking with the other musician members of Killer Velvet. There's no sign of Lori.

'This is from the band's performance last night?' you ask.

'That's right. They'd played "Hell Town" for an encore, so we all thought the gig was over. I think even Aaron did. But keep watching.'

A misshapen figure emerges from the smoke, shambling towards the front of the stage, wielding a knife. The musicians look shocked and surprised. You recognize the Stone Warden costume in which Lori Velvet was found. She steps to the microphone and says:

'This song is for the one who was done wrong. Mark my words: the Stone Warden has a human face.'

The band begins playing, and Lori sings.

'I thought that's what the song was called, at first,' Raven says, pausing the video. '"The Warden Has a Human Face".

But later Aaron said it's called "Eyes of the Warden". Which I suppose is better,' she concludes grudgingly.

'I see. Well, thank you, Raven—'

Suddenly the phone blasts music again. Raven is so startled she almost drops it, then scrambles to shut it off.

'Sorry, sorry,' she says. 'That's my morning reminder alarm. Anti-anxiety pills.'

'You'll have to teach me how to do that,' McAdam says wearily. 'My daughter got hold of my phone and changed the family ringtone to some awful thing from her favourite cartoon.'

Raven smiles sympathetically. 'I'll show you later, but first, watch the video again. See who's there?'

She passes you the phone, then rummages around in her handbag again. While she takes her medication, you re-watch the video from the start. This time when the camera swings over the crowd, you study their faces, then pause the video on a particular face at the back of the crowd.

'Glenn Davis,' you point out to McAdam. 'Isn't it strange that he would attend, given how opposed he was to the band performing?'

'More than opposed,' Raven says, taking back the phone. 'Glenn organized a petition to have them banned from the village. Only got about twenty signatures, mind, and most were from the other Stargazers, those bootlickers. So the gig went ahead, obviously. But I wondered why he was there.'

'Did you ask him?'

She snorts. 'I used to lead the Stargazers, you know. That was *my* group, before Glenn had me kicked out when I opened this place. The shop's done better than I could have hoped, though. Karma is real, Inspector.'

'So you and Glenn don't talk any more,' McAdam suggests.

'Exactly. But he *did* talk to Lori, after the gig. Watch.'

Raven plays another video. This one was filmed after the band had finished playing. It's shaky, dark and filmed from a distance through a doorway, but you can just make out Lori Velvet with her Warden costume hood removed, talking to someone. The camera zooms in: you recognize Glenn Davis again, and can see that they're not just talking. They're arguing.

'Did you hear what they said?'

'No, and when I tried to get closer, Glenn left. But I'll bet he didn't mention this, did he?'

Raven's right. Glenn didn't tell you he'd argued with Lori, or that he was so opposed to the band playing he organized a petition.

From your position at the counter, you notice a side of the shop you didn't see upon first entering. You stroll around a shelf to find a children's section, with a small selection of board games, some dolls, toy cars . . . and a rounders set, with a plastic bat and balls. It might be the sort of thing McAdam is seeking for Douglas, her son.

'A lot of people come here dragging bored kids with them,' Raven says, seeing you browsing. 'There's no toy shop in Grenholme, so I started carrying some instead. Are you looking for something in particular?'

 To suggest McAdam buy the rounders set, turn to **2**

 To forget it and continue questioning Raven, turn to **30**

81

Aaron must be stopped before it's too late. You rush further into the woods, approaching the parking area by the river. From up ahead you hear . . . music?

You freeze, listening. It doesn't sound recorded. Someone is playing an acoustic guitar. The tune is familiar, but you can't quite place it.

Taking care to be quiet, you slowly move towards the sound. Then the drifting haze clears and you see a figure silhouetted against the water, sitting on the riverbank with a guitar. More notes reach you, and with more context you recognize the music: 'Eyes of the Warden', the song which has caused so much pain and trouble.

'Aaron,' you call out, knowing it must be him. 'Aaron, it's the police.'

He doesn't turn, but keeps on playing. 'Inspector. What brings you out here?'

'I could ask you the same question. Where's Patrick?'

He ignores the question. 'I loved her, you know. We had our moments, but I really did. She's . . . impossible to replace.'

'I thought you were planning to do just that. Aren't you singing the songs tonight?'

Aaron puts down the guitar. Then he begins to cry.

'I can't do it,' he says between sobs. 'I thought I could. I thought I didn't need her.' He takes a deep breath and lights a cigarette. His hands tremble so much it takes him several attempts. 'Oh, Lori, I'm so sorry.'

'Aaron, I'll ask you again. Where's Patrick?'

He turns to you, his eyes red with tears. 'Who's Patrick?'

'The landlord. Don't play games with me. Was he there, last night? Did he see you kill Lori, so you decided to silence him before he could tell us?'

Aaron looks bewildered. 'I didn't kill her! I just told you, I loved her. You've got this all wrong.'

Check your notebook in the following order:

If you have A2 written down, turn to **112**

If you have P4 written down, turn to **162**

Otherwise, turn to **70**

82

Your instincts tell you Lori Velvet returned to Grenholme, the site of such tragedy earlier in her life, with a purpose beyond merely making a music video. Perhaps the room where she stayed will help you understand what that was.

'Can we see Lori's room?' you ask Patrick. 'It could prove useful.'

'I suppose.' He takes a key from a drawer behind the bar, then leads you and McAdam up an old narrow wooden staircase.

'You said the band are all staying here?' McAdam says. 'Separate rooms, or shared?'

'Separate,' Patrick answers. 'The singer's is at the end of the corridor.'

To reach it you walk through a wood-panelled hallway,

past several other rooms. While passing one door, you hear the muffled but unmistakeable rhythmic sound of someone having sex.

'Bit early for that,' McAdam says, frowning.

'None of our business, Sergeant,' you say, moving on quietly.

But at the end of the corridor Patrick looks back. 'Actually . . . there's nobody else here except the band. That's the other woman's room, what's her name? The director.'

Julie Grafton. Video director, and Lori Velvet's partner. With Lori gone, who's in the room with her now?

McAdam has the same thought and rolls her eyes. 'Rock stars, eh?'

Patrick unlocks and opens the door to Lori's room. At first, you think someone has ransacked it; clothes and belongings are strewn over the bed and floor, used towels hang from half-open drawers, and jewellery and make-up are scattered across the dressing table and cabinets. But upon second look, nothing appears to be broken or discarded. This room hasn't been turned over by a thief. Lori was just messy.

'Takes me back to my teenage years,' McAdam says with a shrug. 'Won't be long before Nora's room looks like this.'

Patrick watches you both pull on nitrile gloves, then takes the hint and leaves you to it. You keep the door open in order to see if anyone emerges from Julie's room. Then you take photos, before beginning a search through Lori's belongings.

'Expensive taste,' McAdam murmurs as she rifles through the disorganized pile of make-up and toiletries. 'Why is it the people with the most care the least for it?'

'Lori Velvet may have been successful, but losing her twin brother as a child must have haunted her. None of us know what others are dealing with internally.'

'Aye, I suppose. Do you think that's why she wrote that song, and came back here?'

You don't answer.

'Inspector? I said—'

'Yes,' you answer at last. 'I think that probably is why Lori Velvet came back to Grenholme. Look at this.'

Inside Lori's suitcase are more clothes, shoe bags and toiletries, but underneath them all is something quite different. A scrapbook.

The cover has no writing or text. Only a symbol, which appears to have been painted by hand. You've seen it before.

It's the symbol tattooed on Lori Velvet's back . . . and one of those chalked on the Lock Stones.

You still don't know what the markings mean, and you can't be certain who made them. But when you open the book and see its contents, there's no longer any doubt in your mind that this is somehow all connected.

The scrapbook's neat interior is a marked contrast to the messy room in which you stand. It's filled with photos, press clippings, printouts and handwritten notes. The first photograph is of two children, a boy and a girl, five or six years old. Even at such a young age it's obvious they're related. They pose in their school uniforms, smiling and holding hands.

A skim of the following press clippings confirms that the picture is of Daniel and Lucy Isherwood. The stories talk of a concerted search operation and police investigation into his disappearance, but with no result. What torture that must have been for the family. In cases like this, the lack of a body means there is always a sliver of hope the missing person might still be alive . . . but no chance of closure if they're not.

Mixed in with the photos and clippings are articles on the legend of the Stone Warden, photocopied from books and printed from websites. Flipping ahead, you find sketches for a Warden costume, presumably planning for what Lori would wear on stage. You turn another page . . . and stop.

'She was obsessed,' McAdam whispers, looking over your shoulder.

The last entries in the scrapbook fill two facing pages. On one is a sketch of the Stone Warden costume, from head to toe, looking remarkably like the costume Lori was found wearing. In the sketch, the Warden stands in the centre of the Lock Stones circle.

On the second page is a single phrase, carefully written by hand: '*The Warden has a human face*'.

'That's what she said on stage before they played this song,' you say, flipping onward. The scrapbook's remaining pages are blank.

'While she wore that costume, too,' McAdam says.

A thought strikes you. 'I wonder . . . did Lori come back here to search for her brother? This scrapbook almost feels like it builds to a conclusion. Was she conducting her own investigation?'

'Or maybe hoping to provoke something into happening?'

'But then why not reveal who she is? There's no question that Lori provoked a reaction, but she hid her connection to Grenholme from everyone except Raven.'

'And that was only because they recognized one another.' McAdam takes the book and flips through the pages. 'If not for that . . . oh, look.' She points to a press clipping concerning the investigation into Daniel's disappearance, and one of the police's prime suspects: Grenholme councilman Glenn Davis.

🔍 Write **P1** *in your notebook*

🔍 Then turn to **146**

83

Your phone buzzes with a new message from Dr Wash, sending you a photo of the bracelet found on Daniel Isherwood's body. As you noticed before, the wooden beads feature some of the same symbols chalked on the Lock Stones. But what the doctor's clean-up has revealed is that they *also* feature plain letters.

In fact, each bead contains both a letter and a symbol:

You wish you'd seen this earlier, as it would have saved you a lot of effort instead of working out the message by yourself! Nevertheless, you check the bracelet against your notebook and confirm that you were right.

'Danny is here,' you murmur.

'What's that?' Dr Wash and Constable Zwale both ask in unison.

'It's the message that was written in chalk on the stones,' you explain. 'I already believed it was done by Lori Velvet, and this all but confirms it. Her father said both twins wore matching bracelets, presumably each with their own name on it. Lori must have remembered and practised this code over the years. She came to Grenholme and, I believe, wrote that sequence to be a hidden message in her music video . . . but was interrupted by the killer.'

'She was right, too,' the doctor points out. 'Danny was, indeed, there in the forest.'

'Yes. I'm convinced she wrote that song, and wanted to film the video here, in the hope of finding both her brother's body and killer. It might also explain why she was carrying a knife. She may have arranged to meet someone, hence leaving the band and walking to the Lock Stones by herself.'

Dr Wash whistles. 'For all the good it did her. I'll leave you to work on that hypothesis, Inspector. Do pass on my best to Sergeant McAdam when you next speak to her.'

'Thank you, Doctor, I will.'

You end the call and look again at the photograph of the bracelet. Fog drifts across the village square, chasing people into the warmth of the pub.

'Lori told the crowd "The Warden has a human face", didn't she?' Zwale asks.

'That's right. It's why I think she intended to expose her brother's killer. She'd discovered something, or perhaps remembered it after all this time, and wanted to tell the world.'

'So she believed whoever did it is still here in Grenholme?'

'I think so. The symbolism of returning to the site of her brother's disappearance would have been very strong, not to mention confronting his killer.'

The constable takes out his phone and looks something up. 'I saw earlier that someone had uploaded a video of the song from last night. They've even transcribed the lyrics, look.'

He shows you a video taken by a member of the crowd at last night's pub performance. It's shaky, but the music is perfectly audible – as is Lori's powerful voice, screaming and yelling her way through the song. You scroll down to read the transcribed lyrics. With the context you now have, some passages stand out.

Sickened laugh behind the mask
Guardian of lies is cast
Riches that no man could buy
Parading sycophants in mind
Eyes of the warden
Watching you
Stones of a dark veil
Stealing truth
Haunted by a thousand ghouls
Swallowed by a mist so cruel

'I think you're right,' Zwale says. 'Lori had worked out who killed her brother.'

'Or thought she had. She might have been wrong. Regardless,

this reiterates her belief that the Warden is very human, something I'm also convinced of myself after our encounter in the forest earlier. The question is . . . whose face is behind the mask?'

Turn to **178**

84

'I do agree, though,' you say. 'Come along, Sergeant.' With McAdam following, you hurry out of the pub into the village square.

Raven has returned to her shop, while Bill has peeled off down a narrow street.

'Who first?' McAdam asks.

You make a split-second decision.

'Raven will likely stay at the shop for the rest of the day,' you say. 'But we don't know where Bill is going, so let's begin with him.'

You follow the pagan leader at a discreet distance as he walks through the streets of Grenholme, making several turns along the way.

'At this rate he'll be in the forest before too long,' McAdam murmurs.

'I have a feeling Bill is going somewhere rather more prosaic,' you reply. 'Namely, home.'

Your instincts are proven correct, when Bill reaches the outskirts of town and strolls up to the wide gates of a large house, taking a key fob from his pocket.

He stops at the gates, turns and waves to you.

'Come in, Inspector. I'll put the fire on.'

Annoyed that your ability to stealthily follow someone is not what it should be, you force a smile. Bill presses a button on his key fob and the gates swing open with a low, metallic groan.

'You seemed in a hurry to leave the pub just now,' you say, passing through the gates and shivering at a sudden chill.

'I didn't much care for the atmosphere,' he replies. 'I love this place, but there's too much gossip and nonsense for my liking. You shouldn't believe everything you hear in Grenholme, you know.'

'Not even from you, Mr Thomas?'

'Touché,' he says with a smile, and walks towards the house. Check your notebook in the following order:

🔍 *If you have B12 written down, turn to* **135**

🔍 *If you have P9 written down, turn to* **189**

🔍 *Otherwise, turn to* **135**

85

You contemplate talking to another witness, but with their statements all taken, the remaining members of the public have now dispersed.

'I could get some uniforms to drag them back . . .?' McAdam offers with a hint of glee in her expression, but you decline.

'It's very late, Sergeant, and I doubt we'll get much more

sense out of anyone tonight. Including ourselves. We need a decent night's sleep.'

'If we can,' she says gloomily. 'All this spooky nonsense, it gets my goat.' Seeing Dr Wash approaching, she says, 'Not that I expect your goat would be bothered. He'd just munch on the grass around the stones.'

'On the contrary,' the doctor replies, 'goats are very sensitive creatures. If George were here, I'm sure he'd warn me of any ghosts abroad.'

The doctor lives on her late husband's farm, now repurposed as a menagerie. 'George Washington' is her oldest male goat, with whom Sergeant McAdam has what might be called a strained relationship. Normally you'd assume the doctor is joking about goats and ghosts, but given her earlier musings, you're not so sure.

'I came to say I've done all I can here, and I'll see you later this morning,' she continues. 'We'll examine the costume, the hood, and of course the knife found near the body. Meanwhile, I'll get to work on the victim herself. Time and post-mortems wait for no man.'

'Indeed. Good night, Doctor.'

Her forensics team have taken down the white tent while you were talking to witnesses. Now Dr Wash leads them into the woods, leaving behind no trace they were ever here. The police cordon remains, though you doubt there's much more meaningful evidence to be gained from within the stone circle.

'Time for us all to turn in, too,' you say. 'But not for long. News of a rock star's death will travel fast. Fans on social media, then the music press, then perhaps the nationals . . . we mustn't waste time, or we'll soon find ourselves at the centre of a circus.'

McAdam takes out her phone, then swears quietly. 'Forgot there's no signal. I was going to call Emma and tell her we're heading back.'

'I imagine she wasn't impressed with an after-midnight call.'

She shrugs. 'Would have been easier if Douglas hadn't taken hours to get to sleep tonight. We'd barely got our heads down when my phone went. Still, that's the job.'

McAdam swaps the phone for a torch from her pocket and you walk into the dense, dark forest. Constable Zwale finishes talking to another uniformed officer and joins you as you duck under the cordon.

'Pardon me, Inspector,' he says, 'but as I was taking statements a thought occurred to me. What if this is a case of mistaken identity? Because of the costume, I mean.'

McAdam groans. 'As if things weren't confusing enough already! That's all we need.'

'Discouraging though it may be, it's a possibility,' you say. 'If Lori Velvet was dressed as the Stone Warden, including the hood over her head, who's to say the killer didn't assume she was someone else entirely? Good thinking, Constable.' Zwale beams at your compliment. 'Is anyone in the village known to dress as this mythological figure?'

Zwale's expression drops. 'I, um, didn't think to ask that. Sorry. I was just taking statements.'

McAdam sighs. 'Too busy looking at stars instead of thinking about what's happening here on earth. Go on, away with you to bed.'

You reach the parking area, where Zwale joins another

uniformed officer in a marked vehicle. You and McAdam climb into her car, and she pulls away along the forest road.

'We'll need to locate and inform Lori Velvet's family,' you say. 'At least they won't have to go through the awful business of identifying her, seeing as her bandmates have already done that.'

'I'll look them up,' McAdam replies. For once, you notice she's not driving at top speed and throwing the car around corners. Perhaps Grenholme Forest and the Lock Stones have unsettled her more than she'll admit.

Turn to **140**

86

But, somehow, you're wrong.

You expected to find Bill, either in his Disciple robes or perhaps even dressed as the Stone Warden, with Patrick. Instead, a sharp breeze clears mist from the stone circle, and in the light of the full moon you see Patrick lying alone and motionless in its centre.

You rush between the stones, fearing you're too late. To your relief, the landlord is unconscious but alive.

What's going on? Who left him here? You were sure Bill had taken him. He was adamant that you ignore 'village gossip', and even planted in your mind the idea that Lori may have been killed because she claimed to have seen the Warden's face. You believe Bill recognized her as Lucy Isherwood, and knew she was talking about the man who took her brother Daniel all those years ago: not a forest spirit, but Bill dressed as the Warden.

Fearing she would identify him, he arranged to meet her at the stone circle last night, where he made sure she could never tell anyone. But when Patrick told you earlier that Lori had confided in him, Bill realized he had to silence his Disciple as well.

So why is Patrick still alive?

An owl screeches near by in the trees. *No, not an owl.* That was a human!

Turn to **105**

87

'Just one more thing, Mr Davis.' You show him a photo of the speaker you found in the tree. 'Do you recognize this?'

Seeing it, he twitches in surprise. 'Where was this taken?'

'Near the stone circle, inside a hollow tree. Is it yours?'

'It – no, it can't be. I mean, I have one at home that looks the same. But I never take it into the forest.'

McAdam leans in. 'Never? Are you quite sure?'

'Yes,' Glenn protests. 'I keep it in my kitchen, to listen to music. What's this got to do with anything?'

'I'm not entirely sure yet,' you say. 'But I don't believe in coincidences. Constable, would you accompany Mr Davis to his house to check his speaker is there?'

Glenn looks about to object, but relents. He was already

leaving, and he knows that refusing your request would look suspicious.

'Very well,' he says, heading for the door. 'Come along, Constable.'

Zwale makes the universal *I'll-call-you* hand gesture to you, then follows Glenn out of the pub. Through the window you watch them walk across the square, in the direction of his house.

🔎 *Write* **G7** *in your notebook*

Now choose another person in the pub to interview:

🔎 *To speak with Aaron, turn to* **168**

🔎 *To talk to Julie, turn to* **55**

🔎 *If you've already interviewed both of them, turn to* **101**

88

'Everyone seems to be accounted for,' Sergeant McAdam says with obvious disappointment. 'They can alibi each other. The astronomers were all together, the pagans were all together and so were the band members.'

'Apart from Lori Velvet,' you point out. 'Why did she wander away by herself? Was she coming to see the Lock Stones, before they started filming here? A moment of quiet contemplation, perhaps?'

'Maybe she was daring herself to prove the legend wrong.

Youngsters will do that sort of thing.' She stifles a yawn, but you notice. It seems even an energetic sergeant like McAdam can get tired at this time of morning.

You walk the perimeter of the circle together, inside the stones. 'She wrote a song about the Stone Warden, then visited the stones dressed as him. That doesn't sound like someone trying to prove the legend wrong.' You place a hand on one of the stones, its rough surface cool and unyielding. The chalk symbol drawn on it seems to glow in the harsh forensic lamp light. 'No, something doesn't add up here, even apart from the obvious questions around Ms Velvet's death. There's a big question that we're not asking—'

Before you can finish the thought, Constable Zwale approaches. 'I've just been talking to Patrick, one of the Disciples, who owns the village pub.' He looks back at the gathered pagans, and the bald man who insisted to you that the Stone Warden is real gives a tentative wave. 'I asked him if anyone knows what these symbols on the stones mean.'

'The chalk?' McAdam says, peering at the nearest stone. 'Looks like astrology to me. Some old druidic thing?'

'That's just it. According to Patrick, they're not old at all. He's never seen the symbols before, and neither have any of the others. They're a bit offended by it, actually.'

You look more closely at the nearest stone. The chalk symbol upon it is from no alphabet you've ever seen.

'How curious. Constable, when was the last time any of the Disciples visited the circle?'

He checks his notebook. 'Last week. I asked, and they said the symbols definitely weren't here at that time.'

'Well done for checking, lad,' McAdam says. 'It means anyone could have drawn them, though.'

'Not necessarily,' you say. 'Today – or rather yesterday, as we're now past midnight – was Friday. It rained on Wednesday, which would have washed off any chalk. So whoever drew them must have done so in the last forty-eight hours. But who, and why?'

'You did say there's a big question we're not asking,' McAdam prompts. 'Was this it?'

'No. I was wondering: what made the victim scream? Everyone we've spoken to heard it. But her throat was cut. Therefore, she must have screamed before she was killed.'

'Which means she saw her attacker coming despite the dark,' McAdam concludes, 'and it frightened her to death. Well, almost.'

You gaze up at the full moon. All over the world, folklore and mythology link the full moon to unusual and unnatural occurrences: in older times it was werewolves and fairies, nowadays it's psychopaths and road rage. It may be nonsense, but that doesn't stop people believing it . . . and sometimes acting accordingly.

'Here's another question: are we sure Ms Velvet was killed here?' you ask, looking around. 'Is it possible she was attacked in the trees, then brought to the centre of the circle for symbolic purposes?'

'Either way, her killer presumably came from out of the forest,' McAdam says. 'If they were waiting for her in the circle, she'd have seen them when she arrived.'

'That could be why she screamed. Imagine walking out of the trees, expecting to find the stones unattended, but seeing someone standing there.'

McAdam shivers. 'Aye, fair enough. That'd give you the howlers, especially if they're holding a big old knife.'

You know the forensics team will return in the morning to conduct a proper examination. For now, your best course of action might be to talk more with Dr Wash about the victim, and the presumed murder weapon found at the scene. You'd also like to take a closer look at those chalk symbols on the stones, though, so you decide to split the tasks with Sergeant McAdam. One of you will talk to the pathologist, while the other examines the symbols.

   To examine the chalk symbols yourself, go to **41**
   To talk to Dr Wash about the murder weapon, go to **110**

89

You run to follow McAdam, determined to apprehend whoever it is dressing up as the Stone Warden. Perhaps it's someone's idea of a joke, but you fail to see the funny side.

The gloom envelops you, and the deeper you venture into the forest the hillier and more uneven the ground becomes, but you refuse to give up. You leap over a narrow brook, almost slipping on the bank opposite when you land. Still the Warden runs on, and you lose sight of him for a moment in the gloom. Then a movement catches your eye as he leaps over gnarled roots and dodges through trees. McAdam stumbles over a bramble, but you catch her before she falls and run down a sloping hill of dirt to continue the chase.

'Take the left,' McAdam says between ragged breaths. 'I'll go right and we'll pincer him.'

It's a good idea. You veer to the left, trying to outpace and outmanoeuvre your quarry. Both fog and trees thicken, making it difficult to see. You joked to McAdam about Ariadne and the labyrinth, but the reality is closer than you'd like. The stench of rotting leaves reaches you, though you can't tell from which direction. It doesn't matter. You forge ahead.

Then you see him. The Warden has stopped, his shambling layers of forest-grimed fabric rustling quietly in the breeze. He seems to be getting his bearings, something you're confident no ghostly spirit would require. Now is the perfect time to strike . . . but how will you approach him?

    To charge directly at the Warden, turn to **190**

    To sneak up on the Warden, turn to **51**

90

'What do you mean, you can't find Patrick?' you ask. 'Last time we saw him, you were both behind the bar. Admittedly, that was a while ago.'

'Well, he's not there now,' Fran says, fretting. 'Nobody knows where he is. He's not in the bar, he's not out back, he's not answering his phone . . .'

'Is he with the Disciples of the Green? I gather they're planning another ritual at the Lock Stones tonight.'

She shakes her head. 'Not tonight, because we've got so many people in. Besides, Patrick always tells me when he's off with Bill so I can book extra help. I can't cope by myself.'

'Perhaps he's just taking a break,' Zwale suggests. 'If you're going to be really busy, he might be having a quick rest before the madness.'

'Then why isn't he answering his phone?'

You offer to check Patrick's home and see if he's there. Fran gives you directions, then hurries back inside the pub to attend to the impatient crowd.

'Patrick isn't a suspect, is he?' Zwale asks as you walk together through the quiet, misty streets. 'So why are we checking on him? Seems more like something a uniform would do.'

'A uniform that you're still wearing,' you remind him. 'In a case like this, anything out of the usual is worth noting and following up.'

You reach the landlord's street. It's quiet and empty, with only a few lights visible. Patrick's house is dark, and your knock on the door goes unanswered. You and Zwale split up, calling on those neighbours with lights on, but come up empty. Most people haven't seen him all day, and nobody in the past hour or so.

'Curious,' you say. 'I know Fran said it would be unusual, but let's check at Bill's anyway.'

It's a short walk from here to Bill's home, aka Disciple Chambers. Approaching the gates, you see a group of people in robes gathered at the side of the grounds and feel a sense of relief. The Disciples are already here.

But you soon notice that Patrick is not. When you ask after his whereabouts, one Disciple grumbles.

'Pat won't join us until after the band finishes. Assuming Bill lets us in before then, that is.' He gestures at the house. Beyond the closed gates it's completely dark, and Bill isn't out here with his Disciples. 'We normally wait inside.'

You press the gate buzzer several times, but there's no response.

'Have you tried calling him?' you ask.

The Disciple nods. 'Of course. No answer.'

You leave them, with instructions to call you if either Patrick or Bill arrives.

'Next stop, Raven,' you say to Constable Zwale, growing increasingly uneasy. 'Did we take her home address?'

Zwale confirms that he did, and it's on the other side of the village. The quickest route is through the square, so you hurry back. The pub is the only village-centre establishment still open; Stones & Spirits is dark except for a security light.

A group of locals is gathered in the square, and as you cross it one middle-aged man with a backpack slung over his shoulder emerges from the crowd to speak with you.

'Inspector, have you seen Glenn?' he asks. You look at the group and realize they're the Stargazers.

'Is he not with you?'

'No, and he's not at home either. Or answering his phone. We're a bit concerned, to be honest. After what happened . . . earlier.'

Your trepidation grows. Three missing people, one of whom has already been threatened by a mob.

You turn to Zwale. 'Constable, continue on to Raven's and make sure she's at home.'

*If you have R5 written in your notebook, turn to **19***

*Otherwise, turn to **120***

91

You approach the Grenholme Stargazers, looking for Glenn Davis. At first you don't see him, but as you draw near, he emerges from the group to greet you.

'Inspector, we've delivered our statements to your officers. I assume we're now free to go?'

'Yes, but before you do, I wonder if you could help me with something.' You gesture to the Lock Stones, then show him your notebook sketch of the chalk symbols.

'Can you shed any light on these? We're told they're not a normal part of the stones' appearance, and believe they were drawn either today or yesterday. Do you recognize them?'

'Absolutely not,' Glenn replies with disgust. 'I don't hold with the occult, as I believe I already made clear.'

'You think they have occult meaning? Does that mean you do recognize them?'

'I most certainly don't, but what else could they be? It's hardly Christian iconography, is it? No, Inspector, this foul nonsense carries the mark of black magic. Heed my words.'

Turn to 85

92

Sometimes you hate being right.

A sharp breeze clears mist from the stone circle just in time for you to see Patrick on his knees, with the Stone Warden standing over him. By the light of the full moon you watch, helpless, as the Warden slashes a knife across Patrick's throat from behind. Just like how Lori was killed.

As Patrick's limp body falls to the ground, you wonder: is that really Bill under the Warden's mossy hood? Why would he do this?

The Warden turns to face you, and a chill of primal fear wraps around your spine. You came here with nothing. No real evidence, barely even a hypothesis. You were right that the Warden took Patrick, but what good will that do you now?

You turn and run, fleeing blindly into the forest, but you don't know these woods. The Warden has walked them for more than a thousand years. You stumble over a gnarled tree root, and before you can scramble to your feet, the dark, shambling figure is upon you.

He lifts his bloodstained knife, ready to strike. You watch your own terrified reflection in the Stone Warden's mirrored eyes as he stabs down, again and again, all the time in complete silence. You try to speak, to ask why, but your breath is ragged and blood gurgles from your mouth. Darkness creeps in at the edges of your vision, framing the Warden as he stands, nods as if to acknowledge a job well done, then turns and disappears into the fog.

You struggle to rise, to follow, to catch and unmask this ruthless killer. But your body betrays you. You lie on your back, gasping for air and staring up at the dark, whispering branches of Grenholme Forest. Nobody will find you in time.

Wipe your notebook, return to **1** *and try again — this time focusing on gathering clues and evidence against whomever you suspect.*

For now, though, this is . . .

THE END

93

'There's no need for that attitude,' McAdam says. 'Anyway, I went through all the footage you sent us before, and now that you mention it, I do remember seeing shots of the woods with no band members in them. To be honest, I thought it was a mistake.'

Julie rolls her eyes. 'Maybe you should have thought to ask.'

↪ *Turn to* **128**

94

'No sense twiddling our thumbs while we wait,' you say. 'Let's see who's out and about this morning.'

As you walk around the square, the locals continue to avoid you and offer suspicious looks. A more superstitious detective might accuse them of giving you the 'evil eye'. Undeserved, perhaps, but you understand their thinking. Small communities like Grenholme don't mistrust outsiders simply for the sake of it. They live by routines and familiarity, a necessary orderliness which allows them to exist peacefully cheek-by-jowl, seeing the same neighbours day in and day out. Your

presence disrupts that order and makes them see their neighbours in a new and potentially dangerous light.

A young mother passes, holding her toddler daughter by
the hand, and narrows her eyes at you. The girl sticks out her
tongue.

'Charming,' McAdam mutters. 'Anyone would think we're
the killers.'

'We're no less outsiders here than Lori Velvet was,' you
remind her. 'They won't be happy until the killer is behind
bars and we're long gone.'

'Aye, and neither will I.'

You approach the opening of a narrow cobbled street, barely
the width of a car. To one side, in the shadow of a building,
you see two men talking. In fact, their body language suggests
it's a little more than that; they're arguing quietly, trading angry
whispers. They clearly don't want to be either seen or heard.
It takes you a moment, as they're both wearing very different
clothes to last night, but then you recognize Glenn Davis and
Bill Thomas: the astronomer and the pagan.

It was clear from their witness statements that these men
bear no great love for each other, but this argument looks like
more than a mere disagreement over use of the forest.

They haven't seen you yet, but to hear them properly you'd
need to move closer, which risks revealing your presence.
What will you do?

   To move closer, turn to **29**

   To listen from here, turn to **167**

Like the Stone Warden earlier today, Glenn has you at a disadvantage by knowing Grenholme Forest better than you ever could. On the other hand, being in better shape, you move faster. And you're both at the mercy of the drifting fog, which randomly obscures paths and obstacles as you run. The cut he gave you bleeds into your eyes, half blinding you.

Nevertheless, you maintain your pursuit, neither gaining ground nor losing him. By now, you're deep in the forest. Constable Zwale will never find you. If you're going to bring Glenn Davis in, you must do it alone.

Why did he run? Because he knows the game is up. You should have seen it sooner, really. All signs have pointed to Glenn from the start, but your mind should have been finally made up when you discovered that Raven was his ex-wife. No wonder Glenn mounted a petition to prevent Killer Velvet from coming to Grenholme. Even though their divorce predates the band, he probably sees it as a symptom of her fall from grace. Another bad actor, poisoning her mind with Satanic lies. Perhaps the final straw.

When the petition failed, Glenn took matters into his own hands in the only way left to him — by killing Lori, justifying it to himself as a way to save Raven. He must be insane.

As you clamber over a rise in the ground, keeping him in sight, a foul smell drifts upon the damp air. You're close by the bog where Daniel's body was found.

⚲ *Turn to* **169**

<h1 style="text-align:center">96</h1>

'What do you think Lori meant when she told you she "knows more about the Warden than you realize"?'

Bill tries to hide his surprise that you know this detail of his argument with Lori, but you catch his expression before he can mask it.

'I suppose she meant how she was originally from Grenholme. I didn't know that at the time, though. I don't think anyone did.'

'You might never have, if she hadn't been killed while wearing a fancy dress costume.'

⚲ *Turn to* **44**

<h1 style="text-align:center">97</h1>

You answer the call, putting it on speaker so McAdam can hear.

'Morning, Inspector,' Constable Zwale says. 'I've been checking Lori Velvet's phone records like you asked. There's not much here, to be honest. Mostly it's calls to Julie Grafton, some to the band's management company and a few to taxi firms.'

'None to her fellow bandmates?'

'Not calls. My guess is she probably spoke to them through messaging, which means we can't see them without getting into her phone. There is one thing, though.'

'Go on.'

The young constable hesitates. 'Maybe it's not unusual, but Lori made a *lot* of recent calls to a firm of solicitors. Like, none at all until about three months ago, then dozens each month since.'

'Did you call the firm?'

'It went straight to voicemail. I left a message asking them to call me back, and I'll try again later.'

McAdam leans in. 'It could just be the band's lawyers. Every band has them on call, it's standard practice.'

'Not this one, ma'am. The management company told me they use the same firm for all their clients, but this is someone completely different. A-Sharp Legal, they're called. Based in London and specializing in music industry law.'

'Oh-*ho*. Well done, Constable.'

You can almost hear Zwale beam with pride down the phone. 'Thank you, ma'am. I've emailed you their details.'

'I must admit, I was expecting it to be something connected to her pregnancy, but this sounds more like business.'

'Pregnancy?' Zwale asks, so you get him up to speed with what you learned from Dr Wash.

'That's terrible,' he says. 'But you're right, I don't think this firm handles family matters. Maybe the band had a dispute with the record label?'

McAdam shakes her head. 'Then why not use their manager's lawyer? No, I'm thinking maybe she had an issue with the management themselves. We should ask the band members.'

'Not yet,' you say. 'Let's keep our powder dry for now, until we hear from the solicitor themselves. A murder conducted in this manner would be a particularly grim way to solve a legal argument, but it's not unprecedented.'

ᕋ *Turn to* **159**

98

'Not so fast,' you say, preventing Julie from going inside. 'I believe you've taken Patrick somewhere, and I'm concerned for his safety.'

'Why on earth would I take him anywhere? You can check the van all you like, he's not there.'

'Then I'll ask you again: what have you done with him?'

'Nothing!' she protests. 'Look, this is harassment. Before you go any further, I reckon you should see this.'

She takes out her phone, and you think she's going to start filming again, but to your surprised she turns it to face you and presses play.

You watch a video of the moment in the pub when McAdam smashed Julie's camera and destroyed the memory card. You're clearly visible, looking on and doing nothing to prevent it.

'Where did you get this?'

'A source,' she says, smugly. 'They filmed the whole thing and sent it to me. Don't even think about smashing this one too, by the way. I've already uploaded it to YouTube. Along with this one.'

She plays another video. You see yourself earlier, in the village square, accusing Julie of making up the story about McAdam smashing her camera. A pit opens in your stomach.

'I wonder what'll happen when the press see these?' she says, but you both know the answer to that question.

You don't even have to wait long for confirmation. As you stand dumbfounded, watching Julie return inside the pub, your own phone rings. It's the detective chief superintendent.

Not only are you and McAdam both placed on immediate suspension, but you later learn that Bill Thomas and the Disciples of the Green found Patrick's body at the Lock Stones, with his throat slashed in the same manner as Lori Velvet.

Could Julie have killed Patrick before returning to the van where you found her? It's possible, although she'd have had to move fast. His body is found to have been drugged, but otherwise offers no solid forensic evidence, and this time there's no sign of a murder weapon.

It doesn't matter anyway. You're off the case, and potentially off the force.

Lori Velvet's murder, and now Patrick's too, may yet be solved . . . but not by you.

   🔍 *Wipe your notebook, return to **1** and try again – this time acting in a manner more befitting an officer of the law.*

For now, though, this is . . .

THE END

99

'It's my ceremonial knife,' Bill says. 'You saw it last night, and you can see it again if you like. It's over there.' He points to the display cabinet featuring the Disciples' paraphernalia. Inside is a knife that appears to be the same one he showed you at the crime scene, with an intricately carved handle and a slim blade.

'All that blade cuts is ferns and leaves, when we perform a ritual. We're planning one tonight, in fact, seeing as last night's ceremony was interrupted.'

You already have a knife that Dr Wash confidently believes to be the murder weapon – Lori's own, which is quite different – so you're satisfied this one wasn't involved.

Nevertheless, one question remains: is it likely that Bill would simply forget to take his knife on a Disciples outing?

Turn to **115**

100

(If this is your first time reading this section, write **LOCATION:** *1 in your notebook)*

You return to the village square, where a cold breeze whips through the open air, and consider your next move.

'Where to, Inspector?' Sergeant McAdam asks, looking restless and eager to uncover more of Grenholme's secrets. You feel the same way.

*If your LOCATION number is now 4, turn to **187***

Otherwise, choose one of the following options:

*To speak with Glenn Davis again, turn to **49***

*To re-interview Bill Thomas, turn to **151***

*To talk to the pub landlord, turn to **126***

*If you now have P9 written in your notebook, you may also return to Stones & Spirits and talk more with Raven by turning to **76***

101

You re-enter the village square as a haze descends on Grenholme. Nevertheless, through it you see that the village is becoming busier. Many of the new arrivals are young people, clustered in couples and groups, with painted leather jackets and brightly dyed hair. Beneath the jackets, you see many Killer Velvet branded T-shirts.

'What do you think?' McAdam asks. 'Here for tonight's memorial gig, or coming to pay their respects?'

'Perhaps both. That's assuming they're all Killer Velvet fans, of course.'

'If they're not, I'll eat my studded belt.'

You wouldn't like to bet either way if this is merely a turn of phrase, or if the sergeant actually possesses such a belt.

Before you can ask, a figure in the square catches your

attention. A man in his thirties, he isn't dressed like the band's fans, but doesn't seem to be local either. He scans the crowd, then sees you and immediately begins walking towards you. With a sinking feeling you realize too late who, or rather what, he is.

Seeing him approach, McAdam makes the same mental calculations. 'Oh, great,' she mutters. 'A journalist.'

'I'm sure he won't be the last,' you agree, quiet enough that the man can't hear you.

'Hi,' he says. 'Brian Brett, from the *Daily*. Any statement for the press?'

'Why would we?' McAdam says innocently. 'We're just bemused locals.'

'Yeah, and I'm the reincarnation of Elvis. Come off it, you stand out a mile. Is it true she was dressed up like some local myth about a goblin?'

You resist the urge to correct his mistake. 'I'm afraid we have nothing to say at this time, Mr Brett. If you want a formal statement, contact the press office.'

'Oh, come on,' he pleads. 'I think I got here first, but there'll be plenty more coming. Young rock star, killed in some weird cult scenario? That's gold dust, that is.'

'And I'll tell your colleagues the same I'm telling you. We are actively pursuing all avenues in our investigation, and will make a fuller statement when appropriate.'

The reporter leers. 'That means you've got bugger-all, doesn't it? Typical. I wonder how the locals will like that? Or better yet, the fans.'

'Listen, you,' McAdam says quietly. 'If it's cooperation from us you're after, I suggest you wind your neck in.'

'Not how it works, babe,' Brian Brett says, walking away. Just as well, given the look on McAdam's face.

'Ignore him, Sergeant. We mustn't get distracted.'

As you watch the journalist work the crowd of fans, trying to find his story, your phone rings. It's the Family Liaison Officer who's working with the Isherwoods, and to your surprise she says Lori's father wants to speak to you.

'Inspector,' he says when she hands him the phone, 'This is Hugh Isherwood. I gather you've been puzzled by those odd shapes. Where did you see them?'

'In Lori's possession,' you say carefully, not wishing to upset him. 'I feel they may be significant, but nobody here recognizes them, and we've failed to decipher their meaning. Can you enlighten me?'

'I think so. My wife says they look something like a pair of bracelets we bought the twins, on holiday one year. Wooden beads, they were, from a place in Spain . . .'

Mr Isherwood's voice cracks. He may be engaging his best stiff upper lip, but this would be a difficult conversation for any parent.

'For both of the children, you said? We didn't find a bracelet among Lori's possessions.'

'No, you wouldn't. My wife remembers that Lucy broke hers within days of putting it on. She was like that, you see. Always haring around, climbing trees and scraping her knees.' His voice finally breaks. 'Oh, God . . .' he sobs.

'Mr Isherwood, you have my most sincere condolences. Thank you for talking to me, you've been a great help.'

He hands the phone back to the FLO. You thank her, then end the call.

'Did he actually help, though?' McAdam asks after you relate what Mr Isherwood said. 'With the bracelets long gone, we still have no way of knowing what it means.'

'I wouldn't be so sure. Let's go back and take one more look. Perhaps it might jog something loose, and at least it'll get us away from the press.'

'Aye, we'll get lost in the woods instead,' she grumbles. 'Much more of this fog and we'll need a ball of string to find our way out.'

'It's a forest, Sergeant, not a labyrinth. Although I'm sure you'd make a wonderful Ariadne.'

She frowns, unsure if this is a compliment or not, and follows you out of the village square towards the forest.

🔍 *If you have G7 written in your notebook, turn to* **166**

🔍 *Otherwise, turn to* **25**

102

You approach the Grenholme Stargazers, looking for Glenn Davis. At first you don't see him, but as you draw near, he quickly emerges from the group to greet you.

'Inspector, we've delivered our statements to your officers. I assume we're now free to go?'

'Yes, but before you do, I wonder if you could help me with something. Brace yourself.' You show him the bloody knife in the evidence bag, holding it so the light catches the symbol carved into the hilt. 'I wondered if you could possibly shed some light on this. See the symbol? It matches one of the chalk markings on the stones, over there. Do you recognize the knife?'

'Is it the same one that was on the ground when I arrived? I didn't touch it. I assume it's the murder weapon?'

You shake your head. 'We're not sure of anything yet, but it was found near by so it's of interest. Do you recognize this symbol on it?'

'Absolutely not,' Glenn replies with disgust. 'I don't hold with the occult, as I believe I already made clear.'

'You think it has occult meaning? But you said you don't recognize it.'

'I don't, but what else could it be? It's hardly Christian, is it? No, Inspector, this foul nonsense carries the mark of paganism. The only man around here who would carry a knife like that on his person is Bill Thomas.'

You follow his gaze across the clearing, to where Bill Thomas and his Disciples are gathered.

'Thank you, Mr Davis. You've been most helpful.'

Turn to **9**

103

Fog drifts across the village square, chasing people into the warmth of the pub.

'Dannyish,' Zwale says, confused. 'Doesn't make any sense. Why would you write that?'

'I don't think that's it,' you reply. 'We must be missing something. Perhaps it's connected to the three blank stones . . .'

You now have the full 'bracelet code', thanks to Dr Wash.

The answer must lie within, somehow. With pen and note-book in hand, you wrack your brains trying to figure it out.

When you think you've worked it out, there's one more step. Write out the message, then assign each letter a number from 1 to 26 — but counting backwards. So in this case A = 26, B = 25, and so on down to Z = 1. Finally, add together all the numbers to get a total amount between 1 and 200.

*When you're confident you've found the solution, turn to the section matching that total number, but before you do note down section **22** in your notebook. You'll know right away if you've deciphered it correctly. If not, you should turn immediately to 22 instead.*

   *Alternatively, if you can't work it out or don't want to try, turn to **22** anyway*

104

You show Aaron the scrapbook you found in Lori's room, pointing out the symbol on the cover.

'The same as her tattoo,' he says. 'I really wish I knew what it meant.'

'As do I. Had you seen this scrapbook before? It relates to her childhood, when Lori was known as Lucy Isherwood.'

Aaron looks confused. 'That was her real name? Huh. I always wondered, but it was another secret she wouldn't talk about, like the tattoo. I've never seen that book.'

You open it to some of the press clippings and tell Aaron the story of Lori's twin brother Daniel, his disappearance and how the family subsequently moved away.

He turns the pages, amazed.

'I had no idea. She said we had to come here because she'd written the new song, the Warden song, but I just thought she'd read about it in a book. She did that all the time.'

'Not in this case, it seems. Lori had a very personal connection to Grenholme. I wondered if she might have been trying to solve her brother's disappearance, or even find his body.'

Aaron pauses at another clipping. 'Wait – she said this Warden guy took him? But then why wear the costume? It wasn't something she normally did, that's why it took us all by surprise. She dressed up as the thing that took her own brother . . . and someone killed her for it. That's messed up, man.'

You take back the scrapbook. 'We don't yet know why Lori was killed. It seems unlikely that even the local pagans would commit murder simply because she wore a costume. But given her connection to the stone circle where we found her, it does seem more than a coincidence. Are you sure you can't tell us anything about the symbols we found chalked on the stones? I'm convinced Lori herself drew them.'

'No idea.' Aaron lies back on his bed and stares up at the ceiling. 'Three years in a band with her, and now I'm wondering if I really knew Lori at all.'

In the bar downstairs, you discuss what you've learned with Sergeant McAdam, and she reports her interview with Julie.

Contrary to what Aaron told you, Julie claims today was the first time they slept together, due to her feeling fragile and lonely. She also says that Bill Thomas, leader of the Disciples of the Green, initially agreed to help the band coordinate filming but pulled out in protest when they insisted on filming during a full moon, which the Disciples consider sacred. Finally, Julie showed McAdam some video footage from last night that she thinks could be important.

'Notice how they have such different views of their relationship,' you say. 'Aaron makes a blasé claim that it's run for months, which would mean Julie has been cheating on Lori. But Julie insists Aaron seduced her today, which implies he's uncaring about Lori's death.'

'Julie doesn't think the baby is his, either,' McAdam says. 'When I told her about it and suggested it might be Aaron's, she said Lori would "never" do that, but wouldn't elaborate.'

You hadn't expected McAdam to mention the baby to Julie, but the director's response is interesting. 'What complicated relationships these people have,' you remark.

'So much for love, eh? Not to mention that Aaron now conveniently remembers that Julie left for ten minutes shortly before Lori was killed.'

'Love isn't really the word I'd use in this case. It seems few people in this triangle were particularly faithful. Now, I'd like to see that footage.'

McAdam takes out her phone. 'I've got a copy. Julie said she was skimming through it this morning when she spotted something. This was taken at eleven thirty-six last night. Look.'

She plays the video – with the sound off, mercifully – and you watch a recording of the band members, minus Lori, miming playing their instruments in the forest. The full moon is visible behind them, and the camera moves shakily around the scene. Then it ends.

McAdam looks at you expectantly, but you're confused. 'What?'

She swipes her finger over the video timeline to the middle of the scene, then plays it again.

'There, in the trees. Behind the drummer. See?'

You peer at the screen, and this time you do see. A figure in the distance, barely more than a silhouette, moves from one side of the screen to the other. It's indistinct and lacking in identifiable detail, a black shape moving against a slightly lighter black background. You can't tell who it is, or even if it's a man or woman. But there's no doubt that it's a person walking through the forest, without a light, less than fifteen minutes before Lori was killed.

'Could this be Aaron's stalker?' you wonder. 'Or Lori's killer?'

'Why not both?' McAdam says. 'Sneaking around the forest at night is pretty extreme behaviour for anyone.'

McAdam's right, but by definition, stalkers are not in the best of mental health.

'Send that to the digital forensics team,' you say. 'Hopefully Penny can brighten it up so we can identify the person.'

'Already done,' McAdam says with a wink. Your working relationship with the sergeant had something of a rocky start, but she's quickly learned your working methods and can now anticipate them well.

🔍 *Write **A6** in your notebook*

🔍 **Add 1** *to your LOCATION number, then turn to* **100**

105

You're deciding whether or not to risk leaving Patrick alone in the stone circle when you hear another shout, this time recognizing the voice of Constable Zwale. After what happened to McAdam, you can't risk another officer being injured on your watch. You rush into the trees.

Unlike earlier, though, the situation is under control. Not far from the Lock Stones you find Zwale standing over someone wearing a moss-covered Stone Warden costume, handcuffing their hands behind their back. Is it the same person who attacked you and McAdam earlier?

Zwale pulls off the costume's hood . . . to reveal a snarling Bill Thomas.

'I got your message, Inspector,' the constable says, catching his breath. 'Then as I approached the stones, I saw this one creeping through the trees. Look what I found on him.' Zwale holds up a knife with an ornate carved handle.

'Good work, Constable,' you say, ignoring Bill's protests. 'Arrest him on suspicion of murder.'

Zwale uses his phone satellite signal to call the emergency services for assistance. Patrick is taken to hospital, while Bill returns with you and the constable to the station. The knife Bill was carrying is passed to forensics for examination.

But things begin to fall apart when you try to nail down details of what happened. The knife, which Bill insists is only for ceremonial use with the Disciples, comes back clean. While there's transfer evidence of Patrick on his Stone Warden costume, Bill insists that he found the landlord semi-conscious in the stone circle and simply checked to make sure he was OK. He claims he was returning to the village for help when Constable Zwale saw and arrested him.

When you ask why he did all this dressed as the Warden, Bill claims he's been doing it for years. A spiritual calling to appease the forest spirits.

You suspect his real motive is more mundane: to increase sightings in Grenholme Forest and thus encourage tourism to the area, which benefits several businesses, including the souvenir shop he co-owns with Raven.

Nevertheless, you let Bill spin his story, confident that Patrick will give you the evidence you need. But while he recovers quickly, the landlord's memories remain a haze. It seems he was drugged, then taken to the stones while unconscious. Without his testimony, you can't prove anything.

You have a good deal of circumstantial evidence. Bill admits dressing as the Warden, confirming Lori's claim that 'the Warden has a human face'. You're convinced that she saw Bill, dressed as the Warden, take her brother while they were playing in the forest all those years ago, but his lawyer easily counters this as mere speculation. You have no evidence that Bill knew Lori was Lucy Isherwood before today; no confirmation that she believed he killed her brother; no motive for *why* he would kill Daniel in the first place; and, most importantly, he was with his fellow Disciples when Lori was heard to scream. His alibi is rock-solid.

You're missing something. You're sure Bill did it . . . but you can't make a successful case.

*⌐ Wipe your notebook, return to **1** and try again.*

For now, though, this is . . .

THE END

106

'What about what Lori would have wanted?' you ask. 'Didn't you say you're taking her place as the singer tonight?'

'It's just a stopgap,' Aaron insists. 'I'll look for a permanent new vocalist soon.'

Will he, though? Or is this a long-held ambition? You wonder if Aaron always wanted to be the band's singer himself, and killed Lori to get her out of the way. Tragic though her death is, it will also create publicity for the band. Would he be that callous?

As if reading your thoughts, the guitarist sneers. 'Hang on, I see where this is going. First I'm accused of killing Lori for publicity, now you think I did it just to take her place? We were partners. We formed this band together.'

'So did Lennon and McCartney,' McAdam notes. 'Plenty of musical partnerships fall apart eventually, including yours. Your fights are well documented.'

'Those were personal arguments, not about the band. We were always united when it came to Killer Velvet.'

'That's not the impression you gave last night when you told us how she surprised you with the Warden costume,' you say.

Aaron says nothing. You suspect the guitarist is fast creating a new, rosier version of his story for the benefit of fans and press. One that Lori Velvet is not alive to contest.

Turn to **153**

107

'We must find who owns that knife as a priority,' you say.

Dr Wash clears her throat. 'Much as I hate to be the bearer of bad news, the only fingerprints I found on the knife belonged to the victim. Of course, the killer could have been wearing gloves.'

'But if not . . . are you saying she was killed with her own knife?' McAdam is shocked. 'What on earth was she doing carrying it in the first place?'

'Protection in the forest?' you wonder aloud. 'Of course, that would presuppose that she felt in danger. Why would that be?'

Turn to **5**

108

Suddenly, Aaron moves to put himself between Raven and Julie.

'In case you'd forgotten, this *is* our business,' he says. 'It's our friend, our singer, who was killed last night. I don't care how much you like the band, nobody wants justice for Lori more than us. Leave us alone.'

'Don't shut me out!' Raven replies, on the verge of tears. 'You know I want to help you, Aaron. She's not even in the band!'

'I loved her,' Julie protests. 'You didn't even know her, you weirdo!'

'Yes, I did. She deserved better than you!'

Julie slaps Raven across the face.

McAdam quickly separates the women and pushes Julie away, while Bill once again comforts Raven.

'In a way, we all knew her,' he says. 'Now that we know she grew up here, the whole village feels connected to what happened.'

'All the more reason for everyone to calm down and take a breath,' you say firmly. Enlightening as it's been to see things play out, you don't want the situation to escalate any further. 'This is a stressful and emotional time for everyone, but there's no need—'

Before you can finish, Raven shrugs off Bill's arm, turns to Julie and pulls a knife from her shoulder bag!

You quickly block her way, your hands raised. 'Ms Moon-wolf! This has gone far enough. Hand that over at once.'

She hesitates, perhaps wondering if she can duck around you to get to Julie. While she's distracted, to everyone's sur-prise Aaron deftly reaches out, grips her wrist and twists the knife from Raven's fingers. In a single flowing movement, he catches it, flips it in his hand then throws it into the pub's dartboard.

McAdam pulls Raven's arms behind her back to prevent any more mischief. 'One more move out of you, Ms Moonwolf, and you'll be in handcuffs.'

↗ *If you have J1 or A2 written in your notebook, turn to* **152**

↗ *Otherwise, turn to* **23**

109

You want to reassure Aaron, but your hands are tied for now. 'I'll need to apply for a warrant to examine Raven's computer, if you truly believe she's behind this,' you explain. 'Ms Moonwolf, I should warn you that obtaining one won't be difficult under the circumstances, and our digital forensics team is highly experienced. Consider yourself on notice.'

She pouts. 'I don't care how good they are, they won't find anything.'

'Really? So what did you mean just now when you said, "The things I've done for you"?'

'I-I mean stuff like opposing the petition,' Raven stammers. 'Spreading the word, giving the band five-star reviews everywhere, that sort of thing.'

You lean in. 'Nothing else?'

'No, I swear—'

Loud music suddenly blares from her handbag, startling you. She fumbles with it, taking out her phone and shutting off the noise.

'My reminder alarm,' she says simply. 'I'm normally at home by now.'

'She's even got one of my songs as her alarm sound!' Aaron says in disbelief. 'Just arrest her and get it over with!'

'Oh, get lost, will you?' Raven says angrily, turning on her heel. Aaron stares open-mouthed after her.

'Rarely a good idea to anger one's fans,' you suggest. 'I must say, if Raven truly is the one sending you those emails, then she's hiding it very well. Either way, I suggest you keep your distance.'

'I intend to,' he says scornfully, walking away.

Returning to the pub, you don't see Bill or Julie anywhere, but Constable Zwale is at the bar. You beckon him back outside to talk without being overheard and sit together on a bench, watching the mist roll through the square and wrap around your ankles like a needy cat.

He relates what happened: Julie was filming Bill, trying to make him feel guilty about Lori's death. She claims that if Bill and the Disciples had helped the band with the shoot, instead of taking offence because they wanted to film at the Lock Stones, Lori would still be alive because she'd never have gone to the stone circle alone. Bill insisted that's not true; if Lori grew up in Grenholme, she already knew about the local legends.

It's a good point, and suggests that the singer knew exactly what she was doing by coming here to film at this particular time.

You tell Zwale what you overheard from Raven and Aaron,

and your conversation with them. However, you're interrupted by a phone call . . . from the detective chief superintendent.

🔎 *Turn to* **15**

110

You direct Sergeant McAdam to take a closer look at the chalk symbols, then call Zwale over.

'Constable, do I recall correctly that many stone circles were built to be crude astronomical tools?'

'Some definitely were, but I don't know about the Lock Stones. Do you want me to check?'

'Later. For now, stay with the Sergeant and see if there's any connection with these chalk markings.'

Leaving them to it, you make your way back to the white forensics tent. Inside, Dr Wash is finishing up, and Lori Velvet's body is almost ready to be taken to the mortuary.

'Sorry to interrupt, Doctor, but I have a question. Do you think Ms Velvet was definitely killed at this spot? Or could she have been killed elsewhere, then carried into the stone circle?'

Dr Wash considers her answer. 'Difficult to say with certainty. She hasn't been dead long enough for lividity to give a fair indication, and given the damp conditions, the ground may have absorbed a significant outflow of blood. What I can tell you is that a small quantity remained present on the ground, suggesting life was not yet fully extinct when the victim fell.'

'Because if she'd been killed elsewhere then relocated, she'd have bled out before reaching the circle?'

'Exactly so, given the wound she sustained. Do you have reason to believe she was carried in such a manner? If so, there would have been significant transfer to her assailant, defeating the point of attacking her from behind to avoid blood spatter.'

'That brings me to the knife found by the body. Are you confident it's the murder weapon?'

'As confident as I can be absent a full examination,' she says, testily. 'Not enough for you to start going around arresting people. Give me time, Inspector.'

You take Dr Wash's mild rebuke on board. 'Point taken, but could I have it for a moment? It might be instructive to see if anyone recognizes that carving on its handle.'

An assistant hands you the sealed evidence bag containing the bloody knife. Once again, you hold it up to the light and look at the carved symbol in its hilt. You're sure it matches one of the chalk symbols on the stones outside.

You thank the doctor and let her get back to work. It's too early to rule things out completely, but Dr Wash's explanation of the scene increases your confidence that Lori Velvet was attacked where she fell. Sadly, that information brings you no closer to knowing who did it.

Your thoughts are interrupted by a woman's horrified voice from across the stone circle.

'Oh, Goddess! What happened?'

Write **P2** *in your notebook*

Then turn to **183**

I I I

The pub door opens and Constable Zwale enters, looking eager as always.

'Any news, Constable?' McAdam asks.

'Not as such,' he says. 'Everyone in the village still seems on edge, and news about Lori's real identity has travelled.'

'Lori Velvet *was* her real identity. She chose a new name, but that doesn't mean she was hiding something.'

'She was, though, wasn't she?' you point out. 'Lori didn't intend for anyone in Grenholme to know about her connection to the village, and she'd changed so much that nobody here recognized her. If she hadn't been killed, the band would have performed, filmed the video, then left without anyone knowing.'

'Not even the man who fought to prevent Lori coming here at all,' McAdam says, looking over at Glenn Davis. The councilman is nursing a lemonade and gazing out of a window at the village square.

'That reminds me,' Zwale says, taking out his notebook. 'I looked through recent posts on the astronomy Facebook group, and there's some kind of power struggle going on in the Stargazers. Glenn's facing a vote of no confidence as Secretary, so he's in an even worse mood than usual.'

'That's interesting. I wanted to talk to him after today's fracas, anyway.'

'Best be quick, then,' McAdam says.

Glenn Davis is on his feet, about to leave. As he passes you, he regards Zwale in particular with suspicion and says, 'You should arrest that musician. You saw him, he threatened me with a bottle!'

195

'Mr Davis, need I point out that you had just accused him of murdering his former girlfriend,' you reply. 'Aaron's response may have been disproportionate, but was understandable all the same. Now, is it true you're facing a vote of no confidence in your astronomy group?'

His shoulders tense. 'Utter nonsense. Oh, the vote is real, but I'll pass easily. She's wasting her time.'

'"She" being . . .?'

'Raven, of course. I know she's behind it. She's never recovered since I replaced her. But the Stargazers need me. Nobody else could run the group as successfully as I do.'

Check your notebook in the following order:

If you have G9 written down, turn to **163**

If you have G2 written down, turn to **36**

Otherwise, turn to **163**

112

'I don't think so,' you say, pressing home your accusation. 'You've made it clear from the start that Killer Velvet is all you care about. Your career has given you a good life. It's got you where you are now, and there's still more ahead, isn't there? But when Lori told you she was pregnant, you saw it crumbling before your eyes. No more Killer Velvet, no more casual sex with Julie and no more Aaron Warrior the rock star. Just plain old Arjun Shankar, father to a child he didn't want.'

An owl screeches somewhere deep in the forest.

'You're way off base, Inspector,' Aaron says, his contemptuous attitude returning. 'The first I knew about Lori being pregnant was when you told me. The landlord didn't "see" me doing anything. I've hardly even spoken to him – Julie was his main contact. Now get lost and leave me alone, will you?'

Baffling as it seems, he appears to be genuine. You begin to doubt your own judgement. Is he innocent after all? There's no sign of Patrick here. Then again, Aaron would have had time to take the landlord deeper into the forest before returning to the river—

With a sickening churn in your stomach, you realize that what you heard wasn't an owl.

🔍 *Turn to* **130**

113

The astronomers seem to be a diverse group, ranging from teenagers to pensioners, though as they're all wrapped up in hats, scarves and layered warm clothing, you're basing that solely on the patches of face you can see. One particular face, older and silver-moustached, looks at you expectantly as you make your way towards them.

'That's Glenn Davis,' Constable Zwale tells you. 'Secretary of the Grenholme Stargazers, sits on the town council. He'll make an impeccable statement, he's very precise.'

'Oh, you've already spoken to him?'

'No, not yet.' Seeing your confusion, Zwale explains: 'I

know him from online. Glenn's well known in the community, you see.'

'Not really,' McAdam says. 'What community?'

'The Great Britain Amateur Astronomers group on Facebook. Glenn's been a fixture for years. But I've never met him in person before.'

'Does he know you're a policeman?' you ask.

'I don't think so. I don't talk about that online.'

'Very sensible.' By now you've reached the Stargazers and greet them. 'Mr Davis, I assume?'

'Councilman Glenn Davis,' says the silver-moustached man, thrusting out his hand. 'That's Davis without an "e",' he emphasizes to McAdam as she makes notes. She returns a withering look, but says nothing. You're impressed at her restraint; not so long ago the sergeant would have given him an earful in reply.

'I gather you're the local astronomy group,' you say. 'This must all come as something of a shock. You found the victim, Mr Davis, is that right?'

He pulls himself up to his full height, which isn't much, and adopts a grave expression. 'That's correct. It was approaching midnight, 11.47 as I recall, when we heard her scream. I immediately ran here, towards the sound. At first, I didn't see anything. I only had my torch, you see, and she was . . . I thought it was just a mound of leaves on the ground.'

'You mean the costume she wore?' You can see how that would act as a form of camouflage away from the bright lights of a police crime scene.

'Precisely. But as I drew closer, I saw it was a person. I ran over, intending to give aid, and removed her . . . hood, whatever you want to call it. That was when I recognized her as the singer of that group. But it was obvious I was too late.'

'Did she say anything?'

He shakes his head. 'How could she? I'm no medical man, but even I could tell her throat had been cut.'

'Considering what you've seen tonight, Mr Davis, I must commend you on your calmness.'

It's hard to tell under the layered clothing, but you're pretty sure Glenn puffs out his chest a little at your remark. 'In addition to being a councilman, I'm a former primary school teacher. There isn't much I haven't seen.'

No matter how unruly children might be, you don't imagine they often slit one another's throats.

'Did you see anything else when you got here?' McAdam asks him. 'Anyone leaving the scene, for example . . .?'

'If I had, I would have informed you,' he replies, bristling. 'Before you ask, I didn't touch the knife, either. Look, it's no secret I didn't want that rock group coming here, but nobody deserves that. I want to see justice done as much as the next man.'

You exchange a glance with McAdam. 'Mr Davis, could you explain why you objected to the band's presence in Grenholme?'

For the first time since you began talking to him, he looks close to losing his composure.

'They are a corrupting influence, especially on children! I've lived here all my life and it's the same in every generation, seduced by the glitz and glamour of fame. But all people have a responsibility to others, and Satanic rock groups like those people fail to bear it. They peddle sin and debauchery, which have no place in a decent English village like Grenholme. I won't have it!'

'You may be a councillor, but you are not a dictator,' you remind him. 'I fear you must, as you say, "have it". Do your fellow villagers share your feelings?'

'Not enough of them,' he grumbles. 'Especially Bill Thomas and his lot over there.' Glenn looks across the clearing to where the Disciples of the Green stand. 'Mark my words, Inspector, if there's wrongdoing in this village, they're behind it. A more irrational and objectionable group you couldn't hope to meet.'

You doubt that. Standing idly in their ceremonial robes, the Disciples look about as dangerous as a troupe of Morris dancers.

'Mr Davis, how did you come to be so near by that, when Ms Velvet screamed, you were the first to find her, even before her own bandmates?'

He scowls at the question. 'Oh, I see where this is going. But you're wrong.' He gestures at the astronomy group, gathered behind him. 'We were all together in Clearing Delta when we heard her scream. That's two hundred and eighty-two metres from here. It's a regular location because it affords a good clear overhead view while shielding us from the moon's path for much of the night. Very beneficial for viewing the Lyrids.'

'That's true,' Zwale interjects. 'Moonlight can obscure meteors when it crosses the point of origin.'

'Thank you, Constable Zwale,' McAdam says firmly. You wince internally as Glenn Davis turns to regard the young officer.

'Zwale?' Glenn says, incredulous. 'Joseph Zwale? From the GBAA? You never mentioned you're a policeman.'

'It wasn't relevant,' Zwale protests. 'It's nothing to do with my work.'

'Well, it is now—'

Before things get heated, you step between them. 'Only if your astronomy group is involved in Ms Velvet's death,' you point out. 'Now, would you kindly show me this Clearing Delta, from where you heard the scream?'

Glenn huffs in annoyance, then turns on his heel and leads you into the forest, picking his way confidently through the dense trees with the aid of a torch that projects red light.

'The red saves one's eyes from having to constantly adjust from bright light to darkness and back again,' he says, even though you didn't ask. 'Much in the same way that red light doesn't activate the photochemical process in a darkroom.'

You're not entirely sure how accurate that comparison is, but Glenn Davis is evidently a man who likes to talk, and you see no reason not to let him.

'So you and the Disciples effectively share the forest at night?' you ask. 'Do you ever encounter one another?'

'More's the pity,' Glenn grumbles. 'Sometimes I swear Bill Thomas arranges his rituals and pantomimes precisely to interfere with the Stargazers' activities.'

Science versus folklore. A clash of ideologies, certainly, but this also sounds territorial. Grenholme Forest may be public land, but some of the locals seem to regard it as their domain.

You enter a clearing, larger than the one containing the stone circle. Scattered around it are a number of tripod-mounted telescopes, folding tables holding cameras and other equipment, and the sort of canvas chairs you might take camping, with Thermos flasks slotted into cup holders.

'This is my station,' Glenn says, leading you to the largest, and therefore you assume the most expensive, telescope in the centre of the clearing. 'As you can see, from here the view is excellent.'

The sky is dark, each star a single point of light shining in the blackness. A sudden bright streak shoots across the sky, before disappearing as quickly as it came, leaving the void still once more.

Returning to more earthly matters, you face back the way you came and see the illuminated area of the stone circle through the trees. It strikes you that despite appearances, Glenn must be in pretty good shape to have run almost three hundred metres across uneven ground.

'Mr Davis, how did you know Ms Velvet's scream came from the clearing? I'll grant you obviously know these woods very well, but the sound would have bounced around the trees. It could have come from somewhere closer, or in a different direction altogether.'

'It didn't occur to me that it would be anywhere else,' Glenn replies. 'Everything bad in these woods happens there.'

You return to the Lock Stones clearing in uncharacteristic silence. Constable Zwale and other uniformed officers are taking statements from the astronomers.

'GBAA, the Facebook astronomers' group, has apparently been going for years,' McAdam tells you. 'Glenn Davis was a founding member.'

'I can't say that surprises me. He isn't lacking in self-confidence,' you say. 'Nevertheless, unless the entire Grenholme

Stargazers group is covering up a conspiracy, he has a solid alibi – as do the other members, given they were all together in another clearing when they heard Lori Velvet scream.'

- *Write **G4** in your notebook*
- *If you already have B2 written down, turn to **196***
- *If you already have A3 written down, turn to **7***

Otherwise, choose which witness to interview next:

- *To talk to Aaron Warrior, the guitarist, turn to **38***
- *To talk to Bill Thomas, the pagan leader, turn to **148***

114

'You know a thing or two about Stone Warden costumes, don't you, Raven? You even sell them in the shop.'

'So?' she says with a shrug.

'I don't think this is the first time you've dressed up as the Warden. I think you've been doing it for years. Glenn Davis mentioned that Warden sightings in the forest were rare until you opened the Stones & Spirits shop. Then, all of a sudden, the number of sightings just so happened to rise. This benefited everyone in Grenholme who runs a business . . . but most of all you. How fortunate.'

Raven says nothing, watching the fire burn.

'Is that why Lori believed the Stone Warden took her brother? Was it you she saw, wearing a Warden costume?'

The accusation shocks her into reacting.

'What? No! I had nothing to do with Danny going missing!'

'That's why she had to die, wasn't it? She recognized you in the shop, and proceeded to tell everyone the Warden has a human face. You feared she was going to name you, so you silenced her for ever. Now I'll ask you again: where is Patrick?'

To your surprise, Raven laughs.

'I don't know where Patrick is! Go check the pub! Honestly, Inspector. You really have no idea what you're talking about.'

You search her house, but find no sign of the landlord. You arrest Raven anyway and drive her to the station, hoping the shock of being in a cell will loosen her tongue.

But not long after you arrive, a call comes in from Bill Thomas. He led the Disciples of the Green to the Lock Stones this evening, to carry out a cleansing ritual. They arrived to find Patrick, with his throat slashed in the same manner as Lori Velvet.

Your case is thrown into chaos. Could Raven have killed Patrick before returning home to start the fire? It's possible, although she'd have had to move fast. Either way, you have no proof. When examined, the landlord's body is found to have been drugged, but otherwise offers no solid forensic evidence, and this time there's no sign of a murder weapon.

The detective chief superintendent points out that you have no case against Raven Moonwolf; only an accusation from Glenn, and your own gut feeling and speculation. That's not good enough now that a second body has been found while she was already in custody. You're forced to let Raven go, and the DCS reassigns the case to another detective.

Lori Velvet's murder, and now Patrick's too, may yet be solved . . . but not by you.

Wipe your notebook, return to **1** *and try again*

For now, though, this is . . .

THE END

115

You sense this interview is nearing its natural end. While it's a detective's prerogative to apply pressure, you find people tend to talk more easily when you give them room to breathe.

'Let's move on to the matter of Lori Velvet herself,' you say. 'Mr Thomas, if you saw Glenn Davis talking to her at the band's performance then you must also have been present to watch it.'

Bill shrugs. 'Call it semi-professional curiosity. When I was younger, I used to get up on stage and do that sort of thing myself. Strictly part-time, mind you. Their music isn't to my taste, but I could tell they're talented.'

'You didn't recognize Lori at any point?'

'I'd never listened to the band before, so I didn't recognize any of them until they walked on stage. What do you mean?'

You exchange glances with Sergeant McAdam. It's time to tell Bill the truth.

'Would it surprise you to learn that Lori was actually from Grenholme?'

'Oh.' He thinks for a moment. 'OK, now I see why you asked. But no, I didn't recognize her. So she lives – I mean, lived – here in the village? Whereabouts?'

'Not recently. A long time ago, when she was called Lucy Isherwood. Does that name mean anything to you?'

He ponders it, trying to recall. 'Isherwood, Isherw— Oh, wait. The boy who went missing.'

'Daniel Isherwood, yes. He was Lucy's twin brother. You do remember, then?'

'Barely. I was a newcomer to the village, so I didn't know the family. That was her, was it? Well, blow me down.'

'Lucy was seven years old at the time. She claimed the Stone Warden took her brother.'

'Oh, that part I remember. It wasn't long after I'd revived the Disciples of the Green, and I tell you, it poisoned things for a while. Took years to get more than a handful of members, thanks to that.'

'My heart bleeds,' McAdam murmurs.

'I'm sorry, I know that sounds callous,' Bill says. 'But "People flare and live and die, while stone and wood endure under sky," as the poem goes. Everyone feeds the earth in the end, and all that really remains of us is what we pass down the years.'

'I'm sure that's a great comfort to a family who have now lost both of their children,' the sergeant growls.

Before things get any more heated, you stand and thank Bill for his time.

*○ Write **B4** in your notebook*

*○ If you already have P1 written down, turn to **58***

*○ Otherwise, **add 1** to your LOCATION number and turn to **100***

116

It's no coincidence that Lori Velvet was killed in the same place where her twin brother vanished fifteen years ago – and, you now know, where his body remained hidden.

But why? What is it about this place that has invited so much tragedy? You wish you could have deciphered the chalk symbols on the stones. You'll never know for sure if Lori herself wrote them, but it seems almost certain given the bracelet you found.

Then there's the fact that Lori was carrying a knife, and wandered off alone from where the others were filming. Why? Did she hope to confront someone?

Check your notebook in the following order:

*○ If you have A7 written down, turn to **81***

*○ If you have B11 written down, turn to **127***

*○ If you have G8 written down, turn to **171***

117

'Brace yourself.' You show them the bloody knife in the evidence bag, holding it so the symbol carved into the hilt is visible. 'I wondered if you could possibly shed some light on this. See the symbol? It matches one of the chalk markings on the stones, over there.' You gesture at the Lock Stones. 'Do either of you recognize the knife?'

Aaron gasps. 'Yeah, that must be Lori's. Oh, God, is that blood?'

'Is that the knife she was killed with?' Julie asks, staring at it.

You shake your head. 'We're not sure of anything yet. But it was found near by, so is naturally of interest.'

'She had it at the show,' Julie sniffs. 'It was a prop during the encore, when she came out in that costume.'

'Aaron, you said it "must be" Lori's. How can you be sure?' McAdam asks. 'Have you seen it before?'

'No, but I recognize that,' Aaron replies, pointing to the carved symbol in the hilt. 'It matches one of her tattoos.'

Julie nods in recognition. 'That's right. On her back.'

'So presumably the symbol had some special meaning to her,' you suggest. 'What does it signify?'

Aaron and Julie look at one another, as if expecting the other to answer, before simultaneously realizing neither is any the wiser.

'To be honest, I didn't ask,' Aaron says. 'I figured it was something personal.'

'You'd been her partner on and off for quite some time,' McAdam says. 'Weren't you curious?'

Aaron shrugs and lights a cigarette.

'I was,' Julie says, 'but when I asked, she got evasive and wouldn't say. Aaron's right, it was obviously very personal.'

'Is there anyone else who might know? Family or friends, perhaps?'

'We were her family and friends,' Aaron says. 'Lori lived for the band.'

You thank them for their time and step away to confer with Sergeant McAdam.

'Does this mean Lori also made those chalk markings on the stones?' McAdam wonders. 'And if so, why?'

'I'm more concerned by something Aaron Warrior suggested,' you reply. 'If Dr Wash confirms that this is indeed Lori's blood, then we have to ask: how and why was she killed with her own knife?'

    Write **A5** *in your notebook*
    Then turn to **85**

118

You show Glenn a photograph of the stubby folding knife you found on the ground near Sergeant McAdam, after she was attacked by the Stone Warden. The real thing is currently with Dr Wash being examined, but you're already pretty sure of what she'll find.

'Do you recognize this knife, Mr Davis?'

Glenn's eyes widen. 'Is that blood?'

'Please answer the question.'

'Well, of course I do. It's mine. But it went missing last week. I went to my usual spot at the river, and when I opened my tackle box it wasn't there. Where did you find it? Why does it have blood on it?'

'My sergeant was attacked earlier today in the forest, by someone dressed as the Stone Warden. This was found near by and I expect to find that the blood is hers.'

'Good heavens! Is she all right?'

'She's recovering in hospital,' Zwale says. 'So we'll find your fingerprints on that knife, will we?'

'I expect so, yes. I don't deny it's mine, but like I told you it went missing. Oh, can't you see? I'm being framed.'

You'd considered this. It does seem convenient that the Warden happened to drop the knife where you'd find it, complete with blood on the blade. Then again, could it be a double bluff in order to deflect suspicion away from Glenn?

'Who would want to frame you?' you ask.

Glenn gestures in the direction of the street outside. 'Take your pick. You know, we went decades around here with no notable sightings of the Stone Warden. Then, not long before Stones & Spirits opened, we had our first. Then another, and another, to the point that now there are multiple sightings every year. Don't you think that's odd?'

'As I understand it, the shop, and the reformation of the Disciples, has helped to attract many more tourists to the area. It seems reasonable that the more tourists you have, the more will claim to have seen the Warden.'

'I suppose so. But I wouldn't be surprised if one of those so-called pagans, or even Raven herself, is dressing up and wandering about in order to bolster the myth. *Cui bono*, Inspector? Who benefits? That's what you must ask.'

'Thank you, Mr Davis. I'm familiar with the concept.'

Nevertheless, he makes a good point. Could your attacker have been someone wearing a Stone Warden costume to attract tourists? As if murder isn't enough to make a village like Grenholme notorious. And it still doesn't explain why they were carrying a fishing net.

*Write **G6** in your notebook*

*Then turn to **4***

119

'How many people in Grenholme are members of the Disciples, exactly?' you ask.

'Fourteen, I think . . .?'

His uncertainty surprises you. 'Surely you must know?'

'Well, not everyone's from Grenholme. We've also got members who come in from elsewhere, and turnout goes up and down according to the weather, people's family commitments, all that. I think it's fourteen in the village, and another six from outside.'

You think carefully how to phrase your next question. 'Mr Thomas . . . you obviously take the legends surrounding the Lock Stones seriously, but what about the villagers? You told us you speak for them, and often speak *with* them. Do you know there are people in the village who sincerely think the Stone Warden killed Lori Velvet?'

'Inspector, these people have lived with the Lock Stones and

Stone Warden for more than a thousand years. Grenholme is in the Domesday Book, you know. The outside world changes every day, but in places like this, people hold on to what their ancestors knew.'

'What do *you* think happened to Lori?' McAdam asks.

Bill leans forward in his chair to warm his hands at the fire and gather his thoughts. 'I think . . . that you should speak to Glenn Davis. Don't get me wrong, I still say he wouldn't harm a fly. But this morning I remembered that I saw him at the pub last night, watching the band play, and he had an argument with the singer. I don't know what about. You should ask him.'

⸰ *If you have G3 written in your notebook, turn to* **198**

⸰ *Otherwise, turn to* **172**

120

Zwale hurries out of the square, going alone to Raven's house. You follow the Stargazer back to the assembled group.

'When's the last time any of you saw Glenn?' you ask them.

Some shuffle their feet, and you recognize them from the mob outside Glenn's house. That could make for some awkward astronomy.

'Is it possible he's staying away because of the incident earlier?' you suggest.

The foot-shufflers look away, but others shake their heads. 'He wouldn't miss the Lyrids for the world,' says the man who first approached you. 'I'm telling you, something's wrong.'

Trying to make sense of what's happening, you notice another oddity: there's no sound of music from the pub. Shouldn't the band have begun playing by now?

You leave the Stargazers and enter the Watching Warden, which is now completely packed with Killer Velvet fans. You recognize a few journalists at the bar, presumably hoping this performance can form part of their reporting, and even spot a news camera set up at the back of the crowd, aimed over their heads towards the stage.

There's still no sign of Patrick, and Fran is obviously struggling to cope at the bar. Pushing your way towards the stage, you hear grumbles and complaints from the fans – not only concerning the pub's slow service, but also wondering why Killer Velvet haven't taken to the stage yet.

Behind the stage you see Steve, the bassist (you're sure this time, as he has the instrument in his hands) leaning against a doorway, presumably leading to a changing room. You step up on to the stage, eliciting cheers from fans who think the show is starting. The cheers quickly turn into disappointed boos when they see who you are. You walk past the drum kit and catch Steve's eye.

'What's the delay? Why aren't you on stage?'

Confused, he replies, 'Since when is that police business?'

'A restless crowd is always cause for concern, and frankly my officers have more important things to do tonight than worry about rowdy fans.'

He shrugs. 'Aaron's not here yet. We can't start without him.'

Keith the drummer stands near by holding a pair of sticks.

'Haven't seen him for at least half an hour. Or Julie. Not answering their phones, either.'

'You've checked their rooms upstairs?' you ask.

'Of course. I don't know what's got into him.'

Neither do you. You thank the band members and, rather than face the crowd again, leave the pub by the back service entrance.

Emerging into the car park, a terrible feeling of foreboding settles over you. Patrick, Bill, Glenn, Aaron and Julie have all vanished into thin air.

You remember the poison pen letter Patrick received, warning him to 'hear nothing, see nothing, say nothing'. If the letter came from Lori's killer, it means they believe Patrick knows something important – something they don't want getting out. Have they abducted him? Perhaps they intend to ensure he remains quiet . . . for ever.

If your instincts are correct, there's no time to waste. Not only must you save Patrick, but in doing so you can catch the killer red-handed.

The question, therefore, is a simple one: who do you think killed Lori Velvet?

If you think it was Aaron, turn to **72**

If you think it was Bill, turn to **165**

If you think it was Glenn, turn to **37**

If you think it was Julie, turn to **61**

If you think it was Raven, turn to **180**

121

You give McAdam the nod to interview Aaron, then enter Julie's room. You're about to close the door when the smell of sweat and sex reaches you. But there's nowhere else to talk privately, and you certainly don't want her in Lori's room. So you leave the door ajar and open a window, ignoring Julie's shivers as she pulls her bathrobe tighter around herself.

This room is almost as messy as Lori's, with open cases of filming equipment fighting piles of clothing for precious floor space. The bed is obviously unmade. You marvel at how the band only arrived yesterday, yet already their rooms look like they've been here for weeks.

Julie sits on the bed and tucks her knees up under her chin.

'I'll get right to the point,' you say, standing by the window. 'How long you have you and Aaron been in a relationship?'

'There is no relationship. We were talking about Lori, and how much we missed her . . . I could see his aura was troubled, and I already woke up crying this morning. We found comfort in each other.'

'Some might say that's an odd way to commiserate a friend and partner who was killed less than twenty-four hours ago.'

'Lori was very open-minded, and her spirit's still with me,' she says stubbornly. 'I know she'd have wanted me to feel better.'

'And do you?'

Her expression falters. 'Yeah. Sure.'

'So your relationship with Lori was in good shape? There was no jealousy between you?'

Julie scowls. 'Jealousy is for lesser souls, bound by their earthly chains. Like those so-called pagans, for example.'

'Surely having earthly concerns is an integral part of being a pagan, and especially the Disciples of the Green. Why do you say they're jealous?'

'They act like they own the forest and the stone circle,' she says with a shrug. 'We approached them for help ages ago, when Lori said she wanted to film "Eyes of the Warden" here. I found the Disciples online and contacted Bill Thomas for help. Coordinating with the locals, showing us around the stones, that sort of thing. He said he would. Apparently, he used to play in a band himself years ago, so he understood what we'd need. But when I told him the shoot dates he suddenly got angry and demanded we reschedule. Lori said no, we had to film during the full moon. She never backed down. She was like that. Then Bill said we'd be trespassing! He was being totally unreasonable.'

You recall the story of the Stone Warden, and how the legend says he punishes trespassers.

'Obviously you went ahead with filming anyway,' you say. 'Did you see the Disciples while you were in the forest?'

Julie hangs her head. 'Only when we found Lori, in the stone circle.'

'You didn't see anyone else before then?'

'No, not—Oh, hang on. I wanted to show you this.' She rummages through the mess by her bed for a backpack, from which she removes a laptop. 'When we got back here last night, I remembered something and scrubbed through the video footage. I found this, from eleven thirty-six according to the timestamp.'

She turns the laptop to face you and plays a video. You

watch a recording of the band members, minus Lori, in the forest miming playing their instruments to the tinny sound of a song. The full moon shines behind them while the camera moves shakily around the scene. Then it ends.

Julie looks at you expectantly, but you're confused. 'I'm sorry, I don't understand. Why are you showing me this?'

She resets the video to the middle of the scene, then plays it again. 'There, in the trees. Behind Aaron, do you see?'

You peer at the screen, and this time you do see. A figure in the distance, barely more than a silhouette, moves from one side of the screen to the other. It's indistinct and lacking in identifiable detail, a black shape moving against a slightly lighter black background. You can't tell who it is, or even if it's a man or woman. But there's no doubt that it's a person walking through the forest, without a light, less than fifteen minutes before Lori was killed.

'Would you send me a copy of that video? I'll have our digital forensics team brighten it, so we can try to identify that person.' Julie types out your email address as you give it. 'I note that's during a scene where the other members of the band, apart from Lori, are all present.'

'That's right,' she says. 'I told you, the band was together all night filming, apart from when Lori wandered off. We were all—Oh, hang on . . .'

'What is it? You were all what?'

She stares at you over the laptop screen, her eyes widening.

'Before that bit you just saw. I was filming Keith and Steve, the rhythm section . . . and I remember I looked around for Aaron, but he wasn't there.'

'You just said you were together all night.'

'The *band* was, yeah. You know, as a unit. But Aaron must

have gone off by himself at one point . . .' The laptop slips out of her hands on to the bed. 'Oh, I feel sick. You don't think——?'

'At this moment I don't think anything,' you reassure her. 'I'm simply trying to understand what happened. What time did Aaron leave? You said it was before the footage we just watched?'

She retrieves her computer and checks the files. 'Yes, it was . . . hang on . . . OK, so I didn't see him go, and I don't remember exactly when he came back, but it must have been somewhere between quarter past and half past eleven.'

'Then it was at least fifteen minutes before you heard Lori scream. So I don't think you need to worry.'

Julie lets out a heavy breath, and her body relaxes.

'They used to fight all the time, you know. Aaron and Lori. It was so unpredictable, you never knew what would make them kick off. Money, a song, a gig . . . it's a miracle the band's stayed together as long as it has, really. I doubt they'll carry on without her.'

Julie looks like she's about to say something else, but stops as tears form in her eyes.

You don't wish to make things any worse for her, but you'd intended to tell her that Lori was pregnant. Given her seemingly fragile state, though, you're no longer sure if you should.

𝒫 *To tell Julie about Lori's pregnancy, turn to* **35**

𝒫 *To keep Lori's pregnancy secret for now, turn to* **69**

122

You wade into the mob once more, this time joined by Constable Zwale, to restrain Raven and Julie before their argument becomes physical.

'You're nothing but a gold digger,' Raven hisses at Julie. 'Taking advantage of Lori's good heart, and now Aaron as well!'

'You don't know what you're talking about,' Julie counters. 'He came on to me!'

'That's enough,' you say, holding on to Raven. 'What's the issue here?'

'Nothing,' Aaron insists, but the women have other ideas.

'She's got some weird mothering fetish, is the issue,' Julie says, pointing at Raven. 'He's a grown man,' she says, adding smugly, 'and don't I know it.'

'I'll bet you do,' Raven replies, turning to you. 'She's not worth a tenth of either Aaron or Lori. Mediocre director with no future, so she latched on to Lori and slept her way into a job.'

Aaron seems baffled by all this enmity. 'What the hell do you know about it anyway? Who even are you? We'd never met you until yesterday.'

'Wrong,' Raven says. 'I knew Lori as a girl, and I've been following you for years. You once replied to one of my DMs and recognized me from the gig at the Roundhouse, remember?'

He tries to hide it, perhaps simply not wanting to make Raven any angrier than she already is, but it's clear that Aaron has no recollection of this interaction. Instead, he looks alarmed, then scowls.

'That was a good gig, that,' he says. 'Enjoy it, did you?'

'You have no idea,' Raven replies, smiling at the memory. 'It was one of the best nights of my life. I've got the Blu-Ray.'

Aaron leans in. 'Good, because from now on that's all you'll have. You're barred from Killer Velvet gigs, for ever.'

Raven's mouth drops open.

'Bit harsh, don't you think?' Bill Thomas steps out of the crowd. 'Look, we're all on edge—'

'You too, then,' Aaron says, then looks around at the crowd. 'And anyone else who feels like shooting their mouth off, all right? We're doing you a big favour playing here, and we deserve some respect. After tonight you'll never see us again, and that's a promise.'

'Aaron, you're not thinking straight,' Raven pleads, but the guitarist takes Julie from Constable Zwale's grip and leads her away in the direction of the village square. Julie looks back over her shoulder and aims a smug smile at Raven.

The shopkeeper returns a murderous glare, but makes no move to follow. When you release her, she clings on to Bill for support.

The extra police backup finally arrives. You're still outnumbered by the crowd, but the people of Grenholme reassess their chances against a police squad and decide they've already had their spectacle for the evening. They disperse, walking home or back to the pub with a resigned shrug.

The danger to Glenn has passed for now. You'll have your chance to talk to him after all.

⚲ *Write* **R3** *in your notebook*

⚲ *Then turn to* **50**

123

'Not so fast,' you say, preventing Julie from going inside. 'I believe you've taken Patrick somewhere, and I'm concerned for his safety.'

'Why on earth would I take him anywhere? You can check the van all you like, he's not there.'

'Then I'll ask you again: what have you done with him?'

'Nothing!' she protests. 'Look, this is harassment. Leave me alone!'

Despite her protestations, you're convinced Julie did it. You arrest her and wait for Constable Zwale to return, then drive her to the station, hoping the shock of being in a cell will loosen her tongue.

But not long after you arrive, a call comes in from Bill Thomas. He led the Disciples of the Green to the Lock Stones this evening, to carry out a cleansing ritual. They arrived to find Patrick, with his throat slashed in the same manner as Lori Velvet.

Your case is thrown into chaos. Could Julie have killed Patrick before returning to the van where you found her? It's possible, although she'd have had to move fast. Either way, you have no proof. When examined, the landlord's body is found to have been drugged, but otherwise offers no solid forensic evidence, and this time there's no sign of a murder weapon.

The detective chief superintendent points out that you have no case against Julie Grafton, only your gut feeling and speculation, which isn't good enough now that a second body has been found while she was already in custody. You're forced to let Julie go, and the DCS reassigns the case to another detective.

Lori Velvet's murder, and now Patrick's too, may yet be solved . . . but not by you.

🔎 *Wipe your notebook, return to 1 and try again*

For now, though, this is . . .

THE END

124

You stop suddenly, looking around. McAdam almost bumps into you from behind, stumbling when she brings herself up short.

'What is it?' she whispers, scanning the trees.

'The video shoot location was somewhere around here,' you say.

'Yes, in the stone circle.'

'No, I mean the footage with the others besides Lori. Julie showed us the instruments and cameras, remember? If I recall correctly, it would have been somewhere over . . . there.' You point into the trees, perpendicular to your present route. 'Let's take another look before we go on to the stones.'

McAdam grumbles, but follows as you pick your way through the forest. After a few wrong turns you emerge into a small clearing which you're sure is the right one. The sergeant calls up the footage Julie sent earlier and identifies some specific trees that confirm you're in the right place.

'Good. Now let's see that figure in the background that she caught on camera.'

'Digital forensics haven't cleaned it up yet,' she says.

'That's OK. Julie said the footage in question was filmed at eleven thirty-six, less than fifteen minutes before Lori was killed. So there's a good chance she may have caught the murderer on their way to the stone circle. For now, I simply want to see where they went.'

McAdam plays the clip on her phone and zooms in, past Aaron Warrior miming his guitar, on the mysterious shadowed figure walking through the dark wood.

'Zoom back out. Let's determine where the camera was positioned.'

She does, replaying the footage, but none of the trees behind Aaron match what you're looking at.

'How odd,' you remark, looking around. 'Did they film in more than one clearing? Surely not, given how much equipment they had to carry. So what—'

Then you see it and in rapid order experience revelation, deduction and confusion.

'Sergeant, turn around.'

'But the figure was moving right to left,' she says, holding up her phone to show you. 'The Lock Stones are in that direction, so the camera must have been pointing this way.'

You take her phone and pause the footage at a moment when you can see several trees lit behind Aaron. Sure enough, they now match trees you can see . . . on the other side of the clearing.

'We assumed Julie captured someone walking to the stones,' you explain. 'But they weren't. When filming Aaron she was facing in the opposite direction, which means . . .'

'They were walking *away* from the stones,' McAdam concludes. 'But that means whoever it was couldn't be Lori's killer,' she adds glumly.

'Perhaps not. But if this person is innocent, why haven't they come forward? Perhaps we're looking not at Lori's killer, but at Aaron's stalker.'

Taking your bearings, you leave the clearing and its questions to walk on to the Lock Stones.

   🔎 *Write* **P10** *in your notebook*
   🔎 *Then turn to* **71**

125

You run as fast as you dare in this murky, misty forest, but the Stone Warden knows these woods intimately and outpaces you. Before long you're disorientated, unsure of where you are, where the Warden went, or even where McAdam is. And thanks to the lack of phone signal out here, you can't call her to ask.

Then, by some miracle, you hear a familiar voice in the distance shout, 'Stop! Police!' It's McAdam!

You run in the direction of the sound, or at least your best guess. At the bottom of a dip in the land you find a stream blocking your way, but the fog prevents you seeing if it narrows near by or if there's a bridge. There's nothing else for it.

You step into the glacial water, up to your knees, and wade across. It takes only half a dozen steps, but by the time you climb out on the other side your legs are numb.

Then you hear a scream.

Your discomfort forgotten, you race through the trees with a renewed surge of energy, calling McAdam's name. She calls back, her voice weak. Driven on by urgency, you crash through undergrowth and leap over tree roots, until suddenly you're upon her.

She lies on the ground, unconscious. Fresh blood stains one trouser leg, and in horror you see it's her own. She's been stabbed, and is bleeding badly.

You don't have a first aid kit, or even bandages. So you improvise, removing McAdam's jacket and then ripping off her shirt sleeve to tie around her leg and staunch the bleeding. It's not field surgeon quality, but it helps.

Throughout it all she doesn't wake, even though she doesn't seem to have lost enough blood to cause a loss of consciousness. Then you cradle her head, and feel a sticky wetness there. The Warden struck her, dealing a nasty blow and, you assume, concussion.

Anger threatens to consume you. You'd like nothing more than to chase down her assailant and end this charade right away, but pursuit is pointless. By now the Stone Warden, who knows these woods in ways you never could, is long gone.

This deep in the forest there's no signal, so you can't call an ambulance, but trying to carry an unconscious McAdam will slow your movements to a crawl. So you make a hard decision, propping her against a tree before running back the way you came. If that water you crossed is connected to the river that runs through the forest, you can follow it downstream to the parking area and call from there. Or perhaps you'll get lucky and stumble across one of the roads traversing the area.

You plunge into the fog. From the corner of your eye, something glints in the nearby undergrowth, but you'd have to move closer to see what it is.

To stop and examine the object, turn to **31**

To ignore it and hurry to find a way out, turn to **160**

126

You look across the square to the Watching Warden.

'Isn't that where the band played last night, before they went into the woods?' you ask.

McAdam nods. 'Aye, that's the one. Maybe the landlord's worth talking to.'

You push open the pub's thick wooden door and step inside the gloomy, old-fashioned interior, its windows set deep into metre-thick stone walls. A few early locals are already installed at tables, drinks in hand. The low hum of their conversation stops, table by table, as you enter. They watch warily as you approach the bar, where a sign proudly declares that the pub was established in 1752.

'Is that true?' McAdam asks, pointing to the sign.

The landlord pauses wiping his beer pumps. 'There are deeds in the parish records. It was called the Old Stones back then. The Disciples of the Green used it as their meeting house.'

'Is that in the parish records, as well?'

'Can't say I've checked.'

Something in the way he talks triggers recognition in your mind, and you remember what Constable Zwale told you about him. Landlords are often a good source of information, but you'll have to bear in mind that this one is hardly an unbiased witness.

'Patrick, isn't it? We spoke to you last night. You're a Disciple yourself.'

'This is a terrible business,' he says sourly. 'It'll bring in all the wrong kind of tourists.'

'Oh? What are the right kind?'

Patrick stops cleaning and leans on the bar, his expression stern. 'The kind who respect the Lock Stones and the Stone Warden. The kind who come here with reverence for the druids who placed the stones thousands of years ago, and whose spirits still walk Grenholme Forest.' He begins to clean again. 'Not the kind who come here to mock the Warden's rules and film themselves prancing about in the circle.'

Behind you, someone laughs heartily. You turn to see one of the installed locals, nursing a pint and rolling his eyes.

'Pat, you don't half talk some crap,' he says. 'Warden this and fairie that, it's all rubbish. I've lived here my whole life, never seen a thing like it,' he adds in your direction. 'It's all a scam, you know. Nobody really believes the stones are magical; they're just happy to fleece the tourists.'

Patrick scowls at the man. 'Those tourists help keep this pub open. I couldn't manage if it was just you lot in here all the time.'

'Could have fooled me with these prices,' another local says. 'Maybe if we got a locals' discount we'd spend more.'

Patrick snorts in disbelief and returns to cleaning the bar.

There's an edge to this exchange, something deeper than banter between old friends. Perhaps the Disciples aren't as well-loved as Bill Thomas would have you believe.

'Where were you during last night's events?' you ask Patrick.

'I was with my fellow Disciples. We were together all night.'

'Really? All night?' McAdam asks. 'Nobody left the group at any point, not even for a minute?'

Patrick hesitates.

'Lying to or withholding evidence from the police can have serious consequences,' you remind him.

'It was nothing.'

'We'll be the judge of that.'

He sighs. 'All right, Bill did nip off at one point. Said he'd forgotten something, so he ran back to his house.'

'What time was this?'

'About half eleven. But he was only a few minutes, and then he led us on to the stones like normal. Well, until we heard the girl scream, anyway.'

You change tack. 'Tell us about the band, and last night's concert. You must have been shocked to see Lori come out on stage dressed as the Stone Warden.'

'Everyone was,' he says grumpily. 'I was serving last orders at the time, so I didn't pay much attention, but everyone else saw it. They all wanted to talk to her afterwards.'

'Oh? Who is "they"?'

'You know. The fans who'd come here to see them. Oh, and Raven. Makes sense she's into that sort of thing.'

'Raven Moonwolf spoke to Lori after the gig? Are you sure?'

'Well, maybe it was Raven,' he says, busying himself behind the bar. 'I can't be sure.'

'Really?' McAdam says again, her sarcasm on full display. 'In a small place like this, you didn't recognize the woman who runs a shop less than a hundred metres away?'

Patrick glares at her. 'I don't know what they were talking about. I told you, I was dealing with last orders.'

Raven hasn't mentioned this conversation with Lori to you previously. You'll have to follow up on that.

'What about you?' McAdam asks.

Patrick looks blank. 'What about me?'

'Did you talk to Lori afterwards? Or anyone else in the band?'

'Of course I did. Fran had gone home, that's my barmaid, and the band were packing their gear away. So I closed up, then got changed and took my place with the Disciples. I told the director woman I'd see them later.'

You exchange a confused glance with McAdam.

'You locked the band inside the pub? How did they get to the forest?'

Seeing your confusion, he explains. 'I didn't lock them in. They're all staying in our rooms upstairs, so I left them to it.'

'Including Lori Velvet, the singer?'

'That's right.'

First, check your notebook:

If you don't have B4 written down, write **P9** *in there now*

Then, make a choice:

To ask Patrick if you can see Lori's room, turn to **82**

To leave the pub and go elsewhere, turn to **12**

127

Bill must be stopped before it's too late. You rush further into the misty woods, towards the Lock Stones. Even though he's not with the Disciples, you're sure that's where he'll be.

Hurrying through the forest, weaving between trees and stepping over thick tree roots, the full moon lights your way. When you look up, the darkness is punctuated by racing flashes of the Lyrid's meteor streaks.

Dread rises. You fear the worst.

You know Bill moved here almost twenty years ago and formed the Disciples of the Green, installing himself at its head. When Raven left Glenn, Bill was there to comfort her . . . and present her with a business opportunity, which neatly coincided with his own interests in the Stone Warden myth. The shop, Disciples and tourists have enjoyed a symbiotic relationship ever since. The pagans bolster the myth, which attracts visitors, who spend money at Bill's shop and Patrick's pub. Meanwhile, Glenn and Bill argue about the forest, and their respective positions within the community, but by and large everyone gets along and life goes on . . .

Until Killer Velvet decided to make a music video in Grenholme Forest and perform at the pub. Lori's presence threatened everything Bill had worked to build, and he resolved to protect it by any means necessary.

Bill knew that Lori Velvet was Lucy Isherwood and what that would mean for him . . . because, you believe, it was Bill who abducted Daniel Isherwood all those years ago and dumped the boy's body inside a hollow tree.

Fog drifts across your path, stirred by a forest breeze. When it clears you see the familiar clearing up ahead . . . and a figure within.

Check your notebook in the following order:

   🔍 *If you have B7 written down, turn to* **149**

   🔍 *If you have G6 written down, turn to* **57**

   🔍 *If you have B8 written down, turn to* **138**

   🔍 *If you have B9 written down, turn to* **86**

   🔍 *Otherwise, turn to* **92**

128

'We heard Lori threatened to fire you last night,' you say. 'Failing to record the special encore song, taking too long over the shoot in the forest . . . what can you tell us about that?'

'Sounds like you already know everything,' Julie says, huffing. 'Look, they played an encore and went off stage, so I started packing away. We had to get to the forest to start filming.'

'But you told us you'd seen Lori making the Stone Warden costume at your flat,' McAdam reminds her. 'You must have known she was bringing it here.'

'For the video,' Julie protests. 'She didn't tell me she was going to wear it on stage for a *second* encore.'

So Lori really did surprise everyone when she came out on

stage wearing the costume. The fans, the locals . . . even her own band and director.

'By the time I got the kit back out and running I'd missed the first minute of the song,' Julie continues. 'Lori didn't even notice at the time, but on the way to the shoot she asked me how it looked on camera and I told her. She hit the roof.'

'She also threatened to fire you,' McAdam says.

To your surprise, Julie laughs bitterly.

'She wouldn't have, not really. She knew she couldn't.'

'Why's that?' you ask. 'Did you have some kind of hold over her?'

'Does "putting up with her and Aaron's nonsense" count? Look, I know people think I only got this job because Lori and I were in love, but it's not just that. Ever since they split up, the negative energy around Aaron and Lori has been horrible. If they were in the same room, you could feel it. Nobody else will work with them. If that baby really was Aaron's . . .'

She trails off from finishing the unpleasant thought, but you understand. The child's upbringing would have been fraught to say the least.

Julie takes a deep breath, clasping and unclasping her hands. You recognize the signs. She's about to tell you something she's been internally debating.

'That's the real reason she was angry with me, you know. The stuff about filming was just an excuse. It was really because I knew she was pregnant.'

'Lori told you?'

'No, but it's hard to miss when you live with someone, isn't it? I-I accused her of having an affair.'

Julie exhales heavily, as if a burden has been lifted by telling you this. You say nothing, because after all, she was right.

'One last thing,' you say, showing her a photo of the speaker you found in the tree. 'Do you recognize this?'

She shakes her head. 'Bluetooth, is it? I don't use them, because of the control delay. You can compensate for it but it's easier to just use a wired speaker, like the one I showed you. Instant response.'

'So this isn't one of yours?'

'I don't even own one. It might belong to someone in the band, I guess. Why are you asking?'

'All in good time. Thank you, Ms Grafton.'

*Write **J5** in your notebook*

Now choose another person in the pub to interview:

*To speak with Aaron, turn to **168***

*To talk to Glenn, turn to **111***

*If you've already interviewed both of them, turn to **101***

129

You take McAdam to one side within the stone circle to show her the evidence bag containing the knife and relate what you discussed with Dr Wash.

'Hold on,' the sergeant says, producing her notebook. 'I made a sketch of these chalk symbols, in case they get washed away. The weird thing is, there are eleven stones but only eight are marked.'

'Zwale's sure they're not astronomical,' she continues. 'He thinks they might be connected to pagan magic, which I'd say puts those nutters in the frame.' She looks towards Bill Thomas and the Disciples of the Green.

You hold the hilt of the bloody knife next to McAdam's notebook, and see that you were right. The symbol carved into the knife handle does indeed match one of those chalked on the Lock Stones.

'What's the connection here?' you wonder aloud. 'Does the symbol mean so much to the killer that they carved it into a knife used to murder someone . . . then also chalked it on the stones, risking being seen? Or did they chalk the symbols first, perhaps knowing they would use the same knife to kill Lori?'

'Could this have been an opportunistic killing?' she asks.

'Unlikely. Someone just happens to be in the forest, where they just happen to stumble across a young woman in the stone circle, who just happens to be dressed like a local legend, and because they just happen to be carrying a knife they just happen to decide to kill her? It strains credulity.'

'Then why leave the knife behind? If it meant so much, why not take it with them?'

'Perhaps they killed her, dropped the weapon in the struggle, then couldn't find it again before people came running and it was too late.'

McAdam looks around the stone circle, into the dark trees beyond. 'They wouldn't have had to go far to hide. Even with the full moon out it would have been almost pitch black. Half a dozen steps into the trees and they might as well be invisible.'

It's a good point. You've experienced the lack of visibility in the night forest for yourself when accompanying witnesses through the trees. Combined with the forest haze, the killer could be confident of not being seen up to the last moment. They could have been only a few yards away yet invisible to both Lori Velvet and, subsequently, those who ran to help her.

'You're right, Sergeant. So perhaps leaving the knife behind was not carelessness, but a deliberate act. I suspect we won't find any fingerprints or DNA on this weapon.'

'No, but we might get a reaction if we show it to the right person.'

You'd wondered the same thing. Someone here might know of a connection between this knife and the stones. But who should you ask?

    To ask Aaron Warrior, turn to **33**

    To ask Bill Thomas, turn to **67**

    To ask Glenn Davis, turn to **102**

    To ask Julie Grafton, turn to **52**

    To ask Raven Moonwolf, turn to **155**

130

Dread rises as you race to the Lock Stones. The full moon shines down from the night sky, whose darkness is punctuated by racing flashes of the Lyrids' meteor streaks. You fear the worst . . . and your fears are justified.

Mist drifts through the stone circle, then parts to reveal Patrick lying motionless at its centre. You rush to him, but instinctively you already know you're too late. His throat has been cut in the same manner as Lori Velvet's.

The Stone Warden has struck again.

Later, while Dr Wash carries out her sombre duties, you return to the station where the detective chief superintendent hauls you over the coals. Your sergeant is wounded in hospital; a second victim has been murdered; and you're no closer to making an arrest. It's simply not good enough, especially with media attention on this case rising.

You're banished to your desk, and the case is assigned to another detective. Lori Velvet's murder may yet be solved . . . but not by you.

⚲ Wipe your notebook, return to 1 and try again.

For now, though, this is . . .

THE END

131

'Then there's no time to waste,' you say, hurrying out of the square towards Glenn's house. Constable Zwale is already ahead of you, taking long strides, while Bill and Raven follow behind.

'Can one of you explain what's going on?' you ask them.

'Why is there a mob at Glenn's house? Is this why all the locals cleared out of the square?'

Raven talks quickly, anxiously. 'I was afraid of this. Glenn was the prime suspect in Danny's disappearance, all those years ago. He was a schoolteacher, you see, and he's always spent a lot of time in the forest . . .'

'So naturally the police investigated him, as they should have. But he was never charged,' you point out.

'That hardly matters. People were ready to believe he did it anyway. I never did, I always believed he was innocent, but it didn't help. He had to retire from teaching, and we split up because of the stress.'

'Split up?' Zwale asks. 'You mean you were together before then?'

Raven looks at him like it's the world's silliest question. 'Well, of course. We were married for nearly ten years.'

'You didn't think to tell us this earlier?' you say, amazed this is only now coming to light.

'Everyone already knows,' she says with a shrug.

'Everyone local, perhaps. So, you and Glenn were together when Daniel Isherwood went missing, which led to your divorce, and then you opened Stones & Spirits?'

'More or less, yes. But it's all water under the bridge, and now I'm worried about Glenn.'

She has good reason to be. You reach the short terrace of stone houses where Glenn lives, and to your dismay find a large group gathered outside his gate, yelling and shouting.

'Killer!'

'Kidnapper!'

'Nonce!'

'Come out here! You can't hide for ever!'

Glenn's curtains are drawn. Is he even at home? If so, there's surely no way he's going to emerge to face this mob – or the journalists who, you see, have followed the crowd here. You have no doubt they're loving this.

Behind you, Raven whispers prayers to her goddess while Bill comforts her.

'Can't you do something?' Bill hisses.

'There's a lot more of them than us,' Zwale says nervously. 'Not sure they're in the mood to respect the uniform.'

At that moment, Julie Grafton appears from out of the crowd, holding up her phone to film events.

'Why should they?' she says. 'If he killed Danny and Lori, he deserves whatever's coming to him. I bet his aura's black as the night.'

'Whatever his astrological condition, Ms Grafton, we must establish a man's innocence or guilt before throwing stones.'

'Funny you should say that, Inspector . . .' Zwale says, pointing into the crowd.

Aaron Warrior is here, as angry and fired up as any local. While you watch, he reaches through a gap in Glenn's garden fence and picks up a large stone from the ground. He hefts it in his hand, ready to throw it.

To attempt to stop Aaron and the mob, turn to **173**

To stand back and let Aaron throw the stone, turn to **193**

132

You take out the scrapbook and compare the cover with the symbol that matches Lori's tattoo.

McAdam counts off on her fingers. 'The same symbol here on the stones, on the cover of the scrapbook, carved into the knife hilt and tattooed on her back.'

'And now we know it wasn't just chalked on any stone. It was specifically on the stone where her brother's blood was found after he disappeared.' A cold wind passing through the stones makes you shiver. 'That's no accident.'

You both stare in silence at the markings, wracking your brains.

Then inspiration strikes.

'What if we've been looking at this the wrong way? Perhaps these aren't just symbols, but some kind of code. That first symbol could simply be a D.'

McAdam points to each stone in turn. 'D–A–N–I . . . no, that doesn't work. Look, the third and fourth symbols are the same.'

Your mind races; you feel like you could be on the cusp of something. 'Raven Moonwolf called him "Danny", not "Daniel". That would fit.'

'It would! D-A-N-N-Y . . . and then three more symbols, none of which match any of the previous. Damn.' McAdam is deflated.

You look at the stones again, testing your assumptions. It's all too easy to jump to a quick, but wrong, conclusion.

'"Killer" also has repeated letters at positions three and four,' you say. 'Could it be "Killer Velvet"?'

'No, that's too many characters. We only have eight, remember.' McAdam huffs in frustration. 'We didn't find any kind of key to this on her body, did we? So she did it all from memory. Amazing.'

She's right. Drawing such complex symbols accurately from memory is no mean feat. 'Either she made them up on the spot . . . or she'd drawn them many times before. It's a shame she didn't see fit to do so in this scrapbook.'

⚭ *Turn to* 47

133

'Not so fast,' you say, preventing Julie from leaving. 'I believe you killed Lori, and Patrick saw you. That's why you've been causing trouble and stirring things up, isn't it? Not for the benefit of your alleged documentary, but simply to cause chaos and frighten Patrick into silence. You sent him that poison pen letter.'

'Poison pen letter?' Julie snorts. 'I haven't the faintest idea what you're talking about. Why would I kill Lori? I loved her!'

'Yes, you did. So much that I think your feelings became twisted with jealousy when you discovered she was pregnant. Lori denied it, but you knew the baby was Aaron's, and couldn't bear the prospect of having to share her with him. We already know you argued with Lori shortly before she was killed, then went off somewhere unseen by the rest of the band. I believe all your actions since have been designed to confuse, and steer us away from suspecting you killed her.'

Julie stares at you, dumbfounded.

'You're off your rocker,' she says.

'I'll ask you again, Ms Grafton: where is Patrick?'

She refuses to answer, even when you arrest her. Constable Zwale returns and you drive Julie to the station, hoping the shock of being in a cell will loosen her tongue.

But not long after you arrive, a call comes in from Bill Thomas. He led the Disciples of the Green to the Lock Stones this evening, to carry out a cleansing ritual. They arrived to find Patrick, with his throat slashed in the same manner as Lori Velvet.

Your case is thrown into chaos. Could Julie have killed Patrick before returning to the van where you found her? It's possible, although she'd have had to move fast. Either way, you have no proof. When examined, the landlord's body is found to have been drugged, but otherwise offers no solid forensic evidence, and this time there's no sign of a murder weapon.

The detective chief superintendent points out that you have no case against Julie Grafton, only your gut feeling and speculation. That's not good enough now that a second body has been found while she was already in custody. You're forced to let Julie go, and the DCS reassigns the case to another detective.

Lori Velvet's murder, and now Patrick's too, may yet be solved . . . but not by you.

🔎 *Wipe your notebook, return to* **1** *and try again – this time remembering to focus on obtaining the evidence to secure a conviction.*

For now, though, this is . . .

THE END

134

Before you go, though, you have one last point to make.

'By the way, Glenn Davis doesn't share your viewpoint. In fact, he accused you, on the grounds of your involvement in witchcraft.'

Bill shrugs. 'We respect that ancient tradition, but what we do isn't witchcraft. I shouldn't be surprised Glenn would point the finger, though. His feelings about the Disciples are no secret.'

'I see. A religious objection, presumably?'

'Ha! He might say that, but don't believe it for a moment. Glenn's problem is jealousy. Ever since I came to Grenholme he's wanted me out, because the truth is that people around here like me. Glenn wishes he could say the same.'

Leaving Constable Zwale to take Bill's statement, you and McAdam step away.

'He seems very sure of himself,' she remarks. 'A slick customer and no mistake.'

'Yes, as much of a salesman as a druid. A charismatic combination, I suppose.'

🔎 *Write* **B6** *in your notebook*

🔎 *If you haven't yet spoken to Aaron Warrior, the guitarist,
  turn to* **38**

🔎 *Otherwise, turn to* **88**

135

'Drink?' Bill offers. 'I've got Scotch in the cabinet, or beer in the fridge.'

'Neither for us, thank you, but you go ahead.'

He does, pouring himself a finger of whisky from a cabinet in the lounge. You're no connoisseur, but even you can tell it's not the cheap stuff. Meanwhile, McAdam strolls around the cluttered room, peering at the assorted objects and possessions.

'What did Glenn Davis mean when he said you only cared about your pocket?' you ask as Bill sits down with his drink. 'He mentioned "extra business", as if Lori's death would profit you in some way.'

'Surely you don't make money from all this Disciples business,' McAdam adds.

Bill sits facing you and sighs. 'Not directly. But I've got a stake in Stones & Spirits, so in a way I make money from tourists. Glenn's never liked that angle.'

'Raven doesn't own the shop?' you say, surprised. 'She gave us the impression she does.'

'I'm a hands-off investor,' he explains. 'Raven owns half and runs the shop as she sees fit, which she does very well. As for

Glenn, he's annoyed at me because we're going to perform a cleansing ritual tonight at the stones. To compensate for last night's ceremony being interrupted.'

'That's one way of putting it,' McAdam grumbles.

'Presumably that will interfere with the astronomy group's activities,' you suggest. 'Again.'

Bill sips his whisky. 'I'm a servant of nature, not its master. Much as he might think otherwise, so is Councillor Davis. I can't prevent a full moon any more than he can change the date of his precious meteor shower.'

'How did you become interested in Grenholme and its mythology?' you ask. 'Reforming the Disciples of the Green, adopting their rituals, even buying into the local shop . . . you haven't done things by halves.'

'Might have been better for my blood pressure if I had,' he says with a chuckle. 'This place appealed to me when I retired. Both the village and the house, I mean. I wanted to get as far away from the City as possible. It was only after I bought it that I read about the Lock Stones, and that led me to the Disciples. It's an old, proud local tradition, but it hadn't been active for centuries. People have forgotten to respect the old ways, and the ancient spirits. Groups like ours serve to protect and improve the community.'

They also attract tourists who improve Bill's bank balance. He seems sincere in his devotion, but you suspect the business opportunity presented by the Stone Warden and Disciples may have fuelled his interest in local tradition more than he lets on.

'How about you and Raven?' McAdam asks, reaching down to take a cup of tea. 'You seemed close earlier in the pub. Just business partners, is it?'

Bill locks eyes with the sergeant, and for a moment the room is perfectly silent. Then a bird caws somewhere outside, breaking the spell.

'We had a brief thing when I first moved here,' he admits. 'I was newly divorced, and back then we were both younger, slimmer and better-looking. It didn't last.'

'May I ask why?'

You watch Bill debate internally how much to tell you. 'Raven was . . . clingy. Like I said, I was divorced and enjoying freedom. The last thing I wanted was to shack up with someone again right away. So I ended it.'

There's a note of regret in Bill's voice. You imagine him rattling around in this big old house all by himself, essentially living in one room, and wonder if he wishes Raven were here.

'But it's all fine now,' he adds, forcing a smile. 'We're just business partners, as you say.'

If you have both G5 and B7 written in your notebook, turn to **96**

If you have only G5 written down, turn to **181**

Otherwise, turn to **44**

136

'Yet she did just that,' you point out. 'What's this about you helping with the music video?'

Julie wipes away her tears and explains. 'I contacted Bill ages ago, when Lori said she wanted to film the video here. I found the Disciples online, and I thought it would help to get the locals onside, to coordinate things around the stone circle.'

'I said yes,' Bill says with emphasis. 'I was in a pub band myself when I was young, so I wanted to help. But not during a full moon.'

'Because you knew you'd be working with the Disciples that night instead?' you suggest.

'It wasn't just that. The full moon unlocks the stones, drawing back the veil between worlds. To enter at that time, with the Stone Warden abroad, isn't just desecration, it's stupid. I told her not to do it, and look what happened.'

It takes some effort to resist rolling your eyes.

'Mr Thomas, I appreciate your beliefs are sincerely held, but whoever killed Lori Velvet was not a forest spirit or mythological figure. It was a very human act, both cruel and tragic.'

    Write **B8** *in your notebook*

    Then turn to **75**

137

'Would you care to tell us why you were seen arguing with Bill Thomas this morning?' you ask.

Glenn shrugs. 'Bill is an unusually stubborn man who spends much of his time opposing entirely reasonable proposals merely because I'm in favour. As a council member, therefore, I often find myself trying to persuade him. To no avail, I might add.'

'From what we heard, today's "persuading" sounded more like a threat,' McAdam growls. 'Why exactly did you say you'd tell the police you "saw him"? What was he doing?'

Glenn sighs, reluctant to answer.

Turn to 78

138

But, somehow, you're wrong.

You expected to find Bill, either in his Disciple robes or perhaps even dressed as the Stone Warden, with Patrick. Instead, a sharp breeze clears mist from the stone circle, and in the light of the full moon you see Patrick lying alone and motionless in its centre.

You rush into the stones, fearing you're too late. To your relief, Patrick is unconscious but alive.

What's going on? Who left him here? You were sure it was Bill, as he's the only suspect with a prior link to the band that you're aware of. He admitted that they approached him to ask for help coordinating the music video. You suspect that when he recognized Lori as the former Lucy Isherwood, he feared that she'd finally remembered who really took Daniel all those years ago. Not a forest spirit, but Bill dressed as the Warden.

That's why he backed out of helping them, and arranged to meet her at the stone circle last night, to make sure she could never tell anyone. But when Patrick mentioned earlier today that Lori had confided in him, Bill realized he had to silence the landlord as well.

So why is Patrick still alive?

An owl screeches near by in the trees. No, not an owl. That was a person!

Turn to **105**

139

You crawl backwards on your hands and heels, grazing your palms on twigs and stones, as the Warden advances. What are you doing? You can't crawl for ever. Realizing your error, you scrabble around in the undergrowth, seeking a stone or stick with which to defend yourself.

But it's too late. The Warden slashes at you with his knife, cutting through fabric and slicing deep into your shin. You yelp in pain and finally struggle to your feet, hoping to outrun the robed killer.

The Warden laughs, deranged. Blood pours from your leg, burning with pain. You can barely walk, let alone run. The Warden doesn't even have to hurry to catch you. He advances leisurely, the knife blade glinting.

Smothered by fog, the last thing you feel is the sharp, cold steel of the Warden's knife across your throat.

Wipe your notebook, return to **1** *and try again — this time remembering that your job is to confront suspects, not run away.*

For now, though, this is . . .

THE END

140

You have difficulty sleeping through what remains of the night. Questions drift through your mind like the cool mist of Grenholme Forest. Who knew Lori Velvet would be in the stone circle, alone, just before midnight? Who drew the chalk markings on the Lock Stones? Why was one of those markings also carved into the knife that killed Lori? Why didn't the killer take the knife with them?

And what made Lori scream so loudly before she was killed?

When you do snatch a moment of sleep in between tossing and turning, your dreams are filled with dark images of stumbling through a forest, fleeing from a horned beast with eyes of blazing green fire and steel claws dripping blood. You trip on a gnarled, twisted tree root and fall into a circle of stones emblazoned with strange symbols, screaming—

You wake to the piercing wail of your alarm, gasping for breath. Opening the curtains to welcome early sunlight into your room, you shake off the night's terrors and remind yourself it was only a dream.

While you wait for Sergeant McAdam to arrive, you look up Killer Velvet, and lead singer Lori Velvet, online. You watch some music videos, noting that they regularly feature dark, occult-like imagery, and read some interviews with the band. Lori and Aaron were the spokespeople, but while Aaron is garrulous and talkative, Lori is more reserved. She gives little away about herself or her background, creating an enigmatic aura.

You're so engrossed in a YouTube interview with the band, you only hear McAdam the second time she sounds her car horn. She's exactly on time.

As you climb into her car she asks, 'Sleep well?'

'As well as could be hoped for,' you say noncommittally, not wanting to worry your partner with tales of insomnia. 'How about you? You said your son had trouble sleeping before you were called out . . .?'

'Aye, he's not having the best time at school. Spends all day with his head in a book instead of joining in with the other kids.'

'Fewer young boys read than ever, these days,' you say, recalling a recent news article. 'Be grateful he enjoys it.'

She shrugs. 'Emma said the same thing, but he's only seven years old. It wouldn't kill him to play outside once in a while.' She starts the car and pulls away. 'Anyway, let's see what Dr Posh has for us.'

'I do wish you wouldn't call her that. One day you'll do it to her face, and I for one would like to be far away when that happens.'

McAdam laughs in reply.

On the way to the mortuary, you make two phone calls. The first is to Penny in the digital forensics department.

'Morning, Inspector,' she answers. 'What can I do for you?'

'Morning, Penny. I'm calling about the murder at Grenholme

Forest last night, of Lori Velvet. I wondered if it's possible for you to trace people's movements through their phones.'

'It depends on a number of factors, but normally, yes. Who did you have in mind?'

Your spirits are buoyed by her confidence.

'We have a large number of witnesses – not to mention potential suspects – who were all in Grenholme Forest last night around the time of the murder, but they're all giving alibis for each other. Unless the victim was killed by a complete stranger who happened to be wandering through the woods at the time, I'm working on the assumption that one of them is the killer, so it would be very helpful to trace their movements. The catch is that there's no phone signal in the forest itself.'

'Ah.' Penny hesitates, and your previous optimism falters. 'That's a different matter, I'm afraid. We normally triangulate location based on someone's phone pinging off nearby cellular masts. No mast, no ping. The most we might be able to tell is when someone entered the no-signal area, but even that would be an approximation.'

'What about GPS?' you ask, remembering Julie Grafton leading you through the woods.

'And satellites,' McAdam offers from the driver's seat.

'Not all phones keep a history of GPS location,' Penny says, 'and not everyone has it switched on. Even assuming they do, we require the physical device to access that log. If you bring us a suspect's phone, I can try to get inside and take a look, but I can't do it remotely.'

McAdam grunts her disapproval. 'Good luck getting anyone to volunteer their phone for that,' she says, then grins and adds, 'We'll just have to do it the old-fashioned way.'

'No need to look quite so happy about it, Sergeant. Penny, there's one more thing. We found some rather odd markings on the stones themselves, which appear to be recent and which nobody will admit to making. If I send you a sketch of them, could you look into it?'

'You think they're a code?' she asks.

'I have no idea what they are. But if they are a code, there's nobody better than you to try to work out what it means.'

'Flatterer,' she says with a chuckle. 'OK, send them over and I'll take a look.'

You do, then prepare to call Constable Zwale. Before you do, though, you wonder on the best course of action.

'Given his knowledge of the astronomy group, should I ask Joseph to look into their society and talk to them further? Or do you think I should give him the more simple task of looking over Lori Velvet's phone records?'

McAdam shrugs. 'He's still green, but he seems to know the astronomers. Similar interests, and all that. Then again, someone's going to have to go over those phone records sooner or later.'

She's right on both counts, of course. The choice must be yours.

- *If you want Zwale to investigate the astronomers, write* **P3** *in your notebook*

- *If you want Zwale to check Lori's phone records, write* **P6** *in your notebook*

- *Then turn to* **192**

141

'Danny is here,' you murmur.

'Yes!' Zwale cries, seeing it for himself. 'Well done, Inspector. That must be it. But . . . why?'

You look again at the full message. 'That's a very good question. We must assume Lori Velvet herself wrote this message. Her father said both twins wore matching bracelets, presumably each with their own name on. She must have remembered and practised this code over the years. Then Lori came to Grenholme to write that message for all to see in her music video . . . but was interrupted by the killer.'

Did Lori somehow know her twin brother's body was interred in the forest? Presumably she can't have known its exact location, or she would have simply led someone to it . . . wouldn't she?

'Remember, when Daniel disappeared he and Lori were only seven years old. She told everyone the Stone Warden took him, but being so young everyone assumed she was hysterical. What if she was right?'

Zwale looks at you sceptically. 'Inspector, the Warden isn't real.'

'No, but Daniel's killer was. Think about it. Lori wrote a song about the Warden, and insisted they film the music video for it at the Lock Stones under a full moon. She even declared to the crowd that "the Warden has a human face".'

'Danny is here,' Zwale reads again. 'She was right, too, wasn't she?'

'Yes. I think she came to Grenholme hoping to find her brother's body . . . and his killer. It would explain why she was carrying a knife. Perhaps she arranged to meet someone. That's why she left the band and walked to the Lock Stones by herself.'

'So she believed whoever did it is still here in Grenholme?'

'I think so. The symbolism of returning to the site of her brother's disappearance would have been very strong, not to mention confronting his killer.'

The constable takes out his phone and looks something up. 'I saw earlier that someone had uploaded a video of the song from last night. They've even transcribed the lyrics, look.'

He shows you a video taken by a member of the crowd at last night's pub performance. It's shaky, but the music is perfectly audible – as is Lori's powerful voice, screaming and yelling her way through the song. You scroll down to read the transcribed lyrics. With the context you now have, some passages stand out.

> *Sickened laugh behind the mask*
> *Guardian of lies is cast*
> *Riches that no man could buy*
> *Parading sycophants in mind*
> *Eyes of the warden*
> *Watching you*
> *Stones of a dark veil*
> *Stealing truth*
> *Haunted by a thousand ghouls*
> *Swallowed by a mist so cruel*

'You're right,' Zwale says, reading. 'Lori had worked out who killed her brother.'

'Or thought she had. She might have been wrong. Regardless,

this reiterates her belief that the Warden is very human, something I'm also convinced of myself after our encounter in the forest earlier. The question is . . . whose face is behind the mask?'

🔎 *Write* **P13** *in your notebook*

🔎 *Then turn to* **178**

142

Bill Thomas is not best pleased to see you again.

'Can we go home yet, or what?' he says when you approach. 'We've all given statements, and it's very late.'

'I thought you normally hang out here all night anyway,' McAdam says scornfully.

'Yeah, not in these circumstances,' Bill replies. 'Just because we're pagans, doesn't mean we perform human sacrifices.'

You produce your notebook sketch of the chalk symbols on the Lock Stones. 'If I could keep you for a moment more, Mr Thomas, I hoped you could possibly shed some light on these. Your man Patrick says they're not a normal part of the stones' appearance, and we believe they were drawn either today or yesterday. Do you recognize them?'

Bill shoots Patrick a look implying he disapproves of offering information to the police, before turning to you, all smiles.

'Never seen them before in my life. I don't recognize them as pagan or historical. Are you sure they're not astronomical?'

'Apparently not. Does anyone else know what they might

be?' You look over Bill's shoulder to the other Disciples, only to be met with blank faces. 'Very well. Thank you all for your time.'

🔎 *Turn to* **85**

143

Dusk has arrived when you leave Glenn's house, and a cool haze rolls through Grenholme's quiet streets. Much of the village seems to have taken refuge indoors, although there's a marked increase in the number of cars parked on the street courtesy of Killer Velvet's fans and reporters prowling around.

'So much for the forecast,' you remark. 'Glenn and his Stargazers may be out of luck tonight.'

'That's a shame. I really did hope to catch them myself if I wasn't on duty, I didn't just say that for his benefit.'

'How does a young Constable become interested in astronomy, anyway?'

'I've been a stargazer since I was a kid,' he explains. 'We used to visit my uncle in Kano, in northern Nigeria. He's a law professor, and he lives on the outskirts of the city where there's hardly any light pollution. The stars out there are amazing, like nothing you've ever seen in England. We'd sit in the garden and he'd point out constellations, telling me their stories. He even bought me my first telescope.'

This is a side of Zwale you never knew existed. 'It sounds like you're more interested in the romance and wonder of it than the science . . .?'

He smiles. 'That's fair, yeah. If I'd been better at physics I might not have become a copper.'

'Their loss is our gain. You said you "used to" visit your uncle. When was the last time?'

'Not for years. We have video calls on our birthdays and at Christmas, but I don't really have time to fly out these days.'

'You should make time. Calling is one thing, but there's no substitute for visiting a loved one in person.'

Zwale grins cheekily. 'Any chance of a raise, then?'

'For that you should focus on promotion,' you say with a smile. 'You've a bright future ahead, Joseph. Make the most of it.'

Like many other streets, the village square is now largely empty of people. Only the hardiest drinkers remain, and judging by the noise coming from the Watching Warden, Killer Velvet fans are filling out the pub.

You decide to join them, not for leisure but to keep an eye on the band's preparations. The pub is heaving inside, the busiest you've seen it, with Patrick and his barmaid Fran run off their feet to keep up. Remembering the video Raven showed you, you estimate there are at least twice as many people here compared to the band's performance last night.

On the small stage area, you see Keith and Steve, the drummer and bassist, setting up their instruments and equipment. Aaron's guitar is on stage, but he's nowhere to be seen, and neither is Julie.

'Where's Aaron?' you ask Steve.

He shrugs. 'Said he had something to deal with and went off. Probably on the phone to the manager.'

'Are you both on board with this tribute concert for Lori? I gather Aaron's going to sing?'

'It's what Lori would have wanted,' the bassist says, unconvincingly.

Constable Zwale taps you on the shoulder. 'Patrick wants to talk to you, Inspector.'

The landlord stands at the end of the bar, leaving Fran to deal with the four-deep queue of eager drinkers by herself. Previously Patrick has been reluctant to engage with you, so if he's now willing to make paying customers wait it must be important.

Looking ashen, he pulls a piece of paper from his back pocket and beckons you to lean in close.

'Something's happened,' he says nervously. 'I found this behind the bar.' The paper is folded, with 'PATRICK' in computer-printed letters on the outside. He unfolds it, revealing a message in the same printing:

HEAR NOTHING

SEE NOTHING

SAY NOTHING

OR ELSE!

'Do you have any idea who sent this?' you ask.

'No. I don't even know what it's talking about. But it's obviously a threat, isn't it?'

'It implies you know something important. Something the sender doesn't want you to tell.'

'But I don't know anything,' Patrick protests. 'I'm just the landlord. I serve people drinks, then chuck them out at closing time. I don't know anything,' he repeats pathetically.

'Don't you have cameras?' Zwale asks him. 'Whoever sent this must have been able to get inside the pub to place it there.'

He shakes his head. 'We're open all day, so anyone could come in. We don't have cameras. Never needed them.'

Until today. Still, this is odd. What could Patrick know that someone doesn't want him to repeat?

'I'm taking a risk even showing you this,' he says. 'They could be in here right now, seeing me talk to you.'

'If anyone asks about this conversation, tell them I wanted to discuss timings for the band's performance tonight,' you say, reassuring him. 'I'm concerned about their fans leaving and marching straight to the Lock Stones, clashing with the Stargazers and Disciples. Understand?' Patrick nods. 'Good. Now, I'd like to get that letter examined.'

You take a nitrile glove from your pocket, careful to keep it hidden from the pub patrons, though in such a busy place it's unlikely anyone would see. Patrick folds the poison pen letter and hands it to you. You fold the glove around the paper and pocket it. The truth is that anyone cautious enough to use a computer printer for such a letter is unlikely to have left fingerprints, but you'll ask forensics to examine it anyway, and simply the promise of doing so has brought the landlord some relief.

'Oi, mate, you serving or what? We're trying to give you money, here.'

The speaker is a Killer Velvet fan at the bar. Patrick rolls his eyes to you, then turns to the man with a for-the-customer smile.

'Of course, sir. Thanks for reminding me.' You smirk as Patrick walks straight past him to serve someone else at the far end of the bar.

Taking the opportunity to look around the pub from this vantage point, you take in what you can see. The band continues to set up on the stage, though there's still no sign of Aaron or Julie. You wonder if they might be upstairs, together again. Their relationship baffles you.

Killer Velvet fans outnumber locals in the pub by at least four to one, and some locals don't look too happy about it. Despite the sad reason for their gathering, many fans seem to be upbeat and enjoying themselves. Perhaps Steve was right: a celebration of Lori's life, which clearly touched many of the people here tonight, may be a better way to approach such a tragic incident than simply mourning her loss.

Nevertheless, you have a job to do.

You look out the window in time to see two familiar figures across the square. You squeeze through the crowd to get closer and recognize Raven closing up Stones & Spirits for the day, with Aaron talking to her. So he's not with Julie after all. You're surprised to see them talking, though it doesn't look like a friendly conversation. It occurs to you that in these gloomy conditions you could probably sneak up on them without being seen.

Speaking of not being seen, now that you've moved away from the bar you finally locate Julie. She's in an alcove of the pub, having cross words of her own with Bill Thomas. She jabs him in the chest with a finger for emphasis.

You call Zwale over. 'Here's your chance to make yourself useful, Constable. Divide and conquer, as it were.'

While you take one arguing pair, Zwale can take the other. So, how will you divide the tasks?

   To eavesdrop on Raven and Aaron yourself while Zwale talks to Julie and Bill, turn to **13**

   To intervene in Julie and Bill's argument yourself while Zwale listens to Raven and Aaron, turn to **184**

144

You show Raven the scrapbook you found in Lori's room.

'It was you who first mentioned Daniel Isherwood's disappearance, and now we've found this book of Lori's dedicated to him. What more can you tell us?'

Raven slowly turns the pages with a sad expression.

'I remember this . . . well, not quite like it was yesterday, but close enough. I'm not surprised she'd keep something like this. Lucy and Danny did everything together. You get that sometimes with twins, don't you? Either they're thick as thieves, or they absolutely hate one another. They were definitely the close kind. She was devastated when he vanished. I mean, everyone around here was, of course. There was a big investigation and everything. Do you know some people even thought that Lucy had done something to her brother, and made up the story about the Warden?'

'Surely you can understand why,' McAdam says. 'The Stone Warden isn't real.'

Raven looks almost offended by the sergeant's remark.

'That's my livelihood you're talking about, you know. Anyway, I never believed she could have done it. She loved Danny too much to ever hurt him.' She reaches the final completed pages, with the Warden costume design and sketches. 'She should have come to me earlier. I could have helped her make a much better costume.'

Raven closes the book and traces a finger over the symbol on the cover.

'Lori had that same symbol tattooed on her back,' you say. 'But so far nobody seems to know why.'

'I wish I did,' she says wistfully. 'It looks almost astrological, but I'm not familiar with it. Sorry.'

⌕ **Add 1** *to your LOCATION number, then turn to* **100**

145

Raven refuses to tell you where Patrick is. You search her house, but find no sign of him. You arrest her anyway and drive her to the station, hoping the shock of being in a cell will loosen her tongue.

But not long after you arrive, a call comes in from Bill Thomas. He led the Disciples of the Green to the Lock Stones this evening, to carry out a cleansing ritual. They arrived to find Patrick, with his throat slashed in the same manner as Lori Velvet.

Your case is thrown into chaos. Could Raven have killed Patrick before returning home to start the fire? It's possible, although she'd have had to move fast. Either way, you have no proof. When examined, the landlord's body is found to have been drugged, but otherwise offers no solid forensic evidence, and this time there's no sign of a murder weapon.

The detective chief superintendent points out that you have no case against Raven Moonwolf, only your gut feeling and speculation, which isn't good enough now that a second body has been found while she was already in custody. You're forced to let Raven go, and the DCS reassigns the case to another detective.

Lori Velvet's murder, and now Patrick's too, may yet be solved . . . but not by you.

⌕ Wipe your notebook, return to 1 and try again

For now, though, this is . . .

THE END

146

'This must be like déjà vu all over again for Mr Davis,' you murmur.

Behind you, a door opens. You turn to see a figure emerge from Julie's room, pulling a T-shirt over his bare chest: Aaron Warrior.

'Well, well,' McAdam says, startling the guitarist. 'Bit of extracurricular activity, is it?'

'We're consenting adults,' Aaron says, recovering and smoothing down the T-shirt. It's black, with the Killer Velvet logo printed in blood red. He crosses the corridor to another room, presumably his own this time.

'Hold on a moment, please,' you say, knocking on the door from which he just emerged.

Julie opens the door, a bathrobe wrapped around her. 'What—' she begins, then sees Aaron standing beside McAdam. 'Oh.'

'Oh, indeed, Ms Grafton.'

If you have J3 written in your notebook, turn to **157**

Otherwise, turn to **170**

147

You turn to Bill. 'Speaking of the Stone Warden and the forest, Glenn Davis mentioned that Warden sightings have increased in recent years. Ever since Daniel Isherwood went missing, in fact. What do you know about that?'

The pagan leader takes his time to answer, carefully selecting his words.

'Thanks to all the hard work I've put in over the years, more people know about the Warden and so they're more likely to look for him. Our visitor numbers have risen a lot, as well. The more people are out in the forest, the more chance someone will see the Warden. Especially if they keep an open mind,' he adds, gently admonishing.

Turn to **186**

148

The Disciples of the Green wear long robes and heavy cloaks while carrying flaming torches. Their clothing is wool and thick fibres in earth colours. Without the torches it would serve as effective camouflage, especially in the dark.

Bill Thomas stands at their head, the obvious leader. He's around sixty years old, tall and wide-shouldered with a head of tight silver curls. As you approach, he reaches out a hand to shake yours, confident and welcoming.

'All right, Inspector,' he greets you. His voice is rich and baritone, his accent unmistakeably London. 'How can I help?'

'Let's start with all this,' you say, gesturing at the group of around twenty men and women gathered behind him. 'Tell me about the Disciples of the Green.'

'Do you know the legend of the Lock Stones?' he asks.

'Not at all. Do enlighten us.'

He smiles, enjoying a chance to tell the story to someone new. 'So the earliest written record of the Lock Stones dates back to the twelfth century, but they're even older than that. This forest is what they call a Veiled Place, where the worlds of man and fairie meet. The village used to be called "Green Home", and they weren't having a good time. Children stolen, daughters lured away by fairies, curses that spoiled the crops because a villager annoyed the Fey Queen . . . they were dangerous times for mortal folk.'

He looks expectant, so you murmur a noncommittal, 'Indeed.'

'The villagers were distraught, and asked their spiritual leaders for help—'

'The local priest, you mean?' McAdam interrupts.

Bill gives her a withering look. 'Christians wouldn't come near this place in those days. The druids still worked here, and they knew what to do. They used stones from ancient barrow mounds to form a circle, closing the way . . . mostly. Every month, during the full moon, the Veil is lifted again and the path between worlds opens.'

'Like tonight,' you suggest.

'Bingo.'

The legend explains why the circle is called the Lock Stones, and it has a similar ring to myths found in many rural areas of Britain. If you believed them all, it would seem doors to the fairie kingdom are as common as blades of grass.

'Is that why you're all here tonight?' McAdam asks. 'To keep watch in case any fairies appear in the circle? Has that got something to do with Lori Velvet's costume?'

Bill looks puzzled. 'No, that was the Warden, not a fairie.'

'Come again?'

'I was about to tell you. You see, the story doesn't end there. When the Fairie Queen realized the Lock Stones kept her from our world, she was livid. On the next full moon she appeared in the circle, and cursed the chief druid who was watching over the stones. He became her servant. Nobody knows his real name, but now they call him the Stone Warden – an immortal spirit who patrols the forest. If anyone enters the Lock Stones under a full moon, he takes them through the Veil and they become trapped in the fairie lands. For ever.'

'What does the Stone Warden look like?' you ask, an idea forming.

Bill nods, confirming your suspicions, and takes out his phone. 'See for yourself.'

He shows you a drawing of a figure in layered clothes of rough fabric, all holed and torn, under a heavy coat of similar wear. The clothes are festooned with feathers, twigs and cloth banners. The figure's head looks like a demonic scarecrow, formed of leaves and moss with two burning eyes glaring out. Despite some minor differences, there's no question this is the mythical figure as whom Lori Velvet was dressed.

Bill catches your eye. 'Yes, she wore a costume like this. It wasn't very accurate,' he adds, disappointed. 'I don't know where she got it from. She could have bought a better one at the shop.'

'You see him, sometimes, in the forest,' one of the other Disciples pipes up, a middle-aged man with a round, bald head.

'Really?' McAdam says, sceptically. 'Isn't it more likely people are buying those costumes from the shop and wandering about?'

The bald man looks annoyed. 'I think we can tell the difference. The Disciples have been watching the stones for years.'

McAdam snorts. 'I bet you have. Right after you eat your tofu, I assume?'

While her disdain for new-fangled diets and lifestyles is well-known, you're not sure if the contempt in your sergeant's tone here is real or if she's simply trying to get a rise out of the assembled pagans. To your surprise, though, Bill Thomas laughs.

'Think again,' he says. 'Our folk tales are like the natural world: red in tooth and claw.' He realizes what he's said and looks abashed. 'Sorry, I suppose that's in bad taste given what's happened.'

You return to the costume. 'Whether the Stone Warden is

real or not, if Ms Velvet was dressed as this figure, she must have known the legend. So why would she enter the Lock Stones under a full moon, if it's said to be dangerous? Was she trying to prove a point? What is it your Disciples of the Green do, exactly?'

Bill smiles. 'We follow the old ways, and do the druids' work. We protect Grenholme Forest, and every full moon we visit the Lock Stones to make sure nobody enters.'

McAdam snorts. 'You didn't do a very good job this time. There's a young woman in there with her throat cut.'

'We hadn't reached the circle yet,' Bill says tetchily. 'She shouldn't have been there, especially not dressed like that. It's mockery. Like you said, she must have known the risks.'

'Mr Thomas, I'm sorry to tell you that the risk here was entirely human,' you say. 'The Stone Warden may spirit people away, but Ms Velvet is still very much here – and very dead. Whoever killed her, it was not a disgruntled fairie prince.'

Several Disciples murmur disagreement.

'Now, I'd like to know what happened this evening and where you all were.'

'Back there,' Bill says, pointing into the dark trees. 'We met on the edge of the village, like usual, then we walked through the forest towards the Lock Stones. We were about a hundred yards away when we heard the scream. I ran to the stones, and when I got there I saw Glenn Davis on the ground, with the singer.'

'On the ground?'

'Like he was holding her, you know, and praying. She was obviously dead, and there was blood everywhere.'

'Did you see anyone holding a knife? Or anything on the ground?'

He shakes his head. 'I wasn't really looking. Anyway, then those two from the band ran in, so I made an emergency call to you lot.'

'Could you show us the route you took through the forest? Do you remember where you were when you heard Ms Velvet scream?'

'Of course. Follow me.'

McAdam stays with the others while you follow Bill into the trees. He holds a flaming torch high, as if leading a procession for you alone.

'You said Mr Davis was praying when you found him?' you ask.

'Well, sort of. He kept whispering, "Oh, God, this shouldn't have happened . . . oh, God, I'm sorry . . ." that sort of thing.'

'That sounds rather damning. Do you think Mr Davis could have done this to the victim?'

He laughs mirthlessly. 'It's no secret that Glenn and I don't get along, but I'm not going to accuse him of murder. I don't think he's got it in him.'

'So who does? As First Disciple, I assume you know the people of Grenholme well.'

'Exactly,' he says. 'I don't just know them, I speak for them, and I'm telling you this wasn't one of us. Everyone here respects the Lock Stones. They bring tourism to the area, and this sort of thing will only turn people away.'

You're not so sure about that. If anything, a murder at the stone circle will probably increase interest from a brand-new type of visitor.

Bill stops suddenly. 'Here. This is where I was when we heard her scream.'

He turns to face back the way you came, flaming torch aloft. You can picture the scene, with his Disciples dutifully following.

'You're absolutely sure? How can you tell?' To your eyes this looks like any other part of the forest that you've already walked through. Without the police tape that guided you through the other route, you're hopelessly lost.

Bill lowers the torch and moves closer to a nearby tree, illuminating it. At waist height, a burl about the size of a human head bulges out from the trunk.

'We call this one the "belt buckle",' he says. 'I remember I was about to pass it when the girl screamed.'

You turn and look back towards the stone circle, where the police lights are visible. The path to reach the clearing is crooked, winding through many trees.

'Did you see anything up ahead in the circle as you approached?' you ask.

'Not a thing.' He holds up the torch. 'Holding one of these, you can't see much beyond the light of the flame anyway.'

You return to the circle, where Constable Zwale is taking the Disciples' statements. You hear the bald man tell him, 'She shouldn't have dressed up like that. It was only ever going to bring trouble.'

Despite Bill's apparent friendliness, it seems he and the other Disciples had little love for Lori Velvet. If her dressing as the Stone Warden was truly considered mockery, could that be a motive for murder? It's an extreme reaction. Besides, as you've just seen, the Disciples were all together and some distance away when Lori was attacked.

- *Write **B2** in your notebook*

- *If you already have A3 written down, turn to **24***

- *If you already have G4 written down, turn to **134***

Otherwise, choose which witness to interview next:

- *To talk to Aaron Warrior, the guitarist, turn to **38***

- *To talk to Glenn Davis, the astronomer, turn to **113***

149

Sometimes you hate being right.

A sharp breeze clears mist from the stone circle. By the light of the full moon, you see Patrick on his knees, with the Stone Warden standing over him.

He's ready to slash a knife across the landlord's throat from behind, just like how Lori was killed.

Several things made you suspect Bill, not least his musical skills and the way he'd hooked a guitar and amplifier up to the computer you saw at his house. Another was his argument with Lori before yesterday's performance at the pub. He said he warned her not to wear her own Warden costume for the music video, and not to go near the Lock Stones at midnight. He also noted that her vision would be impeded while wearing the Warden's hood. It made you wonder: how would he know? And what did they *really* argue about?

'Bill!' you call out.

The Stone Warden looks up.

And runs at you, knife raised above his head.

Turn to **200**

150

You return to the village square and enter Stones & Spirits, where there's a new sign in the window. Printed out in block letters, it reads, 'VELVET-HEADS WELCOME.' Underneath the words is a fuzzy graphic containing the letters 'KV', which you assume is the band's logo.

Raven's grey cat lies contentedly in its usual window spot. It doesn't even stir as you enter, to be enveloped by the gentle New Age music. The shopkeeper herself is arranging keyrings, featuring pictures of the Lock Stones and Stone Warden, on display pegs in one of the aisles.

'What do you want?' she asks bitterly. 'The band are playing another gig tonight, in memory of Lori. I'm busy getting ready for the fans.'

'We're only seeking the truth,' you assure her. 'Believe me, I'm used to being the least popular person in any given room. But if you don't come clean with us, we can't help you . . . or Ms Velvet.'

Raven's shoulders slump. 'I didn't pin that message to the pub door. I wouldn't do something like that, you have to believe me.'

'I do,' you assure her, and it's true: Aaron was right that it was placed there to generate publicity and outrage, but not by Raven. You recognized it as Julie Grafton's handwriting, like on the filming slate you saw last night. Presumably she thought it would make good footage for her new documentary project.

You continue: 'However, I also believe you owe us an explanation about the knife you were carrying.' You gesture to her handbag, which now sits on the glass counter. 'Should we check it for other offensive weapons while we're here?'

'Don't you dare!' Raven yells at McAdam as the sergeant reaches for it. 'That's my private property.'

'Given the circumstances, I could justifiably arrest you and take it into evidence,' you point out. 'Why do you carry a knife in the first place?'

'For self-defence,' she says plainly.

McAdam snorts. 'In Grenholme? Pull the other one.'

Raven finishes arranging the keyrings and returns to the counter, snatching up her shoulder bag.

'I often go walking in the forest to relax,' she says. 'I always have, and I never used to worry about it. But after Danny went missing I started carrying a knife, just in case.'

'Doesn't sound very relaxing.'

'It is when you know you can defend yourself. Tourist numbers have increased a lot since this place opened. Good for business, but bad for knowing who you might meet in the forest. We get all sorts of strangers around here now.'

'Like the band?' you suggest.

'They're not strangers,' she says, sighing. 'I know I over-reacted, but I'd never do anything to hurt them.'

'Not even Ms Grafton?'

Raven opens her bag at last. She removes a journal-style notebook, holding it protectively. 'This is my diary. As for the rest, take a look for yourself.' She pushes the bag towards McAdam for inspection, then turns to you. 'Julie's a chancer. I would have thought that's obvious. Do you know how she met Lori? She was a photographer's assistant, working on a photo-shoot for the band. Lori took a shine to her, and Julie quickly realized Lori was her meal ticket. She's been clinging on ever since. I'm not even sure Julie's really gay.'

'Are you suggesting Ms Grafton entered a relationship with Lori purely to further her career?'

'I'm not suggesting it, I'm telling you. Everyone knows it. Aaron can't stand her, either.'

That's not the impression you've formed. Perhaps Raven doesn't know the band as well as she thinks.

Having inspected its contents, McAdam returns Raven's handbag. She looks to you and gives a slight shake of the head – nothing dangerous or incriminating found.

   If you have A6 written in your notebook, turn to **62**

   Otherwise, turn to **195**

151

When you met Bill Thomas last night, his attitude struck you as something like a wannabe lord of the manor. He claimed to speak for the people of Grenholme and was confident in his position of village authority, even though you know he's not a councillor or official of any kind.

Seeing his home explains a lot.

Bill lives on the outskirts of the village, close to the sur-rounding forest, in what appears to be Grenholme's largest house. Stone-built and sitting in an acre of land, 'Disciple Chambers' (as the sign on the gatepost informs you) looks like someone took four traditional English cottages and glued them together.

The gates swing open with a low metallic groan. The temperature seems to drop as you pass through them, walking up the path to the front door. The gardens are semi-wild, with little attempt at cultivation. Tall grasses fill the space between flowers, bushes and trees.

Bill opens the door before you can knock. Compared to last night's robes and flaming torch, he looks remarkably normal in blue jeans, a polo shirt and tartan slippers.

'I had a sensor put in the gate,' he explains with a smile. 'Better than a doorbell any day. Come in.'

You follow him inside, peeking into rooms as you pass them. They seem normal enough, lightly furnished and unremarkable.

The sitting room is altogether different. It's the largest room in the house, but that plain fact is obscured by the sheer amount of *stuff* it contains. Overflowing bookshelves, a home office filled with clutter, a large TV and entertainment centre, fishing rods and baskets piled in a corner, chairs and sofas filled with more books and magazines, a guitar and amplifier that appear to be plugged into a large computer, display cases of family photos and more. Much of it is covered in a fine layer of dust, suggesting it hasn't actually been used in years.

Then you see the shrine. It's another display case, but this one is full height and features what appears to be a mannequin of the Stone Warden, as well as a ceremonial robe like the one Bill wore last night, a knife with an intricately carved handle and an enlarged photograph of the Lock Stones in the forest clearing.

'So is this where you all meet?' McAdam asks, peering at the Stone Warden dummy. 'Disciple Chambers? Makes sense, I suppose.'

Bill clears some newspapers off a small sofa so you can sit down, then takes a chair himself. A roaring fireplace draws the chill off your bones.

'That's right,' he says. 'We assemble here, then go into the forest. I named the house in honour of a lost tradition.'

'It wasn't already called Disciple Chambers?'

He shakes his head. 'When I bought this place, Grenholme had almost forgotten the Disciples of the Green ever existed. I wanted to revive the old ways.'

'With you in charge,' you point out.

'Someone's got to lead, Inspector. Your own rank proves that.'

'What does your family think of all this?'

Bill's gaze lingers on the display case containing photographs, his expression hardening.

'My ex-wife took me to the cleaners twenty years ago. That's partly why I took early retirement and came to Grenholme. My children are all grown up, living abroad. One each in Italy, Canada and Singapore. They think I'm a mad old eccentric. Maybe I am, but I wouldn't change a thing. Well, apart from buying a smaller house. I really thought I'd need it, but . . .' He gestures at the room's clutter. 'The truth is I more or less live in one room.'

That explains the unoccupied feeling you got from the other rooms you passed.

'You say you retired. Is leading the Disciples a full-time vocation?'

Bill chuckles. 'Nah. We spend a lot of time tending to the

forest, cleaning up after kids partying, that sort of thing. But most of my time is spent talking to the villagers or checking on the shop.'

'And fishing?' You gesture at the dust-covered tackle in the corner.

He shrugs. 'I thought I'd take it up when I moved here, but it turns out fishing's kind of boring. I don't suppose you're looking to buy some kit?'

'Thank you, but no. I must ask: how do you pay for a house this size? Are you living off your savings and pension?'

He grunts bitterly. 'Hardly. After the divorce I had just about enough left to buy this place. But I was a City trader in town, and I still dabble in the markets.' He indicates the home office desk, where an open laptop surrounded by files and papers plays its screensaver. 'No mortgage, but I've got bills to pay like everyone else.'

You gesture at the guitar, propped up against the amplifier and a rack of computer equipment. 'How about rock and roll?'

Bill laughs. 'My days in cover bands are behind me. Anyway, it's all done with computers these days. It was a fun way to let off steam after a day on the trading floor, but playing to three people and a dog in some stinking pub is a young man's game.'

'Or woman's,' McAdam points out.

If you have P1 written in your notebook, turn to **32**

Otherwise, turn to **119**

152

You expect Julie to be grateful for Aaron's quick action, but instead she looks shocked.

'It's no wonder she didn't tell you, isn't it?' she whispers. 'Imagine what you'd have taught that poor kid.'

'That's not fair,' Aaron protests. 'When I have a son, he won't have to grow up like I did. He'll want for nothing.'

Julie doesn't reply. She seems to have accepted that Aaron was likely the father of Lori's unborn child, and it's clear her remark cut him deeply.

Turn to **23**

153

'That was quite a display you put on with the knife inside the pub,' you say to Aaron. 'Disarming Raven with ease, and throwing it into the dartboard. Where did you learn to do that?'

He blows a final cloud of smoke, then drops the cigarette on the pavement and crushes it under his heel.

'My name is Shankar, and I grew up on an estate in Dagenham,' he says, eyes narrowing. 'What do you think?'

'Is that also how you first came into contact with the police? We've seen your record. Not the musical kind.'

Aaron sneers. 'What can I say? The only thing more racist than the local kids were the local cops. I never went to court for anything,' he emphasizes. 'Music got me out of that world.

It's why the band is so important to me. This is more than just a job, it's my life.'

   🔍 *If you have J2 or J5 written in your notebook, turn to* **27**

   🔍 *Otherwise, turn to* **199**

154

Glenn has a head start, but even with blood running into your eye, you're in better shape. You catch him before he can reach the clearing's treeline, tackling him to the ground. He struggles and fights, wailing like a banshee, but you've dealt with worse. Now safely handcuffed, you march him back through the forest. Constable Zwale has just arrived at the parking area in a car, so you rush Glenn to the station for interrogation while other officers search the forest for Patrick.

Glenn maintains his innocence, and the truth is you have no hard evidence against him. You don't even have a strong motive, other than his admitted distaste for the band.

Then, while you're struggling to get a confession out of Glenn, Patrick's body is found . . . inside the Lock Stones, with his throat cut in the same manner as Lori.

Did Glenn kill Patrick before you found him in the clearing? Or was it someone else after all? Either way, you can't prove it.

The detective chief superintendent hauls you over the coals. Your sergeant is wounded in hospital; a second victim has been murdered; and you arrested someone without the evidence to back it up. It's simply not good enough, especially with media attention on this case rising.

You're banished to your desk, and the case is assigned to another detective. Lori Velvet's murder may yet be solved . . . but not by you.

🔍 *Wipe your notebook, return to* **1** *and try again – this time focusing on obtaining the evidence to secure a conviction.*

For now, though, this is . . .

THE END

155

Constable Zwale has already taken Raven Moonwolf's statement, but she continues to hover on the edge of the stone circle, watching the police activity around her.

'Ms Moonwolf,' you say, approaching her.

'Just Raven is fine, please,' she says. 'How can I help?'

'Brace yourself,' you say, before showing her the bloody knife in the evidence bag and gesturing to the Lock Stones.

'I wondered if you could possibly shed some light on this. See the symbol carved into the hilt? It matches one of the chalk markings on the stones, over there.' She peers at the stone, then back at the knife. 'Do you recognize this weapon?'

'It's not mine, if that's what you're asking,' Raven protests. 'Why would I own a thing like that? Oh, Goddess, is that the knife Lori was killed with?'

You shake your head. 'We're not sure of anything yet. But it was found near by so naturally it's of interest.'

'Well, good luck. I've never seen it before, and I have no idea what that symbol means, either.'

🔍 *Turn to* **85**

156

You decide not to let them know you were listening. Remaining hidden in the doorway, you watch as Raven seems to gather her courage, her shoulders tensing. Maybe you'll have to reveal yourself after all, if she assaults Aaron.

She doesn't. Instead, she simply hisses, 'Go to hell,' and turns on her heel. Aaron stares open-mouthed after her.

You doubt it's a good idea to anger one's fans in such a way, but that's not your business.

Returning to the pub, you don't see Bill or Julie anywhere, but find Constable Zwale at the bar once again. You beckon him outside in order to talk without being overheard. There you sit on a bench, watching the mist roll through the square and wrap around your ankles like a needy cat.

He relates what happened: Julie was filming Bill, trying to make him feel guilty about Lori's death. She claims that if Bill

and the Disciples had helped the band with the shoot, instead
of taking offence at them wanting to film in the stone circle,
Lori would still be alive because she'd never have gone to the
stone circle alone. Bill said that given Lori's now-revealed history with Grenholme, she didn't need him to tell her about the
local legend.

It's a good point, and suggests that Lori knew exactly
what she was doing by coming here to film at this particular time.

You tell Zwale what you overheard from Raven and Aaron.
However, you're interrupted by a phone call . . . from the
detective chief superintendent.

Turn to **15**

157

Last night you decided you'd ask Julie for the video from
the forest, in case she unknowingly recorded something that
would help you identify Lori's killer.

You also want to speak with Aaron about Lori's past, but it's
now clear that he and Julie are closer than they let on, so from
here onwards you decide to interview them separately.

You and McAdam will have to split these tasks, so who will
talk to whom?

*To interview Julie yourself while McAdam talks to Aaron, turn
to* **121**

⚲ *To interview Aaron yourself while McAdam talks to Julie,*
turn to **26**

158

'Not so fast,' you say, preventing Julie from leaving. 'I believe you killed Lori, and Patrick saw you. That's why you've been causing trouble and stirring things up, isn't it? Not for the benefit of your alleged documentary, but simply to cause chaos and frighten Patrick into silence. You sent him that poison pen letter.'

'Poison pen letter?' Julie snorts. 'I haven't the faintest idea what you're talking about. Why would I kill Lori? I loved her!'

'Yes, you did. That's also why you sent Aaron those anonymous emails and messages, because you wanted to eliminate any competition to Lori's primacy within Killer Velvet. That includes Aaron. You hoped that making him believe he had an unhinged, potentially dangerous stalker would force him out of the band. Perhaps out of music altogether.'

Julie stares at you, dumbfounded.

'You're off your rocker,' she says.

'Am I? Earlier you said of Aaron that you "know his signals better than his own mother". Those are the exact words used by his supposed stalker.'

She looks away, nervous.

'I'll ask you one more time, Ms Grafton: where is Patrick?'

Julie refuses to answer, even when you arrest her. You wait for Constable Zwale to return, then drive Julie to the station, hoping the shock of being in a cell will loosen her tongue.

But not long after you arrive, a call comes in from Bill Thomas. He led the Disciples of the Green to the Lock Stones this evening, to carry out a cleansing ritual. They arrived to find Patrick, with his throat slashed in the same manner as Lori Velvet.

Your case is thrown into chaos. Could Julie have killed Patrick before returning to the van where you found her? It's possible, although she'd have had to move fast. Either way, you have no proof. When examined, the landlord's body is found to have been drugged, but otherwise offers no solid forensic evidence, and this time there's no sign of a murder weapon.

An examination of Julie Grafton's computer reveals that you were right; she sent Aaron those 'stalker' emails, and under questioning she admits she was trying to drive him out of the band so Lori could take sole control of Killer Velvet. Damning as that is, it doesn't support a case that Julie killed Lori. All you have is your gut feeling and speculation, which isn't good enough now that a second body has been found – especially as it happened while Julie was in custody. You're forced to let her go, and the detective chief superintendent reassigns the case to another detective.

Lori Velvet's murder, and now Patrick's too, may yet be solved . . . but not by you.

    Wipe your notebook, return to **1** *and try again – this time remembering to focus on obtaining the evidence to secure a conviction.*

For now, though, this is . . .

THE END

159

'Thank you, Constable,' you say. 'We're on our way to the village now, so we'll see you shortly. What's the general mood there?'

He hesitates before replying. 'Fraught, is probably the best way I can describe it. Half the people seem convinced Lori was killed by the Stone Warden, the other half think she was struck down for being a Satanist, and everyone's looking over their shoulder. There's a rumour going around that her eyes were missing, and another that she was mauled by a wild forest creature.'

'Complete nonsense,' McAdam says.

'Of course, ma'am, but short of publishing crime-scene photos, there's not much we can do to convince them otherwise. I've even heard some people talk about needing to buy protective charms from the local pagan shop.'

'The more we deny it, the more we'll be accused of covering something up,' you say. 'When people believe you're keeping something from them, nothing you say can convince them otherwise. Even if we did show them crime-scene pictures, they could claim they were manipulated. Still, we must persevere. Good work, Constable. Keep at it.'

'Yes, Inspector.'

You end the call and sit in silence for a moment, watching trees rush past the car window, before you realize you're driving through the forest.

'Sergeant, where are we going? I think we should pay a visit to the village, not revisit the crime scene.'

'That's what we're doing,' she says. 'Grenholme didn't come

by that name for no reason. The forest completely surrounds the village, containing it. No wonder they're a superstitious bunch.'

'I see. We mustn't fall into such thinking ourselves. We must remain clear-headed, not to mention clear-eyed, throughout. Lori Velvet deserves no less.'

The sergeant grunts. 'What she deserves is justice. I look forward to seeing whoever did this behind bars. Or worse.'

You've had arguments with McAdam before about capital punishment. In some ways she's a throwback to the bad old days, ready to lock people up, throw away the key then lead them to the gallows. But she's a good detective, and mostly keeps a lid on her aggressive nature.

Thinking about what Zwale told you, and what you saw in the forest last night, you make a decision.

'Let's go to the town square and pay Raven Moonwolf a visit. Perhaps she can give us some perspective.'

'Or more likely try to sell us her "protective charms".'

'I'm sure your wife would love one. Regardless, Raven clearly knows the village well. Who better to ask about local legends than someone who sells them all day long?'

Turn to **174**

160

Finding the river is a sensible plan. But it relies on you knowing the forest, which you don't, and you can only see a few metres in the gloom. Two minutes later you're lost again, unable to find the stream you waded across and unsure in which direction you're facing.

You struggle to remember the area map you looked at last night. In desperation you take out your phone, but there's no signal and the map will no longer load. Last night, Bill Thomas managed to call the emergency services via a satellite signal from his phone, but even if yours is capable of that you don't know how to do it.

To stop yourself spiralling into despair, you stop and think things through logically. The forest surrounds the village entirely, but it's not endless. One thing you recall from the map is a road circling its outer edge, in addition to the main road bisecting the woods. If you keep going in a straight line, no matter which direction, you'll surely reach one of them eventually.

The smell of rotting leaves permeates the air again, even stronger than before. Hoping it means water, you turn towards it and run, ignoring the brambles snatching at your ankles and low branches threatening to crack you over the head.

But haste is your enemy. You stumble and lose your footing as the ground suddenly drops away, sliding over the edge of a muddy dell and down a slope. Desperately you grab at a low branch on an old elm, whose roots are exposed where the dell side has eroded. You grip the branch with both hands, holding yourself up. The stench is overpowering. Looking down, you see a foul-smelling boggy area at the bottom of a steep slope – a layer of black mud saturated with foul water which you almost fell into. It probably isn't deep enough to drown in, but it looks thick enough to trap you.

You struggle for purchase and begin to pull yourself back up—

The branch splits away with a loud crack. This tree isn't just old, it's dead and brittle. Staring in disbelief at the rotting wood in your hand, you fall, scrabbling for something to grip. Your fingertips find the exposed roots and grab hold, clutching at them for dear life. Your body stretches down the dell side, your shoes almost dipping in the foul, brackish water. Muscles protesting, you slowly haul yourself up inch by inch until you can wrap an arm around a thick root for stability. The broken branch you were holding on to has already disappeared into the foul-smelling reeds below, swallowed by mud. You look up at the dead tree, wondering if you can somehow use it as purchase to climb the rest of the way out.

As if offering you help, a skeletal hand pokes out from the split bark where the branch broke away. Hanging from its thin wrist is a bracelet of wooden beads.

Two hours later, with a thermal blanket wrapped around your shoulders to warm you up, you watch as Dr Wash and her team carefully recover the skeleton from inside the tree. A separate team has already found McAdam and whisked her away to hospital.

After climbing out of the swamp dell, you ran in a straight a line, or as straight as possible in the forest, eventually emerging on to one of boundary roads circling the area. In fact, you were only a few hundred metres from the edge of the trees, on the far side of the forest from the Lock Stones and Grenholme village.

'Quite an ingenious hiding place,' Dr Wash says as the small, intact skeleton is placed on a stretcher. 'In addition to being inside the tree, the bog would cover up any smell of the body's decomposition. No wonder they searched the area twice over but never found him.'

'You say "him". Without any flesh remaining, how can you be sure it's a male?'

The doctor shrugs. 'At seven years old, there's very little difference between the skeleton of either sex, but very little is still something if you know what you're looking for. I'll be able to confirm when I examine the remains properly, but my initial assessment is that you have indeed found Daniel Isherwood. For one thing, there's the simple matter that his is the only unsolved disappearance in this area. Second, look at this. *Oof.*' She crouches beside the stretcher, groaning as her knees click. 'Impact wound on the upper lateral portion of the frontal cranium.'

She turns the skull towards you, and the wound is clear to see. A head blow strong enough to crack the skull.

'Finally, there's the bracelet you pointed out. Take a look.' She holds up the skeletal hand, carefully removes the wooden beaded bracelet, and places it inside an evidence bag.

Peering closely at it, you see the bracelet is made of dark, solid wood. Burned into each wooden bead is a symbol. They're hard to make out, but match some of what you saw chalked on the Lock Stones.

Are you ready to decipher the chalk symbols on the stones? If so, write them out and assign each letter a number from 1 to 26 — but counting backwards. *So in this case A = 26, B = 25, and so on down to Z = 1. Finally, add together all the numbers to get a total amount between 1 and 200.*

When you're confident you've found the solution, turn to the section matching that total number — but before you do, write **P12** *in your notebook and note down section* **45**. *You'll know right away if you've deciphered it correctly. If not, you should turn immediately to 45 instead.*

🔍 *Alternatively, if you're not ready to decipher the symbols or don't want to try yet, turn to* **45** *anyway*

161

Before you leave, you have one final question.

'You said the song lyrics were about these stones, and the local legends, but none of you were aware of that until you arrived. So how did Ms Velvet know about them?'

Aaron shrugs. 'Probably read it in a book. She was well into witchy stuff and folklore. Even before she met Julie,' he adds, with a scornful look at the director.

'She's always been spiritual, and very knowledgeable,' Julie says with admiration. 'It was Lori who put me in touch with the Disciples of the Green, in fact. We asked Bill Thomas to help coordinate filming here and get the locals onside, but he declined.'

'Because he knew he'd be busy with his own thing tonight?' McAdam suggests.

'It wasn't just that. He sounded kind of offended, actually.

Said we were disrespecting the stones, which is *absolutely* not true. Huge respect, massive respect for local traditions.'

Something about Julie's emphatic insistence makes you suspect the truth is somewhat different. But more importantly, you wonder why Bill Thomas didn't mention his correspondence with the band when you spoke to him.

   Write **B3** *in your notebook*

   If you haven't yet spoken to Glenn Davis, the astronomer, turn to **113**

   Otherwise, turn to **88**

162

'I don't think so,' you say, pressing home your accusation. 'You've made it clear from the start that Killer Velvet is all you care about. Your career has given you a good life and made plenty of money. But you could always make more, couldn't you? Especially if you owned the sole rights to Killer Velvet. We know Lori threatened to sue you for those rights. So you thought, why not simply get her out of the way and take them all for yourself instead? Especially as they'd be worth even more following her death.'

An owl screeches somewhere deep in the forest.

'You're way off base, Inspector,' Aaron says, his contemptuous attitude returning. 'Lori and I co-owned everything. That lawsuit didn't stand a chance, because we signed a contract when we formed the band. And now her family will inherit her share. If you think that's going to make my life easier than dealing with Lori, you don't know the first thing about show-biz. Now get lost and leave me alone, will you?'

Baffling as it seems, he appears to be genuine. You begin to doubt your own judgement. Is he innocent after all? There's no sign of Patrick here. Then again, Aaron would have had time to take the landlord deeper into the forest before returning to the river—

With a sickening churn in your stomach, you realize that what you heard wasn't an owl.

🔍 *Turn to* **130**

163

'Mr Davis, what did you mean earlier when you said Bill Thomas only cared about lining his pockets? Does he profit from the Disciples, somehow?'

Glenn looks confused for a moment, then explains. 'They haven't told you? That's typical, I suppose. No, the Disciples are a loss-leader, as it were, for Stones & Spirits.'

'Raven's shop? Why would that be?'

'Because Bill is her business partner.' Seeing your surprise, he smiles smugly. 'You see, this is why you can't trust either of them. They're deceptive by nature.'

'So Raven isn't the only one who makes money from tour-ists,' McAdam says, thinking aloud. 'No wonder Bill's so keen to keep the pagan stuff front and centre.'

'That's not the only reason,' Glenn responds. 'He also does it to annoy me, by disrupting the Stargazers' activities. Like this evening, with this nonsense "cleansing ritual" he wants to perform at the stones. He's only doing it because he knows tonight's conditions will be ideal for meteor-watching.'

You glance at Constable Zwale, who nods his head in agreement.

'He's right, Inspector. Full moon and clear skies forecast. The Lyrids will put on a great show.'

   If you have G3 written in your notebook, turn to **87**

   Otherwise, turn to **39**

164

You show Aaron and Julie your notebook sketch of the chalk symbols on the stones.

'I wondered if you could possibly shed some light on these. We're told they're not normally there, and believe they may have been drawn some time in the last two days. Do you recognize them?'

Aaron gasps. 'Oh, wow, I – I didn't even notice.' He looks past you, to the stones with their chalk markings, then at your notebook again, with a worried expression.

'Lori doodled symbols like this sometimes,' Julie says, sniffling back tears.

'She's got a tattoo of that one,' Aaron says, pointing to the left-most symbol. 'I'm sure it's the same shape.'

Julie nods in recognition. 'Yes, definitely. The one on her back. And now it's here, on these old stones? How horrible. What does it all mean?'

'That's what we're trying to establish. If Lori had this symbol tattooed, presumably it meant something special to her . . .?'

Aaron and Julie look at one another, as if expecting the other to answer, before simultaneously realizing neither is any the wiser.

'To be honest, I didn't ask,' Aaron says. 'I figured it was something personal.'

'You'd been her partner on and off for quite some time,' McAdam says. 'Weren't you curious?'

Aaron shrugs and lights a cigarette.

'I was,' Julie says, 'but when I asked, she got evasive and wouldn't say. Aaron's right, it was obviously very personal.'

'So who did this?' McAdam says, pointing to the chalked stones. 'Was it for the music video?'

Julie shakes her head. 'Lori didn't mention anything to me. I suppose she might have done it, though. She was spontaneous like that.'

Aaron snorts. 'What she means is, Lori believed it was better to apologize than to ask permission. She was always doing things without asking, even if it caused trouble. Like that business with the costume for tonight's encore.'

You remember what McAdam told you about Aaron and Lori's arguments, and wonder what other things she might have done to engender bitterness in her ex-lover.

'Is there anyone else who might know what these symbols meant to Lori? Family or friends, perhaps?'

'We were her family and friends,' Aaron says. 'Lori lived for the band.'

You thank them for their time and step away to confer with Sergeant McAdam.

'We now have two possible scenarios. Either Lori Velvet was drawing these symbols and the killer interrupted her, or the killer was drawing them but was interrupted by Lori. Whichever of them it was dropped the chalk, presumably before they finished marking all eleven stones.'

'My money's on it being Lori,' McAdam says. 'Especially after what Aaron just told us. How would the killer even know they meant anything to her?'

'That rather depends on *what* they mean, doesn't it? Remember, the knife we found has that same symbol, the one Lori apparently had tattooed, carved into its hilt. That suggests the knife belonged either to the victim . . . or to someone else who knew the symbol's importance to her.'

McAdam looks around the stone circle and shivers. 'Wonderful. We've stumbled on a death cult. I suppose it fits with everything else, doesn't it?'

'It may not necessarily be a cult,' you say, trying to reassure her. 'Just a close, isolated group who don't want outsiders to understand them or their intentions.'

'You say potato . . .'

    Write **A4** *in your notebook*

    Then turn to **85**

165

You've had your eye on Bill since you met him last night in the forest. Something about the pagan leader seemed off to you from the start, and his obsessive interest in the Lock Stones and Stone Warden place him firmly in the frame.

Why would he take Patrick? Did the landlord see something he shouldn't have? Perhaps Patrick witnessed Bill kill Lori. There doesn't seem any question that the landlord is loyal to Bill through the Disciples, but that might not extend to helping him cover up murder. It would explain the poison pen letter. You wish Patrick had been more forthcoming earlier. Now Bill is going to silence him for ever.

If they're anywhere, it must be the forest. You saw for yourself last night how familiar he is with the area. On a fog-cursed night like this, the forest is surely the First Disciple's domain.

   Write **B11** *in your notebook*

   Then turn to **182**

166

Upon reaching the outskirts of the village, McAdam's phone rings. She answers it, then puts it on speaker and holds out her phone so you can both hear. 'It's Zwale. Go on, Constable.'

'I've just left Glenn Davis's house, ma'am. He showed me

the Bluetooth speaker in his kitchen, and it looks a lot like the one we found in the tree.'

'Except for it being in his house. Does he own two?'

'He swears not. Says it must be a coincidence.'

McAdam looks sceptical. 'Aye, and I'm wee Ariadne.'

'Come again?'

'Never mind. Thank you, Constable. The inspector and I are going back to the stone circle, so we'll be out of range for a while. In the meantime, keep an eye on the village square. Killer Velvet fans are starting to gather for this evening's gig.'

'Right you are, Sarge.'

McAdam ends the call. 'Another black mark on Glenn Davis's record. He's looking good for it, if you ask me.'

'We still can't prove anything,' you say. 'To be honest, I'm also struggling with motive. Glenn objected to the band's presence on principle and in practice, but did he hate them enough to murder the lead singer just because his petition failed? It doesn't quite add up. There's more here than we're seeing.'

'Which isn't much in this fog,' McAdam says.

🔎 *Turn to* **25**

167

You signal to McAdam to remain quiet, then press yourself against the street corner, unseen by the two men. Bill and Glenn are too immersed in their argument to notice, but at this distance you only hear snatches of their angry whispers.

'. . . see you anywhere near the forest tonight . . .' Glenn says. '. . . police will hear . . .' Although he's the shorter of the two men, Glenn doesn't look at all intimidated by Bill.

The pagan leader makes a dismissive gesture. '. . . nothing on me.'

'. . . saw you, Bill . . . Understand me?'

'. . . with secrets . . . fifteen years ago . . .'

Suddenly, a voice from behind you calls out: 'Inspector, what are you doing?'

You turn to see Raven Moonwolf standing near by once again dressed all in black, with a handbag slung over her shoulder. She holds a key in one hand and a loaf of bread in the other. McAdam tries to usher the shopkeeper away, but Raven shrugs off the sergeant.

'Hey, don't push me around. What's going on?'

You return your attention to the side street, but Bill and Glenn have already departed. You catch a glimpse of one – Bill, you think, though you can't be sure – turning a corner at the end of the street, away and out of sight.

'Nothing,' you say with a sigh. 'As it happens, Ms Moonwolf, we were looking for you a moment ago. Could we talk somewhere?'

'Of course,' she says, returning across the square to her shop door. 'There are things I need to tell you anyway. Come inside and I'll explain.'

⚭ *Write* **B5** *in your notebook*

⚭ *Then turn to* **80**

McAdam takes out her phone and looks something up. 'Oh-*ho*,' she says, which you know means she's found something interesting. 'Look at this. Arrest record for Arjun Shankar . . . aka Aaron Warrior.'

You skim the record displayed on her screen. 'Several arrests and cautions . . . disorderly conduct, minor assault . . . no convictions, though.'

'Due to no solid evidence and a lack of witnesses. Doesn't mean he didn't do it.'

'True, and I think we should follow up with Aaron anyway,' you say. The guitarist is still standing outside the pub, smoking. When you first step out you see his expression is troubled. Then he notices you and it transforms into simple disdain.

'Julie looks like she could use a friend,' you say.

Aaron shrugs. 'She's been giving me the cold shoulder since this morning. I can't tell whether she's up or down.'

'Her girlfriend was murdered last night.'

'Who was also my ex, my vocalist, and it turns out probably carrying my child. Which is why I know what Lori would have wanted, regardless of what Julie says.'

'Oh? What does Julie say?'

The guitarist tosses his cigarette on the ground, crushes it under his heel and immediately lights another.

'She thinks the gig tonight is disrespectful. She has no idea.'

'Tonight? You mean you're playing here again?'

'Yeah, like a tribute to Lori. I'll sing. And this time I'm making sure everyone knows about it.'

'How do you think the people of Grenholme will like that?'

Aaron takes a long drag, as if giving the question serious thought. Then he grins. 'I don't give a toss. We're here for our fans, not them.'

🔎 *If you have P4 written in your notebook, turn to* **20**

🔎 *Otherwise, turn to* **106**

169

Without stopping, Glenn ducks under the police crime-scene tape surrounding the area and runs past the tree where you found Daniel's body. You feel momentarily overwhelmed by memories. Chasing the Stone Warden through the forest; finding McAdam stabbed; discovering the skeleton inside the wych elm. Now you're back, once again giving chase and exhausted, this time with your own injury. It's almost too much.

You lean against another tree, catching your breath despite the bog stench. Ahead, you see Glenn's silhouette in the haze. He pauses, looks back at you – then continues running. He won't stop until you catch him.

Taking one more deep breath, you push away from the tree, ready to resume your chase. But a sharp stab of pain tells you it's at an end.

Puzzled by the sudden burning sensation in your chest, you look down . . . and see a knife, stuck halfway to the hilt and held by a gloved hand. As if in slow motion, the Stone Warden steps out from behind the tree, his dirt and moss-stained rags unmistakeable even at night.

'Good night, Inspector,' the Warden whispers, bracing a hand against your chest. He pushes with one hand and pulls with the other, freeing the knife and sending you tumbling backwards: past the wych elm, down the steep dell and into the stinking bog. Your blood mingles with the foul water as you sink into the muck. In a moment of dazzling clarity, your mind focuses on one final thought: like Lori Velvet's killer, you may never be found.

    Wipe your notebook, return to **1** *and try again.*

For now, though, this is . . .

THE END

170

Aaron and Julie are obviously closer than they let on last night. You decide that from here onwards you should interview them separately. There's no time like the present, given what you saw in Lori's room.

    You and McAdam will have to split these tasks, so who will talk to whom?

    To interview Julie yourself while McAdam talks to Aaron, turn to **121**

    To interview Aaron yourself while McAdam talks to Julie, turn to **26**

Glenn must be stopped before it's too late. You rush further into the woods, hoping you can find Clearing Delta. Even though he's not with the Stargazers in the village, you're sure that's where he'll be. You only hope Constable Zwale can find his own way there to be your backup.

After a few minutes, you begin to fear you've become lost, but then see a red light flashing in the haze. You hurry towards it, careful not to trip over the gnarled tree roots underfoot, and break into a clearing. Glenn stands in the centre of what you now know to be Clearing Delta, staring up at the sky.

'Glenn,' you call out. 'Mr Davis. It's the police.'

He keeps staring at the sky. 'This bloody fog,' he complains. 'Not a cloud in the sky. Perfect viewing conditions. Instead, we're at the whim of a ground-based impediment.'

There's a bundled shape at his feet. You fear the worst, but upon drawing closer see it's merely a large kitbag.

'Glenn, where's Patrick?'

He finally looks at you, as if seeing you for the first time. His eyes are wild. 'What are you doing here? Go away!'

'Not before you tell me what's going on. Why aren't you with the other Stargazers in the square?'

'They don't want me!' he cries. 'After today, it's obvious how the vote will go. It's never going to stop . . . everyone thinks I did it. They always have. I should have left this place when it all started, with Daniel. But why should I? I'm a good person.' He turns to you as if pleading for absolution. 'I've lived by God's precepts, I've loved my fellow man, I swear . . .'

Now you know what's in the bag, and why Glenn is out here at night. He's not stargazing. He's escaping Grenholme. You wonder what his final departing act might have been.

'Glenn, what have you done with Patrick?'

'Nothing! Nothing . . . I don't know what you're talking about. I'm innocent!' He backs away from you, but stumbles over a rut in the dirt and falls to the ground.

You press on. 'You've always maintained your innocence, haven't you? But you weren't the prime suspect in Daniel's disappearance for no reason. Is that the real reason Raven divorced you? Did she suspect there was some truth to the accusations? Now here comes Daniel's sister, whom you surely recognized, and just to really stick the knife in, you discover your ex-wife is obsessed with the band.'

He scrambles backwards on all fours. 'No, no, you're twisting everything around! That's what you do, I know it is, just like before! You make everything sound bad . . .'

'I don't need to, Glenn. When the others came running last night, they found you holding Lori's dead body and muttering about how sorry you were. I should have arrested you there and then. So I'll ask you again: where's Patrick?'

'No!'

In the dim light you didn't see his hand close around a large stone on the ground. He throws it at you, catching you unawares. The stone strikes your forehead and you stagger backwards. Blood runs into your eyes, obscuring your vision.

Glenn takes advantage of your disorientation and gets to his feet, running into the trees. You wipe away the blood and give chase.

Check your notebook in the following order:

๑ *If you have G6 written down, turn to* **42**

๑ *If you have G1 or B5 written down, turn to* **95**

๑ *Otherwise, turn to* **154**

172

'All in good time,' you say. 'I assure you our investigation will be thorough.'

McAdam looks up from her notebook. 'Did Lori dressing up as the Stone Warden offend you, Mr Thomas? Did you feel she was mocking your beliefs?'

'No, you've got it all wrong. Village kids dress up as the Warden all the time, and there are costumes for sale in the shop. It's good for publicity. Anything that spreads awareness of the stones benefits the village.'

'And you, as First Disciple.'

He shrugs. 'Like I said, I've got bills to pay. For me, reviving the Disciples was a calling. But opening the shop, changing the pub's name, attracting more visitors to the area . . . that's about putting the community in a position to take advantage of the tourism trade. I drew a line at the band filming inside the Lock Stones, under a full moon, while wearing that costume. It was too much.'

'So much that you took matters into your own hands, to prevent it?'

'I don't like what you're implying.'

McAdam scowls, leaning forward on the sofa. 'I don't like young women being murdered, so today we're all disappointed.'

She's pushing hard, but you've seen this aggressive approach work before, so you wait for Bill's reaction.

Avoiding the sergeant's gaze, he looks into the fire. 'Not half as disappointed as you'll be when I remind you I was with the Disciples all night. They'll all vouch for me. In fact, if I remember right, they already did.'

↺ *If you have P9 written down, turn to* **54**

↺ *Otherwise, turn to* **115**

173

'Call for backup,' you say to Zwale, before shouting, 'Aaron, put that down immediately! Don't make me arrest you!'

You push your way through the mob, ignoring their insults and reciprocal shoving, to stand before Glenn's gate.

'That goes for everyone. I understand you think justice is overdue, but you must let us do our job.'

'You didn't do it fifteen years ago,' someone shouts. 'You should have arrested him then!'

'You don't know who's responsible. At the time, the police decided it wasn't Mr Davis. You may not like that decision, but I promise you it wasn't made lightly. We haven't even positively identified the body in the forest yet.'

A groan ripples through the crowd. 'Come off it,' someone else calls out. 'Of course it's Daniel – and now little Lucy's dead, as well!'

This appears to cause some confusion among both the mob

and watching reporters. Evidently, not everyone had yet heard that Lori Velvet and Lucy Isherwood were one and the same. Constable Zwale takes advantage of this lull in hostility to stand by your side in a show of strength.

'See?' You say to the muttering crowd. 'This shows that you don't all know everything. Now please disperse and return home before doing something you might regret. There are more officers on the way, and I won't hesitate to arrest you all at the first sign of trouble.' You glare at Aaron, who has the decency to look sheepish. He drops the stone back in Glenn's garden and retreats into the crowd.

The gathered villagers consider what you've said, and for a moment you're confident they'll see sense. Then a wave of energy seems to pass through them, and they surge forward towards the house. You think they're coming for you, but then notice they're all looking past you. You turn to see the front door open – and Glenn walk out on to his doorstep.

'Go away, all of you!' he shouts. 'I've done nothing wrong, then or now, and you all know it! Leave me alone!'

Brian Brett, the reporter from the *Daily*, steps forward and holds out his phone like it's a microphone. 'Mr Davis, is there anything you'd like to say to the press?'

Glenn glares at him. 'Nothing fit for you to print,' he says disdainfully. 'If you want to go and hound someone, look no further than those horrid pagans! They've ruined everything!' Glenn points an accusing finger at Bill, still lingering at the back of the crowd.

The crowd turns as one, but Bill scoffs. 'Don't be daft, I barely knew the kid. Glenn, you can't throw accusations like that around just because you're still mad about what happened. She was going to leave you anyway. Go on, Ray, tell him—'

But Raven is already engaged in an argument of her own, one which quickly becomes heated. She and Julie are yelling at one another, with Aaron in the middle trying to keep them apart.

The altercation draws the crowd's attention. While they're distracted, you could slip inside the house and talk to Glenn about Daniel in private. Or you could break up the fight, and hope to speak with Glenn afterwards.

⚲ *To break up the fight between Raven and Julie, turn to* **122**

⚲ *To ignore the fight and go inside to interview Glenn, turn to* **50**

174

McAdam parks around the back of Grenholme town square, behind the Watching Warden pub. You walk through a narrow alleyway beside the building to reach the open space. A stone fountain stands in its centre, surrounded by wooden benches. The square around it is a combination of large grey flagstones and cobbled sections, many uneven and with missing cobbles, and low stone walls.

Although a main road approaches at one side, and another continues on from its opposite side, the square itself is pedestrianized and lined with local businesses. A bakery, a grocer, a newsagent, a cafe, a hairdresser, and of course the local pub itself. Beyond the square lie several rings of village streets, and beyond those the surrounding forest is visible in all directions.

Locals eye you carefully and take a wide berth when they see you. You may not be wearing uniform, but it seems everyone here still recognizes you as police. Unwelcome police, at that.

'It's like stepping back in time fifty years,' McAdam says.

'Except with added mobile service,' you note, checking your phone. 'We may be in the heart of the forest, but unlike the stone circle, the village has a good signal. Now, where's the shop . . .?'

You remember Raven's directions from last night: '*Across the square from the Watching Warden.*' Sure enough, on the other side of the square from the pub is a small shopfront whose sign reads 'Stones & Spirits', and underneath 'Souvenirs / Guidebooks / Crystals / Esoterica'.

You approach the shop, watched by a cat with glossy grey fur who sits in the window atop a display case of gem-like crystals, next to several books on local mythology. A photocopied poster in the window advertises last night's Killer Velvet performance at the pub.

The door, however, is closed. Its hanging sign declares Stones & Spirits to be open, but underneath is a handwritten yellow sticky note which informs you the proprietor will be 'Back in 5 mins'.

'Just our luck,' McAdam says. 'Now what?'

To wait here for Raven to reopen the shop, turn to **18**

To look for Raven elsewhere in the village, turn to **94**

<h1 style="text-align:center">175</h1>

Now that you look at it, the message in the chalk symbols seems obvious. You've cracked it – and what a strange message it is.

   If you have P12 written in your notebook, turn to **28**

   Otherwise, turn to **141**

<h1 style="text-align:center">176</h1>

You recall what Constable Zwale told you he'd learned from members of the Stargazers. It's time to present Glenn with that information.

'Mr Davis, you've maintained that you were with the astronomy group all night last night, correct?'

'That's right. Until I heard the girl screaming, at which point I ran to the stones.'

'But members of your group have told us you left them for several minutes last night, and from 11.25 until 11.38 you were nowhere to be seen. How do you explain that?'

Glenn doesn't answer, instead gazing out across the river. You're about to ask him again, when he says:

'Yes, I remember now. I returned to my car, to fetch my camera. I'd forgotten it, you see. In all the excitement.'

McAdam views him sceptically. 'You forgot your camera.'

'That's right. I retrieved it, returned to Clearing Delta, and nine minutes later I heard the girl scream.'

You find it hard to believe a man as precise and orderly as Glenn Davis would forget his camera, especially on a night supposedly so important to the Stargazers. On the other hand, he's right that Lori was still alive at 11.38.

   Write **G9** *in your notebook*

   Then turn to **43**

177

Realizing you're not following her, McAdam stops.

'Come on, he's getting away!'

'Let him go, whoever he really is,' you say. 'We have more important things to do.'

'It could be Lori's killer! I never took you for a coward, Inspector. I'm not letting him escape!'

She turns back and runs into the trees. Her words cut deep, and with a reluctant sigh you follow, not wanting to leave your sergeant high and dry. But the gloom envelops you, and the deeper you venture into the forest the more disorientated you feel. The ground becomes hilly and uneven, exhausting to navigate. Before long you have no idea which way you're facing, where McAdam is, and certainly no idea where the Stone Warden has gone. The sun has dimmed overhead, and dusk will soon arrive.

After climbing another hill and clambering over twisted

roots you stop to catch your breath, leaning on the nearest tree. Your breathing is loud and laboured in the forest's quiet, and perhaps that's why you don't hear the footsteps approaching from behind you.

A sharp pain lances through your head, then everything goes black.

You wake in hospital the next day, having suffered severe concussion and a head wound that requires stitches. Worse, rather than commending your bravery, the detective chief superintendent berates you for letting the Stone Warden go and not backing up Sergeant McAdam when she gave chase.

You're under doctor's orders to remain here while you recover. Not that it matters, because the DCS has lost confidence in you. Lori Velvet's murder may yet be solved . . . but not by you.

> 🔍 *Wipe your notebook, return to **1** and try again – this time remembering that your job is to apprehend suspects, not let them go.*

For now, though, this is . . .

THE END

178

You close your notebook and look up from the bench in the village square to find that you've been so absorbed with matters you didn't notice time moving on. Night has truly fallen in Grenholme, bringing a sparse gloom to the village.

Killer Velvet will be ready to take the pub stage soon. You consider attending, in order to understand them better. The manner of Lori's death suggests it had something to do with the local mythology, but could that be deliberate misdirection? What if the Stone Warden is a distraction, and her death was actually connected to her professional life? Aaron and Julie may have had their own reasons for wanting Lori out of the way.

While you ponder this, your phone rings with a call from Sergeant McAdam.

'You promised me you'd get some rest,' you say, gently admonishing her.

'And you promised me you'd keep me updated,' she counters. 'What's the story?'

You tell her about the mob descending on Glenn Davis's house, Patrick receiving a poison pen letter and Dr Wash cleaning up Daniel's bracelet.

'Oh, so nothing much,' she says sarcastically. 'Could Glenn have sent that letter?'

'It's possible. When you and I ventured into the forest, our suspects were all here in the village. Any of them could have slipped it behind the bar when Patrick wasn't looking.'

'Apart from Julie Grafton. She followed us in, still filming, remember.'

'True, but we also sent her packing. She could have returned here long before I returned to Grenholme following your injury.'

'You make it sound like I fell over. He stabbed me!' Zwale suppresses a chuckle, but McAdam hears it. 'You can stop smirking, Constable. You're supposed to be our eyes online for that astronomy lot. What are they up to?'

He hurriedly checks his phone. 'The usual, it seems. They're going to be at Clearing Delta tonight, hoping the fog doesn't play havoc with things, and they'll be setting off . . . fairly soon, actually.'

'Does Glenn Davis still intend to go with them?' you ask.

Zwale shrugs. 'The notice they've posted doesn't say one way or another.'

That suggests he will. The group leader, a man about to face a leadership challenge, not attending would be unusual and worthy of a mention. You wonder if the forest would be a better place to spend the evening after all. Perhaps you could leave Zwale here in the village while you go.

'Dr Wash sends her best, by the way, Sergeant,' you say to McAdam. 'I believe she's finally warming to you.'

'She wants to be careful with that. Ice queens melt if they warm too much.'

'Very droll. Now go back to bed, and I'll speak to you soon.'

'I'm already in bed. That's the problem,' she says glumly.

You end the call, ready to make a decision about your actions this evening. But before you can, Fran the barmaid emerges from the pub, sees you and rushes over.

'Inspector,' she says, 'I can't find Patrick anywhere.'

⚷ Turn to **90**

179

Constable Zwale has already taken Raven Moonwolf's statement, but she continues to hover on the edge of the stone circle, watching the police activity around her.

'Ms Moonwolf,' you say, approaching her.

'Just Raven is fine, please,' she says. 'How can I help?'

You gesture to the Lock Stones, then show her your notebook sketch of the chalk symbols.

'I wondered if you could possibly shed some light on these. We're told that they're not a normal part of the stones' appearance, and believe they were drawn either today or yesterday. Do you recognize them?'

'I didn't draw them, if that's what you're asking,' she protests. 'No, I don't recognize them. I suppose they might be something used in a ritual. But I've never seen symbology like that before, and I know a thing or two.'

'You don't say,' McAdam grumbles cynically.

↻ *Turn to* **85**

180

You take out your phone and type Raven's address into the Maps app, trusting there's enough signal to point you in the right direction. You recall her saying she lived on the edge of the village, near the trees. Could she have taken Patrick into the forest, planning to kill him and leave him there?

No sooner have you started walking towards her house than you see a column of fire and smoke rising from the same direction.

You break into a run, calling Zwale as you go.

'Constable, where are you?'

'Just arrived at Raven's house, Inspector. She's not answering, but there's smoke coming from somewhere.'

'I can see it from here. What's the source?'

A pause. 'Can't tell, sorry. I'm going to see if I can get round the back.'

'Be careful, and call me if you find anything. I'm on my way.'

You keep running. Zwale hasn't called by the time you're almost at the house yourself, and you fear the worst. It's an old terrace of a dozen houses, above which smoke continues to rise. Fortunately, there's an alleyway halfway along the street, leading to the back. You hurry through it, your nostrils rapidly filled by a foul burning smell.

'Over here, Inspector,' Constable Zwale calls when you emerge. You look over a fence to see him standing in Raven's back garden. The shopkeeper is also there, and between them both is the source of the smoke: a fire pit, its flames burning strong and high.

You hurry into the garden. 'What's going on? What are you burning?'

'None of your business,' Raven retorts.

'I couldn't put it out,' Zwale complains. 'She doesn't have an extinguisher. I saw CDs and DVDs in there.'

The fire is hot enough to drive you back. You get as close as you dare, peering into the flames. What you see confirms your suspicions.

'She's burning all her Killer Velvet material,' you say. 'Why, Raven? You told us you're a big fan.'

Raven scowls. 'Aaron barred me from their gigs! Me! He's nothing without Lori anyway. Good riddance to all of it.'

This is quite a turnaround from the love she professed for the band earlier. But being barred, along with Lori's death, seems to have made something snap.

'Raven . . . where's Patrick?'

'How should I know?'

'Don't play games with me. You're the one person in Grenholme who recognized Lori Velvet as Lucy Isherwood, and I don't think it's because she called you "Angela". I think you've always known who she is. Is that why you followed the band? Or were you watching their career anyway, and worked out who she was?'

She stares into the flames, saying nothing.

You press on. 'Everything that's happened here benefits you, doesn't it? Lori's death will bring more tourists to the Lock Stones than ever before. Not only people interested in myths, but true crime fans and murder tourists. It will be very profitable for you. Is that why you killed Lori?'

Raven turns to face you, her features cast into hard shadows by the light of the blaze.

'You're a fool,' she says.

Check your notebook in the following order:

   If you have J4 written down, turn to **53**

   If you have G6 written down, turn to **114**

   If you have R1 or R3 written down, turn to **77**

   Otherwise, turn to **145**

181

'What about Lori Velvet's interest in the Stone Warden?' you ask. 'We have a witness who saw you with her yesterday, before the band performed. Were you debating the finer points of local mythology?'

'Careful, Inspector, your sarcasm's showing. As it happens, you're closer than you think.'

'You don't deny arguing with the victim?'

'It wasn't an argument per se,' he says, sighing. 'I was in the pub, talking to Patrick, while the band were preparing. He was busy, so he asked me to fetch a box of crisps from the storeroom to restock the bar. When I walked out back, I saw the singer carrying what was obviously a Stone Warden costume. I asked her what the hell was she playing at, but she stormed out the side door, so I followed her.'

McAdam looks up from her notebook. 'To make her see sense?'

'In a way, yeah. To provoke the wrath of the Warden, last night of all nights, under a full moon . . . it was reckless. Stupid.'

'But she didn't listen.'

'No, she didn't. And look what happened.' Bill gazes at the Stone Warden mannequin in his display case.

'So what do you think Lori meant when she told you she "knows more about the Warden than you realize"?'

Bill tries to hide his surprise that you know this detail of his argument with Lori, but you catch his expression before he can mask it.

'I suppose she meant how she was originally from Grenholme. I didn't know that at the time, though. I don't think anyone did.'

'You might never have, if she hadn't been killed while wearing a fancy dress costume.'

⚲ *Turn to* **44**

182

Breaking into a run, you head for the forest and call Zwale along the way.

'Inspector, I was just going to update you,' he says, answering. 'Raven Moonwolf's not at home.'

'Forget Raven,' you say, and tell him where to meet you in the forest. 'On the double, Constable.'

You end the call, but keep your phone out to use its flashlight. You cross the forest threshold, running through lazily drifting mist and wishing your legs could move faster.

Lori Velvet's murder, and now Patrick's abduction, are both linked to the death of Daniel Isherwood fifteen years ago. You're sure of it. The only remaining question is how to prove what you suspect. But that can come later, once the killer is in custody. The immediate priority is to prevent a third dead body.

You recap yesterday's events in your mind. There was trouble from the moment the band arrived. When they performed, Lori surprised everyone, even her bandmates, by donning a Stone Warden costume and declaring, 'The Warden has a human face' – causing even more arguments. The band, Stargazers and Disciples then all entered the woods separately. Lori left her colleagues to visit the Lock Stones, upon which she chalked symbols – until someone killed her with her own knife.

Several of those who were in the woods have 'missing time', where their movements are uncorroborated, and you only have their word for it where they went. Confusingly, all of them were missing *before* Lori was heard to scream. But you think you can explain that, and why it doesn't exonerate anyone.

The forest closes around you. A break in the gloom reveals the night sky, and as you glance up a bright, brief streak of light sears through the darkness. Tonight's Lyrids have begun to fall.

   If you have P13 written in your notebook, turn to **48**
   Otherwise, turn to **116**

183

A middle-aged woman stands on the other side of the clearing, held back outside the crime-scene cordon by Constable Zwale. She has long dark hair and is wrapped in several layers of dark clothing, with a purple scarf wound around her neck and shoulders.

Sergeant McAdam crosses the stone circle to join you as you approach the woman and introduce yourself. Not wanting to alarm her, you say, 'I'm afraid there's been an incident. May I ask who you are?'

'Is it the band? Is Aaron OK?' she asks.

'Everyone's understandably shook up, but yes, Mr Warrior is unharmed. Is he a friend of yours, Ms . . .?'

'Moonwolf,' she says inexplicably, then clarifies: 'Raven Moonwolf. I run the souvenir shop, and I live on the edge of the woods, so I saw all the lights and cars go by. What's happened?'

McAdam checks her watch. 'It's near enough one in the morning. You just happened to be looking out of your window?'

Raven fixes her with a withering glare. 'I'm a night owl.'

'I thought you said you're a raven.'

'That's enough, Sergeant,' you warn McAdam. Her attack-dog nature can be useful, but there's a time and a place for it. You turn to Raven. 'Why did you assume something had happened to Aaron Warrior? Do you have a connection to his band?'

'No, I'm just a fan, I . . .' She trails off, looking at the white forensics tent with horror. You turn to see Dr Wash exit the tent, along with a forensics officer carrying evidence bags. 'Oh, no. It's Lori, isn't it?'

'What makes you say that?'

'Because I can see the others over there.' She gestures across the clearing. Sure enough, Aaron and his remaining bandmates stand by the trees. Raven waves at them, but nobody returns the gesture. In fact, Aaron Warrior turns away and talks to one of the other musicians. 'The Stone Warden got Lori, didn't he? She shouldn't have come here, messing around with things . . .'

'What do you mean by that? Is there something we should know about Ms Velvet's actions?'

The shopkeeper looks at you, McAdam and Zwale in turn

as if the answer is obvious. 'You do know about the song, right? And the gig, at the pub earlier? She even came out dressed as the Stone Warden for the encore. I mean, it was really cool, actually. I think they've got a hit on their hands. But dangerous, you know? These stones have a strong energy. I've lived here all my life, and I'm telling you, don't mess with it if you don't know what you're doing.'

You look at Raven again. She's a decade or more older than McAdam, but has a youthful zest. Perhaps it's down to her music tastes.

'Tell me, Ms Moonwolf, where were you around midnight this evening?'

She looks confused by the question. 'At home, watching a film . . .' Then she understands why you're asking. 'Oh, Goddess! Don't be silly, I'm not a suspect. I'd never hurt Lori or do anything to the band. I told you, I'm a fan. Ask anyone, I was down the front at the gig earlier.'

'Then I advise you to return home and finish watching your film. We may want to speak to you again in due course. Is the souvenir shop easy to find?'

'Of course. Stones & Spirits, across the square from the Watching Warden. Open every day.'

You leave Raven in Zwale's hands and confer with McAdam on your next steps.

If you have P5 written in your notebook, turn to **60**

If you have P2 written in your notebook, turn to **129**

Leaving Constable Zwale to slip out of the pub and eavesdrop on Aaron and Raven, you weave through the crowd towards the alcove where Julie and Bill are arguing. It can't be seen while standing at the bar. Perhaps that's why they chose to talk there.

You can't hear them over the hubbub of the crowded pub, but the conversation clearly isn't friendly. Julie appears to have her phone out and pointed at Bill, who puts up a hand to block the lens. So when Julie suddenly bursts into tears it's unexpected, and Bill seems equally surprised. He looks around for help, sees you approaching, and shrugs in bewilderment.

'Ms Grafton, are you all right? Can I help?' you ask.

'Yes,' she sobs, pointing at Bill. 'Arrest him! He killed Lori!'

'That's quite an accusation. Would you care to explain?'

Bill looks apologetic. 'She blames me for the girl's death. And I suppose she's right, in a way—'

'It's your fault!' Julie cries, jabbing him in the chest again. Bill has a good head of height over her, but she isn't intimidated. 'He was supposed to help us shoot the video,' she wails. 'But because he backed out, Lori went into the stone circle alone! If he'd been with her, she'd have been OK!'

'Haven't you heard?' Bill says, rolling his eyes. 'She grew up here, and knew all about the Lock Stones. She didn't need me to tell her not to go there at midnight.'

If you have P1 written in your notebook, turn to **17**

Otherwise, turn to **136**

You decide it's time to intervene.

'That's enough, Sergeant.' You rest a hand on McAdam's shoulder. She reluctantly backs away from Julie. 'That goes for everyone else, too. Let's all calm down and be sensible. On the one hand, Ms Grafton has a point; there's little expectation of privacy in a public establishment like this.' You turn to the director. 'On the other hand, it's clearly upsetting people and the owner has asked you to turn the camera off, so I'd be grateful if you'd comply.'

To your surprise, Julie refuses your olive branch and sneers.

'I'm sure you would, but that's not how it works. This is in the public interest.'

'It's not in *our* interest!' Raven cries. Before you can stop her, she snatches the camera from Julie's hands and flings it to the ground. Once again you hear the sound of breaking glass, this time from an optical lens. Julie shrieks in horror, but Raven isn't finished. She reaches down to retrieve the memory card from the camera's wreckage, then snaps it in two.

The others look on in shocked silence.

'You can't do that!' Julie yells. 'Inspector, arrest her!'

'At least you won't be filming any more,' Raven says, mocking her. 'Now mind your own business.'

🔎 *Turn to* **108**

'Can you explain to me why the Stone Warden would carry a fishing net?' you ask Bill. 'I don't recall seeing such a thing in any drawings I've seen.'

'He's a creature of the forest,' Bill says impatiently, evidently wanting to end the conversation. 'Maybe he enjoys a fish from the river now and then.'

Munching on raw fish, or even using a net to catch one in the first place, strikes you as a rather mundane activity for a forest spirit cursed to roam eternally by a vengeful fairie queen.

At that moment, you look out of a window on to the square and see Constable Zwale returning.

'Thank you, Mr Thomas,' you say. 'I'm sure we'll speak again.'

You head outside and intercept Zwale so you can talk without being overheard in the pub. Instead, you sit on a bench, watching mist roll through the square and wrap around your ankles like a needy cat.

He relates what he overheard: Aaron accusing Raven of stalking him, and threatening to tell the police. At that point the constable revealed himself, but Aaron backed down and said all he wanted was for Raven to leave him alone. For her part, Raven denied everything and even turned the tables, telling Aaron to get lost before she stormed off.

'I wonder if we should get a warrant for Raven's computer,' Zwale suggests. 'If she really is stalking Aaron, she might have killed Lori out of jealousy.'

It's a fair point, but Lori and Aaron split up months ago.

You have a hunch they might have got back together in the future, once he discovered she was pregnant with their child, but that time hadn't yet come. Now it never will.

You tell Zwale about your conversation with Julie and Bill. However, you're interrupted by a phone call . . . from the detective chief superintendent.

Turn to **15**

187

Your phone rings with a call from Dr Wash.

'Doctor,' you answer. 'What news?'

'I've just had more blood results back from the knife found at the crime scene,' she says. 'Not only is the blood on it a match for Lori Velvet's type, but it's the only type present. It's possible there could be a second identical donor, but the chances of that are low.'

'What about DNA?'

'I'm not a miracle worker, Inspector,' she says frostily. With her diamond-cut accent, it's like being reprimanded by royalty. 'Those tests are under way, but will take time.'

'Understood. You're still confident the knife in question is the murder weapon?'

'More than ever, but the lack of prints besides the victim's implies whoever wielded it wore gloves, so I don't know how much help that is.'

Dr Wash has a point. Finding the weapon is always import-ant in a murder case, but whether it meaningfully advances the investigation depends on what it can tell you. In this case, the evidence raises as many questions as it answers.

'We know the knife was part of her act,' you say. 'She was holding it on stage, while wearing the Stone Warden costume during their final song. She even carved it with a symbol that carried some significance for her. Why was it part of the performance? Why carry it into the woods? Did she fear for her safety?'

'Perhaps she just liked knives,' McAdam suggests. 'Too many youngsters do, these days, if you ask me.'

'I think the symbol may be the key you're looking for, Inspector,' Dr Wash says. 'Lori Velvet had many tattoos on her body, so we can't read too much into that alone. But the fact she also carved it into a knife hilt, not to mention that it matches one of the stone circle symbols, suggests to me it would be worth focusing your efforts in that direction. For all we know, that sequence of chalk marks is a message of some kind.'

The mysterious, almost ubiquitous symbol keeps nagging at you, but until now the notion that it could hold a message hadn't occurred.

You thank the doctor and end the call. 'Sergeant, let's have a break from interviews for now. I want to take another look at that stone circle.'

McAdam is far from thrilled about going back into the forest, though at least this time you can see where you're going, with the midday sun high in the sky.

'I don't think you'll meet any owls in daylight,' you say, making your way from the parking area to the stone circle on foot. She isn't amused.

Despite the sun, mist continues to hug the forest floor, making the going slow underfoot. Dense trees deaden the forest sounds, cloaking you in an uneasy silence.

⚬ *If you have J2 or J5 written in your notebook, turn to* **124**
⚬ *Otherwise, turn to* **71**

188

Your phone buzzes with a new message from Dr Wash, sending you a photo of the bracelet found on Daniel Isherwood's body. As you noticed before, the wooden beads feature some of the same symbols chalked on the Lock Stones. But what the doctor's clean-up has revealed is that they *also* feature plain letters.

In fact, each bead contains both a letter and a symbol:

'This is the code,' you murmur.

'What's that?' Dr Wash and Constable Zwale both ask in unison.

'The symbols written in chalk on the stones,' you explain. 'I don't think they're random. I believe Lori Velvet wrote them as a message of some kind, and this bracelet will help us decode it. Her father said both twins wore matching bracelets, presumably each with their own name. Lori must have remembered and practised this code over the years. She came to Grenholme and, I believe, wrote the sequence on the stones to be a hidden message in her music video . . . but was interrupted by the killer.'

Dr Wash whistles. 'I'll leave you to work on that hypothesis, Inspector. Do pass on my best to Sergeant McAdam when you next speak to her.'

'I will. Thank you, Doctor. This is invaluable.'

You end the call and look again at the photograph, comparing it to the drawing you made of the chalk symbols in your notebook.

They're a perfect match.

   First, use the cipher shown to decode the chalk symbols found on the stones

Then check your notebook:

   *If you have Pʃ written down, turn to **59***
   *Otherwise, turn to **103***

189

A sign on the gatepost of Bill's house names it as 'Disciple Chambers'. It's the largest dwelling you've seen in Grenholme, stone-built and sitting in an acre of land. It looks like someone took four traditional English cottages and glued them together. The gardens are semi-wild, with little attempt at cultivation. Tall grasses fill the space between flowers, bushes and trees.

Bill beckons you inside. You follow him through the house, peeking into rooms as you pass them. They seem normal enough: lightly furnished and unremarkable.

The sitting room is altogether different. It's the largest room in the house, but that plain fact is obscured by the sheer amount of *stuff* it contains. Overflowing bookshelves, a home office filled with clutter, a large TV and entertainment centre, fishing rods and baskets piled in a corner, chairs and sofas filled with more books and magazines, a guitar and amplifier that appear to be plugged into a computer, display cases of family photos and more. Much of it is covered in a fine layer of dust, suggesting it hasn't actually been used in years.

Then you see the shrine. It's another display case, but this one is full height and features what appears to be a mannequin of the Stone Warden, as well as a ceremonial robe like the one Bill wore last night, a knife with an intricately carved handle, and an enlarged photograph of the Lock Stones in the forest clearing.

'So is this where you all meet?' McAdam asks, peering at

the Stone Warden dummy. 'Disciple Chambers? Makes sense, I suppose.'

Bill clears some newspapers off a small sofa so you can sit down, then busies himself starting a fire.

'That's right,' he says. 'We assemble here, then go into the forest. I named the house in honour of a lost tradition.'

'It wasn't already called Disciple Chambers?'

He shakes his head. 'When I bought this place, Grenholme had almost forgotten the Disciples of the Green ever existed. I wanted to revive the old ways.'

'With you in charge,' you point out.

'Someone's got to lead, Inspector. Your own rank proves that.'

'What does your family think of all this?'

Flames rise in the fireplace, and Bill turns his gaze to the display case of photographs. His expression hardens.

'My ex-wife took me to the cleaners almost twenty years ago. That's partly why I retired early and came to Grenholme. My children are all grown up, living abroad. One each in Italy, Canada and Singapore. They think I'm a mad old eccentric. Maybe I am, but I wouldn't change a thing. Well, apart from buying a smaller house. I really thought I'd need it, but . . .' He gestures at the room's clutter. 'The truth is I more or less live in one room.'

That explains the unoccupied feeling you got from the other rooms you passed.

'And also in the forest,' you suggest. 'Your dedication to the Disciples is clear. Which makes me wonder why you left them for some time last night, at around half past eleven?'

Bill eyes you suspiciously. 'Says who?'

'That's not important. Is it true?'

'Yeah, it is, as a matter of fact. We'd started walking to the stones when I realized I'd forgotten my ceremonial knife. So I came back for it, picked it up, then ran back. It only took about ten minutes.'

'Then why didn't you mention this last night?'

'Not relevant, is it? This was all before we heard the girl scream, and I hadn't been anywhere near the stones.'

↪ *Write* **B12** *in your notebook*

↪ *Then turn to* **135**

190

It's times like this you wish you didn't have the detective's habit of leaving your baton and pepper spray at the station. Technically, every officer should carry them, uniformed or not, but you can count on a couple of fingers those detectives who do. Besides, they tend to spook witnesses.

So there's nothing else for it; you'll have to take on the Stone Warden barehanded. He stands unnaturally still, like a statue of twigs and moss, so you take a deep breath . . . then charge at him!

But the sound of your approach gives you away. At the last moment, the Warden turns and strikes out with his gloved hand. The blow hits you across the face, and you fall to the ground in pain. With a clattering sound, something else drops near by a cloth sack, poking out of which you see some kind of plastic handle.

But your attention is soon drawn back to the Warden as he draws something from under his robe. With a metallic click, a blade unfolds. He has a knife.

You're on your back, hands pressing into dirt and stones, with the Warden standing over you. What will you do?

   To scramble backwards and try to escape, turn to **139**

   To look for a weapon and defend yourself, turn to **40**

191

'Raven, we already spoke about this,' you say. 'Do you still deny sending Aaron those emails?'

'Of course. I promise, I don't know anything about them.'

'Hang on, you already asked her?' Aaron says. 'Why the hell didn't you tell me?'

'You may have noticed that we've been busy with other matters. Yes, I spoke to Raven after you showed me those emails. I did wonder if she might be the anonymous sender, but she denies it.'

'She's hardly going to say, "Yeah, I did it, it's a fair cop"! Can't you check her computer?'

Raven speaks up. 'Over my dead body. That's personal and private. Aaron, I don't know who's sending you horrible messages, but I swear that it's not me. I wouldn't.'

   Turn to **109**

<h1 style="text-align:center">192</h1>

You call Constable Zwale and tell him what you want him to do. Then you sit back and relax. Or you would, if not for McAdam turning on the car stereo to blast loud rock music as she drives.

'Rather early for this, don't you think, Sergeant?'

She frowns and gestures at the stereo. 'This is Killer Velvet's last album. Thought it might be useful for you to hear them. Get some context.'

You're not sure how much useful context you can draw from the cacophony issuing forth out of the car speakers, but you do your best. You reflect that McAdam meant this album is the band's latest release, but it really will also be its last. That is, unless they find a new singer. But hearing Lori Velvet yell, scream and bellow to be heard above the raucous, pounding music, you're not sure anyone could replace her.

Halfway through the second song you arrive at an unassuming single-storey building, on this occasion grateful for McAdam's fast driving. She parks next to a van wrapped in paramedic livery, near what might otherwise be mistaken for a warehouse-style roll-up door, and you make your way into the mortuary building.

After signing in, you proceed to Dr Wash's lab. A central metal table holds the body of Lori Velvet, now cleaned and naked, under a crisp white sheet. You note how different she looks here, devoid of make-up and costume, to the young woman you saw in those music videos and interviews.

The doctor is washing her hands as you enter.

'Good morning, Inspector,' she greets you. 'I'd ask you to sit down, only I don't have any chairs. Nevertheless, you should prepare yourself for a few surprises.'

McAdam practically rubs her hands with glee. She and Dr Wash haven't always seen eye to eye, but all differences are forgotten when a juicy mystery is afoot.

'Please proceed, Doctor,' you say. 'We're all ears.'

The pathologist walks to Lori's body and points out her wounds.

'First of all, what's not surprising is that my initial hypothesis was correct. The victim died of exsanguination due to a single, deep cut from a knife across her throat, severing both the jugular and carotid artery. She would have been rendered unconscious very quickly, with death following rapidly.'

'Can you say with certainty that she was killed from behind?'

She shakes her head. 'No, but it's highly probable. The cut goes from right to left across the throat, suggesting either a right-handed person from behind, or a left-handed person from the front. As we discussed last night, the balance of probabilities supports the former. In addition, there are no other blade injuries on the body, not even defensive wounds.'

You understand her meaning. It's unthinkable to imagine that, faced with a knife-wielding assailant, an unrestrained and fit young woman like Lori Velvet wouldn't have at least tried to block the knife with her arms or hands. But if she was taken by surprise from behind, she would have had no chance of defence.

Dr Wash lifts the singer's arm, which you notice bears several black-inked tattoos. 'The sole other injury, in fact, is a light bruise on her wrist which I believe was inflicted very shortly pre-mortem.'

'Inflicted by force? Wouldn't it be more severe if so?'

'For a bruise to form, blood must be flowing. This to me looks like a forceful contact which didn't then have time to bruise fully before death. What's puzzling is how there's no corresponding bruise on the other wrist, or anywhere else. If the victim had been restrained, I'd expect to see deeper bruising from a longer period of time, not to mention other marks to represent a struggle.'

You peer at the bruise. 'Leaving the most likely explanation: someone roughly grabbed her wrist, but only one of them, almost immediately before killing her.'

'At least it was quick,' McAdam says. 'Poor lass. What about the knife, Doc?'

'I'm now confident it was the murder weapon,' Dr Wash replies. 'We're having DNA run to double check, but blood sampled from the blade matches the victim's type, and its profile matches the wound. The DNA check will tell us if there are multiple blood donors, of course, but I wouldn't count your chickens.'

If you have A5 written in your notebook, turn to **56**

Otherwise turn to **107**

193

Aaron draws back his arm, then throws the stone with surprising force and accuracy. For a moment the mob falls silent – then the stone smashes through Glenn's front window, splintering glass shards against the curtains. You hear a cry from inside. Glenn is indeed at home.

The sound seems to energize the mob, who shout and yell with renewed fervour.

'We should break this up,' Zwale says, but doesn't actually move to attempt it. You can't blame him. As he pointed out, there are a lot more of them than you and the village mob is now at fever pitch.

The front door opens. Glenn takes half a step outside and yells.

'Go away, all of you! I've done nothing wrong! You're all—'

Another hurled stone hits him square in the head, cutting him off. Glenn falls to the ground like a puppet with his strings cut, and you hear a sickening *crack* as his head hits the front doorstep.

Glenn is lucky. The fall merely rendered him unconscious, and after a few days under observation in hospital he returns to Grenholme, where the contrite villagers, having come to their senses, offer him their apologies and aid.

You're not so fortunate. After you broke up the mob and rushed Glenn to hospital, the detective chief superintendent reprimanded you for not stepping in when you should have. Worse still, Julie Grafton recorded the incident on video and sold her footage to the media, embarrassing the police. You're suspended, pending an internal investigation.

Lori Velvet's murder may yet be solved . . . but not by you.

*Wipe your notebook, return to **1** and try again — this time remembering that your job is to keep the peace, not let mob rule run amok.*

For now, though, this is . . .

THE END

194

You see that you missed a call from Constable Zwale while you were in the forest, so phone him back.

'Inspector,' he answers. 'The solicitor from A-Sharp Legal got in touch. She was tight-lipped until I informed her of Lori Velvet's death, then she confirmed her as one of their clients. It definitely wasn't a family matter.'

'We assumed not. So why did Lori engage them?'

'Turns out she was going to sue Aaron Warrior for rights to the Killer Velvet brand. Apparently, they co-own the name, but Lori told the lawyer that she came up with it originally. It's why she changed her own name.'

'If Lori named the band herself, why is there a dispute?'

'Because there's no documented proof. She and Aaron were together when they formed Killer Velvet, so they agreed to be musical partners too, but she maintained it was all her idea.'

This sheds light on a possible motive for Aaron Warrior to want Lori out of the way. But would he really kill her just to own the band's name?

'What were her chances of winning, I wonder?'

'I thought you'd ask that, so I checked with the solicitor and she said Lori's chances were pretty good. She has the name, and is – was – the band's figurehead. Look at any publicity photos, it's always Lori who's front and centre. Aaron was second because he writes most of the music, but Lori contributed some too, and she also wrote all the lyrics.'

'A lawsuit strikes me as something that would only be necessary in the case of a split,' you say, thinking through the ramifications. 'Now that they were no longer officially a couple, perhaps Lori also intended to fire Aaron from the band.'

'The solicitor didn't mention that, but she said Lori was determined to go through with it and planned to formally file the suit next week.'

You thank Zwale and end the call, then update McAdam.

'That's a motive and a half,' she says. 'Name rights can be worth a pretty penny. It would mean Lori could ditch Aaron and go her own way, still playing and releasing records as Killer Velvet, while he'd have to start over again with a new band. If Aaron found out, he might have killed her to prevent the suit.'

'But then the band's figurehead, as her solicitor put it, would be no more. Isn't that cutting off his nose to spite his face?'

McAdam shrugs. 'When rock stars die, their sales go up. A dead Lori Velvet could be worth more to him than a live one.'

What a chilling thought. You make a mental note to ask Aaron Warrior about this next time you speak to him.

○ Write **P4** in your notebook

○ Then turn to **6**

195

'Let's talk about your relationship with Bill Thomas,' you say. 'How did he come to be an investor in your shop?'

'It was partly his idea,' Raven replies. 'We came up with it in the pub one night. I was working there at the time, waiting for the universe to send me a sign.'

'And did it?' McAdam asks sceptically.

'Yes,' Raven insists. 'After Bill revived the Disciples of the Green, more tourists started visiting. I said we should have a village shop to cater to them and Bill said, "Why don't you open one?" I had a sudden flash – it was like a shiver passing through my whole body – and I realized that was it. That was the sign. The problem was, I couldn't afford it on my own. So Bill offered to invest, and guarantee me to the bank.'

'How generous of him,' you say. 'Was this before or after you and Mr Thomas had a "brief fling", as he described it to us?'

Raven frowns. 'If you're insinuating I slept with him for the money, you're way off base. Bill and I had an immediate mutual attraction, so naturally we became intimate, but it didn't suit us. We consciously separated, and have remained close ever since.'

'As well as business partners.'

'Sure. He takes care of the publicity side, with the Disciples and everything, to encourage visitors. The music helps, too.'

'Music?'

Raven gestures to the air. 'He records it on his computer, then sells it online and gives me copies to play in the shop. I wouldn't know where to start, but Bill's an experienced musician. The albums are all named for aspects of Grenholme, by the way. This one's called . . .' She peers at her tablet, propped on the shop counter. '. . . *Green Kingdom*. It came out last month.'

You take a moment to listen to the New Age music, which has been playing whenever you've been inside Stones & Spirits, with a new interest.

'So Bill is more than just a financial investor.'

'We're partners. He drums up customers, and I sell them what they need. Everyone's happy.'

You have some doubts about that. 'Including Glenn Davis? He doesn't strike me as a man overly fond of the commercial side of local tourism.'

'I couldn't care less. Glenn had me kicked out of the Stargazers after I opened this place, remember. But karma is real. Did you know they're holding a vote of no confidence in him soon?' Raven's smile is full of unspoken implication.

'You wouldn't have anything to do with that, would you?'

'My lips are sealed.'

The music continues to play, reminding you of what Penny's team found in the forest. You show Raven the photo you took of the Bluetooth speaker.

'Do you recognize this?'

She peers at it, as if trying to remember, then shakes her head.

'It does look familiar, to be honest. I might have seen it before. But I don't recall where, sorry.'

'What about here in the shop?'

She points to a large speaker sitting on a high shelf beside the counter. 'That's what you're listening to right now.' The speaker looks nothing like the one you found. Furthermore, it's here in Stones & Spirits, not lodged in a tree.

The shop door opens and a young couple enters, looking around. Judging by the leather and denim they wear, these are not hikers. One even has 'Killer Velvet' painted on the sleeve of their jacket.

Word, it seems, is beginning to spread.

Write **R2** *in your notebook*

Then turn to **101**

196

As you turn to leave, you recall what Bill Thomas told you.

'Mr Davis, you seem like a traditionalist,' you suggest to him. 'You say you've lived here all your life, so you must be familiar with the legend of the Lock Stones, and the Warden. I'm told they bring tourism to Grenholme, too. So what do you have against Bill Thomas and the Disciples of the Green?'

Glenn sighs. 'My issues with Bill are not personal. It's commendable that after moving here he became closely involved in the community, but he's also a fraud. The Lock Stones may be centuries old, but the Disciples are not, and his claims of continuing a local tradition are nonsense. Besides, it's unseemly. The stones are traditional British folklore, not a children's cartoon.'

'He claims to speak for the villagers, though . . .?'

'He most certainly does not speak for us all.' Behind Glenn, the other astronomers frown and nod. The battle lines between these two groups seem clearly drawn up.

'Then I have one final question. When he found you with Ms Velvet, Bill Thomas says he heard you whispering, "Oh, God, this shouldn't have happened, I'm sorry." What did you mean by that, exactly?'

Glenn looks momentarily shaken. Perhaps he hadn't known Bill could hear him.

'I – did I say that? I don't remember . . . look, I didn't want the band to come here in the first place. I prayed last night for God to show them the error of their ways, but I didn't expect anything like this. It's a tragedy.'

'They do say He moves in mysterious ways,' McAdam remarks drily.

🔎 *If you haven't yet spoken to Aaron Warrior, the guitarist, turn to **38***

🔎 *Otherwise, turn to **88***

197

Your phone rings. It's McAdam.

'Inspector,' she says, 'I've just spoken to Killer Velvet's manager.'

'Which part of "rest and recuperation" escaped your understanding, Sergeant?'

'It's my leg that's done in, not my head,' she protests. 'Lying here all day, I'm bored to death.'

You check your watch. It's barely been two hours. 'Never mind. What did the manager say?'

'He corroborated Aaron Warrior's story about that phone call during the video shoot. They talked around half eleven last night, discussing legal stuff.'

That matches the time Aaron told you he went to the edge of the woods to make a call. His alibi for that part of the night holds up.

'Was there anything else? Did the manager hear anything untoward, perhaps?'

'I asked him that. He said no, and that he's pretty sure he'd have heard if Aaron was killing Lori at the time.'

'How droll. Thank you, Sergeant. Now put your phone away and get some rest. That's an order.'

🔎 *Turn to* **143**

198

'As it happens, we've already spoken to Mr Davis,' you say. 'Funnily enough, he told us he saw *you* arguing with Lori Velvet yesterday, before the band performed. So, before you throw stones at others, perhaps you'd like to tell us what that was about?'

Bill huffs, obviously annoyed. Perhaps he expected you to leap to your feet and march to Glenn's house immediately.

'I told you, Glenn's never liked me. You'd think living here for almost twenty years, getting involved in the community, and giving my own time to help the village's reputation and economy might buy me some slack. But not from Councillor Davis, oh no. He'll take any opportunity to bad-mouth me.'

'So, you deny arguing with Lori yesterday?'

'It wasn't really an argument,' he says, sighing. 'I was in the pub, talking to Patrick, while the band were preparing. He was busy, so he asked me to fetch a box of crisps from the storeroom to restock the bar. When I walked out back, I saw the singer carrying a Stone Warden costume. I asked her what the hell she was playing at, but she stormed out the side door, so I followed her. I suppose that's what Glenn saw.'

'What did he see, exactly? Tell us in your own words.'

'I was trying to make her see sense, that's all. To provoke the Warden, last night of all nights, under the full moon . . . it was reckless. Stupid.'

'But she didn't listen.'

'No, she didn't. And look what happened.' Bill gazes at the Stone Warden mannequin in his display case. 'It was a bad costume, anyway. When I saw her wearing it on stage I wondered how she saw out of the mess she'd made of the hood. But that's neither here nor there. Like I said, it's Glenn you should be speaking to, not me.'

    🔎 *Write* **B7** *in your notebook*

    🔎 *Then turn to* **172**

199

Aaron shivers in the crisp air of the village square, and looks towards the pub door. 'Are we done here? Only I think I'm getting a headache. I want to get some rest.'

'One last question, Mr Warrior,' you say. 'Do you recognize this?'

You show him the photo you took of the speaker found in the woods.

He peers at it. 'What is that, a Bluetooth box? Nah. Never use 'em, except for video shoots. The sound quality's pathetic.'

'Have you seen this particular speaker before?'

Aaron shakes his head. 'I just told you, I never use 'em.' He pushes past you and re-enters the pub. You follow and watch him go straight past the bar, ascending the stairs to the bedrooms.

'Get some rest? More like tell everyone he knows to come to the gig,' McAdam says drily. 'I don't think there's much Aaron Warrior wouldn't do to achieve success.'

She's right. But does that include killing his own bandmate and former lover?

Now choose another person in the pub to interview:

To speak with Glenn, turn to **111**

To talk to Julie, turn to **55**

If you've already interviewed both of them, turn to **101**

'Wait!' you shout as the Stone Warden advances. 'I told my colleagues everything. If you kill me, they'll know. You'll go down not just for Lori and Daniel, but for killing a copper too. That won't go well for you.'

His head twitches left and right, as if looking for an escape route.

'Don't think about that, either. We have officers all over the forest looking for you. The game's up. And this time there's no Bluetooth speaker to help you.'

The Warden snarls, taking another step forward. You're very conscious of the ornate, ceremonial dagger in his hand. Does he know you're bluffing about backup? Even if he does, mentioning the speaker should give him pause. If you know that, what else do you know? That's the seed you wanted to plant in his mind.

'Yes, I know how you did it,' you continue. 'I also know why. In a way, Lori herself told me. Not through spiritual means, but by leaving clues that a good detective could follow. She was devoted to her brother Daniel, and to his memory.'

The snarl becomes a deep-throated growl, and you wonder if you've pushed too far. Hard as it is to read body language under the Warden's layered, ragged robes, nevertheless you sense rising tension. Around you, the night grows still and quiet. Fog envelops the Lock Stones, like a veil being drawn over the world. It feels as if you and the Warden are now the only living beings in the forest, lost in a place where twilight reigns and inhuman eyes keep watch. No wonder locals came to believe it was a gateway for fairie folk.

The Warden takes another step—

And collapses with a grunt, brought down from behind by Constable Zwale.

The young officer got here in the nick of time, leaping out of the gloom to tackle the so-called mythical figure to the ground. The Warden drops his dagger, which you immediately retrieve.

Zwale presses down on the Warden, kneeling on his back while drawing his hands behind his body to handcuff him. You walk over and grasp the Warden's hood, the hessian cloth rough beneath your fingers, and pull.

Bill Thomas's face glares up at you, wild and manic in the silver moonlight.

'I don't see a thing,' McAdam complains. 'It's just black.'

'You have to wait, ma'am,' Zwale says, showing more patience in one moment than the sergeant has all evening. 'They don't fall on demand.'

You laugh as Dr Wash shoos McAdam away from the telescope and takes her place in the garden chair, sitting and pressing her eye to the viewfinder. Soft light from Constable Zwale's kitchen spills out through the patio doors into his small garden, where you've all gathered for the last night of the Lyrids meteor shower. His large stargazing telescope is set up to watch for shooting stars, but much to her annoyance, McAdam has yet to catch any.

'Ooh, there's one!' Dr Wash cries.

You all look up in time to see a streak of light shoot across the sky, leaving a retinal imprint as it fades.

'Typical,' McAdam complains, leaning on her walking stick. 'I was sat there for ten minutes and nothing happened.'

'Wait there, ma'am,' Zwale says. 'I've still got my starter scope inside the house somewhere, you can have that to yourself for the night.'

'No need, Joseph. *Oof.*' Dr Wash stands, groaning as she straightens her knees, and relinquishes the chair back to McAdam. 'One was enough.'

Zwale turns to you, sitting at his garden table. 'Fancy a look, Inspector? By tomorrow the Lyrids will be gone until next year.'

You decline with a smile. 'I'm quite content to watch them with my own eyes.' You pull your coat tight against the night. 'Another cup of tea wouldn't go amiss, however.'

A general murmur of agreement goes up, and Zwale heads inside to boil the kettle. Dr Wash joins you at the small table, slowly lowering herself into a garden chair.

'I hear Bill Thomas confessed,' she says. 'Well done.'

'It was a team effort,' you reply. 'Catching him red-handed with Patrick made the rest easy.'

'Perhaps, but you still had to know it was him in the first place. I must admit, my money was on Glenn Davis.'

You nod. 'Bill was banking that we'd all think that. He publicly insisted it couldn't possibly be Glenn, while subtly pointing the finger at him and attempting to have him framed. He even used the same model of Bluetooth speaker Glenn owns, and carried a fishing net when we encountered him dressed as the Stone Warden.'

'You mean the net was meant to throw us off?' McAdam says, eye once again glued to the viewfinder.

'Partly. Glenn isn't the only fisherman in the village, of course, but he's one of the best-known. When Bill went back to collect his Bluetooth speaker, he carried a fishing net in case he was seen. Which, of course, he was.'

McAdam winces at the memory. 'We'd already found the speaker by then, though.'

'Why was it there in the first place?' Dr Wash asks.

'First, Bill didn't know we'd found it,' you remind McAdam. 'But doing so was the key to understanding how Lori was killed, despite all of our suspects having alibis.'

'That's right. They were all with someone else at the time of the murder.'

'Not quite. They were all with someone else when Lori Velvet was heard to scream . . . but in fact she was already dead by then.'

The doctor shakes her head, not understanding. 'Perhaps you'd better start from the beginning.'

'For that, we must go back a very long time. Fifteen years, in fact, to Daniel Isherwood's disappearance. I suspected his death was linked to Lori's, but I wasn't quite sure how until Bill confessed. I thought he'd abducted Daniel, but he insists the boy's death was an accident. Bill had recently moved to Grenholme and revived the Disciples of the Green, with himself as leader. He secretly made a Stone Warden costume and began wearing it around the forest, hoping to be glimpsed by locals and thereby stoke interest in the legend.'

'Which in turn attracted people to the Disciples, increasing his own standing and influence in the village,' Dr Wash suggests.

'Not if they knew he was running around wearing twigs and moss like a nutter,' McAdam says.

'Indeed,' you agree, 'which was itself the problem. Lucy and Daniel Isherwood snuck out of their house to play in the forest one evening and saw Bill dressed as the Warden, taking a break with the hood off. Instead of keeping quiet, though, Daniel ran out from their hiding place to confront Bill, who chased him through the trees and into the Lock Stones . . . where Daniel tripped and fell head first against one of the stones.'

Constable Zwale returns with tea for everyone, placing three mugs on the table and handing another to McAdam.

'That explains the cranial injury,' Dr Wash says. 'I expect he died more or less instantly. Small mercies.'

'Perhaps, but what happened next was far from merciful. Panicking, Bill decided to hide the body. He had no idea Daniel's sister had seen the whole thing. Having only recently moved to Grenholme, he barely knew the family. So he carried Daniel to the wych elm by the bog and deposited him inside. Presumably Lucy was too traumatized to follow, and instead ran home.'

'Where she told everyone the Stone Warden had taken her brother,' Zwale says. 'So she wasn't mistaken, or making things up.'

'Not at all, but being so young, people naturally assumed she was hysterical. By the time Bill realized what she'd seen, it was too late to do anything about it. Luckily for him, Lucy's memories of the event were so mixed-up and confused that she genuinely seemed to think the Warden himself had taken her brother. Glenn Davis was arrested and accused, as we know, but never charged. It all became too much for the Isherwoods, who took Lucy and moved away. Meanwhile, Glenn's wife Angela left him, changed her name to Raven and opened the souvenir shop in partnership with Bill.'

McAdam shakes her head. 'He went right back to dressing up as the Warden to attract business. He knew he'd got away with it.'

'That's right. The whole episode became a distant memory to all involved . . . except for Lucy Isherwood and her family, of course. Quite understandably, Lucy never forgot her brother and carried his memory with him throughout her life, even as she became Lori. She committed the odd symbols of his bracelet to memory, and even had the symbol for "D" inked as one of her first tattoos.'

'I can't even imagine that loss,' McAdam says sympathetically. 'Their poor parents.'

'Perhaps it will be some small comfort to them knowing that Lori died attempting to find justice for Danny. She wrote a song about the Stone Warden and decided to film the video at the Lock Stones. When Killer Velvet then contacted the Disciples asking for help with the video, it set everything in motion again.'

Dr Wash looks puzzled. 'Lori Velvet hardly resembled her seven-year-old self. Surely Bill Thomas didn't recognize her?'

'Not at first. But then Julie sent him a copy of the song, and he heard the lyrics. They're not literal, but they make clear reference to the Stone Warden being a liar and a fraud. Suspecting Lori might know something, Bill backed out of helping them by pretending that filming on a full moon offended him. The band came anyway, and when Bill spoke with Lori, she told him outright that she knew it was him. At that moment, Bill knew Lori was Lucy and arranged to meet her later that night, at eleven thirty in the stone circle.'

'That's why she said, "The Warden has a human face".'

'Exactly. Bill claims he thought she would simply blackmail

him, but he arrived to find her dressed as the Stone Warden, writing chalk symbols on the stones and brandishing a knife. When she saw him, she attacked him in a frenzy.'

'Wait a moment,' Dr Wash snorts. 'Don't tell me he's trying to claim self-defence.'

You smile. 'He did . . . at first. Then we showed him the Bluetooth speaker.'

'I still don't get how that's connected,' Zwale says.

'To be honest, I'm kicking myself for not taking action as soon as we found it,' you say. 'Bill is a musician, remember. As a young man he played in cover bands, and now he makes music for Raven's shop using a computer. Computers, you see, can be used to make all kinds of music . . . and to isolate sounds.'

You look around, waiting for someone to pick up on it, but are met with blank faces.

'Sounds like Lori Velvet's scream, on the very song Julie sent to Bill. He isolated it from the background music, and turned it into a sound that would play as a phone alarm. We heard Raven do something similar – her alarm reminder to take medication plays an old Killer Velvet song. So, after entering the forest with the Disciples, Bill left them, claiming he'd forgotten his knife. In fact, he already had it, as well as his phone and the speaker. He rushed to the stone circle, where he killed Lori. Then he placed the phone and speaker on a nearby tree before rejoining the Disciples. When we found the speaker, I noticed the branches were high enough to not be easily seen, but still low enough to reach. Fifteen minutes later, at 11.47, the phone alarm went off and played the sound of Lori screaming at maximum volume through the speaker.'

'Which everyone heard, and they came running,' McAdam says. 'So our presumed time of death was completely wrong.'

'Unfortunately so. Glenn reached the circle and tried to administer help to Lori, but it was too late. Bill then stepped out of the trees, pretending to have just arrived. Aaron came next; he said Bill seemed to be in shock, swearing to himself and backing out of the stone circle. Julie followed shortly afterwards, at which point Bill was calling 999 via satellite.'

McAdam shakes her head. 'I should have noticed that Bill was the only person in the forest that night with a phone. Everyone in Grenholme knows there's no regular signal.'

'If Bill's phone was up a tree, how did he get it back?' Zwale asks.

'The crucial moment happened between Aaron and Julie arriving,' you explain. 'Bill wasn't backing away from the body out of shock. He was retreating to that same tree, while Glenn and Aaron were distracted by the body. Unluckily for Bill, in the process of retrieving his phone he accidentally knocked the speaker . . . and it fell inside the tree, which he hadn't known was hollow.'

Dr Wash watches the night sky. 'There's irony for you.'

'It also brings us back to the start, and the other reason Bill was carrying a fishing net when we encountered him. He planned to use it to lift the speaker out from inside the tree. The fact it could implicate Glenn Davis was a bonus.'

'He didn't know we'd already found it,' McAdam says, rubbing her leg. 'Found him, too.'

'Can you prove it's his speaker?' Dr Wash asks.

You smile. 'As soon as we had him in custody, Penny simply brought Bill's phone within range of the speaker and it immediately connected. It's not irrefutable proof of ownership, but it shows that his phone has connected to that particular speaker before. I'll wager nobody else's in the village has.'

'There's still one big question to answer,' Zwale says. 'Why was he going to kill Patrick?'

'Because Bill thought Lori had told him. Patrick said Lori had confided in him that she "knew the Warden's face", remember? Shortly afterwards, he received that poison pen letter. Bill had become convinced that Patrick could now identify him, and would tell us if he wasn't silenced. He called Patrick to his house, under the guise of preparing for the Disciples' ritual that evening, where he drugged him and then took him into the forest. Bill dressed as the Stone Warden in case anyone happened to see him.'

'A disguise and myth-builder all in one,' McAdam grunts.

'What a terrible waste,' Dr Wash says. 'None of this would have happened if Bill Thomas had simply come clean about the accident with young Daniel fifteen years ago.'

You nod in agreement. 'He was too selfish. Bill moved to Grenholme to reinvent himself in retirement, determined to win over his new neighbours and become a popular local figure. Daniel's death threatened to undo that almost before it had begun, and Bill simply couldn't face it.'

'Ooh, got one!' McAdam cries, as a shooting star blazes across the dark sky.

'That reminds me,' Zwale says, and ducks back inside the house. A moment later he returns, carrying a child's plastic rounders set. 'Raven asked me to give you this, Sarge. For your son.'

McAdam sees it and smiles. 'Just put it there on the table. I'll give it to Douglas in the morning.'

Dr Wash cradles her mug. 'Joseph, tell me about the night sky at your uncle's house.'

'I'll do better than that,' he says, and takes out his phone to make a video call. Moments later you're all greeting the professor, who's watching the Lyrids from his own garden in Nigeria.

While Zwale's uncle charms Dr Wash with tales of Yoruba deities among the heavens, you sip your tea and enjoy the spread of its warmth against the cool night air. Overhead, a streak of light cuts through the dark.

THE END

Scoring

Congratulations – you *could* solve the murder! You'd make a fine detective ('Aye, with a little help,' McAdam says).

But *how* fine a detective, exactly? Here's where you find out.

Below and overleaf is a table of Clue Numbers you may have noted down while reading *The Forest of Death*. Check each Clue Number you found (including any you may have later crossed out) and add the number of points it's worth to your total.

Not all of these clues were necessary to solve the crime, but they reflect well on your investigative powers. Note also that some clues were red herrings and missteps, which are worth *minus* points!

Finally, not every clue in the book is listed in this table, as some were benign and don't affect your score either way.

CLUE = SCORE

A1 = +5
A2 = +5
A4 = +5
A6 = +5

B3 = +5
B4 = +10
B5 = +5
B7 = +10

B8 = +5
B9 = +10

G1 = +5
G2 = +5
G3 = +5
G5 = +5
G6 = +10

J1 = +5
J2 = +5
J3 = +10
J4 = -10
J5 = +5
J6 = +10

P1 = +5
P2 = -10
P3 = +5
P5 = +10
P7 = +5
P8 = +10
P10 = +10
P11 = -10

R1 = +5
R2 = +5
R3 = -10
R5 = +5

If you copied out the chalk symbols into your own notebook, award yourself an extra **+5 points** for diligence.

If you deciphered the message *before* Dr Wash sent you the photo of the bracelet, award yourself an extra **+10 points** for ingenuity.

If you deciphered the message *after* Dr Wash sent you the photo, award yourself **+5 points** instead.

If you failed to decipher the message at all, deduct **-10 points**.

Now check your score to find out how well you did:

20 OR FEWER POINTS: AMATEUR

Phew – it's amazing that you solved the murder at all! You must have done so by the skin of your teeth. We suggest you go back to the beginning and try again, to improve your score.

20–60 POINTS: DETECTIVE CONSTABLE

You are a good, hard-working, competent detective. You may not be flashy, but you quietly get solid results. Why not have another go at solving the case? Focus your investigation more on following the right path, and you could potentially score much higher.

60–120 POINTS: DETECTIVE INSPECTOR

You're a great detective! You followed all the right paths, asked all the right questions and uncovered the killer. What's more, you avoided many of the red herrings and dead ends that were thrown in your path along the way. You are a credit to the police force, and promotion lies in your future.

Incredible. You weaved a near-perfect path of deduction by avoiding red herrings, expertly cracking codes and following the most relevant and correct lines of enquiry. An outstanding, almost impossible achievement – but you did it!

So, how did *you* solve the murder? I'd love to know! You can find me on social media **@AntonyJohnston**, or email me via my website **antonyjohnston.com**.

The only remaining question is: could you do it over again and get a higher score?

There's only one way to find out . . .

Acknowledgements

There's something ineffably magical about an English forest, and I've always enjoyed the way our mythology and folk tales are woven into the landscape, especially our once-great forests. My idea of a good time is walking in woodland and visiting a pile of old rocks, be it a stone circle, ancient barrow or ruined building.

When I was young, I spent a lot of time running around in the woods. Growing up in the West Midlands, it was inevitable that I'd eventually learn the story of the skeleton found inside a Hagley Wood tree, immortalized by the graffiti '*Who put Bella in the wych elm?*' on Wychbury Hill.

This was long before the internet or Wikipedia, so folk tales inevitably changed and grew in the telling. However, as that's the age we now live in, I'll let you look up the story for yourself. Suffice to say it stuck with me, particularly after I visited the location in the 1990s, and when I needed a plausible reason why Danny's body could remain undiscovered for so long, I remembered the wych elm story. Raven Moonwolf might call that fate.

Any author will tell you that writing books never seems to get any easier. In fact it somehow becomes more difficult, not less, with time and experience. Writing the second book in a series also brings its own unique challenges, this time including a desire to refine and improve the interactive game mechanics – not normally something one needs to worry about in a crime novel!

Thankfully, I had the help and trust of my UK editor, Finn Cotton, who once again went above and beyond with brainstorming help, not to mention editing the story's flowchart alongside my US and Canada editors, Jeramie Orton and Bhavna Chauhan, before I'd even written a word of the manuscript.

The reception from readers to the original *Can You Solve the Murder?*, as well as to the interactive events I hosted at bookstores and festivals all over the country to promote it, was beyond what I could have expected. Thank you for all your kind words.

At Transworld, thanks to the indefatigable Emma Fairey, whose help organizing and running those events was invaluable, and to everyone on the team who's worked to bring *The Forest of Death* to life: Phoebe Llanwarne, Eleanor Rhodes Davies, Marianne Issa El-Khoury, Cara Conquest, Nekane Galdos, Judith Welsh, Barbara Thompson, Katrina Whone, Kim Young, Bill Scott-Kerr, Tom Chicken, Mathew Watterson and Molly Openshaw.

My agent Sarah Such is a powerhouse. Everyone should have an agent with her commitment and wisdom on their side. My thanks to Sarah and her colleagues at the Sarah Such Literary Agency, as well as to Jessica Buckman of the Buckman Agency, for helping *Can You Solve the Murder?* travel the world.

My final thanks, as always, go to Marcia, who likes looking at piles of old rocks even more than I do.

You can find and follow me on most social media platforms as @AntonyJohnston – be sure to let me know whether you could, indeed, solve the murder!

Antony Johnston
February 2026

Detective Notes

About the Author

Antony Johnston is the multi-award-winning, *New York Times* bestselling author of more than fifty books, graphic novels and comic series, including the popular *Dog Sitter Detective* murder mysteries. His graphic novel *The Coldest City* was made into the multi-million-dollar blockbuster movie *Atomic Blonde*. He is also a celebrated videogames writer and is credited with many franchise-defining titles. Johnston is a former vice chair of the Crime Writers' Association, a member of International Thriller Writers and the Society of Authors, a Shore Scripts screenwriting judge and sits on the Writers' Guild of Great Britain's videogames committee. He lives and works in Lancashire.